Kamrynn Bellary

The Ravenell Dynasty Trilogy

· · · ·

Book Two
Raptured Love

· · · ·

Lenevar Publications

• • • •

REFERENCE TO THE SONG, "His Eye is on the Sparrow":
Abecasis, S. The Sparrow. Ditson, C. H., New York, monographic, 1884. Notated Music. Retrieved from the U.S. Library of Congress, <www.loc.gov/item/sm1884.06589/>.

Raptured Love

Dedication

This book series is dedicated to all ladies on Earth, who endeavor a world of equality, diversity, and inclusion, and who believe in love and romance, and have taken a chance at love, only to have experienced heartbreak, and yet, maybe if even only deep down, still believe in the possibility of true love.

· · · ·

THIS STORY AND BOOK series is a work of fiction.

All characters and situations are purely fictional.

Unless otherwise indicated, all the names, characters, businesses, places, events and incidents in this book are either the product of the author's imagination or used in a fictitious manner. Any resemblance to actual persons, living or deceased, or actual events is purely coincidental.

· · · ·

THIS FICTION STORY series is for adult readers/ audiences, and contains elements of human life, including love, sex, violence, sexual assault, abuse, rape, suicide, death, grief, and spirituality.

· · · ·

"TW" IS FOR TRIGGER warning, and is placed at the beginning of each chapter where the author feels the reader may want a trigger alert warning for very emotional parts of the story that may deal with abuse, sexual violence, or suicide. This courtesy is not a guarantee that every possible trauma trigger is alerted in this fiction work, however, it is with good intentions that this author places the alerts for the reader.

Author encourages anyone with suicidal thoughts, or any victims of sexual assault to reach out to your local community resources to receive help.

Chapter One

The bright sun beams through the beautiful artwork on the stained glass windows of the Austin, Texas hospital chapel, casting illuminating and heavenly colors throughout the small sanctuary. Nicolaus Ravenell and Deirdre Omari draw near to each other. Emotions are high, after Nicolaus' wife, Marguerite, the Latvian woman he was forced to marry to save the family empire, has just outright rejected their newborn baby, as he himself was rejected by his own mother when he was a child.

Nicolaus' mind plays upon the words she deliriously screamed at them in the hospital room, 'I hate you! I don't want him! Take it away!' Marguerite said of her newborn son.

Nicolaus and Marguerite have been married a little over a year, and their forced marriage has been contemptuous from the beginning. Nicolaus was forced to marry Marguerite through a company merger created by his mother, Ceil Ravenell. It was marry her, or their family would lose everything and suddenly become penniless, giving away everything their ancestors and his father worked so hard to create.

The adversary company is Drone Pharma, the Latvian company owned by Marguerite's father, Andrejs Drone. Ceil turned a friendly merger into a spiteful scheme against Nicolaus. Marguerite was also forced to marry. She had to marry a rich American, in order to receive her million dollar inheritance left to her from her mother, or remain penniless. This marriage, for Marguerite, promised her independence. Yet, this marriage, for Nicolaus, though he had to sacrifice his destined and devoted love for Deirdre, saved the family empire, of which he is now the Vice-President, replacing his father, Nigel Ravenell, who is now retired.

Deirdre, a brilliant lawyer, and elegant beauty, though jilted by her future mother-in-law, depriving her of the destined marriage to the dreamy, pious, and valiant Nicolaus Ravenell, has just promised him the unthinkable. She promised to mother his newborn son, as if he were her own; their own, as it should have been from the beginning.

Nicolaus looks upon Deirdre with the greatest love in his heart for her, through his pained tears of indignation, as he is trying to figure out if God is playing some kind of cruel joke on him or place him in a cruel test of character. It is unfathomable to him that the woman he does not want, birthed his son then pushes the baby away as if he were some type of object, not wanting him, while the woman he truly loves is willing to step into that gap and protect his son from the hurt that comes from a mother's denial of love. Such a hurt he's known very well, his whole life.

Deirdre offers the most of herself to him, selfless love. She stands before him, looking ever so beautiful, her soft curly black hair strewn to her shoulders, playing off her lightly toasted skin color, with sparks of love jumping from her light green eyes.

The electricity of love between them is palpable. Deirdre unmistakably felt it, and yes, she could see it there through his tears; that eternal look of love for her. That look that is beyond comprehensible words.

Suddenly, what the Bishop had previously told Deirdre is manifest before her. Deirdre knew, in that very moment, that no one, on earth, in heaven, or in hell, could ever take their love. Their's is the love of a million years. The love that is their destiny which has been written in the stars from the beginning. No matter what scenarios tried to block them, or which bridges were destroyed, their love could never be denied.

Deirdre exhales in Nicolaus' loving arms that wrap her up in an instant. That warm love that she'd missed so much, and she knew he'd missed it too.

In silence, they meld together, their bodies against each other, her womanly figure fitting perfectly to his muscular manly frame, as is supposed to be.

Nicolaus basked in God's love and Deirdre's love inside that chapel. He held onto the only woman who owns his heart. He realizes that because of her presence, everything is going to be okay. His son is going to be okay. Indeed, his life is going to be okay.

Tears still stream from his eyes at the treacherous hurt caused by his wife. The rejection of their son is prompting a generational scorn from the same action that was set upon him by his own mother. Prayers begin to pour from his mouth.

As usual, he begins in the Latin tongue, and then transitions to English, asking specific blessings upon Deirdre, his hold on her getting tighter. He kisses the top of her precious head. He asks for protection upon his son, and for his bond with Deirdre to never be broken. He also prays for Marguerite, that in time, she could have some healing and be a better person.

When the prayers end, it is Deirdre who reaches up and wipes his tears away. She shakes her head slightly, admiring and knowing that this man she truly loves is a very special person. They remain standing close, in each other's space, in silence, his hands enrapture hers. He could feel the engagement rings he'd given her still upon her wedding finger. This touches Nicolaus deeply, as their marriage had been denied more than a year ago. The few minutes that pass seem timeless, as they stare into each other's eyes, in silence, no more words needed.

Someone else's family member enters the chapel to pray, breaking their concentration. Remaining silent, living in the moment, they rejoin their family in the labor and delivery waiting room. The nurses and the doctors continue to care for Marguerite, though her hateful hysterical screaming is still heard through the hallways.

Quickly Nicolaus steps away and makes a call to Andrejs Drone, Marguerite's father. Deirdre has followed him and is right by his side. "We have a boy!" he tells the new grandfather with enthusiasm.

"And my daughter, how is she?"

"Well... physically she is fine, mentally ... she ... she is ...," Nicolaus pauses in thought. How does one tell a father that his daughter is hysterical and may be unhinged from reality? "She is having a hard time. I think you should get here," he offers.

"Hard time?"

"Andrejs, she is rejecting the baby. I don't know. I'm sure you can help her."

"Oh no. Is that the baby depression?"

"Yes, perhaps," Nicolaus sighs, trying not to get emotional again. "I'm sure she'd feel better if you were here. We will support her in any way we can. We have been doing so."

Andrejs nods, "Yes, okay. We'll be there as soon as my jet can get me there. We leave right away," he says in broken English, with his thick Latvian accent.

"Okay. See you soon."

When Nicolaus ends the call, no words are needed, as he and Deirdre are on the same page about supporting Marguerite. She briefly hugs him again, and they rejoin the family in the labor and delivery waiting room.

Ishani, an East Indian American, whose family has ties to important dynasties and dignitaries in India, is Deirdre's law school colleague. They graduated the same year, and have always kept in touch. Ishani resembles a real-life action doll, with mellow brown eyes, thick straight silky hair that shines and moves with the slightest breeze, and a smile that lights up any room.

Maggie, Deirdre's longtime friend, and daring mother hen, has always kept an eye out for Deirdre. Deirdre and Ishani tease her, calling her, 'Never Married Maggie', because she is childless, usually dateless, and takes care of everyone around her.

Both Ishani and Maggie have been supporting Deirdre in the background of all the happenings with Nicolaus. And now, they arrive to the hospital to support her. They hug Deirdre, worried about her. They both also greet Nicolaus with a hug.

Maggie pulls Deirdre aside. She shakes her head, frowning, as Marguerite's hysteria can occasionally be heard through the hospital hallways. "Deirdre, what's happening now?"

"Well, Marguerite doesn't want the baby, so I'm going to take care of him."

They both frown at Deirdre. It is Maggie who is the one who always speaks up first. She whispers in the corner, so that only the three of them could hear. "Deirdre! How is that supposed to work? Nicolaus is still going to be with her."

Deirdre nods. "I know, ... I'd do anything for Nicky. It's his son."

"You'd do anything for him, somehow, I'm not sure he'd do the same for you."

"Maggie!"

"Deirdre, Maggie's right. Nicky should have given his all to you in the beginning. He should have left his family for you," Ishani asserts.

"Oh that's not fair. Remember, I told you he offered for us to leave and marry when all the trouble started to break. It's me who told him no. And anyway, how could he walk away from everything his ancestors have done to build up their family and their company. It's an unfair burden, and I wouldn't have accepted him doing that.

It is me who kept putting him off. You've got to give Nicky a break," tears roll from her eyes. This whole situation is painful. "Anyway, I already promised him. His son needs a mother, and I'm going to step in and be that mother. If nothing else, doing so will cement me to Nicky, even more."

Maggie sighs, not feeling satisfied at her explanation, "I guess." Maggie scopes out Nicolaus from across the room. She sees him being surrounded by people. Even at a time like this, his natural charisma and striking good looks draw people towards him.

"Stop chastising me! I need your support right now," Deirdre gripes at her ladies.

They nod and hug on her. "Of course you'll make a great mom," Ishani tells her.

The hospital staff, like the many people in the city, knew of the couple, and were thrilled to have the ever handsome Nicolaus Ravenell, Vice President of the Villamae Medical Corp, (VMC) clinics, and his stellar father, Nigel Ravenell, co-founder of VMC, amongst their patient guests. Some staff members just could not pass up the opportunity to go to Nicolaus and offer their congratulations on the baby. Others ask for autographs. Nicolaus is still amazed and sometimes overwhelmed at peoples' reaction towards him. He hardly thought himself famous, or a star, though he seems to be well known, even in Latvia, where their pharmaceutical partnership with Marguerite's father is located.

Nigel draws the line when selfies are requested. He nicely tells the staff, "Well we are waiting to see my grandson. Please, now," he waives his arms at them, "it's just not a good time ... maybe another day."

Graciously, the staff takes leave of them. Suddenly, Manfred, the security detail for the family, appears. Somehow, Manfred has a knack for appearing just at the right time. His tall muscular frame, and strong Native American jaw could be intimidating. No one ever questioned his authority.

Nigel greets him with a hold of his shoulder, "Ah, Manfred, thank you so much for being here."

"Of course! Congratulations on the baby. Now you are a grandfather, like me," he gives a toothy grin to Nigel. "How does it feel?"

Nigel frowns, thinking about all that is happening, "Hmm, I don't know yet," he jokes. "Seriously though, it really is wonderful. Amazing. My grandson looks like Nicolaus, like us men."

After another half hour, the whole family is invited into the hospital room, intended to bring cheer and support to Marguerite. Deirdre lovingly holds Nicolaus' newborn son, as Marguerite continues to refuse the child. As much as she could with everyone present, Marguerite shut herself off from the family. The sedatives calmed her delirium.

Chapter Two

Marguerite is released from the hospital in good health the following day. The small army of helpers Ceil hired accompanies them home. The team includes two nurses, a nanny, and a teacher for the newborn.

Once home, Nicolaus attempts to move himself and the baby into Marguerite's bedroom, only to be run off by her hysterical screaming. Her behavior concerns him greatly, so he arranges for a woman psychologist to immediately assist her. Nicolaus is surprised when Marguerite accepts this help.

Andrejs is unable to fly into Austin, Texas from Riga, Latvia as quickly as he thought he could, due to weather delays.

"Marguerite is having a hard time," Nicolaus tells Andrejs, after he has finally arrived and settles into the guest room in Nicolaus' wing of the mansion. Nicolaus is hoping Andrejs' presence might change Marguerite's disposition. "She's asked for Deirdre to care for our son. Deirdre agreed ... we know Marguerite needs a break," he explains, using Deirdre's words.

Andrejs had not seen his oldest daughter since the wedding, as Marguerite had refused a visit from him and her sister, Penelope. Marguerite's feelings of abandonment made her anger overflow. Although her supposed abandonment left her with this rich American family, and a handsome and pious husband, for which many women would trade places with her.

Andrejs and Penelope enter Marguerite's bedroom, seeing her dressed in luxurious bedclothes, her hair disheveled, as she has not been out of bed.

Andrejs is very happy to have a grandson. After Penelope's antics of obnoxious hugging on Nicolaus ends, she happily accepts the baby from the duty nurse, holding him gently.

"Wow, he is beautiful." Penelope observes the baby's face, nose, and hair line. She chuckles, "He looks exactly like his papa. No?" Andrejs agrees, however, this does not sit well with Marguerite. Nicolaus takes this as a cue to leave them, and hopes they can talk Marguerite through her troubles.

Rachel, his aunt, appears from nowhere, and hugs Nicolaus to her. It pains her to see him suffer the awful events he is going through. She knows this is all her fault, and she cannot do anything about it. If only she had been stronger when he was born, she could have kept him in her care, instead of turning him over to the care of Ceil, her sister, whom she knew would reject him.

Rachel did realize that she is much luckier than other women in that she is able to be part of Nicolaus' life. She had seen Nicolaus on a daily basis since he was a child, she knew where he was, how he was doing, and she watched him grow from a baby to the man he is today. Nigel would never deny her access to their son. She knew that Nicolaus was well taken care of and had everything he needed, well ... except a mother's love. He was never going to get love from Ceil, even though Ceil is her sister. It has always been very hard for Rachel to see Ceil continually abuse and mistreat Nicolaus. She could say nothing about it, as Nigel had to be the one to control all the situations. It pained her that mostly he had not.

By no means had Ceil ever gotten over the fact Nigel had always wanted Rachel, even though he married her. Since Nigel had been in their family's circle, Rachel felt that he was always supposed to belong to her. They had intended to marry, except, their mother had other plans. Their mother decided that Rachel was not strong enough for Nigel, even though, at that time, they were already together.

Rachel and Nigel suffered the same cruel injustice that Ceil now inflicted upon Nicolaus and Deirdre. Ceil purposefully flaunted her schemes and good fortune in Rachel's face at every chance, even now, hiring a nurse, a nanny, and a teacher for the few day old grandson. Actions that Rachel could not afford.

Rachel is tired of Ceil using Nicolaus as a pawn, using the secret of his parentage against him. Rachel knew that one day she'd tell Nicolaus the truth, but today is just not that day. Tears well in Rachel's eyes.

"Auntie Rachel, you okay?" Nicolaus asks her with great concern, his hand lightly touching her back.

Rachel smiles up at him, shaking the crying spell away, waving at her eyes, trying to make the tears stop. Nicolaus gives her a big hug, conveying the love and concern he has for her. This only makes her want to cry more.

Rachel looks up at her son, smiling on him. She is so proud of him. Rachel sees Nicolaus as highly manly, more than Nigel, being strong, brave, and fearless. Exactly like Nicohls, their ancestor. She felt regretful for his emotional suffering. She fake laughs to ease his concern, "That baby ... he looks just like you." She touches his chest and can feel the taunt muscles, "Just like Nicohls, except for the coloring, a shade or two darker" she reminds him.

Nicolaus chuckles, "Yes. I thought about that. The Kiviste genes."

Rachel wipes her eyes, chuckling, feeling a little better, "Yes." She sought a tissue from a nearby table and wipes her face. "Have you thought of names yet?"

Nicolaus shakes his head, "No." He sighs, "With all the drama, I just wanted to get through her birthing him without hurting him, you know?"

Rachel nods, "Yes. I'm so sorry about all this. It should be a happy time for you."

Nicolaus smiles, "With Deirdre around, I think everything will be okay. I thank God for Deirdre every day. Auntie Rachel, I couldn't have made it this far without her."

"She's your true love," Rachel whispers to him.

"Yes, she is!"

"Well, when you begin to think about names, you may want to look at the family book Francesca has. The family names run deep, just like our genes."

Nicolaus smiles at her, "Okay, I will."

Rachel joins Nicolaus, going into the room with the Drone family.

Chapter Three

The following day, Andrejs felt that Marguerite was in good enough condition and being well cared for, so he could get back to his Drone Pharma headquarters in Latvia. In his daughter's lavish bedroom, he once again touches his grandson, tousling his curly hair, as the nurse held him. Andrejs smiles, then he sits at the foot of his daughter's bed, where she lay in her depression.

He looks at Marguerite, with Penelope standing behind him.

"So now daughter, I want you to know I think you have done well. This baby holds firm the merger. And here, I brought something for you," he tells her as he reaches into his inside suit jacket pocket. He pulls out a sealed envelope. Smiling, Andrejs hands Marguerite the envelope.

Marguerite sits up, the same disheveled look about her. She had a feeling this is the trust fund money that her mother had left her. She didn't know when her father was going to release the money to her, she'd been waiting for nine months now, since the day she had begrudgingly consummated her marriage.

She opens the envelope and feels a little relief at seeing a check for five million U.S. dollars, a quarter of what her mother had left her. The check is signed by her father. She looks up at him, then frowns. "The rest?"

Andrejs chuckles and speaks in broken English. "Well, when you stronger, you visit to Latvia and get it yourself." He touches her hand. "For now, you continue to be good wife. You get out of bed. You wash yourself. You eat. You visit your friends. You shop. Don't worry about baby, you have plenty help," he waives his arms around at the professional women waiting for their turn with the Ravenell baby to prove their worth.

He touches her hand again, "You no more cry. No more whine. Nicolaus is good to you, just look around. You want for nothing.

He take care of you. For this, I am pleased. He is kind to you. Deirdre is very kind to you." He saw a frowned look appear over Marguerite's face at the mention of Deirdre's name. "No, no," he tells her, his chastisement making the frown leave, "Deirdre is kind to you, doing what you want, taking on care of baby. And that is okay. When you ready, you take over. If never ..." he bobs his head from side to side with pursed lips, "well, we see, that probably okay too. Marguerite, that baby is your baby. You and Nicolaus. No jealousy needed. Right?"

Marguerite nods understanding what her father is saying.

Penelope frowns, "If Nicolaus was mine, I'd do everything to keep him close, not push him away," contradicting what she'd previously told her sister to do, while in cahoots with Ceil to ensure the marriage is ruined.

Marguerite frowns again, "Father, he wants cheat," she complained in her broken English.

"Ah, no, Nicolaus is good man. He is here for you. He not cheat. That's thoughts in your mind," he tells her pointing to his head. "If Nicolaus cheat you drive him to that." Andrejs then shrugs, "Anyway, most men lie ... and cheat, eventually, it's our nature, some cannot resist," he gave a nagging laugh. "No, you not bring shame to this family, you will be good wife. Tend to yourself, get strong, then tend to your husband. Now, no more talk of negative thoughts. You get out of bed, and get strong to spend your money."

Andrejs stands and takes Marguerite by the hand to help her out of the bed. One of the two nurses is quickly by her side to help her walk to the extravagant bathroom.

Chapter Four

I t is at Sunday dinner, with all family present, when Benjamin decides to make an unusual announcement. Benjamin is the younger Ravenell brother. Everyone present includes Ceil and Nigel, Francesca - the brother's loving cousin, Constance - Deirdre's mother, Deirdre, Rachel, Elsa - Deirdre's dear friend who works at the company and is dating Benjamin, and even Ishani and Maggie.

Benjamin has not had the best behavior in his lifetime. As the younger brother to Nicolaus, jealousy has been his forte most of his life. His covetousness of Deirdre has unfortunately morphed into an obsession, for which he has started to become bold in his pursuit of her, now that Nicolaus is married to another. He cannot understand and does not accept that Deirdre continues to turn down his marriage proposal, despite her undeniable love for his brother.

Benjamin smiles, glad everyone is in attendance, so that he would not have to repeat himself. He motions to the server to fill his glass with bourbon. After taking a long drink, he interrupts the conversation that centers around Nicolaus' son.

"Umm, excuse me everyone," he says loudly to bring the attention to himself. The talking stops, and all eyes are on him. He smiles. "I want everyone to know, that I have decided to use my middle name, Niall, from now on. So please, instead of calling me Benjamin, address me as Niall. I will be changing everything, including all my documents. I want to be known as Niall Ravenell."

Ceil smiles. "Yes well, I like both of the names I've given you. Benjamin Niall."

Francesca giggles, "What's with the Irish names? I thought we are Estonian!"

"Niall is the special name I have given, after your father", Ceil continues, "a derivative of the name Nigel." She smiles at her younger son. "You are special. And it is about time that you have recognized that about yourself."

"I feel that I want to walk a different path in life now," he momentarily looks at his glass, thinking about what Helena had told him previously, "thanks to Helena, my new friend at the children's home. I want to transform," he says with arrogance, missing out on his own gesture.

"Walking a different path?" Francesca grills him. "So, ... that includes changing your despicable behavior towards women?" she asks him directly, with her thick British accent.

Niall smiles at her question, wanting to say something nasty, then recoils from his previous behavior. "Yes," he answers. "I know I have not always ... been ... proper with women, Francesca. That is why I want a name change, for a fresh start."

"A reset of behaviors can be a good thing," Nicolaus supports his younger brother's thoughts. "Your actions need to follow the name change, though, Benjamin."

"Don't envy me because you don't have a middle name to follow suit, brother." His comment gets chuckles. "Of course, I know my actions need to change."

"I'm all for good things of good people. I support you, Niall," Nicolaus tells him, earnestly. He looks to Deirdre, noticing she is quiet about all this, not voicing her opinion.

"I agree with Nicolaus, and am very glad that you have recognized that you can do better and are making strives at it. Makes me proud of you, my son," Nigel tells him.

Niall feels a rush of gratitude at his father's words.

"Lots of kumbaya going around this table," Ceil states. "No matter what your name is, or what name you use, or what you change your name to, you are still my much loved and adored son," she declares for everyone to hear, never having said such a thing to Nicolaus in his whole life. "You are my special son, and one day, you'll be in the place where I want to see you. One day you will be, I just know it."

Nicolaus nods at his mother's words. "We all support you, and will help you get there," he sweetly tells his younger brother.

The dinner continues, and talk is now all about sports.

Chapter Five

N iall stands against the door frame and admires Deirdre as she cradles Nicolaus' son in her arms. The distinctive and beautiful aroma that is special to Deirdre envelopes the room beyond the new baby smell, as she tells Little Nicky affirming words, just as she does every morning. "You are special, aren't you, my little one? Yes you are. And so very smart. And handsome too, just like your daddy. We'll have to keep the girls off you."

Nicolaus' son responds to Deirdre the best he can, looking into her eyes as he drinks his breakfast. Most likely, he thinks Deirdre is his mother, just as Deirdre promised Nicolaus. She promised him the baby wouldn't notice his mother is missing. She believes she is accomplishing her promise to Nicolaus and is glad for it. She also does hope she is being of help to Marguerite.

Deirdre feels someone's eyes on her. She looks up to see Niall, grinning wide. "What?" she asks him with a smile, unashamed of her baby talk. She smoothes the baby's hair while she feeds him baby formula milk from a glass baby bottle.

Niall looks down for a moment, then back at Deirdre. "I am just thinking ... just imagining how you'd be with our children." Niall may have changed his preferred name, however, his character mostly remains the same, including his irksome obsession with Deirdre. Niall's jealousy of the pure love between his brother and Deirdre has been festering from the time of his youth. Niall has always been jealous of Nicolaus' natural goodness, his high achievements, and his easy ability to attract women. He loathed the fact that Nicolaus did nothing to draw women to him, while he himself found it difficult to get women's attention; especially that of Deirdre.

Deirdre frowns at him, thinking he mis-spoke. "I'm sorry, what?"

Niall sits in the chair next to her in the dining room. It's just the two of them, and the nanny across the room, in case she is needed. The nanny knits to keep herself busy. Niall sighs. "Yep. Our children. Yours and mine." He motions between them with his fingers, "You know, you and me."

Deirdre rolls her eyes. She thought this was over with him. "Niall ..."

"Just hear me out, Deirdre," he gently touches her arm. The feel of her soft skin makes him want to grab her up against him. Niall controlled the urge, and continues his explanation. "I'd make a pretty good father, and of course," he gestures over Deirdre and the baby, "you are a wonderful mother. Our children will be beautiful. And we could raise them to do good in the world."

Deirdre looks at Niall strangely, never having heard this raising children argument from him before. "Oh, I think you miss the kids at the children's home. You should go by and see them! I'm sure they'd be happy to see you."

He shakes his head. "Deirdre, I'm talking about the children you and I will make. You know I want to marry you. Having changed my name does not and will never change how I feel about you. I still love you Deirdre. And well ... you can't really marry Nicolaus now, since he's already in a marriage."

Deirdre sighs, not expecting to have to deal with this again. Niall moves closer to her. Quickly, he kisses her cheek, hardly able to resist this action. Next thing Deirdre sees, Niall gets down on his knee, just as the baby finishes his formula drink.

Wanting to ignore what she knew would be coming out of Niall's mouth, Deirdre keeps her attention on the baby. Deirdre places a cloth on her shoulder, then places the baby up for burping. Gently, she pats the little darling who exactly resembles Nicolaus, her true love; while Nicolaus' brother is trying to get her to marry him. Deirdre frowns at her uncanny situation. She wonders what her mother will think when she tells her later.

Since Deirdre's hands are busy with the baby, Niall touches her denim covered knee. "Deirdre, I have professed my love for you to the world on international television; I have explained my love for you to my mother; and Nicolaus also knows that I have interest in you."

"Niall, we have already talked about this. I ..."

"And," he interrupts her before she can finish her sentence. "I want to protect you, and be your lover, your husband, your ... everything. I love you, Deirdre. Let me take care of you. Our children will be strong. I will love you and our children. And we'll have a great future together. And ..."

"Ah, Niall, ..." Deirdre stands with the baby, not able to take much more of Niall's love speech. "That is really thoughtful and all," she continues her attention to Little Nicky. Suddenly, the baby gives a large belch, as expected. He makes a satisfied cooing sound. Deirdre kisses his sweet little head.

The nanny rushes over to assist, "Deirdre, I'll watch him now, so you and Niall can speak. I'm sure he's ready for a nap." The nanny is very happy to earn her money as she eases the baby from Deirdre.

"Oh, yes, thank you!" Deirdre smiles at the nanny, and lets her take whatever she needs: blankets, cloths, etc.

Niall grabs Deirdre's hand, getting her attention back on him and on the matter before them. "I love you, Deirdre."

Deirdre sighs, gently retrieving her hand and waving it in the air to question him. "Where does that leave Elsa? Elsa is the one who loves you, Niall."

"I love you, Deirdre."

Deirdre smiles, "Look Niall, I told you, I only think of you as a brother. I could never marry you, or anyone else. For me it's Nicky or no one." She sighs, and then smiles again. "I really appreciate the gesture, but Niall, it's just not going to happen. Please, use this wonderful, positive energy on Elsa. I'm more than sure she'd appreciate it, and be happy to hear those words from you. Anyway, I would not want to do anything that would hurt Elsa. She's like my sister."

She touches Niall's face with both hands, smoothing his hair back. "Thank you, but no, sweetie." She tugs at his arms so he would get up off his knee. "I think you should focus on Elsa, and the kids at the children's home. And Niall, if you don't love Elsa, or you don't want her, please, don't string her along. Don't hurt her. Just talk to her. Tell her how you feel."

Niall rose, feeling wounded by her rebuff of him, yet again. He just doesn't understand why Deirdre doesn't want him. He thought of himself as a prized catch. After all, he is a rich bachelor with connections. He cannot understand her total devotion to his brother, who cannot marry her.

"I just don't get it," he blurts out to Deirdre, as if her rejection pained him. "I just ..."

"Niall, we talked about this already. Look, I'm going to get some rest while the nanny has the baby." Quickly, Deirdre kisses Niall's face, and pats his arm, hoping it would settle him down, and make him drop the subject. She exits the room, almost at a running pace. She doesn't want to discuss this with him any longer, or ever again, if she could help it.

Chapter Six

Several days after Andrejs and Penelope left, Marguerite slowly became more herself, however, she still refuses to have anything to do with the baby. Nicolaus watches his mother as she makes absurd demands on Marguerite.

"I will not have my grandchild drink formula milk. Breast milk is always better and healthier," Ceil chastises Marguerite, not caring if she may be depressed.

Marguerite turns away, as Ceil nudges the breast pump at her, insisting the demand be followed.

Ceil scoffs, "If you don't cooperate, I'll get that milk myself! I'll not have you mistreat my grandchild."

Nicolaus steps up for his wife. "Mother, please stop badgering Marguerite. Give her some breathing room." He stands between the ladies, as if to protect Marguerite from his mother's foolery. "I'm fine with the baby drinking formula. He doesn't seem to mind," he tells Ceil, wondering what revenge she will exact upon him for his words and his actions.

Ceil looks at Nicolaus, the military hero, with disdain, then backs off. Now she fell into a different upset because every time she plots against Nicolaus, he finds a way to navigate through it. She is annoyed that Nicolaus is still around, and still holding on as Vice President of Nigel's firm, even with all the troubles she created for him.

Ceil is disappointed that Nicolaus has not run off with Deirdre by now. She blames herself for miscalculating his loyalty to Nigel. She vows to keep working at making his life as miserable as possible.

Chapter Seven-TW

Niall drove his Italian sports car to the mansion, having Elsa entrapped.

"Niall, you promise to take me home after our nightcap, right?"

Niall smiles at her, "Sure, sure," he says so she'll stop complaining. He wants to get her into the house and pressure her.

It is late, so most of the family have retired to their respective rooms. Niall is gentlemanly, opening the doors for Elsa. He makes them drinks of blackberry Bourbon.

Niall pulls Elsa on his lap as they enjoy their drinks. "Hey babe, I want you to stay here tonight, with me, in my bed," he tells her, not holding back.

His words made Elsa tense up. She has the urge to leap right off his lap. His arm prevents her from getting up. Elsa rolls her eyes, having staved off Niall for so long, however, his behavior towards her was a little different than usual. In the last few days, he seemed a little more aggressive towards her. "Niall, no, it's time to take me home."

"You know, with all the drama in our family, I have learned one thing. Life is short. None of us really know when it may be our last day." Niall's grip on Elsa tightens as she tries to get out of his lap again. He draws her closer to him. His eyes on Elsa, he puts his drink down, then takes hers from her hand and sets it down, so he can properly gripe. "Elsa, you know I love you, right?" he says frowning, looking into her eyes.

Elsa sighs and closes her eyes, wishing this away. However, when she opens her eyes, she is in the same predicament. She gently touches Niall's face. Her brain suddenly reacts 'did he just tell me he loves me?' Elsa feels his hands on her as he grips her tighter. She knows she isn't going to be able to get away from him, he is much stronger than she. "Say that again," she whispers to him, trying to turn this awkwardness into something beautiful.

"I love you, girl. You hear me?"

Elsa nods. "Wow! I love you too, Niall."

"I don't want to wait any longer to have you, Elsa."

Elsa smiles, putting her forehead against his. "Babe, we talked about this. We wait until we are married. Remember?"

"No! No more waiting!" Now he sounds agitated.

Elsa giggles at his frustration, "Oh, is that a marriage proposal? Oh it just went right over my head. Ask me again."

Niall sighs, not giving up. He turns Elsa's back to him, as she is still on his lap, and he does not let go of her. He is pleased that she doesn't try to fight him. "Elsa, stop. I'm serious. Look, you stay with me tonight, or it's over. No more waiting. I'm not built like that. I need women around me. I need to have sex. So, either we have sex, or ... you're out," he tells her coldly. After all, they had been dating for six months now, and once Niall was helping at the children's home, Helena helped him turn over a new life, and reset some behaviors. In exasperation, Niall confirms, "I'm not like Nicolaus. I will not wait any longer."

Elsa frowns, scared of what might happen. Scared of giving herself to him, then he walk away, thinking of her as another notch in his sex tally board. Or if she calls his bluff and resists him, he still might actually walk away. It's a lose-lose situation for Elsa.

Slowly, Elsa reaches back, and pulls his face next to hers, their skin touching. "Okay, so are you proposing then, Niall? We should at least be engaged before having sex."

Niall is silent for a long moment. He nods. "Okay, okay", telling her what she wants to hear, and not really meaning it. His body and his mind is in tune with his engorged member, especially as he is thinking of Deirdre. Niall seems to have already forgotten his speech about changing his life. Currently, he only has one thing on his mind.

Elsa turns herself in his lap. She could feel that he is already aroused. She chuckles, "Well, what does that mean?"

Niall nods again, feeling tortured in his loins. "Yes, we can be engaged."

Elsa lets out an excited squeak, holding her left hand out, accentuating her ring finger. "Okay, great, where's the ring, baby? You already have one for me, right?"

Niall doesn't like where his lying is leading, however, right now, he'd do anything to have Elsa. "Well ... I have one in mind for you. I have it on hold at the jewelry store. I need the size of your finger," he boldly lies to her again.

Elsa wiggles excitedly in his lap. Her movements are a horrid tease for him, almost making him cry out. He is ready to hold her down and go into her.

"When do we go get it? Tomorrow? Oh babe," she kisses his lips, "that is so sweet of you. And of course, yes, I will marry you," she answers the question Niall never asked her.

Their lips connect, Niall jamming his tongue in Elsa's mouth, harshly kissing her. He stands with her in his arms, not letting her feet touch the ground. He quickly carries her up to his bedroom.

Once inside, Niall is glad the staff had cleaned his room, still following Nicolaus' standing order to do so, as he had left it in the usual messy state. In no time he had Elsa on the bed, and out of her clothes. There was little foreplay before Niall clumsily and harshly rams himself into Elsa's vagina, unable to wait a second longer. Elsa moans loudly... in pain. Niall hushes her moans with his mouth on hers.

Tears fall down the sides of Elsa's face as Niall harshly sexes her. Elsa lets him have his way with her, not fighting him at all, though she did think the experience was going to be different. Perhaps romantic. A little gentle loving. No, it is fully the opposite.

Elsa thought his ravenousness may have been her fault for making him wait so long. She feels disappointed. She figures he probably couldn't control himself at this moment, and perhaps it would get better with time.

Niall groans loudly as he ejaculates into Elsa. Her body brings very good sensations to him. Roughly, he flips her onto her belly, and enters her vagina again, not having yet had his fill of her.

Elsa's mind suddenly fears that this may be Niall's way of doing this. Perhaps he is sexually rough. Niall goes into Elsa as far as he can go, and roughly pounds her, wanting to make her scream.

"Niall, ... wait ... Niall..." Elsa flails her arms about trying to stop him.

"No more waiting." Roughly, he continues to enjoy Elsa's slim body, holding onto her curvy hips, not stopping until he ejaculates again, controlling his moan this time, hoping he somehow satisfied Elsa as well. Out of breath, he pulls Elsa upon his chest, facing him, and holds her tightly.

Angry and in pain, Elsa tries to get away from Niall, and he won't let her. He lightly laughs as she tries to get away. "Niall, it's not funny. You were too rough," Elsa complains, as he forces her to lay down on him.

"Oh, that wasn't rough. You feel really good, babe." Forcibly, he grabs a fist full of Elsa's thick, black hair and pulls her head back, force kissing her sweet, soft mouth, tasting her again. Niall takes a deep breath to relax, going to sleep, his grip on Elsa remaining tight.

Chapter Eight-TW

The following night, Deirdre heads towards the Ravenell family library to grab a book that peaked her interest, to read in bed, as she now is back to spending nights at the mansion. Staying at the mansion made it easier for her in the mornings when Little Nicky awoke.

As she came to the opened library door, she stumbles upon the silhouettes of Niall and Elsa, against the moonlight that shone through the windows, in the dark room.

The couple were quiet and in a lover's moment. Not to disturb them, Deirdre backs from the opened door, into the unlit breezeway space before the room entrance, out of their sight, and out of the moonlight. Deirdre just wants to cherish the sweet moment for Elsa, before turning to leave.

Niall held Elsa to him, as the light from the full moon completely illuminates the unlit library, through the twenty-foot window. He is at her neck, making her moan in pleasure. In an instant, Niall roughly throws Elsa flat on her back, upon the large table which is an antique from somewhere in the world. The table is thick and strong, and sturdy enough to hold much weight. Niall's monstrous behavior led him to hold Elsa down on the table by a handful of hair from the back of her head.

Deirdre could hear Niall tearing her clothes away from her body, exposing her womanly bosom. Niall greedily handles her, making Elsa shriek. Her distressed sound causes Niall to quickly backhand her face and grab her neck. "Quiet!" he tells her, kissing her nape, then returning to her bosom. Suddenly, he stops, and looks up, jerking on Elsa's head so she could not move, as his body pins her down.

Deirdre is appalled at Niall's behavior. She fears he can see her through the window next to the library door, in the dark shadows of the corridor. She freezes, knowing if she moves, or walks away now, he will certainly be able to see her. What might he do to her for being there? What might he say? Would he hurt Elsa more than he is hurting her now?

Actually, Niall cannot see Deirdre, though he can smell her beautiful aroma. Knowing she is nearby or walking somewhere in the hallways of the house, her aroma drifting to his nostrils, even more so heightened his already high sexual tension, making him more impatient. He returns his attention to Elsa. Quickly tugging at his own clothes, Niall harshly thrusts himself deep into Elsa, wishing she is Deirdre. He breathed in Deirdre's sweet scent with closed eyes, trying to imagine her with him now. Imagining that it is Deirdre he is deeply thrusting into, not easing up, driving his stamina over the top.

Niall is so rough with Elsa, she gasps and whimpers quieted moans throughout this torrid lovemaking, which is not enjoyable for her. However, Elsa swallows this disappointment of Niall, along with the other moments in time he has disappointed her, and replaces it with gladness believing he wants her so much. Elsa does love Niall, and despite this setback, she wants him to be her husband. She imagines she can work on this issue once they are married, as she continues to whimper.

Tabu intrigue entices Deirdre to watch the couple. Niall covers Elsa's mouth to quiet the noise, though he does not let up on her. He began to grumble and moan in ecstasy. To stop himself climaxing, Niall slaps Elsa across the face again, making her cry out. Then he flips her on her stomach. Deirdre frowns, terrified by Niall's behavior, waiting for the opportune time to run from this awful scene.

Without hesitating, Niall roughly enters Elsa from behind, making her shriek again. Roughly, Niall intensely grinds Elsa as hard and as deep as he can, swiftly increasing his tempo. Elsa is no longer able to make a sound. She reaches for something to hold on to. The table is bare and too wide to reach the edge. All she can do is endure his harsh sexing.

Niall then grabs Elsa by the throat, with monstrous behavior, pulling her head back. Although Elsa is unable to breathe, this does not seem to bother Niall. His intensity increases even more so, as he simultaneously shakes her by the throat, as if he were a maniac. He goes faster while he thinks about what he wants to do to Deirdre. Niall finally ejaculates inside of Elsa, exploding in quiet orgasm and a soft moan.

Out of breath, Niall collapses on top of Elsa, finally releasing her throat so she can breathe. Elsa gasps for air under the weight of Niall, her love. Elsa's body also releases orgasm, making her shudder beneath him.

Niall's cruelty and the harshness towards Elsa made tears stream from Deirdre's eyes, because she feels bad for Elsa. Deirdre feels guilty for feeding Elsa's fantasy about Niall. Deirdre knows Niall is harsh, never realizing he is so abusive. She worries for Elsa. Quietly, Deirdre is finally able to get away.

Chapter Nine

The next morning, as Deirdre is escorted to breakfast by Nicolaus, with Marguerite alongside him, she watches for Elsa to appear, as she is almost certain she would have stayed overnight with Niall. Moments later, Elsa and Niall enter the breakfast room. Elsa clings to Niall with a big smile on her face, and Niall does not look amused. Deirdre pulls on Elsa's arm. "Elsa, walk with me!"

"Oh, okay," Elsa went along, understanding Deirdre needs to talk to her.

Deirdre walks them out to a faraway place on the property, where the evergreen bushes lined the grass, out of hearing distance from everyone. The morning sun shone in the clear Austin sky, illuminating the bruises on each side of Elsa's face and neck.

As they sat on the bench, the site of the bruising made Deirdre put her forehead in her hand. "Oh God," Deirdre starts.

Elsa frowns, "Oh no, what is it? What's happened?"

Deirdre sighs, to calm herself. "Elsa, I'm glad you seem to be happy in this relationship with Niall, uhm ... is everything going okay? I mean ... like the way you expect?"

Elsa frowns at her again. "Well, yes ... I think so. Why? Has Niall said something?"

"Elsa, I guess what I'm trying to ask is, does Niall treat you properly?"

"Well ... oh!" Elsa touches her cheek, feeling this is what Deirdre is talking about.

"Is it showing? I thought I covered it with makeup."

Deirdre is bothered by the nonchalant attitude Elsa has of Niall's abuse of her. "The fact that we are having this conversation has me really worried, Elsa! You can't let Niall treat you like this."

"Okay, okay, slow your roll my sister. I can handle Niall."

"Elsa!"

"What? This is nothing. He just gets a little rough sometimes. That's all."

"A little rough? Elsa! Now you know that is not okay."

"Deirdre, relax! I can handle Niall. I would never let him hurt me. This is nothing." Elsa sighs. "I'm sorry this is a worry to you. Look, I'll talk to him about it. I was going to anyway." She sighs again and grabs Deirdre's arm. "Anyway, he asked me to marry him! I'm so excited, Deirdre. We're engaged!"

"What?" Deirdre hugs Elsa. "Oh ..." not sure she is happy about it. "I'm happy for you, if that's what you want."

"Well, yes, it's what I want. I want him to be my husband," she exclaims excitedly. She kisses Deirdre's face. "I owe you, Deirdre! If it weren't for you, Niall and I probably would have never gotten together."

"No, you don't owe me. For sure, you've got to talk to Niall. Elsa, you promise you'll talk to him and get everything straight?"

"Yes. Yes!" Elsa jumps to her feet. "Now, can we get some breakfast? I'm famished!"

Deirdre tightly hugs Elsa to her. The ladies make their way back to the breakfast table in the mansion. The brothers had waited for the ladies to return before eating.

"Everything okay?" Nicolaus asks them.

Elsa nods. "Oh, yes, fine. Thank you, Nicky."

"Anything I should know about?" Niall asks, not to be out done by his brother.

Elsa shakes her head. "No, babe, all is well. We'll talk about it later." Both brothers were standing and waiting to seat the ladies at the table. Elsa gave Niall a kiss, "Thank you for waiting, babe."

Chapter Ten

The next day is sunny and hot in Austin, though it is only February. A cool breeze is felt at times, making the weather feel like early spring.

Niall is not as discreet about Elsa as he should have been.

Ceil frowns, while on the huge back patio, entertaining guests, she hears what sounds like two people having sex in the nearby bushes. Ceil can tell by the looks on her guest's faces they hear the couple as well. Her guests of three people are the mayor's wife, the wife's next door neighbor, and an up and coming young lady who represents a local charity organization.

"Ceil, is that your son? The younger one?" the wife asks, being familiar with his voice.

Ceil blushes with embarrassment. "Why don't we ..."

The couple run from the bushes, Niall chasing Elsa through the maze of shrubs. They didn't seem to notice that other people were around. Elsa giggles and runs like a young, giddy schoolgirl, as Niall chases her. Happily, she throws her shoes at him. Niall catches up to her, and they kiss. Niall leads Elsa to another set of bushes, where they lay on the ground, and he makes love to her again.

"Yes, let's take our meeting inside. We can let them have their space."

Later that day, Ceil complains to Nigel about Elsa's behavior. Nigel frowns at his wife. "Well, she was not by herself, was she?"

Ceil crosses her arms, "Well, no, she ..."

"Ah, so Niall, her man, and let me emphasize the word ... man ... was not acting responsibly either. Do I have that right, Ceil dear?"

Ceil huffs, unable to defend her Niall. "Okay, okay, I hear you."

Nigel chuckles, "They seem to be doing it everywhere. I caught them in the kitchen pantry, of all places, you saw them in the bushes, the staff saw them in the garden. Elsa seems to be holding

Niall's attention, and Niall can't seem to keep his hands off her. Perhaps Niall is actually in love. Elsa is a good girl! A bright young woman, with a career. An ambassador's daughter." Nigel kisses Ceil on the face. "Don't worry dear, I think this will all work itself out."

Chapter Eleven

"**B**abe, we are going to look at rings today, right?" Elsa pressures Niall at the breakfast table the next morning, in front of everyone. Niall had been putting her off about the ring for a few weeks now. However, Elsa is desperate not to let Niall trick her. "Mother Ceil, Mr. Ravenell, Niall and I are engaged for a few weeks now, has he told you?" Elsa grabs onto Niall's arm, with glee in her voice and spirit.

Nicolaus stops eating and puts his financial paper down to see his parents' reaction, as Niall focuses on his food and says nothing. However, this is a first where Niall is concerned.

"Well ...no, actually. Niall hasn't said a word. Niall?" Ceil addresses him.

Niall stops eating and looks up to see all eyes on him, including Deirdre. Niall sniffs, then smiles and nods, looking to Elsa. He moves towards her for a kiss, and they smack lips, as if this is a sign of them being engaged.

Ceil eyes Elsa, and thinks to herself, 'Perhaps Nigel is right. Elsa is always fashionably dressed, and she is a beautiful young woman. Everyone knows Elsa is smart, organized, and she gets things done. Nigel sings praises about Elsa's work all the time.'

Ceil's same thoughts of Elsa could almost be used word for word to describe Deirdre, except that Deirdre, more so, has been around their family since she was a child. And Deirdre is educated and a well-known lawyer. However, because Deirdre is for Nicolaus, Ceil's mind and spirit does not have concern for Deirdre because she is consumed with hatred for Nicolaus. Ceil has been intent on making the destined couple as miserable as possible, hoping to run them off.

Ceil smiles, grateful that Niall seems to be moved along from the previous call girls he usually brings to breakfast, a different girl for a different day. Ceil remembers that Niall hasn't been with any other woman since he began seeing Elsa, and has not brought anyone else home with him, either.

Ceil slightly nods, agreeing with her mind's eye. Elsa did seem to be a positive influence on her Niall. There hadn't been any incidences or actions of weird people showing up trying to hurt Niall for his womanizing ways, since he'd been with Elsa. Nigel made no complaints about Niall lately, nor had Nicolaus. The brothers had not had any quarrels lately, actually not for quite some time. And Elsa would do well for Niall, once Ceil had him seated as head of the company, to replace Nicolaus, once she is able to run Nicolaus off.

"Well ...," Ceil reaches for Elsa's hand, grasping it, she gently shakes it, "that is wonderful, dear. Wonderful."

Nigel chuckles, "Elsa! It will be an honor to add you to our family!" Nigel takes a breath, feeling that Elsa would be able to ground Niall. He hadn't seen any other women hanging around his youngest son lately, though he is a little concerned about the bruises he can see on Elsa's face.

Deirdre touches Niall, as he is closest to her. "Congratulations to you both," she tells them, as she keeps her eyes on Elsa, while Niall keeps his eyes on Deirdre, a smirk on his face as he feels himself get stirred at her touch.

"Yes, congratulations to you both!" Nicolaus offers, noticing Niall's behavior towards Deirdre, frowning, hoping he is wrong about what he thinks he sees Niall doing, while announcing his engagement to Elsa. "Though, I clearly have to point out, that I didn't see mother follow the family tradition of picking your bride, Niall. Not sure why that step was missed for you, and not for me."

"It's because you're the oldest," Ceil snaps at Nicolaus, trying to cover for what she'd done to him and Deirdre.

Deirdre touches Nicolaus' arm and shakes her head with a frown, not wanting to get his mother riled up. She doesn't want things going wrong for Elsa, as they did for her. This discussion put a little damper on the topic.

Nicolaus sighs, "I'm just saying ... it was such a big deal ..." his words fall off as Deirdre tugs at his arm with a frown.

"Oh goody, another wedding," Marguerite comments sarcastically, as she notices that Niall is not thrilled about any of this.

"Like I said," Ceil says loudly, to dismiss Nicolaus and his complaint, "it's wonderful! We can sure use some good news around here," Ceil adds, frowning at both Nicolaus and Marguerite.

"Okay, Ceil." Nigel wants to stop her before she tries to distress Nicolaus.

"Well, I have to get to the office. Love, you have something to do today, away from here?" Nicolaus openly asks, expecting Deirdre to catch on that he wants her to leave the same time he leaves, and not hang around the mansion, because of Niall's behavior.

Both Deirdre and Marguerite answer in unison. "Well ... I ..." both stop talking, Marguerite scowls deeply at Deirdre. "Well ... I ..." another fail, so they both stop again.

Nicolaus sighs, understanding his mistake. He puts down the paper again. "Sorry," he says, sure Marguerite is going to be offended.

"I your wife," she reminds him in her broken English. "You ask me, or you ask her?" she yells at Nicolaus, infuriated that he'd be calling Deirdre "Love".

"Well, okay Marguerite, you go first," he ignores her agitation.

Marguerite straightens her back, feeling superior to Deirdre. "I going shopping with Kelly." Her usual action nowadays, as she never spends time with the baby.

Nicolaus smiles at her, not wanting conflict. "Okay. Relax and have fun. Call me if you need me," he tells her flatly, wondering why she goes shopping every day, all day. Nicolaus then places his attention toward Deirdre. He has the usual look of love for her.

Deirdre nods "I'll be at the children's home today."

Nicolaus drops another hint. "Okay, you leaving now? Can I give you a ride?"

Elsa sighs at the lovely husbandry communication Nicolaus gives to both Marguerite and Deirdre, and she wishes Niall would do the same for her. She could just see the obvious of how Nicolaus and Deirdre are meant for each other, even in the presence of Marguerite. Everyone sees it. Everyone knows it. Even Marguerite knows it, perhaps that is why she keeps reminding everyone that she is Nicolaus' wife.

Deirdre smiles at her love. She wants to kiss his face, and obviously cannot since Marguerite is present. "I have my car." Deirdre looks at her watch, "I'm leaving in about a half hour."

"Okay." With all eyes on them, Nicolaus smiles and kisses Marguerite on her cheek, and kisses Deirdre on her hand. "Just keep to your schedule," he tells Deirdre. "I'll see everyone later."

Chapter Twelve-TW

Despite being dressed for breakfast, Elsa gets into the shower to get ready for ring shopping with Niall. Deirdre is gathering the last of her things to head towards the children's home. She has her purse under her arm. She grabs her keys from the large glass heart dish where the family keeps their keys, so they can easily be found. Deirdre grabs her phone, then remembers she needs to check for calls. Looking at her phone and not paying attention, Deirdre bumps into Niall. "Oh Niall, I'm so sorry," she touches his chest apologetically.

Niall catches Deirdre by both arms. "Just the person I was looking for. Can I talk to you for a minute?" Without her permission, he ushers Deirdre into the library. They are alone, and Niall closes the heavy door. Deirdre's beautiful aroma quickly fills the whole room.

The beautiful smell of Deirdre plays with Niall's mind. He wants to take Deirdre and make her his, right then and there. His mind reminisces of how she always looks so beautiful. Her aroma just takes his breath. And knowing she is untouched ... is just too much for him. As most men would want ... Niall most of all, wants her virginity.

"Look Deirdre, I need you to know that I still love you." He steps closer to her, they are less than an arm's length away from each other. "I still want to marry you, Deirdre." He gently touches her shoulder. "I bring this up now because of Elsa's announcement. And I know you think you'll do anything to marry my brother, if ever he was divorced or something."

Deirdre looks at Niall, feeling a little astonished. She frowns, "What?"

Niall begins having trouble controlling his desire for Deirdre. Suddenly, Niall finds himself kneeling on one knee. "Will you be my wife?"

Deirdre is shocked. "Niall, what are you doing? You literally just announced your engagement to Elsa."

"You are the one I love, Deirdre. I'd do anything for you. I want to hold you, and make love to you, and satisfy you."

Alarmed at his words and his behavior, Deirdre stands back from Niall.

Niall stands and takes Deirdre's hand. "I love you," he softly tells her again. Gently pulling her towards him. His hands gently begin to stroke her face, her hair, her arms, her shoulders, and crossing the line he touches her chest. His obsession for her is in full swing.

His touching horrifies Deirdre. She is afraid he will grab her up into a cobra hold again, as he'd done several times before. "Niall ..." she tries to step away from him, and disturbingly, it is too late, and he won't let her. He backs her up against a wall out of sight of the door window and traps her with his body.

"I understand why my brother is so in love with you," his hands encase her neck, another red flag for Deirdre. "My love for you is stronger than his. Let me love you, Deirdre. Let me take care of you." Niall sees what he thinks is the opening of Deirdre's heart to him, and quickly leans forward and kisses Deirdre's mouth.

Deirdre tries not to respond to Niall's kiss, although, somehow her mouth reacts, maybe because of the hold he has around her neck.

Excited at her response to him, Niall's breathing increases dramatically. He takes Deirdre into his arms and holds her tightly, still pinning her body to the wall. He believes he finally has gotten somewhere with her. Finally!

Deirdre pushes back on him, "Oh Niall, I am so confused and tired. I don't know what I am doing." A tear falls from Deirdre's eye. She is tired of crying and tired of hurting. Niall kisses the tear away, amazed at this moment with Deirdre. He is trying really hard not to do the wrong thing, although his hand does not leave her throat. Nevertheless, he is unsure of himself, and his desire is over the top for this particular woman. "It's simple Deirdre, be my wife. I will take care of you, and love you."

Deirdre sighs, trying to push Niall away from her. She wants to remove herself from being cornered to the wall, remembering how he is abusive to women, and remembering how harshly he treated Elsa, in this very room, not so long ago. She tugs at his hand around her throat. She is surprised when he doesn't release her. "What about Elsa?"

"Elsa?"

"Yes Niall, Elsa! Don't you love her? Aren't you engaged to Elsa?"

Niall looks at her, "My heart has only enough room for one woman, and that woman is you, Deirdre. Always has been you."

Deirdre frowns at him, still trying to get away from him. "You do not care for Elsa?"

"Elsa is a good friend," he tells her, his mouth close to hers, his hand still on her throat.

"Niall, haven't you had relations with Elsa?"

Niall sighs, trying to bring her back where he wants her. "Why do you ask me that? I am talking about you and me."

"I want to know Niall. Have you had relations with Elsa?" Deirdre already knows the answer. She wonders if Niall has any integrity at all. Would he be truthful?

Niall sighs, momentarily dropping his gaze from her. "Yes, ... yes, I have had relations with her," he gives in. " Except Deirdre, each time I am with Elsa ...," he pauses, not sure if he should tell her his thoughts, "I imagine I am with you." His throat hold finally released, he gently rubs her neck now.

"Well ... that's ... terrifying, actually," she responds to his twisted thoughts.

Suddenly, Niall drops to his knees before Deirdre again, kissing both of her hands. He desperately wants to sex her. "I love you so much, Deirdre. My heart is only for you." As Deirdre is overcome with emotion, Niall can see that he is wearing her down. He stands, and quickly pins her to the wall again. He has her in a place where no one could see them unless they walk into the room.

Niall kisses Deirdre again. This time Deirdre does not respond to his kiss. In a flash of an instant, Niall's hand is caressing her bosom, and his right hand is tight around her throat again. He uses his body to pin her to the wall again, so she cannot move.

Deirdre freezes, as she doesn't understand what is happening as she feels Niall tugging at her blouse. She grabs his hand to stop him.

Niall is in a fantasy state from the dark side of his mind, wanting to expose her body, and look upon her nakedness. He wants to immediately put his mouth on her, to taste her and tease her relentlessly. He imagines how she would respond to him.

"Niall, stop!" Deirdre yells at him, as he tugs at her blouse trying to rip it off. She doesn't understand why he is doing this. "Stop!" she yells at him again, hitting and pushing his hand away. Deirdre is terrified, not sure what action to take, afraid of what he might actually do to her, his hand tightening around her throat.

Trying to remain calm to think of a way out of this, Deirdre flatly asks him, "Why do you try to take what belongs to your brother?" Her words bring Niall back to reality. He sees that Deirdre looks frightened of him. Her words stop his assault on her.

Breathing heavy, Niall looks at her. "You do not belong to him, Deirdre. I want you to be mine." He continues his menacing assault of her again, pulling at her blouse, wanting to live out what he sees in his mind.

"I have always belonged to Nicolaus."

Saying the name of her beloved made him stop again. Frowning, Niall looks to her, "I'm the one who loves you, Deirdre."

"No!" she turns her head away from him.

Niall abruptly becomes agitated. "I know you may not have me now, Deirdre, " he harshly tells her, tightening his grip on her throat while turning her face to him, "one day ... you will," he threatens her.

Tears seep from Deirdre's eyes again, her fear of Niall grows immensely. He left her no wiggle room for getting out of his trap. She can't lift her leg to knee him in his manhood, she cannot move to either side, nor turn her back to him. Niall's large hands caress the small of her little neck, tightening, then loosening, repeating the motion.

"Niall, please ... just let me go," she begs him softly.

He releases her and takes a step back.

Deirdre straightens her clothing, and pushes Niall away, using all her might, her dainty weight hardly moving him. "Why are you doing this, Niall?" She yells at him in anger and disbelief. Quickly, she grabs her things and moves towards the door. She holds her finger up towards him, "Niall, you better get that ring you promised Elsa. You are not going to break her heart."

Wanting to sound strong, though terrified to the bone, as he could easily grab her up again, Deirdre swallows her sobs and adds, "And Niall, there is nothing here for us, and there never will be, so just stop your clowning! Leave me alone! You try to touch me again, I'll tell Nicky what you've done," she yells at him.

Quickly, Deirdre leaves the mansion. She feels herself unsettled and shaking with fright on the drive all the way to her house, as there is no way she can go to the children's home now. Mentally, she is perturbed by Niall's latest assault on her. She is glad to be alone, her mother elsewhere. Several times she picks up the phone to dial Nicolaus, however, each time, she ends the call before it can register on his phone.

She takes a hot shower to try to calm herself. In the shower, she decides she will hold onto this information about what Niall has done to her, if ever she would need it to thwart his future sexual advances.

Exhausted, Deirdre cries herself to sleep.

Chapter Thirteen

"**D**eirdre, that's it! You've got to tell Nicolaus what Niall did. That is just beyond crossing the line," Maggie comments angrily, as they sip their coffee on the patio at their usual spot at the coffee shop. It is Saturday morning, and the sun is beaming on them. They each have their designer sunglasses on to protect their eyes from the Texas sun rays. "What you're describing is sexual assault. He can't just grab you up like that and try to rip your clothes off!" Maggie is incensed at Niall's behavior. She had such a hard time understanding the behavior differences between the brothers. She knows Nicolaus would never do anything like this.

Deirdre moves her curly hair out of her face, as a cool breeze flows over their table.

"I agree with Maggie, Dee. Niall is getting out of control."

"You don't understand. I can't tell Nicky. He'd get really angry. He'd probably hurt Niall. I don't want to be the cause of any riffs between them."

"Well, yeah, except Niall is hurting you!" Maggie half yells at her frowning.

"He's just threatening." Deirdre denies what she knows is true.

"Dee, that's playing with fire. You don't know if he'd really be able to control himself next time. Niall's been obsessed with you for years."

"Obsessed?"

"Yes, girl, obsessed. Almost like a madman. I've seen how he looks at you," Ishani confronts her.

"And he hurts Elsa, too," Maggie reminds them. "He's volatile."

"I already talked to Elsa. She said she could handle it, and she'd talk to Niall to make him stop."

"Says every battered woman." Maggie rolls her eyes, the worry not leaving her. She breathes aloud, "You should tell Nicky. Hey, you want me to tell Nicky? I'll do it for you," Maggie offers.

"No, no. I ... I don't think we should tell him."

Ishani sighs, "Deirdre, you should say something before Niall gets more out of hand. Nicky warned you about him before. Maybe you should notify the police and get a restraining order on Niall. He needs to stay away from you."

"The police?" Deirdre questions with a raised eyebrow. "Ishani, are you crazy? We are black people in the United States of America. The police will not help us. They'd probably just shoot us. Imagine if the media discovered that I put a restraining order. I can just see those headlines now, 'Shoot out at the Ravenell mansion over lovers' quarrel' ... or 'Ravenell lovers triangle'. Doing something like that would involve more people than just me."

"Nicolaus' mom knows people in city hall, and ..."

"You think the police who respond would care anything about any of that? They'd take one look at us, see we are people of color, and would just burst in with guns blazing! No! No police!" Deirdre tells her sternly.

"Yes, Deirdre's right about that, Ishani. No police!" Maggie agrees. "Deirdre, you should let Nicolaus take care of it. Nicky would want you to tell him, and will probably be upset if you don't tell him."

Deirdre is quiet for a long moment. She sips her coffee. "I don't want to think about this anymore right now," sounding a bit wounded, and uncertain. "We need to get some things for the children's home. Will you help me shop for the little ones?"

"Of course!" her ladies say in unison, both of them hating to leave this issue unresolved.

Chapter Fourteen

As many weeks passed, not much changed with Marguerite. After a long day at work, Nicolaus sat with Nigel in the sitting room. They share Nigel's favorite cognac.

Deirdre, the nanny, and the nurse are in another room tending to the baby, while Marguerite is off with her friends.

"So how do you make your marriage work, father? I mean, mother doesn't seem like the easiest person to be married to," he frankly asks Nigel between sips. It would be another hour before dinner is served.

Nigel looks at his son, feeling for him. "You know, I've been through a similar situation, like the one you are dealing with."

Nicolaus frowns at his father, not sure what he means. "How's that? You got to choose mother for your wife."

Nigel shakes his head, "No, your mother and I were matched. I was engaged to someone else at the time we were put together."

Nicolaus looks at Nigel with extreme shock. "What?" He can't believe what his father has just told him. "What?" He scoffs. "You're kidding, right?"

Nigel did not want to reveal much, though he does want to help Nicolaus through all of this. He nods one time to confirm his words. "We were matched."

Nicolaus sighs with a deep frown, "My God!" he sighs again, still in shock, "Why have you never told me about this?" He sighs again, "No wonder! No wonder mother won't let go of this making me marry someone else thing. My God!" he repeats, feeling as if a load of bricks from an unknown puzzle was just dropped on him. "Father ..." Nicolaus stands and steps away from Nigel, feeling somewhat betrayed by him, yet again. Standing by the large fireplace, he shakes his head in disbelief, at a loss for words.

Nigel remains calm, "All right, I know, I should have told you. Sit down, ... please." He wants them to keep talking. Nicolaus breathes deep to compose himself, and sits down again. "You are correct, that your mother is not easy to get along with. Ceil has a mean streak. If it were up to me, I would not have chosen her. However, we were matched to make good things happen, and I think, for the most part, we have succeeded."

Nicolaus nods in agreement. He shakes his head again, with squinted eyes, "Well then, why was I match with Marguerite and forced to give up Deirdre? What good is supposed to arise of that?" he asks, almost spiteful, already knowing the answer.

Nigel sighs, "Well ... I told you, Ceil is after you because of something I did. She resents me and takes it out on you."

Nicolaus stands again, his large muscular frame unable to remain seated. He is getting upset. The injustice of his situation creeps up in his chest making him want to lash out. However, his military training helps him control his emotions. Besides, he does not want to make an enemy of his father after the opportunity he'd given him to be Vice President of the company. The Vice President position embodies a great amount of trust and responsibility.

Nicolaus holds onto the fireplace mantle, his back to his father, still wanting information that can help him. Frowning, trying to reconcile his mind with his predicament, "So, then, how do you make things work?"

Nigel smiles at Nicolaus, feeling he'd get passed everything that is being thrown at him. It's times like these that Nigel feels most proud of his son. "Well, really, what it all amounts to is choice. All women will eventually make you choose."

Nicolaus' frown grows deeper as he turns to look at Nigel, "I can't. I can't choose between them! How am I supposed to do that? One choice is family and business, and the other choice is pure love. In my situation ..."

"Yes, well, ... you will have to choose. And son, my best advice is that if you want some semblance of peace, you'd better be sure to choose your wife."

Nicolaus' heart ached as the injustice against he and Deirdre immensely increased, and took away more of his soul.

Chapter Fifteen

Nicolaus and Deirdre stepped up their financial donations and their activities at their church, having invited Helena to bring the foster children, for spiritual learning. Ishani and Maggie are already members and participants of the church as well.

The church has a diverse congregation. Having a mixed marriage, when Helena and Joel attended, they felt they fit right in with everyone else, though Joel mostly attended more so to keep his eye on his wife around Nicolaus. Helena, with her Puerto Rican roots, and Joel, with his American Caucasian self-assuredness, felt comfortable in the congregation.

Nicolaus also provided Helena with a personal donation of ten thousand dollars for holiday gifts for the children, when the time came for them to be purchased. He'd also ordered the mansion kitchen staff to be prepared to make a holiday feast for the children's home when the proper time was upon them. Helena is again breathless at Nicolaus' generosity. Her heart grew with love for him, as she is infatuated with him more than ever.

Nicolaus had his son blessed and baptized at the church. It upset him greatly that Marguerite refused to participate, and that she still had not given their son a name. All the Ravenell family were present at the baptism, except Marguerite. Deirdre, of course stood in for her, which also upset Marguerite. Even though the bishop did not approve of the true mother being absent, he carried on with the neonate baptism, understanding Nicolaus' difficulties, as he'd rather have God's blessing over the child, taking care if something should happen.

Nicolaus and Marguerite seemed to be in a cycle of psychological pain and anger, of which Marguerite continued to feed, no matter what Nicolaus tried. His son is three months old now, and Marguerite is still rejecting both of them.

The week after the baby's baptism, is when Marguerite finally tired of being ignored. Though it is her own doing, she felt left out and alone. Ceil approached Marguerite, seeing she is ready for a change, and provided guidance on what to do about her situation. Ceil cautioned her that she must follow her every instruction to the very letter.

Monday evening, Marguerite watches the clock. It is now a little after five, and she knows Nicolaus will be home from the office around six to join the family for dinner, his usual pattern, as he never works late on Mondays or Fridays.

Marguerite goes downstairs after bathing and doing up her hair, having had the maids change her bedsheets and clean up her room. Marguerite tired of hearing her grouchy baby cry. Without words or warning, she rudely takes him from Deirdre's arms.

Deirdre gasps and smiles at Marguerite. "You ready to take Little Nicky?" she asks excitedly for her, with only good intentions in mind.

Marguerite places her son on her hip, "I tired to hear him cry all day," she says ungratefully, and of course, this is not true. "And his name is not Little Nicky. His name is Thaddeus."

Deirdre raises her eyebrows, wondering why she would insult Nicolaus' baby with such a name, "Thaddeus? Oh!" She takes a breath, to keep her comments to herself. "Well, he is a little cranky today. I'm sure he'll be glad to be with you."

Without words of thanks or appreciation, Marguerite goes to her side of the mansion. After closing the connecting door, she runs up the stairs with the baby, as she had to work quickly, to be ready by the time Nicolaus returned home.

She puts Thaddeus in the basinet she had placed beside her bed. Taking the bottle of fresh formula milk, she adds a few drops of liquor she had stored from the family sidebar to make him sleep, just as Ceil unethically advised her to do. Such action is a medieval trick of calming a baby, something one could be arrested for in these modern times. Without holding Thaddeus, she fed him the bottle, which he happily drank, his little hands touching that of his unfamiliar mother. He didn't seem bothered by Marguerite, as if he knows she is family. It is not long before he is sound asleep, breathing evenly.

Then Marguerite changed into her sexy nightgown, which is shiny gold, almost touching the floor, with a long slit, exposing her legs, just as Ceil suggested, telling her to wear something that is easy for powerful seduction. Marguerite sits at her vanity table, and waits. Soon, she hears Nicolaus downstairs.

As usual Nicolaus greets Deirdre with a loving hug and a kiss to her head. The two of them are back to peck kissing, after all, she is the surrogate mother to his son. He holds her hands, "My son is sleeping?" he asks, noticing the quiet and not seeing Thaddeus around. For three months, the family has been calling the baby alternate names such as 'his son', 'little baby', 'grandbaby', and Deirdre named him 'Little Nicky' since Marguerite had refused to give him a name.

Deirdre shakes her head, "No actually, he's with Marguerite. She was here to get him. She actually looks good, Nicky."

Nicolaus frowns at her, "Marguerite?"

Deirdre chuckles, "Yes! She says his name is Thaddeus."

He frowns again, "Thaddeus?"

Deirdre nods, with a smile.

Nicolaus looks at the connecting door to his wing of the mansion. He releases Deirdre's hands, "I must go to her," he says to no one, and yet to everyone. The tether of loyalty propels his body forward to be with his wife. He knows he's got to check on things to be sure Thaddeus is alright. Already, he feels the weight of owing Marguerite for paying some attention to their son. A behavior he does want to encourage.

And just as Ceil had told Marguerite, Nicolaus goes straight to her. He knocks on her bedroom door, and enters before she can say anything. He enters gingerly though, looking around to see that all is okay. The room is dark, only lit by numerous candles, giving the illusion of possible romance. He sees his son asleep, in the basinet, next to Marguerite's bed, unaware that he'd been given alcohol for quelling. The room is clean and smells of fresh gardenia.

"Wife, you okay?" he asks her. The smell of perfume also permeates the air. Nicolaus sees Marguerite sitting at her vanity table, her hair down and to one side. Her gown is off her shoulder, exposing the bare skin of her neck.

She does not answer him. Marguerite remains unmoving. She watches Nicolaus through the reflection of the mirror on the vanity table. She can't believe it when he does exactly what Ceil said he would do. He kneels behind her on one knee, gently touching her arms, as if he is drawn to her. His action makes her understand that Ceil is wise, and she decides to do exactly what Ceil had instructed her to do. Ceil wants her to get out of the hole she'd dug herself into, and most of all, Ceil wants Deirdre and Constance out of her house.

"Marguerite," he calls her name softly.

Finally, Marguerite moves to look at him briefly, then turns her back to him again. She sees the confused expression on Nicolaus' face when she does not answer him. His hands gently touch her arms.

"I hear you named our son." He breathes in the smell of her perfume.

"Yes," she finally responds to him, "Thaddeus Ulvis," she announces to him.

"Thaddeus Ulvis? Thaddeus Ulvis Ravenell? Hmmm," Nicolaus does not like that name for his son. He quickly understands that Thaddeus is a Greek name, and Ulvis is a Latvian name, however, the child would be living in Texas. "Can we discuss that name?" he offers, hoping to talk her out of such a name for their son.

"No," she says sternly.

Nicolaus, still on one knee behind her, nods, not wanting to argue the point, he is just very glad she finally paid attention to his son. "Okay, Thaddeus Ulvis Ravenell, it is!"

He frowns, knowing he'd find a nickname for his son like "Tee", or "Teddy", or "Ulie".

Marguerite remains unmoving again. She continues to watch her husband's reflection in her oval vanity mirror. She sees that he begins to move closer to her.

Nicolaus is not sure what to do. By this scene she set, he believes she finally wants to connect with him. Nicolaus' handsomeness and charm begin to affect her. Gently, he begins to stroke her arms. Nicolaus sees the opportunity to choose between the women in his life, just as his father had described to him.

Desperate for peace, and for the sake of Thaddeus, he forces himself to take action, hoping her mood doesn't backfire on him. Nicolaus forces himself into the moment with Marguerite, as his military commander negotiator mind takes over. 'Remember, what do women want?' he thinks to himself. Softly, he kisses the side of her face, then slowly, he kisses her neck. "What can I do for you? What can I do to make things better?"

Marguerite briefly smiles, because Ceil had told her he would ask her something along these lines. His touch, and his kisses, his being so close to her, made her stomach drop with want for him. His closeness always gets to her. Nicolaus' innate charm affects women in ways he does not even realize. He doesn't even have to try to bid for women's affection, he only has to be himself. A trait divinely imparted upon him. The one thing that is out of Ceil's control. This is the part Marguerite knew she'd have trouble with. Why is it that he always makes her feel this way?

Marguerite feels herself awakening with each of his hand strokes. Her breathing grows heavy, her chest rising and falling. She tries to remain unmoving at his soft touch, finding it hard to do so. A quiet tornado is brewing inside of her.

His being close to her, no matter how mad she is at him, or how much she hates him, his closeness, his charm, his handsomeness just makes her want to jump him and take all of him. However, she is aware she would never have all of him because he truly belongs to Deirdre.

As he continues to touch her, she feels her body temperature rise, and she cannot quelch it. They literally hadn't touched for almost one year, the last time leaving Nicolaus absent of the memory. Marguerite gasps as she feels herself very eager with want for him. Another kiss makes her lose her breath. He nuzzles her between her neck and her shoulder, making her gasp again, unable to resist him. She gets hotter every time he moves his hands on her. She leans against him, breathless, desiring him.

Marguerite is suddenly very confused. How could such a beautiful man, who has soft hands and a gentle touch, be the monster both Ceil and Penelope say he is? Is he a monster?

"Tell me what you want." Nicolaus whispers to her. He can see she is getting excited. Softly, he puts short licks on her neck, making her pant with each movement, her arms reaching for him. Nicolaus is unsure what to do, as he still does not fully understand Marguerite, so he just keeps going. He reigns light kisses to her face, until he reaches her lips, then taking a chance, again forcing himself, he kisses her mouth softly.

Believing he is betraying Deirdre, Nicolaus pushes the feelings of self-loathing down deep, to pay attention to Marguerite, who is actually his wife. He kisses her again, and to his surprise, she responds to him in a rush of desire.

Marguerite is unable to resist his kiss, she just can't, regardless of her thoughts. Her head is spinning with confusion. Her gorgeous husband's breathing has become elevated, his hands are on her belly, and touching her thighs. She stands to face him, and they kiss more, and deeper.

Marguerite's desire for Nicolaus grows greatly, though she knows she has to somehow stick to the plan, and she is very glad sex is included. Still unable to resist his kissing, she pulls at his clothes, his designer suit jacket falling to the floor, and then his shirt pulls off easily. Her hands roam his muscular chest and his manly arms.

Nicolaus bends to pick her up, and Marguerite stops his kind and romantic action. Ceil told her she had to be in control. Quickly, she maneuvers herself, twirling them around, to be able to back him towards the bed, as she tugs at his pants, while still kissing him.

Nicolaus is surprised at her tugging on his pants. She sees his hesitation, so she guides his large frame backwards with her legs, and works his pants loose. Nicolaus tries to relax, letting her take the lead. In an instant, she jumps on him, her legs around his waist. Nicolaus holds on to her, catching her, then letting them both fall onto the bed. Quickly Marguerite is on top of him.

"Marguerite," Nicolaus murmurs her name, not sure what to make of this. However, it is clear to him that they are going to have sex when she grabs his member. Fighting against his impulse to make her stop, it is not long before he is completely ready for her.

Marguerite wastes no time. She places him inside of her, making him moan loudly at the feel of her, just as she moans at his size.

This time, Nicolaus is fully aware of what is happening. Marguerite faces him, watching him. She begins rocking her body, moving quickly, making him moan again. Though she loves the feel of him inside of her, as he touches her legs, she pulls herself off him, and goes to the side of the bed, not touching him, and out of his reach, just as Ceil had told her to do. Nicolaus frowns, baffled, as expected, having unknowingly already fallen into their trap. Nicolaus covers himself with his hands, not understanding why she has stopped.

"Oh, ... I don't know," she says, as if in doubt, standing. She looks at the baby, who is still sleeping, then slowly she looks toward Nicolaus. "You sure you want this?" she asks him, whipping her hair, putting her hands on her hips, atop her golden negligee, as if teasing him.

"Yes, yes, I'm sure," he reassures her, his manhood throbbing. He reaches for her.

Marguerite climbs back onto him, squeezing him tightly inside of her, then moving harshly on him, making sounds escape his mouth. He grabs her legs, liking the feel of her.

Nicolaus' eyes are closed when she removes herself from him again. "Hmm, oh, ... I don't know," she says again. She can see Nicolaus is pained this time. She turns from him, sitting herself on the side of the bed. She breathes deep, pretending to want to cry, following Ceil's script.

Marguerite can't believe the plan is working. Ceil told her to use Nicolaus' sexual inexperience against him. As she hears Nicolaus groan with manly discomfort, his demeanor towards her remains calm. He gently touches her, scooting right behind her on the bed. Marguerite touches the baby basinet for dramatics.

Nicolaus gently holds her around the waist and begins to kiss her shoulders again, trying to pull her back in. He is at a loss, not understanding what is happening. When she stands away from him, he feels his chance for trying to change the dynamics of their relationship slipping away, and his manhood is becoming pained for the waiting. He wants to be back inside of her warm moisture.

Marguerite stands quiet and unmoving, waiting for his question. She understands that she has him in the trap created by Ceil. 'All men have a weakness regarding sex, and Nicolaus is no different,' Ceil told her.

Nicolaus sighs, feeling as vulnerable as he is naked before her. "What do you want me to do? What do you need?"

"It is not me you want."

Nicolaus is surprised by her answer, as he thought they were talking about sex. He reaches his hand out to her, "I do. I want you," he tells her, though his mind is on Deirdre, and on God. He wonders if somehow he is conveying this in some way. His mind is questioning if Marguerite is the path his children are to be born now, instead of Deirdre. He is trying to figure out God's plan for him, as he could see that Marguerite is trying to control his manly function of impregnating her.

"You not thinking of me."

"Yes, Marguerite, I am thinking of you. I want you," his pious mind not understanding he is being deceived. "Now, please. Be with me."

Marguerite smiles, takes a step towards him then stops. "You want me?" she asks him with sexy eyes, teasing him again. She steps closer, taking his hand.

"Yes, I want you," he tells her what he thinks she wants to hear, trying to be a good husband, and doing what is expected of him, desperate to find a space for peace between them. Again forcing himself to act, he pulls her into him, landing her on his lap. He kisses her lips again. Soon they are ready, Marguerite assuming her position on top of him.

Again, Marguerite climbs onto him, and puts pressure, making him moan loudly. She isn't sure if his moan is due to relief or pleasure. She went to work, moving for her own gratification. "You put her out," she tells him harshly, moving quickly, making him moan from the sensation of her soft internal walls.

Nicolaus grabs onto the thighs of his wife, helping her along. "What ..." he frowns, not wanting to break his concentration, "let's talk about that later."

"No!" she yells at him, stopping her movements. They are both breathless. "You put her out! I want her out!" she harshly demands.

"Okay, okay," he frowns and moans when she resumes the sex. Nicolaus tries to flip her to the missionary position, she refuses, pushing at his chest, moving him deeper into her. Ceil told her not to let him be on top, that she must remain in control. She applies physical pressure on him again, and works more. Finally, they climax, together, for the first time, both moaning from the sensation of each other.

And then Marguerite starts up again, not letting up on him.

Ceil watches with a smile, feeling satisfied, seeing that Marguerite is having her way with Nicolaus. She observes them through the peep glass that peers into Marguerite's bedroom, that she had installed in the secret passage hallway, to be able to spy on the couple. She watches for what seems to be a little too long.

Deirdre waits and waits. When neither Nicolaus nor Marguerite emerge from their wing of the mansion an hour after dinner, she suspects they are having relations. This realization is a wound to her heart; the world again reminding her that Nicolaus no longer belongs to her. Although this information is not new to Deirdre, it crushes her spirit.

Constance notices that Deirdre's mood had changed with the absence of Nicolaus at dinner. She saw Deirdre quickly become withdrawn, not eating or drinking anything, just moving the food around her plate.

Constance made excuses for them of why they just couldn't stay, and she whisks Deirdre out of the mansion as quickly as she can. Constance did what any loving mother would do, protect her daughter's heart. Though Constance knows it is already too late, that her daughter's heart is mortally wounded with love for Nicolaus.

As Deirdre and Constance enter their own home for the night, Constance is fairly sure that Deirdre is never going to be able to get over losing Nicolaus.

Chapter Sixteen

The following morning, Maggie and Ishani provide Deirdre emotional support during their early morning telephone conference. Their conversation gives Deirdre strength to face Nicolaus after his all night rendezvous with his wife, and also to actually face Marguerite.

Deirdre drives to the Ravenell mansion, in case she is needed for Thaddeus. She thought Marguerite may have changed her mind about caring for him, or she might want some pointers.

The morning light brought deep regret to Nicolaus, as Marguerite reaches for him, yet again. He'd lost count of how many times they'd had sex throughout the night, letting her have her way with him. This time, Nicolaus takes control and enters her in the missionary position, having caught her off guard. Marguerite forgot about the plan, until it is too late when he ejaculates inside of her; his intent and what he thinks of his husbandry duty, to impregnate her.

Just then, Thaddeus begins to cry from hunger. Trying to be a thoughtful husband, Nicolaus sweetly kisses his wife's cleavage before climbing off her. He retrieves a towel to wrap himself, and picks up his son, bouncing him in his arms. Immediately, Thaddeus responds to Nicolaus, cooing and cackling, as if he were trying to tell him something. Suddenly, he begins to cry, his tummy hungry.

Nicolaus takes Thaddeus to Marguerite. When he hands her the baby, Marguerite turns from him, pulling the sheet over her, as if to ignore them and go to sleep. Nicolaus frowns at her action. He takes Thaddeus with him to go to the kitchen for formula. When Nicolaus opens the bedroom door, the newly hired nanny is there, her arms out for Thaddeus.

The help Ceil hired for the baby, the nanny, the nurse, and the teacher, were all present and ready to care for him. Nicolaus had told Ceil it wasn't necessary to hire these people, though Ceil insisted, despite Deirdre filling in as the mother.

When Deirdre is present, the three ladies stand around with practically nothing to do, as Deirdre provides genuine care for Thaddeus. With Deirdre not yet present, the nanny is overly happy to relieve Nicolaus of the baby. "Don't worry, Sir, I will take good care of little Thaddeus." She even already knew his name. He let her take the baby, and then went to his own room to change to his running clothes.

Suddenly, Nicolaus realizes it's crazy to go running because he is exhausted, however, the guys are scheduled to meet up with him. Personally, Nicolaus feels guilty, as if he cheated on Deirdre with his wife, and the guilt cloaks him as he leaves for his early morning run.

Chapter Seventeen

E ven more exhausted after his two-mile run, Nicolaus enters the mansion just in time to hear Marguerite badgering Deirdre.

"Why you here? I take baby."

"Marguerite, I'm only offering to help, if you should want ..."

"I want no more of you!" Marguerite yells at Deirdre, while dressed in her luxury, silken robe. "I want you leave. I want you get out!"

Nicolaus touches Marguerite on her back with a frown, especially after seeing that she is addressing Deirdre in such a manner. "Hey, hey ..." he looks to Marguerite, to stop the bickering between the ladies, standing between them. He didn't think he'd have to deal with this so quickly, or so directly. He isn't really ready.

"Tell her," Marguerite yells to Nicolaus, "Tell her!"

Deirdre looks to Nicolaus with a frown, wondering what is going on.

"Marguerite."

"Who is your wife?" she asks him sternly. Marguerite is determined to carry out Ceil's plan. She steps closer to Nicolaus, touching his torso. "Who is your wife?" she asks him again more slowly.

Nicolaus cringes inside, closing his eyes, wanting to wish the nightmare away. He opens his eyes to Marguerite closer to him, rubbing his torso. Her touch reminding him of their lovemaking. "You tell her, or I will," she tells him sternly, with certainty.

"Tell me what?" Deirdre stands with crossed arms. That stance she knows Nicolaus hates. She sees the look across his face once he looks at her.

Nicolaus sighs. "Can we talk in the sitting room?"

Nicolaus and Deirdre walk side by side to the sitting room in silence, which felt like walking a mile barefoot on broken glass to Nicolaus.

When they enter the room, Nicolaus' attempt to kiss Deirdre on the forehead is thwarted by her upset mood, as she moves away from the kiss, not letting him touch her. She is only all too aware of where his lips may have recently been.

"What's going on, Nicky?" Deirdre demands of him, her arms crossed again, closing herself to him.

Nicolaus turns his head to the side, his eyes staring out the large glass window. He is as distant as he feels in this moment. He sought for words to lighten the heavy action. Nicolaus looks to Deirdre, then holds his hands in a calming motion. "Honey, she's just intimidated by you, that's all."

"Intimidated?" Deirdre frowns, "How's that? I have been very kind to her, even when she rudely ripped Thaddeus from me yesterday."

"She thinks you are going to watch her, and judge her over Thaddeus," he improvised, making this up on the spot.

"Why would she think that, Nicky? I've been extremely supportive. I've ..."

Nicolaus touches her arm to stop her from talking. "She wants ... she wants ..." Nicolaus had a tough time getting his mouth to say the words. Suddenly, he feels the heavy weight of his marriage. He is afraid of severing his relationship with Deirdre by having chosen Marguerite. However, he also realizes this is part of the choosing.

"What?" Deirdre grows impatient, moving away from Nicolaus, away from his beguiling touch.

"She wants you to move out." Immediately, he saw the look on Deirdre's face change. He can tell she is shocked by his words. He steps forward to comfort her, and she draws back away from him. His betrayal of Deirdre on full display.

"Are you ... throwing me out?" She can't believe it! She cannot believe what she is hearing from the only man on earth her heart pines for, the only man on earth for which she would do anything. How can he even say such a thing to her, after all she has done to assist with the baby? She is hurt to her core. She is very surprised that he'd let Marguerite put him up to something like this.

"I don't want you to leave." He shakes his head. "I don't want you to leave," he reiterates, seeing how Deirdre looks hurt.

"You are ... throwing me out!" She states, as if she completely understands.

"Please, Deirdre, don't' take it like that. She just needs ..."

"How am I supposed to take it, Nicky? What am I supposed to think?" Her upset is apparent. She wipes the tear that rolls from her eye. "You're letting her get between us."

"Deirdre," Nicolaus steps towards her again, only to have Deirdre step away from him, and turn her back to him.

Deirdre sighs, willing herself not to cry, wiping her face. Angrily, she twirls to him, and stares at him with no words.

"Deirdre," Nicolaus whispers her name. He doesn't know what to do, or what else to say. Obviously, she is not going to let him touch her. "Please ..."

Deirdre storms past him and out of the sitting room, not wanting to hear another word about this from him. "I suppose you'll have mine and mother's things delivered to my house.

I will expect to receive my things in two days' time." Deirdre grabs her purse and keys, and runs out of the mansion.

Nicolaus is at a loss for what to do. The pain of the situation engulfs him. He watches Deirdre leave out the open front door. He stops himself from going after her, though it would have been a natural thing for him to do so. Nicolaus has a keen awareness that this is also part of the choosing. His father did not mention to him how much this was going to crush his heart.

Marguerite's hand touches his back, as she stands next to him. As a couple, they both watch Deirdre drive off. Nicolaus looks at his wife and leans to kiss her cheek, however, now it is Marguerite who moves away from him, not letting him kiss her. She looks at Nicolaus with a cold stare, turns, and walks away. Nicolaus feels more confused than ever, his pious mind not understanding that he'd just been played.

Unbeknownst to the couple, Ceil has been watching the wild scene unfold from the upstairs balcony, since the beginning. She is very proud of Marguerite for having brilliantly carried out her plan. She knows she'll have to think of a reward for her. Ceil is thrilled to finally have Deirdre and Constance out of her house.

Chapter Eighteen

"What the fuck, Nicky? How is it that you throw Deirdre out the mansion? What the fuck is wrong with you?" Francesca accosted Nicolaus in his sitting room, where he'd gone to get away from everyone after a long day at work. Francesca is right upon him, without warning. She rightly defends Deirdre, crossing her arms, standing over him, waiting for his answer.

Nicolaus stands to address his cousin. "Ya' know,... that mouth of yours ... that language has got to stop! It's very unbecoming." He admonishes her.

"Don't you try to change the subject, Nicky."

Nicolaus sighs, "No! We're going to talk about this first."

"Piss off, Nicky! So what, you're my daddy now? Last time I checked, I ain't never had a daddy," Francesca yells at him in her thick British accent.

Nicolaus frowns, "Francesca, that's exactly what I'm talking about. That mouth ...."

"What? So now bossy Nicky is going to tell me what I can and cannot say? We live in America, Nicky. I can express myself however the fuck I want. Anyway, we're all adults here."

"Francesca," he sounds exasperated, "You're a professor, with standing in the community. Young people look up to you, they listen to you, and I'll bet even some of them ask for your advice. Do you address them with curse words? Do you lecture with curse words?"

Francesca scoffs. "Well, of course not. Of course I don't! That's not professional."

"Well then why do you curse in your everyday language? I don't like to hear it. And frankly, Francesca, it's disrespectful to our parents."

"Nicky, ..."

"I'm going to pray for healing of that tongue of yours." He touches her shoulders, as if he were laying hands on her.

Francesca giggles, knowing he is being serious. "All right, I'm sorry. I'll stop. I didn't know I was bloody offending you." She rolls her eyes. "You make your soldiers walk the straight and narrow? You were controlling over them, too?"

Nicolaus nods, "As much as I could be. It's easier to deal with folks under your command if they aren't drunk and brawling, and if their attitudes are even. You know what I mean?" Nicolaus pulls his cousin into a hug, "You stop altogether. No more cursing! It's just a bad habit. You're much too pretty for those words to be emulating out of your mouth."

Francesca looks up at Nicolaus. "So you going to answer me? What happened with Deirdre? You threw her out?"

Nicolaus frowns, looking sad at such an assumption. "No. I'm sorry she's taking it that way." He moves away from Francesca, deeply frowning. "Now that Marguerite has somewhat accepted Thaddeus, she feels Deirdre will be judging her, and she doesn't know how to handle it."

"So just like that, out with Deirdre? How is that fair?"

"No, I ..." he sighs. "I ...." He sighs again. Is Francesca correct? "I didn't want her to move out ... Marguerite is insisting. I don't know ..."

"Nicky, making Deirdre leave is not the answer, and..."

"I know, I know ..." he interrupts her, almost unable to bear hearing what he believes she would say. He leans on the fireplace for support. "I'll go to them. I'm just giving time to let their tempers cool down," he tells her.

Francesca stands next to Nicolaus and hugs him again. "That's probably wise."

Chapter Nineteen

After a few days of painful sulking, Nicolaus shows up at Deirdre's doorstep, not sure how he'd be greeted, or if the door would even be opened for him.

Constance pulls Nicolaus inside with a hug and her usual motherly kiss, the only comfort he'd received since the day he'd told Deirdre she had to move out. He and Marguerite were back to their separateness, with her not letting him touch her. Their separation within their marriage seems to be the very essence of their loveless union.

"I just want to apologize for having to move you and Deirdre from the house. It's just that Marguerite is intimidated, now that she ..."

Constance stopped his speech, having heard it from Deirdre, for which neither she nor Deirdre believed a word of it. "Nicky, ... don't." Constance nods at him, "I completely understand that you have to appease Marguerite. Deirdre will be all right. All this mess Ceil created has been hard on all of us. It's a consequence of the marriage."

"I'm not trying to hurt you, or Deirdre, or anyone." He frowns, "Sometimes I don't know what to do."

Constance touches his arm and chest, "We know, honey." She worried that too much burden is being placed on Nicolaus. He still had to move forward in his profession as well, to carry on the company his father built from the ground up. She worried about his mental health.

Nicolaus sits down and relaxes himself on the couch, feeling quite at home. "Where is Deirdre? Is she home?"

Constance smiles, "No, actually she's out on a date. At my insistence."

Nicolaus' relaxed stance is gone, he sits straight up. "A date? With who?"

Constance chuckles at his reaction. She wasn't about to tell him that Deirdre is out with her visiting cousin. "Now, Nicky. You should be glad that she is able to move forward. Certainly don't want her milling around here like some rejected old woman. She still needs to live life, you know."

Constance's words hurt Nicolaus. Did Deirdre feel like he is rejecting her? He'd never do that. He frowns, not sure how to respond. Nicolaus grappled with words, realizing what he thought of as impossible is happening. Deirdre may choose someone other than himself, just as he chose Marguerite a few days ago.

Nicolaus stands, feeling helpless. "Who is this guy? I want to check him out to make sure he is safe."

Constance touches him again, "Oh never you mind dear. Deirdre will be all right.

You will be all right."

Chapter Twenty

S everal days later, Maggie's daring self went off the limb, inviting Deirdre and Ishani to skydive for her upcoming birthday. Nicolaus had been wrangled to join them for lunch at a little restaurant in the famous Austin outdoor shopping center, as Deirdre is to talk him into arranging everything.

Nicolaus is more than glad to meet the happy ladies, who are abounding with giggles when he joins them. Nicolaus, of course, sits next to Deirdre, after rounds of kiss greetings, feeling timid, not sure if she is still angry with him. His greeting to her is unreturned, and she does not look at him.

Appetizers are set before them, and Maggie gets right to the point.

"Nicky, I have this wonderful notion for us to go skydiving for my birthday in two days."

"Skydiving? Like for real?"

The ladies giggle. "Yes. And my dear, that is where we need you. Can you help us arrange this?"

Nicolaus takes a drink of his water and sits back. "Hmm, maybe. What do I get out of it?" he asks with a mischievous smile.

The ladies giggle and Deirdre grabs his leg by his knee, looking at him, finally giving him some attention.

"You can jump with us!" Maggie offers, happily.

"Hmm, what's my ROI?" He teases them.

"We'll bond you into our group," Maggie tells him, as if he wasn't already part of them. The ladies giggle again.

Nicolaus sits back and pretends to think about it, teasing them. "Okay, all right," he finally says.

Maggie claps, "Yay! Drinks all around, and on me!"

Two days arrived quickly, and the ladies are very excited as the plane takes off. However, their excitement quickly turns to fear as the plane climbs in altitude.

"Oh my God, Maggie, how did I let you talk me into this?" Ishani asks her.

They are seated, attached to their tandem helper person, with their parachute gear, helmets, and goggles on. Nicolaus is closest to the door, and is not attached to a helper, as he's had professional training in skydiving through his military service, and accomplished an extensive number of jumps. The ladies have an instructor who explains to them, for the third time, what to do. The group has already been through twelve hours of simulated training at the skydive center. Maggie seems to be the only lady excited. Ishani is scared, and Deirdre is nervous. Nicolaus grabs Deirdre's shoulder to reassure her. She looks up at him and feels better just seeing the confidence in his face. At this moment, she decides to stop being nervous and to enjoy the jump.

When the instructor stops talking, Nicolaus stands to give them additional directives.

He touches Ishani on her shoulder. "Don't worry, it will be okay. It's fun," he smiles at her. She nods, not exactly convinced. "Okay, my ladies, when the door opens, each go after the instructor. Be sure to watch for his signal, like he says, that's when your helper will pull your chute lever. This is all going to go really fast, so enjoy it."

Time arrives to jump. Maggie and her tandem helper are the first out after the instructor, then Deirdre, Ishani, then Nicolaus. Nicolaus watches over the ladies, and is happy to see they are relaxed and enjoying their time in the sky, as having the tandem helper provides extra assurance. Then his eyes drift directly to Deirdre. When her eyes find Nicolaus, they both hold each other's gaze. She knows she can't be mad at him. They love gaze at each other at ten thousand feet in the air. Something they would never forget.

The instructor gestures the signal to pull their levers. Maggie gives Nicolaus a huge smile and a thumbs up, then her helper pulls her lever. The opening chute lifts them up and away, as happens for all of them. Slowly, they glide to the ground in the expected area. Nicolaus remains close to Deirdre. As Deirdre and her tandem helper touch down to the ground, Nicolaus is right next to them.

Nicolaus helps Deirdre detach from her helper, then he lifts her in his arms, their eyes locked on each other. The adrenaline from the jump is running through both of them, exacerbating Nicolaus' desire for Deirdre. She can see he wants to kiss her, and she wants that kiss. She is so happy that he is holding her in his arms, against his muscular chest. She breathed the moment, her heart pounding. They are so close.

Gently, Nicolaus eases Deirdre's feet to the ground. "There you go," he tells her sweetly, making her fast beating heart melt.

Maggie's excited screaming and jumping interrupts their moment. "That was so awesome! Oh my God! Did you see the birds pass us?" Jumping, not able to calm herself she hugs Nicolaus to her. "Thank you so much!" She kisses his face. "Let's do it again!" They chuckle at her as Ishani joins them as well.

Nicolaus touches Ishani. "Ishani, you okay?"

Ishani puts her hands to her head, smiles brightly, and jumps around like Maggie. "That was fantastic! Why did I get scared? Oh my God, let's do it again!" Her arms in the air in glee.

Nicolaus chuckles at the ladies, knowing it is the adrenaline rush they are feeling. They drift off to speak to their helpers and the instructor, happy about the jump. This leaves him and Deirdre alone for a few minutes. Even though Nicolaus has placed Deirdre on the ground, she is still in his arms.

Deirdre touches Nicolaus on his chest. "Thank you for making my friends so happy.

You make lots of us happy," she tells him. Deirdre does not know where this conversation is going. She does not want Nicolaus to release her. She wants to remain in his arms the whole of the day.

Chapter Twenty-One

C eil has planned Marguerite's birthday party. This party is Ceil's reward to Marguerite, for getting Constance and Deirdre out of her house. In usual fashion, Ceil planned a large party, and invited two hundred guests. The party is held at an upscale hotel in downtown Austin. As typically expected, the number of guests who attend does not disappoint Ceil.

Marguerite is dressed in a royal blue minidress, with her hair done up, and girlfriends in tow. Nicolaus' expensive suit jacket matches Marguerite's dress color, and is paired with a grey shirt, black slacks, and no tie. Nicolaus looks and smells enchanting. The women guests greet him with hugs and kisses. Thaddeus is being tended to by the nanny, who has a full space in the corner, for guests who want to see the little one.

Nicolaus made sure that Deirdre, as well as Maggie and Ishani attended the party. Deirdre glows as the beauty she is. She appears sexily stunning in her lilac ruffle wrap cami strapped dress, with a daring slit ruffle that runs diagonally along the front of the dress to the side of her left hip. She is accompanied by her besties.

Several men, other than Nicolaus, flock to Deirdre, bidding for her attention, knowing she is no longer engaged, and a good deal of time has passed since she'd been tied to Nicolaus. Several men also give attention to Ishani and Maggie. Ishani is dressed in a designer chiffon, ankle length white dress, with a golden embroidery of flowers. Maggie looks smart in her dark emerald colored, v-neck jumpsuit with sequenced embroidery.

Annoyance befalls Marguerite, as she feels that Deirdre and her friends are upstaging her.

She grows enraged when she sees how Nicolaus observes Deirdre, kissing her hands.

Marguerite's girlfriends hold her back from confronting Deirdre, as eligible Austinite bachelors surround the lovely beauty for attention.

When Nicolaus realizes his wife is upset, suavely, he crosses the room to her, leaving Deirdre's side, and the attention that swarmed around her, and her friends.

Nicolaus walks up to his wife and kisses her on the cheek, before her friends, taking her hands, giving her the attention she wants from him. A romantic move Marguerite's girlfriends approve of, through their smiles and nods to Marguerite.

Nicolaus smiles at Marguerite, his back to Deirdre. This action seems to calm her quickly. He keeps his attention on her for quite some time, reminding her that she is his wife, answering the unasked question she posed to him so many times. He attempts to do the thing the husband is supposed to do, make his wife feel appreciated, and doing this to the witness of others, despite her cold nature towards him. Nicolaus is getting the understanding of what his father had told him, even though he has to force himself to do these things with Marguerite. He is sure if Deirdre were his wife, it would just be natural for him.

Niall does not like that so many men are attentive to Deirdre throughout the whole evening, despite the fact that he has Elsa on his arm. Deirdre's accentuated beauty greatly stirred him. Deirdre does have a shapely body, however, the dress she wears does not show it. Deirdre has a knack for choosing fashionable clothes that provide a mystery of her body frame, giving a tease to the men. Despite being with Elsa, Niall feels prangs of jealousy about Deirdre.

The party continues through the next two hours without incident. Nicolaus coaxes Marguerite to dance to a slow song, the first time they'd ever danced together since their marriage. The guests clap for them at the end of the song.

The gift table is piled high with nicely wrapped boxes, gift bags, and envelopes. Catered food is served, despite a buffet set up. At the end of the party, cake is passed to all the guests.

Francesca, intrinsically known as the high society family cousin with British ties, who closely resembles the brothers, enters the glamorous party room with three men on her arm, while wearing a white frock top and a white swirl skirt which swishes around with her every move. Despite her professorship tenure, Francesca is always herself, as her natural soft afro makes it seem that she has an auburn halo around her head.

Francesca and the men on her arm appear before Niall's across the room stare at Deirdre. She knocks Niall on the shoulder. "Niall!" she says loudly with a huge smile. Francesca kisses Niall on his face, "Cuz!" Then she kisses Elsa too. "You two seem to be having an awful time!" she loudly observes with her British accent. She remains before Niall, purposefully blocking his view of Deirdre to remind him of his manners. She hates it when Niall behaves this way.

"Yeah, well, you know, we're not really a fan of these parties."

"Ah, speak for yourself, babe. This is the time I network. Remember babe, Deirdre says we've got to network more," Elsa reminds him.

"Yeah, yeah, okay, I know," he tells her.

"Look who I got!" Francesca says happily, pulling the three men forward. "You remember our cousins, Ned, Cato, and Bobby?" The look on Niall's face changes to wonderment at the appearance of his cousins, whom he has not seen since he was a child. Niall's expression brings joy to Francesca.

"Hell yeah, I remember!" Niall proceeds to lock hands and man pat each cousin. "I haven't seen you guys in forever, man!"

"Benjamin! You're all grown up!" Ned offers with a laugh.

"Dude, I go by my middle name now. I'm known as Niall."

"Oh, that's cool!" Bobby says with a smile. "Nigel, Nicolaus, and Niall. A Ravenell force to be reckoned with!" The other brothers laugh and nod, liking the change.

"My father know you're here?"

"Nah, man, we're going to surprise everybody! Who's your little lady here?" Bobby inquired of Elsa.

"Oh, this is Elsa Baird," Niall introduces her, without additional descriptions.

The three brothers gently shake her hand. When they see Nicolaus, they make their way towards him.

"Oh my God! No way! Bobby, Cato, Ned!" Nicolaus exclaims, going over to his cousins, as they meet him halfway to the middle of the extravagant room.

"There he is! Military man in the flesh!" Cato says aloud.

They each hug and man bump with chuckles. "When did you guys get here? Why didn't you call me? How long you staying?" Nicolaus is excited with questions.

They laugh at Nicolaus' reaction to them. "Man, we just got here! Francesca told us we should travel out and see about you and Deirdre." Nicolaus nods with a smile. He sees Francesca across the room making her way to Marguerite, however, she became preoccupied by a handsome man who wants to talk to her. Francesca is popular around town, outside of her university professorship.

Nicolaus takes his cousins with him to meet Marguerite and her friends. By the time he gets across the room, Francesca has made her way to greet Marguerite. "I'm so sorry I'm late," she tells Nicolaus, kissing her handsome cousin on the face, and touching Marguerite's hands.

"Oh no don't worry about that," Nicolaus tells her. "We are very glad you are here. Never a party without you! And you brought me the most wonderful surprise!" he gestures his hand towards his cousins. "This is my wife Marguerite," he opens his hand to Marguerite.

"Your wife?" Bobby is quick to ask shocked. "Your wife?"

Nicolaus nods. "Yes. Marguerite, these are my cousins, Cato, Ned, and Bobby." They nod to Marguerite.

"Hello." Marguerite notices that all four of the cousins look very much alike. Cato, Ned, and Bobby have darker skin than Nicolaus. Bobby is clean shaven and has short, cropped hair, and a muscular build. Cato is thin, like a rail, with long curly hair, and flipflops. The type of shoes he wore every day. Ned is tall with a bald head, and a medium, dark beard. Their facial features were all the same, however, she does notice that Nicolaus is the most handsome.

"You guys still living out in California? I haven't seen you since we were kids!. Oh my goodness, why is that?"

Bobby walks them towards the direction of Deirdre, and stops short before they get to her, out of the hearing distance of both ladies.

"Dude, we know all about you. You're all over the entertainment news in California, seems like every night. You and Deirdre."

"What?" Nicolaus is shocked to hear this.

"Yeah man, you and Deirdre are celebrities."

Nicolaus shakes his head, "That can't be. No, we're not."

Cato chuckles at Nicolaus' reaction, pointing his thumb at him. "He's gonna tell us!" he says to his brothers, laughing. "Man, the two of you are all over the news all the time. We saw Deirdre in her wedding dress. Benjamin ... ah, Niall, jumped in and was all over her. I told Ned, I bet you kicked his ass for that." They laugh.

Nicolaus couldn't help chuckling. "No, I did not."

"What?" They laugh more.

"So what happened man? How is it that you are not married to Deirdre?" Ned asks.

Bobby grabs onto Nicolaus. "So what the hell? Marguerite is your wife? Who is she? Aren't you supposed to be married to Deirdre?" He frowns deeply, knowing this could not possibly be. "You and Deirdre been together for years. Suddenly there's someone else? The media covered your little wedding too. And the part when you mentioned it was a business transaction. What the hell, man?"

"Yeah man, what happened?" Cato questions.

Nicolaus sighs, folding his arms, suddenly feeling very somber. He frowns, "Well, ... my mother ... prevented us from marrying."

"Aunt Ceil?" Cato couldn't believe it.

"Ah man," Ned states, "that ain't right. Everybody knows you and Deirdre are supposed to be married."

"Yeah man, everybody knows that," Cato agrees with simplicity.

"My mother arranged for my marriage to Marguerite to be tied to a merger that risked everything we have. I had to do it," Nicolaus briefly explains to them.

"See, that's why my mom don't like Aunt Ceil. That's why we haven't seen you guys all these years. My mom is afraid of Aunt Ceil. She thinks she's a witch. I mean a real witch. She's like – stay away! And it's stuff like that, what Aunt Ceil did to you, that makes her feel that way. That is just all kinds of wrong. I don't even know the details, and I can see your hurt, Nicolaus. I see it. Mom doesn't even know we're here. She'd be freaking out."

Nicolaus frowns at this new information. He sighs. "My mother may have done something to Auntie Zahra." He sighs again. "Please apologize for me. Better yet, if you give me the number, I'll call her. We probably need to go see her. Is she well?"

Cato nods, "She's all right."

"And just what are you apologizing for?" Deirdre's voice is right behind him.

"Oh, there she is!" Bobby smiles at Deirdre.

"Oh my God," Deirdre frowns with a smile, and Ishani and Maggie are right next to her, "is that who I think it is?"

"It's me, the one and only Bobby Ravenell!" His arms open up to give Deirdre a big hug. "Whoa! Last time I saw you, you were a little girl. Now look at you! Beautiful and shapely!"

Deirdre laughs. Ned picks her up into a hug, lifting her feet off the ground. "Ned!"

"Girl! Look at you!"

Marguerite watches the happenings from the other side of the room. Not only does she feel left out and upstaged again, she also feels her jealousy grow one hundred-fold.

Cato is last to greet Deirdre with a light hug.

Nicolaus still can't believe his cousins are in Austin, before his eyes. "I'm so glad you guys are here. You should stay with us so we can catch up. Then we'll go to California to visit you. I imagine you each have families, wives, kids."

"Yep, sure do! Deirdre you'd love my wife!" Ned informs her.

"Oh, I'd love to meet your wife and kids. And these are my close friends Ishani, and Maggie."

"Nice to meet you," he nods and smiles at the two ladies. "Yep, Cato is about to be a grandfather."

"What?" Nicolaus is surprised. His cousins are not that much older than he.

Cato nods, "These teenagers! They don't listen, man! They done made me a grandfather already. I'm too young for that, man!" They all laugh.

When Nigel sees his only brother's sons at the party, he immediately goes to them. "Ned? Oh my goodness!" They hug.

"Uncle Nigel!"

"Xavier didn't alert me that you'd be here."

"No, he doesn't know we're here. Neither does mom."

"Neither Xavier nor Zahra know you're here?" Nigel hugs onto Cato and Bobby.

"I owe a visit with Auntie Zahra," Nicolaus informs his father. "My cousins can stay with me at the house. Hey, guys, let's get you some food and drink. There's plenty of it. Please help yourselves!" Deirdre and her ladies lead the men to the food and assist them in getting plates and drinks.

Chapter Twenty-Two

After another thirty minutes, the four hour long party ends. The family stands in the usual line to thank each guest for attending. This time, Deirdre sits out the line. She bids Ishani and Maggie goodbye, and stays with Elsa, and Francesca. The three ladies chat and laugh, catching up with each other.

All seems usual until Nicolaus looks up and sees a strange sight enter the hotel room door, as people are going out. "Brigadier General Coventry! It's an honor to see you here, Sir." Nicolaus greets the well-known general he's never met before with a strong man's handshake.

Brigadier General Coventry has his assistant with him, who also shakes Nicolaus' hand. Coventry nods, "I'm here to see you, son," the General says without emotion, as matter of fact.

Nicolaus is taken aback. "Oh, okay, well, we are wrapping up here. We should be done in about ten minutes." Nicolaus sees that most people are gone. He motions to the buffet that still has plenty of food, "Please, help yourselves to some food and drink," he offers them, feeling as though he's repeated that phrase at least a hundred times to various guests.

Coventry nods. He and his assistant have some water, and have the wait staff make them plates to go, while they wait on Nicolaus.

After about ten minutes, the family follows Nicolaus to the lounge area couches where Deirdre, Elsa, Ned, Cato, Bobby, and Francesca are sitting, as they want to know what is happening. Nicolaus sits himself next to Deirdre on his left, pulling Marguerite to his right. His cousins shake their heads in disbelief of Nicolaus' actions, seeing how he tends to both of his women. Nigel and Ceil seat themselves as well. Coventry and his assistant stand before the family.

"So what can I do for you?" Nicolaus asks Coventry, his curiosity peaked.

"We need to talk, Sergeant Major Ravenell," Coventry points out with obvious flair, wanting a private audience with Nicolaus.

Nicolaus nods, "Just tell me what you can before my family," Nicolaus spreads his arms to include everyone. "They would have to know what's happening anyway. So, tell me why you are here?"

Coventry sighs with an eye flicker, agreeing to the terms. "Well, Sergeant Major ..."

Nicolaus stops him, "Hold on! You do know I'm retired. I work for my father now. We're in private industry. In healthcare."

Coventry nods, "Yes Sir! Sergeant Major Ravenell, I'm here on behalf of the President."

"The President?" Nicolaus interrupts him again.

"Yes Sir! The President of the United States is asking for your assistance."

"Jesus, Almighty!" Francesca exclaims, what everyone else is thinking.

"The President?" Bobby repeats, in awe.

"The President needs your special skills to lead a team in the rescue of two diplomats, the American Ambassador to France, and the Ambassador of Kenya, have both been abducted and taken to Milojastan."

"Milojastan?"

"Yes Sir! We believe if they are not rescued within the next forty-eight hours, they will not survive."

"Milojastan? Where the hell is that?" Bobby asks, frowning.

Nicolaus chuckles at his comment. "It's a small obscure country near the Balkans."

Nicolaus stops in thought for a moment, realizing this is a huge ask ... from the President. He looks at Coventry and his assistant, his brain calculating military risks. "Do you know where they've been taken?"

Coventry nods. "They were taken to ..." he stops himself from saying it aloud, and leans forward to whisper the place in Nicolaus' ear. In earnest, Nicolaus looks at Coventry with great concern. "Yes Sir." Coventry knows Nicolaus understands the urgency.

All eyes are on Nicolaus as he nods, agreeing to take the mission. "Yeah, okay. Can I pick my team members?" he asks Coventry.

Coventry nods again. "Yes Sir, we can accommodate up to four team members total. We have already made contact with Strictland."

Nicolaus nods, "Yes. I want Sanchez and Washington as well."

Coventry points to his assistant, "Yes Sir, we'll make contact right away."

Nicolaus' cousins and Francesca are fascinated and discuss how the officers know who Nicolaus is talking about by last names only. After all, how many people in the United States military have the last names of Sanchez and Washington? Must be hundreds. Francesca is amazed to watch this taking place in real time.

"Please, give me ten minutes with my family, and I'll be right with you."

"Yes Sir!"

As Coventry and his assistant step away to contact the other team members, Francesca couldn't help herself, "My God, Nicky! That General is calling you Sir! What the ... hell?" Francesca is being more mindful of her language these days, inspired by Nicolaus. "Aren't you supposed to be calling him 'Sir'?"

"Clearly, Nicolaus is a very important man!" Ned clarifies.

Nicolaus chuckles at his open-minded cousins. "Well ... I don't know about all that," he humbly tells them, trying to make nothing of it. Nicolaus is aware that the observations are correct. This is a big deal. He is not exactly sure what he will be getting himself into. Certainly, it is highly dangerous.

"Well, I don't have much time," Nicolaus stands before his family to brief them. "Obviously, what you just heard is confidential and you cannot tell anyone."

"The President sent for you? The President." Francesca points out again.

Nicolaus sighs, "Yes, well, this rescue is going to be very tricky. And it being in Milojastan makes it very high risk. You have to know ... I may not make it back," he tells them. The gravity of this situation hits Deirdre and Elsa. Niall looks a little shocked by all this.

"Son, perhaps you shouldn't take this mission. Let someone else go," Nigel wants to immediately change his mind.

Nicolaus folds his muscular arms before his chest, "Well ... I would hope that if I or any of you were abducted and taken to Milojastan, or anywhere else, that someone would step in to help," he tells them. "Father, if you don't hear from me in seventy-two hours, you should assume the worst. You should hear something from the state department. I'll have Coventry's team send you contact information. Also, if I don't make it back, Alexander knows everything I've been working on at the office. We work on most things together. And you are the beneficiary on all my military benefits. I never changed any of those documents."

Nicolaus bids the family to stand so he can begin his goodbyes. Every mission he'd ever been on had its risks. This one seems different, it weighs heavier on his mind, perhaps because he had to go into Milojastan without any backup. Abruptly, the weight of finality hits Nicolaus. He looks at his family, realizing this may be the last time he sees them. His gut slightly knots at the thought that this may be the last time he sees ... Deirdre. His Deirdre. The suddenness of leaving left no time to mentally prepare for the going away.

Francesca is the first to cozy Nicolaus with love as she hugs him tight, and he does the same for her. She rests her hand on his chest, "You better not let them keep you, Nicky. You use your special agent tricks to get you outta there," she half-jokingly tells him in her thick English accent. "I want you back my sweet cousin." She kisses his cheek.

Elsa unexpectedly hugs Nicolaus. "I think of you like a big brother, Nicky. Please be careful and stay safe."

"Thank you, Elsa."

His cousins are quick to grab him up. "Man, you owe us some catching up," Ned tells him. "I just know we are gonna see you back here."

"Yeah, we'll see you when you get back," Bobby says. Cato gives him a light hug.

Nigel grabs Nicolaus by the nape of his neck, bringing him into a brief hug, clearing the father's worry in his throat. "I have no doubt that you'll rescue those ambassadors, and return safely to us." He smiles with pride, "I'm very proud of you, son."

Nicolaus smiles at his father's belief in his abilities, "Thank you, father."

Next in the goodbye line is Ceil. Nicolaus looks upon his mother, observing her beauty through her cold stare at him. He gently touches her shoulder. "Mother, I've never asked anything of you. Today I ask you to please look after Marguerite, as you always do. She needs your support," he tells her with a smile.

"Of course," Ceil nods. Nicolaus accepts her nod as her hug to him.

The cousins watch Ceil from afar, and know they will have to get around to speaking to her.

Marguerite stands before Nicolaus, no smile about her, Thaddeus in her arms, brought over by the nanny. Nicolaus touches his son's head, rubbing his dark hair. He holds the small of Marguerite's back, "Wife, ... please ... behave while I'm gone. Take care of my son." Nicolaus kisses the soft baby cheek of his son, taking in his baby smell. Then he kisses Marguerite's lips, as a husband should do. She reacts to him, so they kiss again, then he moves to the next person in line.

Niall still has a stunned countenance for Nicolaus going away like this. He knows there is a military helicopter outside somewhere, ready to jet his brother away. He shakes his head in disbelief, sorry for having belittled his brother's past missions. He understands the gravity of Nicolaus being called on by the President to rescue someone. Unexpectedly, Niall grabs Nicolaus and hugs him, in a tight, strong hold. The action surprises Nicolaus, as his arms fling around his younger brother, bringing emotion to the surface. They man hug for a good minute. When they break their hug, Nicolaus sighs away the emotion in his chest. "Niall, please help care for my wife and my son. Marguerite needs all the support available for her." Niall nods. The brothers smile.

Last in line is Deirdre. Nicolaus grabs his precious angel to him, hugging her, his back to the family, as if they were the only two in the room. They hold each other tight, tears seeping from Deirdre's eyes. When they part, Nicolaus gently wipes her tears. Suddenly, Deirdre removes her gold medallion necklace. She sometimes wears it when she thinks about her missing father.

"I want you to take this, Nicky. As you know, it belongs to my father. I am told it brought him good luck when he wore it. He did not have it on the day he disappeared."

Nicolaus looks at it, knowing it is familiar to him, having seen her wear it so many times. The gesture made emotion choke him. "Deirdre, I'd be honor to wear this."

Quickly, she puts it on him. "Bring it back to me. You return, Nicky," she whispers to him, in a shaky voice, trying not to blurt out cries. "My love," her voice low, only for the two of them to hear.

Nicolaus tightly hugs Deirdre to him again, cradling her within the space of his middle chest, the space that is exclusively hers, not wanting to let her go. He plants a passionate kiss on her lips, possibly their last, then tears himself away from her, leaving his love to go serve his country, yet again. He is not able to look back.

"Now that is true love," Ned quietly observes to his brothers. "There is no way those two should not be together. This is all messed up."

Quickly, Nicolaus steps right up to the General and his assistant. "Let's go," he tells them. The general understands the pain of saying goodbye to family to go on a dangerous mission. Abruptly, he ushers the men to leave the building.

Deirdre's legs carry her after Nicolaus, as he goes out the door. "Nicky," she calls after him, her hand to her face. She is perplexed of his leaving and the true possibility of not seeing him ever again. She is only stopped going after Nicolaus by Elsa, who puts her arms around the crying Deirdre, and turns her from the direction of the door.

Deirdre's high intelligence could not quelch the mourning moan within her, because of her most precious love, her precious Nicolaus, leaving. Somewhere from the depths of Deirdre's heart and soul, an uncontrollable loud wail of love and longing escapes her mouth, in hope for Nicolaus' safety.

This is too real for her, as thoughts race through her mind, 'What if she never sees him again? What if he gets hurt and can't make it back? What if he were captured during the rescue mission?' She wails loudly again, falling to her knees on the floor, her hand over her very heart, unable to contain the emotion. "Nicky! Nicky!" she calls for him again, crying uncontrollably.

Francesca quickly joins Elsa to try to console Deirdre, getting on the floor with them, holding onto her. The party, nor their fashionable clothes no longer matter.

As grief eludes Deirdre's body, Marguerite has the opposite reaction, displaying obnoxiousness to Deirdre's lamentations. The brother cousins stand back and watch the scene unfold. They know Ceil is responsible for Deirdre's literal heartbreak.

Niall grabs Marguerite to stop her from going after Deirdre. Marguerite is flaming hot with anger again, ready to hurt Deirdre, with Thaddeus riding on her hip. "You hussy!" she shouts at Deirdre in a nastier demeanor than usual. Niall holds Marguerite back as she yells at Deirdre, "You dare touch my husband. I told you, you no touch him! He not your husband!"

"Calm down, Marguerite!" Niall yells at her, trying to outshout her rants.

"I'm the wife!" she shouts at Deirdre, trying to get away from Niall. "You want cry? I make you cry!"

Niall shepherds Marguerite to a corner on the opposite side of the room. "Calm down!" he yells at her again.

Marguerite screams, ignoring Niall, "Nicolaus my husband!" She tries to get her point across, as if no one has understood this. "I hope he not be back, and you never see him again!" she screams with all her might and angry energy to Deirdre, her words shocking the family. "The enemy fix him!"

Francesca voices what most of her shocked family members are thinking, "Shut up, Marguerite!"

"They fix him, and you to never see him again!" Marguerite adds for more shock value.

"Shut up!" Francesca angrily yells right back at her, deeply frowning, "Don't say those things! Don't wish Nicky harm! Are you fu ... freaking crazy?"

"Oh God, help him!" Marguerite's ugly words and ugly demeanor do not change Deirdre's disposition, as she continues to wail for Nicolaus, her hand to her heart, as if to stop it from leaping out of her chest. "Nicky! Oh God! God, please protect Nicky!" she laments aloud. "Please God, keep him safe," her faint words melt into tears. "Nicky."

Ceil doesn't know what to do. She helps Niall calm Marguerite. Thaddeus screams at the commotion, and Ceil takes the upset baby from Marguerite, gesturing the nanny to help.

Nigel sighs, closing his eyes to the chaos. He backs away from his family to go find himself a drink.

Feeling for Nicolaus, Ned, Bobby, and Cato decide to sidestep the dramatic commotion and return to California on the next available flight.

Chapter Twenty-Three-TW

Nicolaus and his team, Sanchez, Washington, and Strictland-of which Strictland is also his close friend, made their plan of rescue on the light military plane while enroute. The ambassadors were taken to an underground prison in a heavily populated city, just north of Bulgaria, on the southern border of Milojastan.

Nicolaus and his men are loaded up with the equipment of their choice, which they jammed into military grade backpacks, camouflaged as regular backpacks, before boarding the U-28A Special Forces military plane. The plane is to drop them off just before the Milojastan border. They will be on their own, until giving the secret signal for the plane to retrieve them at the agreed upon pickup point.

Their extremely capable pilot is Captain Bessie Coleman Browning. Her mother named her Bessie Browning, her first name in honor of the first African American woman aviator. However, once Bessie decided she was going to be a pilot, she legally changed her name, adding the Coleman, wanting to fully honor Bessie Coleman. Captain Browning, one of the few African American woman military pilots, has flown and retrieved Nicolaus and his teams on several previous missions. Nicolaus has the utmost respect for Captain Browning, and knows she is the best pilot to get them in and out of Milojastan unseen.

The men spend their flying time heavily studying the maps to get their bearings of the geographic location. They repeatedly discuss the plan to each other several times to be sure they each understand what to do. Once dropped off on the border, at two in the morning, disguised as tourists, they have to get to Milojastan in an unconventional way, by foot. It takes them most of the day to get to their destination, as they trudge non-stop through the frigid city of Vidin.

It is nightfall again once they are inside Milojastan. Ice cold artic winds rip through the air. The men need to work quickly under the cover of darkness to gain access to the ambassadors.

Back in Austin, Nigel and Deirdre are cemented to the phone the whole time Nicolaus is gone. Deirdre feels herself adrift between terror and fear of the high possibility of Nicolaus getting captured by foreign authorities. What might they do to him? She could not sleep, she could not eat, she could not work, she could not do anything. She is very anxious. Ishani and Maggie support Deirdre as much as they can, as they know this is very difficult for her. This type of situation would be difficult for any family member or loved one of a military member.

Nigel is in a similar state as Deirdre, not able to eat or sleep, though his anxiety is not as extreme as Deirdre's. Nigel is not only worried about Nicolaus' safety; he is also worried about the future of his corporation. What would happen if Nicolaus does not return, or if he returns injured and unable to carry forward with his work?

Deirdre wonders how Marguerite continues to go about her life, as if she doesn't care what happens to Nicolaus. This upsets Deirdre, though she says nothing of it. She pulls out the rosary beads the Bishop had given her the day she was jilted. She remains constantly prayerful for Nicolaus.

Francesca appears in and out of the mansion between her classes. She is also a nervous wreck. Today is forty-eight hours that Nicolaus has been gone. She had a substitute cover for her for the remainder of the week, as she is unable to concentrate. Francesca has been checking all the news she can find, especially anything about Milojastan or American spies, or Special forces activities in the area, and found nothing. Francesca plops down on the sofa next to Deirdre, and watches quietly as she sees her praying.

Francesca brought the family ancestral book with her, the only one of their entire family lineage. Her great Aunt Clara of Estonia tasked her with keeping the family history. She bought a special pen for scribing into the book, which she is doing now, about Nicolaus' mission. She believes this mission must be noted in the book, especially since it is a request of the President.

Nigel is standing by the fireplace when his phone beeps. Deirdre and Francesca quickly stand next to him to see what the message is. "It's a text message," Nigel announces aloud for all the family present to hear, "from the state department. It says there is no news to report." Nigel frowns in frustration. "Well ... at least we know they will contact us if needed," he mutters, sighing.

As Nicolaus' team stealthily finds their way into the underground prison compound, they are glad to see that it is not heavily guarded, most likely because it is three in the morning, and there were only political prisoners held here. They shed their tourist clothing, ready to get this mission done quickly.

After taking out two security cameras, and rendering three guards unconscious, who were in the way of getting to the ambassadors, they go right to their destination, having been provided the information.

Captain Browning is tuned into their microphones, which are connected to their helmet cameras, as worn by all special force agents. She can hear what is happening and will receive the signals directly from the team.

The team swiftly make their way through the interior of the prison, and to the inside prison door of the small cell where the ambassadors are being held. Quickly, Nicolaus identifies the ambassadors.

"Get back, and get down, we're going to blow the door open," Nicolaus instructs the men who are overjoyed to see American military there to rescue them.

Noting the United States flag insignia on their right shoulder, the usual mark of the United States military, the French Ambassador says words of blessings to the men, "Oh bless each of you. Bless America."

Washington works quickly to set the wrapped C4 explosive. Other prisoners are awakened by the voices and unusual noises. They begin to beg for rescue as well when the team takes shallow cover. The door is abruptly blown clear off its hinges, causing a loud explosive noise, and lots of dust.

The force of the explosion set off alarms throughout the prison. The men have exactly two minutes to get full clear of the outer prison walls, or they most likely will not make it. Getting outside the walls within two minutes ensures a large enough lead from running guards, running dogs, and flying bullets, that are sure to be tracking them.

The team enters the cell to find the ambassadors in bad shape, having been brutalized and tortured. "Can you run?" Nicolaus asks them, as they need to leave quickly, beyond walking. One of the ambassadors has a cracked leg.

Without hesitation, Strictland and Sanchez, drop their heavy backpacks and offer their bodies for the men to climb onto their backs to be carried.

Nicolaus retrieves the weighted backpacks. Quickly, he apologizes to the other prisoners for having to leave them behind. He assures them he will inform the embassy and the state department of their whereabouts. Nicolaus leads his men out the prison through a different route from which they entered. They are outside in no time. Immediately they are under gunfire.

Swiftly, they make their way through the nearby wooded area, and keep moving out of gunfire range. Sanchez and Strictland kept pace, despite carrying the injured ambassadors on their backs. Washington is the protector in the rear, and it is up to Nicolaus to get them to their pickup spot.

After an hour of hurried traveling through the frigid cold without stopping, Nicolaus can see the pickup spot in the distance. He has been making chirp noises in code for Captain Browning to understand their distance. "Yellow Bird," he says the code words one time as they are now about fifty feet from the pickup point.

"Roger that," Captain Browning responds one time.

Within minutes, the plane lands, the men board, and they are off to Germany to the United States Airforce base where the ambassadors will receive medical treatment; and they will all be debriefed. It is not until they enter German airspace, well out of reach of the Milojastans, that the men feel they can celebrate their accomplishment with laughter and relief.

"As usual, you guys are top notch!" Nicolaus tells them.

"Did you see how neat and clean I blew that door right off its hinges?" Washington gleefully comments, with a wide smile, showing his pearly white teeth.

"Didn't know I could run so fast carrying someone," Sanchez chuckles. The French Ambassador shakes his hand in gratefulness.

"I felt such jubilation when I saw that American flag patch on your uniform," the Kenyan Ambassador notes, "You just don't know! Whoa! You just don't know!" He grabs Nicolaus' hand. "I don't know how you got in there. Thank you for risking your lives to save us. Thank you," he somberly tells them. Then happily, he brings Nicolaus into a shoulder hug.

As Captain Browning lands the military plane in Germany, Nigel receives another text message. He reads it to the family. "Oh, here we go, it says they are safe, having accomplished the mission.

They are in Germany. We can expect to hear from Nicolaus within twelve hours."

"Oh, ... thank God!" Deirdre is so relieved tears fall from her eyes. She feels as though she might collapse from the relief of knowing that Nicolaus is all right. Constance is beside her, holding her up in one arm, hugging Rachel to her with the other, as they both had joined the family in waiting for news on Nicolaus. "Thank God! Thank God!" Deirdre repeats.

"That's our Nicky!" Francesca cheers.

"Another extraordinary accomplishment, and the world will never even know it was our Nicolaus who saved those very important people," Rachel comments.

"Well, I think this calls for celebration!" Francesca feels the stress leave off her mind and body. "I'll get us all drinks. God knows I need one!" Immediately, she begins the efforts of pouring drinks for everyone.

Ceil watches as everyone seems relieved, even Niall, who helps Francesca. However, she does notice that Marguerite appears a bit off. Ceil observes as Marguerite stares into space as if in a daze, with Thaddeus hanging off her hip.

Nigel's phone chimes another text. "Oh, I just got a text from Nicolaus! Says mission successful. We are in Germany. We shed no blood and shot no bullets. Always my preference. Team is all okay. Be home in twenty-four hours. Love to all." Nigel chuckles and sighs with even greater relief for hearing directly from Nicolaus. "Wonderful, just wonderful!"

Deirdre couldn't stop herself from hugging Nigel with joy, her tears still falling. She is so in awe of how wonderful, as Nigel put it, Nicolaus really is.

Across the room, believing she is unnoticed, Marguerite quietly walks out. She has Thaddeus on her hip, and doesn't seem to pay attention to him. A looming feeling of despair has taken over her.

Marguerite had hoped, and prayed, and bargained with God to take Nicolaus from her, from all of them. She just wants to be free of him. She was so hoping he'd meet a horrid fate in Milojastan. 'How is it that he escaped the enemy?' she wonders to herself, having no understanding of the audacious caliber of her husband. She is agitated, feeling that now Nicolaus will be returning home, not to her, only to Deirdre, and she will matter less and less. After she witnessed his action towards Deirdre upon his leaving, Marguerite believes it will be impossible to continue with him. She feels that she cannot compete with Deirdre, and she no longer wants to be in this constant struggle with Nicolaus. She walks through the mansion listlessly, thinking about her situation.

That kiss he'd given Deirdre stirred up the foulest hatred she has for him; that hatred which seems to always be present within her. It is the same hatred she felt for him during her pregnancy, and at the birth of their son.

Marguerite stops at the foot of the stairs to their wing of the mansion, and she looks upon Thaddeus. Thaddeus exactly resembles Nicolaus. She cry chuckles at this, thinking about the liaison on the night this child was conceived. He was not conceived out of love, or even out of husbandry duty, but from drunken anger, on both their parts, only to fulfill a contract, a business transaction. Thaddeus was conceived against both their wills. She looks upon him, thinking of him as an unwanted conception.

Marguerite notices just how much this unwanted child resembles Nicolaus: his fingers, his coloring, his eyes, his nose, his chin, even his hairline. What irony. Irony Marguerite has to live with every day. Her mind is full of discontent. She abhors having gone through with the pregnancy. She loathes the thought of ever having let Nicolaus touch her, that night and the only time after. She bemoans her situation, one which she cannot see a way out of.

Listless, Marguerite looks up the stairs. The steps stretch the long height of the mansion, at least twelve feet up the curvature design. It seems like a chore, a heavy burden, to carry the baby she does not want, up all those stairs. This baby is the only thing which keeps her tied to Nicolaus. Thaddeus coos to his mother. She looks upon him again, this time frowning upon him with scorn.

Since Nicolaus beat out death in Milojastan, Marguerite now has to face him returning home. She does not want to deal with Nicolaus anymore. She is tired and defeated. Even God didn't listen to her or help her, so she thinks, as she slowly ascends the beautiful staircase which has detailed railing banisters and wooden steps. The beautiful steps in the beautiful mansion, that held her beautiful things, and all things she wanted that her money could buy, which were stored in her beautiful bedroom, that held her comfortable and beautiful bed, where a nurse, a nanny, and a teacher waited their turn to help her with the baby. Yet Marguerite feels she is not helped by God. In her delusional thinking, Marguerite feels unlucky, unwanted, and uncared for.

Ceil does not feel right about Marguerite, so she follows her, and is stunned to see her slowly gliding up the stairs. Ceil can see that Marguerite does not seem to be acting properly. "Marguerite, what's the matter? You need something?" Ceil calls to her. "Marguerite ..."

At the top of the stairs, Marguerite hears the sound of Ceil's voice below, however, in her frenzy of self-imposed misery, everything is a blur. Marguerite is dazed and confused, as she turns to the sound of Ceil's voice.

Suddenly, Ceil sees a change about Marguerite. Marguerite runs into the baby's room. "Get out! Get out!" she deliriously shouts at the nurse and the nanny. The ladies abide by her demand, and they leave the room. Quickly, Marguerite locks the door. She is determined to release herself of the only thing that ties her to Nicolaus.

Ceil quickly climbs the stairs, and finds the door to the room is locked. She frowns as she hears gurgled cries from Thaddeus. She can hear strange noises made by her grandson, then she hears nothing, then something, then nothing.

"Marguerite, you open this door!" Ceil yells in a panic, knocking and banging on the door. "Marguerite, you open this door! Right now, young lady! Open up!" Ceil turns to the nanny. "Go get Nigel. Hurry!"

The nanny flies down the stairs, and she quickly returns with Nigel. Several family members, including Deirdre are right behind him.

"Hurry Nigel, the door is locked, and she won't open it."

Nigel frowns, then loudly knocks on the door. "Marguerite! Marguerite, open the door please. Marguerite!" They hear a blood curdling scream. Nigel steps back, then rushes the door with all his weight, busting the door open.

Promptly, realizing what she'd just done, Marguerite shrieks another loud blood curdling scream, her hand to her mouth. She drops the pillow, then blackness falls over her, and she falls to the floor. It is too late to save little Thaddeus.

Chapter Twenty-Four-TW

Nicolaus and his men are dismissed by Brigadier General Coventry, with happy gratitude, confirming he knew this team would be successful for the President. His joyful handshake ends in handing each man a sealed envelope, and their plane tickets back to their home destinations.

After several connecting flights from Washington D.C., Nicolaus and Roddy are greeted at the Austin airport by a government agent, and driven home in a private government vehicle.

On the ride home, they receive text messages from their comrades Washington and Sanchez who are glad about the payment received, and verification that they arrived home safely. Nicolaus opens the envelope to find a letter of thanks signed by the President, and a hefty check for services rendered. He smiles with a headshake, never having thought about payment. He knew he would have done that mission for no pay at all, his intention was rescuing those ambassadors, getting them all safely out of Milojastan, and returning his team home.

Roddy is dropped off first. Roddy's wife happily runs to the vehicle to greet them. After kissing and hugging her husband, she hugs Nicolaus, grateful her husband is safe.

"We deserve a rest for a day or two after all that running we did!" Nicolaus chuckles with Roddy. "I'll see you on Friday, to get back into our morning runs."

"Yeah, man, sounds good." They give each other a man brace, with hard pats to the back, and Nicolaus gets back into the vehicle for his ride home.

As the government vehicle drops Nicolaus to the door of the mansion, he opens the door and enters to eerie silence. He'd left with nothing, and returned in a new set of casual clothes, dressed in jeans and a simple shirt. He also purchased a small duffle bag which held the clothes he wore the night he left, and a few German made gifts: a beautiful hair clip for Marguerite, a collector's item for Francesca, and a handmade necklace for Deirdre. He places the small duffle bag by the fireplace in the sitting room. Suddenly, he is rushed by Nigel, who greets his son with a man hug.

"Nicolaus!" Nigel stands back, grabbing his son's shoulder, admiring him, feeling proud and sad at the same time. He seems to be choked with emotion.

Nicolaus smiles at his father's reaction to him, though it is unusual. He hands Nigel the envelope, knowing his father likes reading through his military letters of commendation.

Ceil appears. Nicolaus touches her forearm. "Hello, Mother!"

Ceil nods, "Yes, hello. Hello."

Nicolaus looks around for other family members to trickle in behind her to greet him. "It's so quiet. Where is everyone? Where's Deirdre?"

Ceil looks at him frowning, for not having asked about his wife. She sighs heavily.

Before she can speak, Nigel hugs her to him. "Deirdre is upstairs as is your wife. Son, I'm so proud of you, and so very ..." he pauses to find the words to express his emotions, "grateful that you have returned safely."

"Thank you, father. I'm grateful to be out of there myself."

Nigel touches his shoulder again. "Drink?"

Nicolaus chuckles. "Sure."

"Nicolaus, sit down, we ... need to talk to you," Ceil instructs him, in a kind manner.

Ceil's nice tone immediately gives Nicolaus worry. He brushes the worry away, and sits down as Nigel hands him the drink of whisky. He swallows the two ounces as his parents sit across from him. Nigel swallows his drink as well, not his first for the day.

Nicolaus feels a little weary of what this conversation may bring to him, now that he is back home after having left so abruptly. "So ... let me guess. Marguerite did something."

Nigel nods, grabbing Ceil's knee so she would not blurt out the situation, "Yes."

Nicolaus sighs to brace himself, hoping whatever it is, may not be bad or undoable.

"Okay, just tell me."

"Well ..." Nigel begins slowly, "It's Thaddeus," he says in a defeated tone, shaking his head at the horrid actions of his son's horrid wife.

Nicolaus frowns, "Is he okay?"

Nigel slowly shakes his head, "No. She ... she ... smothered him ... then fainted. I'm so sorry Nicolaus."

Nicolaus pops up to stand in shock at his father's words. Frowning, "Wait a minute ... what are you saying?" Emotions immediately grip him. He cannot believe what he'd just heard.

"With a pillow," Nigel inserts the ghastly information.

Nicolaus breathed hard, a tear spilling from his eye. He frowns. "No."

"I heard it, but she had locked herself in the baby's room. But I heard it!" Ceil says sternly, wanting him to get the full information, "she smothered my grandson. By the time we got the door opened, she still had the pillow in her hands."

"What?" he whispers loudly. His mother is talking about murder. He had to sit himself down again. "What ...why ... why would she do that?" Nicolaus grasps for words.

"Oh, I do not know," Ceil says nastily, "perhaps it has something to do with your behavior towards Deirdre."

Nicolaus' frown grows deeper. He leans forward, wondering if his mother is being facetious with him. "Are you saying that she smothered Thaddeus because of Deirdre? Why? That does not make sense. Deirdre helped us."

"Oh Nicolaus, you still have so much to learn about women." Ceil's nasty tone had not changed as she insults Nicolaus. "Deirdre has been here the whole time you were gone. I know what I saw, what we all saw. She had that pillow in her hands. I tell you she smothered my grandson, and then she fainted."

Nicolaus felt incensed. He'd been halfway around the world to rescue men from death, while his baby son was home, with all of his family present, yet still suffered tragically at the hands of his wife. "Where's my son?" he asked faintheartedly, his voice breaking with tears, he suddenly felt weighted with his son's tragic death.

"He's upstairs, in the guest room, with who else, except Deirdre," Ceil snipes.

Nicolaus eyes his mother, her words and tone greatly bothering him, though he said nothing about it to her. He knew Ceil didn't understand that Deirdre thought of herself as his son's mother, in the absence of Marguerite.

Nigel attempts to soften her words, "Nicolaus, the police have ruled Marguerite's actions unsolved, because of her mental state. I've already talked to Andrejs, he will be here in the morning. Deirdre is sitting with Thaddeus. She did not want to leave him alone. I told the coroner no autopsy. And I instructed the funeral director to get him around six," he chokes back emotion. "I hope it's enough time for you to be with him, before ..."

Nicolaus sighs at the horrible words he had to endure in this tragic situation. "Yes, father, ... thank you," he says softly.

As Nicolaus is leaving the room to go to his son, Niall catches him in a hug, "Glad you're home safe, Nicolaus. Really. So sorry about all of this."

Nicolaus nods at Niall's words, as they release each other from the hug. He went upstairs.

"Mother, you stop attacking Deirdre," Niall chastises his mother. "You forced Nicolaus to marry Marguerite. You brought her here. Now the Ravenell name will be tainted, beyond anything I could have ever done."

"Don't you speak to me that way, Niall! You sound just like your brother," she harshly tells him.

"Enough!" Nigel shouts. "We are all upset! Ceil, we have just lost our grandson! Nicolaus needs our support."

"Ha!" Ceil turns from him.

Nigel turns to Niall, "Niall, please go assist your brother."

"Sure, father." Niall goes to the room where Thaddeus lays. He stops at the doorway to observe, as Nicolaus has just entered.

Thaddeus is laid in a cherry wood baby coffin, provided by the funeral home. The lid is off, and Deirdre is softly singing lullabies through her tears, gently touching Thaddeus' arm.

Ishani and Maggie are each at her side, grieving for the child, as well.

"Deirdre," Nicolaus softly calls to her.

"Oh Nicky!" In a flash Deirdre embraces Nicolaus. Her dainty arms go tightly around his waist, as his strong muscular arms wrap her in warm love. Deirdre lays her face to his chest to listen to his strong beating heart. Nothing and no one could ever take away the love she has for this man. Not even Marguerite. She revels in his arms, taking in the clean smell of him, clinging to his body. She revels in his love, even at such a horrendous time as this.

Maggie and Ishani stand and half hug Nicolaus as well, their hands to his back.

Nicolaus kisses the top of Deirdre's precious head, then acknowledges Maggie and Ishani, touching them on the shoulder. He releases himself from Deirdre's loving embrace to attend to his son. Slowly, he walks to where the lifeless, little body lay. Gently, Nicolaus picks up his son from the small wooden coffin. Nicolaus recognizes his own baby blanket which Deirdre had placed over Thaddeus.

Nicolaus holds his son, who is stiff with death. Facing the open window, sorrow escapes Nicolaus as he cries prayers over his son, praying in the Latin language, blessing his son. He gently touches Thaddeus' chest, where breath no longer emanates from. Touching his little chest seems to make his prayers stronger and louder.

Deirdre and her ladies stand on the opposite side of the coffin box. Following Deirdre's lead, they hold their heads in prayerful solace, listening to Nicolaus' voice. They cannot understand what he is saying, however, Deirdre is sure his prayers are powerful. She imagines he is calling on the angels to protect Thaddeus and lead him on the journey he is now forced to make at such a young age. Tears stream from the ladies' eyes. Deirdre sees Niall in the doorway, standing and watching them.

As his prayers fall silent, Nicolaus' tears fall on his child. He kisses his son for the last time, then places him back into the coffin. Sorrow grips Nicolaus hard as he knows this child should have been that of he and Deirdre, and if so, this never would have happened.

In silence, Nicolaus stares at his son. He could not understand how Marguerite would do such an awful, ungodly thing. Several moments pass before he can pull himself together, only as Deirdre's arms return around him again.

A long sigh escapes Nicolaus. He did what he must, and all he could do, having asked for holy protection upon his son. Nicolaus picks up the coffin lid, and puts it gently in place.

Nicolaus looks up to see Niall approaching him. Suddenly, Nicolaus feels weak and sickened at all of this. "Niall, will you go with me to speak to Marguerite?"

Niall nods, "Of course."

Deirdre reseats herself in the rocking chair, next to the bed that holds the baby coffin. Ishani and Maggie stay with her. The ladies sit without words. Deirdre is doing what she knows Nicolaus would want her to do.

In an unusual move, Niall holds onto Nicolaus' shoulder, in support of his older brother, as they make their way to Marguerite's bedroom.

The door is open, however, Nicolaus knocks before entering. Marguerite is alone, sitting by the fire, looking and feeling despondent. She knows what she has done, and she knew she would eventually have to face Nicolaus.

The brothers enter the room, and Nicolaus directly goes to where Marguerite is. He gently sits down across from her in the chair. Niall stands by the fireplace, watching, not sure what this woman might do, though aware of what she could do.

Marguerite stares at Nicolaus, wide-eyed, waiting for the accusation.

Nicolaus' eyes meet those of his unstable wife. He sighs, vowing to himself to stay calm. "Help me understand ... what happened?" he asks her softly.

"Did your mother not tell you? She saw me," Margarite growls spitefully.

Nicolaus closes his eyes, and holds his hand up to silence her. He does not want this hateful energy from her. Not now. He nods. "She did tell me what she saw. I want to know from you what really happened?" he explains, still in disbelief, hoping she'd tell him something else had transpired, instead of her having smothered his son.

Marguerite stands, "You want to know what happened? I tell you what happened," she shouts, "I kill him! Okay? I kill him! I take pillow, and I stop him breathing." Hatred seethed through her. Tears of hysteria and guilt fell from her eyes, as she threw her angry words to Nicolaus. "Yes, I did! Just like your mother say. I kill him!" Marguerite feels as though she wants to jump Nicolaus and beat on him, her anger growing uncontrollable.

"Why?" Nicolaus asks her loudly, shocked at her callousness. She did not even seem to be grieving, or remorseful.

"Why? Because ... I hate you, that is why. I hate you, and I wish damnation on you."

Nicolaus rubs his forehead with his fingers. He sighs, not wanting to escalate her further, as he can clearly see she is agitated, heading down that road of hysteria.

Marguerite sits down, trying to regain control of herself. The hatred within her for Nicolaus makes her look around the room for something to stab him with, in the hopes of taking him from Deirdre. Her breathing is heavy.

"Okay, okay," Nicolaus' tone is calm again. "I understand that one day you hate me, the next day you do not, then you do again. I can accept that. I thought we had an agreement in the marriage." He sighs, at a loss, trying to understand. "I accept if you hate me. I don't get why you hurt ... wanted to kill Thaddeus."

"The day you left I wish you dead by enemy hands. I want free of you!" She yells in her Latvian accent.

Her words of wanting him dead by enemy hands brings shock to Nicolaus. He is absolutely feeling the hatred she has for him, even though she has voiced this to him hundreds of times. "The day I left?" Nicolaus shakes his head remembering their kiss goodbye, remembering their night of nonstop sexual activity.

Marguerite stands again, "You did not care for leaving me or Thaddeus. Is that hussy, Deirdre, concern you. Is that hussy you cry for."

Nicolaus stands to defend Deirdre. "Now, hold on. You don't talk about Deirdre like that!"

Marguerite points at him, stepping closer, wanting to hurt him. "You see? Even now ..."

"Wait a minute! You killed Thaddeus because of Deirdre? Deirdre helped us with Thaddeus, at your insistence when you didn't want to take care of him. Deirdre has always only tried to help you. It's what you wanted, for her to look after Thaddeus." He still couldn't understand her logic. His frown was deep. "You killed him for that?"

"No," she yells. "I kill him because I hate you!"

"Uh ..." Nicolaus is at a loss for words, "he is an innocent child. A baby, Marguerite. If you didn't want him again, why didn't you give him to the nurse or the nanny?"

"He no so innocent if he of you," Marguerite yells at him, in her broken English, ignoring his question. She is so angry she wants to rip that charm right off Nicolaus' face. Marguerite finds herself jumping on Nicolaus, and hitting at his tall frame about his chest and arms.

Nicolaus bares her blows, barely defending himself. He let her hit him.

Niall wasn't sure how it became his job to corral Marguerite off the people she wanted to attack. He pulls her off Nicolaus, trying his best to be supportive of his brother through this horrid ordeal.

Marguerite feels herself out of control, as she wrangles in Niall's arms. "I want release from you ... you bastard!" she yells at Nicolaus, feeling her neck veins throbbing. As usual, Marguerite tries to jerk herself away from Niall for another bodily attack on Nicolaus and is getting nowhere. Tired from the stress and struggle, she stops moving and breathes to calm herself down.

Nicolaus takes Marguerite from Niall, and guides her by the arm to the chair to sit down again. She does not fight against him.

Nicolaus stands by the fireplace, turning from her, thinking what to do. It is obvious things cannot continue on like this. It only takes a minute for Nicolaus to face her with his decision.

"Very well, Marguerite, you will get your wish. I will release you. I am sending you back to your father. After we bury Thaddeus, I will demand your father take you back home with him."

"No!" Marguerite seems shocked. "You cannot send me back to my father!"

Nicolaus is solemn in his response. "I won't divorce you because that will put everything at risk. We obviously cannot live together anymore. You should go back home. You'll probably be happier."

"No!" she stands in protest.

Nicolaus frowns, puzzled by her reaction. "Perhaps your father will legally release us of this marriage. Surely, your father will understand ... "

"It will disgrace me and my family if you send me back!"

Nicolaus scoffs, now feeling impatient with Marguerite. "Woman, you have killed my son ... our baby, and happily admit to it. What you have done is called murder," he harshly whisper yells at her, to keep himself from yelling aloud, wanting to respect Thaddeus. "You are lucky you are not in jail. Now, I have made my decision," he says sternly, "you will go back to Latvia after the funeral. Your father will be here, and he can take you with him. I will go to Latvia to see about you at a later time."

Marguerite falls to her knees before Nicolaus, crying in sudden despair, ready to plead on her own behalf. "No, Nicolaus, please! Please not to disgrace me. Please ..." she begs him.

"Me? Disgrace you? It has been two years and you have disgraced yourself every day since the first moment you have been here," Nicolaus harshly whisper yells at her.

Marguerite cries, grabbing onto her husband's leg. "Please Nicolaus, not to send me back. Please, Nicolaus!"

Nicolaus is moved by Marguerites' pleads. "Get up now! The decision is made!" With some struggle against her grip on his leg, Nicolaus lifts Marguerite off the floor, and gently places her in the chair again. Kneeling before her, he hugs her to him, "I forgive you," he tells her softly. "I forgive you. I forgive all the hate and anger. You'll feel better at your home in Latvia. We'll work this out together."

Nicolaus gets up and backs away, out of Marguerite's arm reach for him, as he feels he can do no more. He turns and leaves the room. Niall follows, amused by the whole scene. As they leave the room, Marguerite falls on her knees again, reaching towards them. She melts into a blubbering ball of hysterical crying.

Nicolaus is so upset his breathing is heavy. He seeks out and finds a bottle of liquor in the empty sitting room. Niall follows Nicolaus as he takes the bottle with him to the nursery room he played in as a child with his own nanny. His childhood toys remain put away in the toy chest. Toys he'd thought his own son would play with.

Niall is speechless when Nicolaus slides his back down the wall, to the floor, in a corner. He opens the liquor and drinks from the bottle as if it were water. He offers Niall the bottle, however, surprisingly, Niall passes. Niall is suddenly very grateful he is not Nicolaus.

Niall realizes his brother has been through a lot, all in one day. Especially after returning from his Milojastan mission, for which he is sure he was probably shot at, and maybe almost captured; however, they didn't know any details because Nicolaus hasn't had time to talk about it to any of them. Niall thought about how crazy he'd be by now if he were in Nicolaus' shoes. Already he felt half crazy, just from witnessing it all.

No words pass between the brothers. Niall can see that Nicolaus wants to be away from the family, to be alone for a while. In silence, Niall leaves Nicolaus to rest and to grieve. He goes to sit with Deirdre.

Chapter Twenty-Five

Nicolaus remains in his childhood playroom. He mourns his son, never having thought such a terrible thing could ever happen.

"Why?" he frowns, asking aloud, still not understanding how Marguerite could so cruelly harm Thaddeus, even at the height of her hatred for him. He wonders if his son suffered. It is too much for him. Slowly, he closes the bottle of liquor, deciding not to drink anymore, knowing that drinking will not solve anything or bring his son back to life.

Overcome with emotion, Nicolaus lays on the floor. Tears of guilt and sorrow flow from him, as did more prayers for his son's soul and for Marguerite's soul as well, until the liquor and jet lag casts sleep over his emotional and physical exhaustion.

Niall sits with Deirdre, Ishani and Maggie now gone. Deirdre also appears exhausted, though she stays at her post, not leaving Thaddeus alone.

Anytime Niall is near Deirdre, his sexual desire for her is greatly heightened. Niall uses the new skills he'd learn to control himself when Elsa used to constantly deny him. Niall very well knows this would be an awkwardly inappropriate time to flirt or make a move on Deirdre. He is sure she'd think the worst of him if he tried such action and would never forgive him.

Niall breathes deep to calm himself. Quietly, he takes more breaths, focusing on the matter at hand. He touches Deirdre's shoulder, "Deirdre ... "

Deirdre glances back at him. "Niall .. where's Nicky?" she asks softly.

Niall sighs, "He's up in the old nursery. I think he wants to be alone right now."

Deirdre nods in understanding. She turns to Niall, tears seep from her eyes, "Poor little Thaddeus."

Niall hugs Deirdre as a gentleman, surprised and happy that she let him. He softly rubs her beautiful, curly hair. "Nicolaus is sending Marguerite away after the funeral."

"Away?" she whispers, frowning. "How?"

"She is to leave with her father."

"What's that you said?" Ceil asks, as she and Nigel enter the room. They thought Deirdre could use a break and were entering to relieve her, and sit with the baby.

"Oh Mother, I was just saying that Nicolaus decided Marguerite must leave with her father after the funeral."

"What right has he to make such a decision without consulting us?"

"Consult you for what, mother? There is nothing else to be done! And I agree with him, she should go with her father."

"I was thinking the same thing, and was going to discuss this with Andrejs. Good to know Nicolaus feels the same as I do," Nigel notes.

Deirdre left the area as the funeral home personnel arrive to take the baby. She is not strong enough to watch them take Thaddeus. She and Francesca go to the pool at the back of the house where they can neither hear, nor see anything that is happening.

Ceil and Nigel oversee the sad activity of handing their grandson over to the funeral home Director.

Chapter Twenty-Six-TW

The following morning, during breakfast time, a scream is heard with calls for help, inside the mansion. Most of the family, Deirdre and Constance, are present, though none had the appetite to eat any food. Nicolaus is absent.

Everyone rushes to the calls for help, coming from Nicolaus' wing of the mansion. They enter, nearing the nurse who is standing in the doorway of Marguerite's bedroom, where Nicolaus and Marguerite had discussed what happened with Thaddeus. The fire is still ablaze in the fireplace, placing the room at a warm atmosphere. Beyond that, everyone stops in devastated disbelief at the sight before them.

"My God!" Deirdre exclaims, turning away, unable to look. She puts herself in Francesca's arms, hiding her sight from the unthinkable.

Nigel and Niall enter to assist. "Get her down," Nigel provides the obvious demand.

"No!" Ceil yells at them, looking at Marguerite. "Leave her. Get Nicolaus first. I want him to see this."

Niall shakes his head at his mother's behavior. "Oh wow, that is just cruel mother!"

"Bloody mean, Auntie Ceil, even for you!" Francesca chastises her.

It is obvious to everyone that Marguerite is beyond saving. No telling how long she'd been deceased, as her face and hands are now discolored.

"Let him see what he has done to her! He needs to see this. I don't want him to put blame on anyone. Where is he?" she demands harshly.

Niall sighs, "I think I know where he is."

Niall turns to go get Nicolaus, however, Ceil stops him. "I will get him," she says firmly. "Just tell me where he is."

Niall looks at Ceil in disapproval, knowing she is taking this too far. "The old playroom," he says, dropping his gaze to the floor. Then Niall looks to his father to intervene, however, as usual, Nigel says nothing, nor does he try to stop Ceil. Though Niall loves his mother, and appreciates all she's done to support him and take care of him, he is disappointed at her current behavior. She never backs down from hitting Nicolaus with emotional pain, though he knows she is doing this for him. Niall sits and waits for the spectacle he knows his mother is planning in her cunning mind. Again, Niall finds another reason to be glad he is not his brother.

Ceil goes to get her oldest son, gloating for another chance to bring Nicolaus down. She finds him shut in the old playroom, which is on the backside of the wing of the house, void of the noises from the other wing of the mansion.

Ceil sees Nicolaus sitting on the window ledge, staring out onto the acres of land attached to their property. Their closest neighbors are very far away, and down the hill. To get to the front of the mansion from the highway entrance, one had to drive up a long, cobblestone road, after being let in the barrier gate by a security guard, after previous entrance through the secure passcode gate. The secured gate which keeps the press away from the family.

"Here you are!" she says loudly, trying to startle Nicolaus, which she does not.

"What is it, mother?" Nicolaus asks dryly, not breaking his gaze out the window. His pious mind is confused about God's plan for his life. Again having trouble understanding why he had to give up Deirdre for Marguerite. Nothing is making sense to him now that Thaddeus is taken from them, and he is sending Marguerite back to her father.

"So, what exactly did you tell Marguerite about the baby?" she asks him, curious.

"I told her she needs to go back home with her father."

Ceil nods. "Uh-hum. And what did she say to that?"

"Why?" he looks at Ceil, feeling she is up to something, annoyed that she is interrupting his thought process and his meditation on God.

"Just tell me. What did she say?"

Nicolaus sighs, "She said it would disgrace her. And I told her she'd already disgraced herself, and that my decision is final. Why all the questions?"

Ceil smiles, "Well, your wife calls for you. She has a message for you."

"I am not interested in anything else she has to say."

"Oh I think you will be interested in this. Marguerite has just put one up on you."

"Mother, what are you talking about?"

"She has won."

"This is not a game, mother. My son is dead. My decision is final."

"Not this time. Marguerite has made the final decision," Ceil taunts him, despicably, even at such as sad time as this.

"Mother, what are you talking about? I'm not in the mood to play your silly games!"

"Go see for yourself. She is waiting for you."

Nicolaus frowns, confirming for himself that his mother is up to something by the tone of her voice. Slowly, Nicolaus gets up from the window, and follows his mother. He slowly climbs the stairs on his side of the mansion, stopping for a moment, thinking of his son. He follows Ceil to the bedroom where everyone is gathered. He looks inside for Marguerite and does not see her. He looks to his mother, who touches his shoulder, and points up.

Nicolaus looks up, and shock ceases him. He quickly goes to Marguerite, and lifts her body by the legs to ease the strain off her neck. Marguerite had managed to get an electric extension cord around the chandelier. It held her weight, as she had been there for some time.

"For Christ's sake, someone help me get her down. Please!" Nicolaus yells at the men in the room, who quickly go into motion, and help him release Marguerite.

Nicolaus lays her on the floor and immediately begins the resuscitation process, pumping on her chest, and breathing air into her lifeless body. "Wake up, Marguerite! Wake up!" he talks to her. Everyone else stands and watches, knowing it is too late to bring Marguerite back.

Andrejs and Penelope have just entered the mansion, and are led to the commotion where the family is. The staff thought it only right, that he may want to assist his daughter.

Nicolaus has been tirelessly working on Marguerite for quite some minutes, yet she is still unresponsive.

Penelope's cries could be heard. Deirdre and Elsa tend to her.

Andrejs can clearly see that nothing can be done for Marguerite. She cannot be saved or resuscitated. He sees the cord wrapped around the chandelier, and an antique chair that is turned on its side, nearby. He understands what has occurred. Andrejs touches Nicolaus' shoulder. "Let her go," he tells him.

Nicolaus does not stop trying to revive her. "No."

"Let her go!" Andrejs harshly yells at Nicolaus.

Nicolaus ignores the words and keeps working on Marguerite.

"Stop!" Andrejs grabs Nicolaus around the upper body, including his arms, making him stop. "Let her go. Please! Let my daughter go," he tells him again. "She already gone", he says near tears. "She already gone," he repeats, much calmer.

Nicolaus freezes. He shakes his head, the reality being unthinkable. He sits back on his heels, and stares at Marguerite. She is blue from having no oxygen. Her lungs are closed, her heart had stopped, his efforts were futile. Marguerite is gone. Nicolaus stands and looks at Andrejs, at a loss for words. He opens his mouth, ... no sounds are heard.

Andrejs understands that Nicolaus is probably in shock at what has happened. It is obvious to Andrejs they had just found Marguerite. Rachel and Francesca are crying, consoling each other. Andrejs touches Nicolaus, he nods at his speechless son-in-law. "I know you try to save her. She is gone."

Nicolaus frowns, then closes his eyes, emotion gripping him again. He steps back, away from everyone.

"You kill my sister!" Penelope shouts at Nicolaus, in an accusatory manner. Deirdre and Elsa are barely able to hold her back. "You kill her!" she screams at Nicolaus.

"No ...," Nicolaus begins, again at a loss for words.

"You did this! You!" she shouts at him, her voice raging.

The room starts spinning for Nicolaus when he sees Ceil smile and nod in agreement with Penelope's words.

Niall grabs his brother, and gets him out of that room.

Nigel is already contacting emergency services.

Chapter Twenty-Seven

A ndrejs and Penelope are welcomed to stay at the Ravenell mansion. Andrejs is fine with this arrangement. However, it is at the funeral home that Andrejs makes his wishes known, as he, Nigel, and Nicolaus go to pick out a casket for Marguerite. It was decided that Thaddeus would be buried in the coffin he currently lays in.

"They should be buried together, here in the U.S.," Andrejs blurts out.

"Of course", Nigel agrees. "We have a family cemetery on the property."

"Buried together? No," Nicolaus disagrees softly. "I want my son to be in peace."

"Your son? He is her son too," Andrejs quickly corrects him, upset by Nicolaus' words. "My grandson!" he emphasizes. "What she has done, no matter! They should be buried together, mother and son!" Andrejs demands, now yelling at Nicolaus.

Nicolaus turns from him, trying not to be overwhelmed with emotion. He quickly understands that he is not going to win this argument. The thought of his son having to be buried with the person that caused his death, is ... unbearable to Nicolaus. 'Is this another twist in the cruel joke from God?' Nicolaus wonders to himself, sighing to keep from expressing his thoughts.

Nicolaus turns to face Andrejs. "Please Andrejs, just hear me out ..." he tries to stand up for his son.

"No!" Andrejs yells at him again, sounding much like Marguerite. "Do not you think you cause enough damage?" His forceful yelling caught Nicolaus by surprise. "I left my daughter to your care, thinking she okay. And my daughter now is dead!" he shouts at Nicolaus, feeling angrier by the minute about this whole situation, fully putting the responsibility of her death on Nicolaus.

Not only is this looking bad upon him and his company back home, his stock took a large hit on the news of Marguerite's death.

Nicolaus frowns, "Wait a minute. Are you blaming this on me?" he scoffs. "What the hell?" Nicolaus expected such a ridiculous accusation from Penelope, not from Andrejs. "It was you that agreed to ..." Nigel pulls Nicolaus away from Andrejs before he can finish his sentence.

"Son, please ... don't. Andrejs is hurting as much as you are. Give him this one thing."

The shocks keep falling upon Nicolaus, as his father backs up Andrejs, instead of his own son. "Oh, so my son, your grandson, can be buried with his murderer? Why is that okay?"

Nigel takes a strong hold of Nicolaus' shoulder. "Nicolaus, please. Let him have this."

Nicolaus sighs, seeing how now both men are against his wants for his son. "Fine!" he angrily tells his father. "I don't agree with it. I'll let it go."

Nigel nods, "Thank you, son."

"I'll be outside." Unable to bear much more, Nicolaus goes outside and sits on a bench next to the mortuary wall. His large, dark sunglasses hide his face from the public. It hides the tears of anger, of hurt, and of sorrow that unexpectedly fall from his eyes.

Nicolaus is sorrowful as he thinks about how his baby son didn't have a fighting chance with Marguerite as his mother. He feels inward anguish for having left Thaddeus alone with her. Though he asked the family to watch over Marguerite while he was gone, it wasn't enough to prevent her from harming their baby. Not even the availability of the extra help his mother hired prevented her from harming little Thaddeus. Nicolaus is enveloped in sadness at the thought of Marguerite hating him so much that she was willing to kill their son, then take her own life.

What is to happen now?

Chapter Twenty-Eight

eil tries to keep the funeral services quiet, to save herself from public embarrassment, as everyone knows it is she who matched Marguerite to Nicolaus. Niall has no loss of love for Marguerite, and siding with Nicolaus, is not going to let his mother have her way on this. Niall is raw over Ceil bringing someone like Marguerite into the family in the first place. He feels it ruined his chances with Deirdre. So, no, he is not going to let this be a quiet funeral.

Niall announces the services in the city newspaper, and through press releases, inviting everyone to attend. Many people answer the funeral announcement with their presence, just like they answer when Ceil throws a party.

People of all classes and races fill the large church. The same church on Martin Luther King Jr. Boulevard, where Nicolaus and Marguerite wed. The same church Deirdre was to wed Nicolaus. The wind begins to blow, and clouds form as the funeral proceeds. The church service is officiated by the bishop and takes about an hour. During the funeral service, Nicolaus receives many condolences and hugs and kisses, however, mentally, he is not present to accept them.

Nicolaus, unaware of the crowds of people, did not feel himself, as he stands at the Ravenell estate family cemetery. The graveside ceremony ends with family members placing roses on Marguerite's and Thaddeus' coffins, before they are lowered into the grave. Nicolaus doesn't notice the press taking many pictures of him in his time of sorrow. After a while, Manfred ushers all the journalists and photographers away.

Nicolaus stands there, looking at the coffins that were to be set next to his grandfather and his grandmother, who both died before he was born. These are his Kiviste ancestors, who began life in America with Ceil and Rachel. It pained him that he had not met them. Nicolaus also looks upon his grandmother's grave on his father's side. And now, his own son is to be lowered in the ground, next to them.

Deirdre stayed by Nicolaus' side the whole day, her tears flowing for little Thaddeus, whom she cared for. She thought about how he wiggled in her arms and smiled at her every morning. She is very worried about Nicolaus, as she knew Nicolaus had been unable to sleep or eat for a few days now, the same as she. Nicolaus stands still, trying to wrap his mind around everything that happened. Alexander grabs onto Nicolaus' shoulder. He stands with him, wanting to make sure he doesn't feel alone.

Deirdre wonders what Nicolaus is thinking as he stares into the grave. She hugs him, and leaves him to grieve and to think, as Constance motions for her to do. Alexander stays with Nicolaus for a little longer, then leaves him to grieve in his own way.

Much time has passed that Nicolaus motionlessly stands at the grave site, as his mind quietly repeats Latin prayers for his son. The hired team of burial men, nod at Nicolaus to acknowledge his presence, and begin to lower the caskets down into the earth, as instructed.

Suddenly, Deirdre and Alexander are by Nicolaus' side again. Deirdre can feel the loss, and her heart pains for Thaddeus. She places an arm around Nicolaus' waist, quickly wiping her eyes, wanting to be strong for him.

Sorrow fills Nicolaus. Alexander gives him a shoulder squeeze of support, as dirt is thrown into the grave on top of both coffins. Thaddeus' baby coffin is atop the middle portion of Marguerite's coffin, their feet in the same direction. Nicolaus feels sorry for Marguerite and wishes he had never met her. However, his sorrow is for his son who has suffered in the hands of his mother.

"Wait!" Nicolaus shouts to the burial men. Just then, the sky opens up and heavy Texas rain pours over every living thing and every structure, as if to wash the city. In the torrential rainstorm, Nicolaus works the wedding ring off his finger. He looks at that ring which brought him much misery, as the rain drenches him. Without hesitation, he tosses the ring into the grave, and it lands on Marguerite's coffin. "Now you may continue," he tells them.

Nicolaus walks some steps away from the grave, holding onto Deirdre's free hand, and Alexander by his side. Nicolaus sighs the bittersweet emotion somewhere between relief and sorrow, throwing his head back as if to let the rain wash him, wash away his torrid troubles. He wants a nature cleansing from the Almighty God who carried him through the harsh trial of Marguerite Drone, though he really does not understand it all.

Nicolaus hopes that this pouring of rain, at this very time of day, meant that he'd passed the holy trial. After about two minutes or so, Deirdre grabs her love around the waist and Alexander coaxes him inside the Ravenell mansion. Deirdre hands some cloth napkins to Alexander and Nicolaus, so they could each dry themselves off. Nicolaus does not dry off, he remains drenched.

Chapter Twenty-Nine

The repass of serving guests food and drinks has begun. There must have been at least one hundred guests, who are everywhere inside the mansion. Once Nicolaus is spotted, people, mostly women, go to him to provide their condolences. Each gesture their love for Nicolaus in different ways- taking his hands, kissing his face, kissing his lips, hugging him, talking gently in his ear. The older ladies are particularly comforting with words of wisdom and hugs. This time, Nicolaus pays attention to each guests' comments.

Alexander is amazed at the skilled grace of Nicolaus, as he individually thanks each person for their presence at the funeral, and support of his family, with Deirdre by his side. Deirdre also receives greetings and kisses from the guests. Alexander sees Nicolaus military comrades, and he goes over to sit with them, and chat about the day and other topics.

The scene of guests made Ceil's stomach churn as she watches from the other side of the large room. She observes how the guests begin to form a long line to provide their condolences to Nicolaus and Deirdre, as if the pair are royalty. She believes this means her plan to be rid of Nicolaus isn't working. It seems no one, besides Penelope and Andrejs, officially blames him for what happened with Marguerite.

Ceil peers outside through a front window, and sees more people wading through the rainstorm, approaching the line to give condolences. She can't believe it, and doesn't understand why Nicolaus is so popular. She frowns in his direction. "Why are all these people here?" she angrily asks aloud. "Why the hell are they so loved?"

Suddenly, Nigel is by Ceil's side. He'd been watching his wife. The look on her face made him aware he'd better run interference.

"Ceil, you need me to get you something? Or perhaps you'd like some fresh air, away from everyone?"

Ceil drops her thoughts, and accepts Nigel's hand to go outside, away from everyone. Since it is still raining, they go to the private enclosed patio, where they are sheltered from the rain. They are immediately served drinks and snacks by the wait staff.

The long condolence line takes two hours to finish hearing from everyone. Penelope is on her head to interrupt the line, and is repeatedly stopped by Andrejs. She tries to remove his hands from holding her back, "Papa, let me go!" she groans at him. "I want to talk to Nicolaus."

"I know what you want, and you will not go now. Now not the time!" Andrejs knows Penelope is angry. "You will not dishonor me in public like your sister!" he yells at her.

His words get her attention, as Penelope stops struggling against him. She breathed a harsh breath. "Now, you wait until everyone gone. Then you can have your say."

Penelope nods, believing her father may be right. Perhaps she doesn't want to make a scene in public. She just knows that as she looks upon Nicolaus, she has a strong urge to smack him. She's been in love with him for so many years, and now she is so angry with him. She is a ball of confused emotions. She saw what he did at the gravesite, and she intends to confront him about it. "Okay Papa, okay." In a huff, she sits down next to her father and waits.

Finally, most of the guests left. Alexander knows Nicolaus has not eaten or had any hydration the whole of the day. Alexander and Roddy guide Nicolaus to the drink bar, as the staff are still assisting the family. "A bourbon, please," he tells the staff, then changes his mind, not wanting to get back into drinking again. "Sorry, on second thought, an iced coffee." The staff nod, and provide what he needs.

As Nicolaus takes a sip of his coffee that he really doesn't want, Penelope is upon him.

"You kill my sister!" she starts in strong, with the same accusation as before. "You did this! You kill her!"

"Penelope, you've got it wrong. I ..."

Penelope's frustrated love obsession with Nicolaus is full center. She acts on her feelings of attacking him. She slaps his face as hard as she can, not letting him complete his sentence. Penelope proceeds to throw punches anywhere she could. Nicolaus' coffee is on the floor, as she continues her attack. Nicolaus let her hit him a few times, so she could get it out of her system, as he understands she is grieving. Deirdre and the rest of the family begin to rush over to stop her.

After several seconds, Nicolaus grabs Penelope by both arms to stop her hitting him. She is out of breath, and she struggles against him, his touch bringing more confusion to her mind. She remains upset, unable to get her arms loose, she uses her feet to kick him where she could. She aims for his groin, however, the kick lands on his bad knee.

Nicolaus releases her hands, and grabs his knee as her kick pains him greatly, "Ouch! Damn!" Quickly, Nicolaus attempts to hug Penelope to him to try to calm her, to show her he is not her enemy, "It'll be all right," he tells her softly, frowning, not sure what else to do.

"No!" Penelope yells, wrenching herself out of his arms, surprising even herself. Her breathing is heavy.

Niall is quickly behind Penelope pulling her off Nicolaus. Niall twirls Penelope away from his brother. However Penelope is too much for Niall, and she gets away from him, landing another slap to Nicolaus. Roddy and Alexander take action to stop Penelope attacking Nicolaus. Andrejs finally makes her stop, standing between the two of them.

Penelope heaves her breath, her body rampant with all kinds of emotions, mostly anger. She points to Nicolaus, "You kill my sister!" she yells at him again. "You even not care. I saw you take off wedding ring and toss it to the grave. I saw you!" she shouts, wanting everyone to know this detail. "You bastard!" She wants to hit him again. Her father and Roddy stop her actions.

"Penelope, enough!" Andrejs yells at his daughter, grabbing her by the forearms, as Nicolaus had done a few minutes earlier. "Enough!" he shouts at her.

"I say when it's enough!" She yells at her father for the first time ever, now struggling against him, wrenching herself loose. "I'm not through yet. I say when it's enough!"

Andrejs looks at Penelope as if she's lost her mind. She'd never spoken to him in such a rude manner. He did not move from protecting Nicolaus from his spit fire daughter.

"I promise you, Nicolaus Ravenell, I promise," she points a shaky angry finger at him, still held off by her father, her eyes focused on him, "I promise you pay for kill my sister! I promise you."

"Penelope, I didn't kill Marguerite. I ..."

"You drove her to kill herself. You!" she shouted, "and you alone. I promise I make you pay at some time in your life." Feeling finished, Penelope jerked herself around, turning her back to her father. "Let's go, Papa. I will not stay here another night." Penelope looks a little disheveled, her hair having fallen loose from its bun. Anger is still on her as she walks out the door of the mansion.

Andrejs looks down, not wanting to meet the stares of any family members. He feels embarrassed by Penelope's actions, disturbed that she seemed to be in charge of him. Andrejs is heartbroken over the loss of his daughter and grandson. However, he is thankful the press was already gone, not to have recorded this scene. Andrejs leaves the mansion without a word to anyone.

Everyone seemed to dissipate to their respective spaces in the mansion.

"Guys, thanks for being here today. I really appreciate it," Nicolaus tells Roddy and Alexander. They give him a man hug as they also leave the mansion.

Francesca hugs Nicolaus to her, finally getting him alone. She kisses the red marks Penelope's strikes left on his face. "You okay, love?"

Nicolaus sighs. "No, not really. Can you believe that bull?"

"We may need to think of a way to help Penelope deal with all this," Francesca suggests.

Nicolaus sighs again, trying to relieve some of the pressure and guilt that is in his heart. He is glad the day is over, as the rain has stopped, and now the sun has set over the Austin skyline. The staff clean the floor of the coffee spill.

"I'm sorry about that." Nicolaus tells the staff.

Exhausted, Nicolaus does not want to do anything else for the evening.

Deirdre hugs Nicolaus around his waist, laying her head on his back. She can hear his strong heart beating, as he touches her arms around him, in solidarity of their love.

Deirdre had seen that Nicolaus is still wearing her father's medallion, bringing it back to her. He left it on as he had not had a chance to properly return it to her or to discuss his mission. She is so thankful that Nicolaus returned safely to her. Deirdre's arms tighten around her precious Nicolaus. Without words, she holds him tightly, and listens to the rhythm of his heart.

Chapter Thirty

The following day, Nicolaus escorts Deirdre to breakfast. The Ravenell family are mostly quiet. Though they are aware of each other and are present for breakfast, none of them really have an appetite. The chair Marguerite usually sat on remains empty.

Deirdre touches Nicolaus on the arm, smiling at him. "I see my father's medallion remains around your neck. Did it bring you luck?"

Nicolaus smiles at Deirdre with the eyes of love that he always gave her, making her blush. He touches the medallion, and nods, "Yes, it did. As we were leaving we came under heavy gunfire. And thank God, none of us were hit. I'd say that was pretty darn lucky."

Nicolaus removes the medallion from his neck, and places it onto Deirdre, where it belongs. He gently kisses her cheek, wanting to kiss her lips, though knew better of it due to place and time; and his mother's narrow-eye stare at him.

Deirdre touches the medallion, her eyes on Nicolaus. She also wants to kiss his lips, also knowing it would be inappropriate at this time.

They both return to the meal before them.

"Nicolaus, it is very well that you had good success in Milojastan. I can imagine the ambassadors were happy to see you," Nigel adds, realizing they had not had time to discuss his mission.

Nicolaus lightly chuckles, "They were! We were more glad to see them. It always helps when the intelligence is correct."

Chapter Thirty-One

T he following week contains Valentine's Day, on the upcoming Friday. Today, being Monday, Nicolaus not quite ready to face the world, nor had his head into his work, strolls the Ravenell property, holding onto Deirdre's hand. She'd been by his side all day, every day since the funeral. They rarely parted company, except for personal breaks, if someone needed to talk to them privately, or to sleep in their respective beds.

Though it is February, the Austin weather is intermittently cold or somewhat warm. As Nicolaus and Deirdre walk together, the sun shines onto the hundreds of evergreen trees and bushes that line the walking path on the property. The busy birds who live in these beautiful trees chirp away as they create nests, chat with each other, or lay their eggs.

Nicolaus and Deirdre walk in silence, just enjoying being in each other's company. When they make it back to the back patio door, Nicolaus stops and pulls Deirdre into a tight hug, placing her in the space that is hers alone, the natural masculine cut of his chest, the space closest to his heart, where she fit snuggly.

Deirdre savors the loving, warm arms of her dream man, as he embraces her. She is happily surprised when Nicolaus softly kisses her neck. Deirdre melts more in his arms, relishing in his love, wanting every bit of him. At this moment, Deirdre briefly feels glad for having her man back, though she wishes it could have been under other circumstances, instead of Marguerite's demise. She wishes life had been easier for she and Nicolaus. She feels her joy of life starting to become depleted with their troubles.

"Stay with me tonight," Nicolaus whispers in Deirdre's ear, ready for more of her love. He doesn't want to be apart from her any longer. He is tired of waiting to be with his true love. He wants to express his love to Deirdre, and cherish her the way she deserves to be cherished. Nicolaus wants to begin bringing about their destined children.

Deirdre bites her lip, remembering that this is a wiser, more experienced Nicolaus talking to her. Somehow, in her hesitation, Nicolaus manages to pull her even closer to him. He kisses her neck again, playfully, making her shiver with the delight of his lips on her.

"Nicky," she whispers, "you already know I cannot do that."

Nicolaus chuckles, "My innocent Deirdre. When can I ever have you?"

"On our wedding night!" Deirdre frowns up at him. What is he thinking? However, her mind ponders the worry of their life together, under his mother. She worries for her future children, knowing that Ceil has a never-ending vendetta against Nicolaus. She frowns again, wondering how she could possibly be considering not marrying Nicolaus Ravenell, her one and only, sweet love.

Suddenly, the hands of Niall gently pull Deirdre from Nicolaus' embrace, interrupting her thoughts. He gently tugs her by the hand, walking her to the nearby sitting room. Deirdre giggles, not resisting him, and only feeling safe because Nicolaus is there with them. Playfully, she wonders what Niall is up to. Nicolaus is right beside her, although now he is frowning.

The actions of his brother jolt Nicolaus to remember that Deirdre is not automatically his any longer, especially since he gave her up to marry Marguerite, to save the family empire. Followed by him having made the conscious decision to choose Marguerite instead of her, to try to get some peace in the marriage. Nicolaus' mind remembers the other day, at the birthday party, that several suitors were vying for Deirdre's attention.

Niall sits Deirdre in the chair, next to the fireplace. He sits himself on the floor, and with a smile on his face, he gently removes her shoes. Niall takes the flower petal soft foot of Deirdre and begins massaging it. Niall's smile grows bigger and mischievous when Nicolaus gives him an awkward look, and remains quiet. Niall knows Nicolaus can say nothing, and he is loving this situation he placed his all-powerful brother in.

"Oh, wow," Deirdre feels a little nervous for Niall to touch her.

Nicolaus closes the sitting room door. In seconds, he is standing behind Deirdre, gently massaging her shoulders. Niall continues to work on her foot, moving upward to her ankle.

"To what do I owe all this attention?" Deirdre asks, letting the two brothers comfort her. She thinks this is hilarious, and now wonders if somehow they are trying to compete for her. Niall already knows the answer to a competition between he and Nicolaus. However, the foot massage feels great.

Niall begins to massage her other foot. "I want to apologize if I have ever done anything to offend you, Deirdre. I want you to know that I too can be sweet," he tells her softly.

Niall's apology is very shocking to Deirdre. However, her attention is promptly swooped away by her true love, as Nicolaus' mouth is upon her. He knows she will not refuse him.

In direct competition with Nicolaus, Niall finds himself gently kissing Deirdre's feet, and tugging at her toes, making her moan.

Nicolaus' tongue gently probes Deirdre's mouth, making her moan more.

Niall's hand goes to her middle leg.

Nicolaus' hand goes to her cleavage.

Quickly, Deirdre pushes both brothers off her, and stands away from them, panting, feeling herself flush and hot, her hand to her chest, her eyes a look of surprise, feeling herself fully aroused. How far was Nicolaus going to let this go? "I ... ah ... I think ... ah ... I believe it is time for me to take a nap," she says, unable to think of anything else to say that would remove her from the room.

Quickly, Deirdre turns and leaves the brothers, knowing Nicolaus would take care of defending her if needed. A smile covers her face, and she giggles with giddy delight, as she runs barefoot to her regular guest bedroom and locks the door.

Chapter Thirty-Two

After about two hours, Deirdre emerges from the room, only to find Nicolaus guarding the door. "Honey?"

Nicolaus chuckles, "I just wanted to make sure you were not accosted while getting your beauty rest. That's all." He smiles and puts down the financial newspaper he was reading onto the end table which is next to the chair he'd placed beside the bedroom door. Since Deirdre actually let Niall touch her, Nicolaus is not so sure if Niall would behave properly. It was a good surprise for him when Niall did not show himself to bother Deirdre.

Nicolaus kisses Deirdre on the head, and pulls her into an all loving, consuming hug. "I think we should get married next Friday, especially since it will be Valentine's D...," his words drop when Deirdre pulls away from him and looks at him doubtfully.

"Nicky," she touches his chest, "no! It's too soon!"

"Too soon? I've been delayed an extra eighteen months since our first wedding plans. If I married you today, maybe it'd be too soon; but next Friday?"

Deirdre sighs, "Nicky, you're not thinking clearly right now. We cannot wed ..."

"What's this talk?" Ceil rudely interrupts their private moment, appearing from nowhere. "Have you two forgotten what just happened?" Ceil spitefully says, annoyed at their happiness. "Look at you Nicolaus! The dirt has not even settled over your dead wife's coffin yet, and you're making wedding plans?"

Nicolaus does not have an answer for his mother. He sighs, holding his head down, closing his eyes, not wanting to engage her.

"Why did you toss your ring away, as if you cared nothing for Marguerite? She did birth my grandson, after all."

Nicolaus quickly wraps his arm around Deirdre, his hold on her waist tightens. "I tried to care for her, mother. The ring and all the misery it has brought is exactly where it should be. I want no reminders of her. I have locked her room, and will allow no one to enter it until it's fully remodeled and her things taken away."

Ceil looks at him with amazement. "You embarrass me!" she tells him nastily, then takes leave of them. Ceil is upset, having worked herself up again over Nicolaus. She stops her mean strut momentarily in thought, holding onto the wall, suddenly realizing she needs to work out another plan to be rid of him.

Deirdre looks upon Nicolaus with love, as she removes herself from his embrace. She points in the direction Ceil had left them. "See? That ... my love, is exactly what I'm talking about. It's too soon to discuss us getting married. For once, I agree with Mother Ceil. It's just too soon. And anyway, maybe I don't want that anymore." There. She said it to him. Even though it pained her to say it, now it's out in the open. She looks up at Nicolaus and more pain hits her at his expression.

Nicolaus looks at Deirdre, an intense frown on his face. "What ... what are you saying, Deirdre? You don't want to be married?"

"I ..." Deirdre sighs, not wanting to hurt Nicolaus farther, "I don't know. I'm not sure ... I mean ...yes ... of course I do ..." she sighs, "I mean no ... it's not you, I mean ... I want you ..." she struggles to explain her jumbled thoughts which were as unclear as she thought they would be. "Oh honey! I still love you," she frowns at his frown, he almost looks devastated. She knows that he had only truly loved her his whole life, just as she had only ever loved him. Nicolaus is the only man for Deirdre. However, ... his family, well ... that is a whole lot to deal with. She touches his muscular torso, and then his impeccable chest, "I will always love you ...", she sighs again, "I just don't know anymore."

"What are you saying? You don't want to marry me?" This is all Nicolaus heard.

Deirdre kept her hand on Nicolaus' chest. "Babe ... I'm not really sure I want to be joined to the Ravenells forever." Nicolaus is looking at her bewildered. She knows she is hurting him. "What I mean is ... maybe I don't want Mother Ceil to be my mother-in-law. I'm terrified when I think of her as my children's grandmother! Frankly, I can hardly imagine it working smoothly. She would not be nice to them. They'd be frightened of her ... kind of like I am."

Nicolaus takes both of her hands, and he kisses one, in a begging motion, "No, no, no! You cannot let my mother come between us. That's what she wants."

"Nicky, your mother went halfway around the world to get someone else to force you to marry. She risked your family's fortune, and the company. Your mother really went to a lot of trouble to separate us."

"Deirdre, please ..."

"I'm sorry, honey, I really have to think about this. I need to sort this out."

Nicolaus sighs, his heart is racing. He feels as though he has to talk her into marrying him, ... a first. She'd always been very responsive to him, their love undeniable. "Deirdre, of course we should be married! And anyway, your mother will also be grandmother to our children. So it will even out, like it's always done for us. They will have one really mean granny, and one really lovely granny."

Deirdre shakes her head no, which surprises him that she is not following along with him as usual.

"Look, you know I'll do whatever you want. We don't have to live here. We can live at your house. We can get our own new house. We can even move to another city."

Deirdre takes her hands from Nicolaus, so that she could be present, in the moment, as his touch melts her and makes her weak. She takes a step or two back, knowing he isn't thinking clearly again. "Nicky, you know good and well you are not going to abandon your father. Not even for me."

"Hey, that's not fair," he complained of their previous broken engagement, "what choice did I have? We worked that out together, you and me."

"I know babe, and that is exactly what I mean. You are Vice President now. You are not going to step away and stop helping your father with the company because of me. And frankly, I wouldn't want you to. You'd be miserable."

"I'd do anything for you, Deirdre."

Deirdre looks up at her love, and gently touches his face. "I know you believe that, and I thank you for saying it."

"I mean it. I'll commute. Whatever you need me to do."

Deirdre sighs, "Okay, well ... right now I need you to let me think about it." She tells him boldly, trying to be strong, needing him to hear her. Deirdre sighs again. "In fact, I've decided I need to leave to think things over. I'm going to our castle in Estonia for a while.

By myself."

"Deirdre ..." she hushed his words with her finger, not wanting to discuss it anymore.

She goes inside the bedroom, and grabs her packed bags. She had packed after an hour of tossing and turning in her sleep deprived nap.

Nicolaus is again surprised by her actions. He realizes she has been thinking about this for a while. "Can I at least take you to the airport?" he offers in anguish, shocked that she is thinking about not marrying him, and that she seems to be running away from him.

Seeing her with suitcase in hand, ready to leave his side, brings panic to Nicolaus, something he's never felt with Deirdre, before now. He wants to respect her decision, although he doesn't want her to go, and definitely not alone.

Could he blame her for wanting to run away? The case she set out for him does make sense. Most likely, any woman would run away from such circumstances.

Deirdre smiles at him, and lifts herself on her tiptoes to kiss him. "Manfred is going to take me. I love you. I'll be back soon. I promise to call you after I arrive."

Nicolaus catches Deirdre by the arm as she tries to scurry from him. He pulls her into another embrace, and kisses the top of her precious head. "I'm going to miss you," he whispers to her. He bends down for a mouth kiss. "Just remember that I love you, Deirdre, with all my heart. You are my first and only love. We should be married as soon as possible." Nicolaus gently touches the middle of Deirdre's exposed cleavage. "Keep my love for you right here, near your heart. Never forget that you belong to me! We belong to each other. We are meant for each other, babe," he frowns, feeling emotional.

Nicolaus' sappy, love filled, romantic words make Deirdre want to cry, because she knows he means what he says.

Nicolaus touches their foreheads, "Promise me, love, you'll return to marry me. Promise me."

Deirdre doesn't respond to his demand. She swallows down the tears, throws him one more kiss, and quickly hurries herself away, through the house to the front door. She has to leave now, before he weakens her resolve, or before she changes her mind again. Deirdre desperately needs a break from everyone.

In astonishment, Nicolaus watches his angel leave him.

Chapter Thirty-Three

The evening emerged quickly. Niall pulls his Italian sports car into Elsa's townhouse, having got himself all hot and bothered about Deirdre. When Elsa opens the door, Niall greets her with a bouquet of roses and a kiss. He hopes the roses impress upon Elsa how much she means to him, and that he enjoys being with her.

"These are beautiful, Niall, thank you." Elsa gives him another kiss, as he gently holds her by the waist.

Niall follows Elsa into the kitchen, as she looks for a vase to place the flowers. Her back to Niall, he wraps his arms around her and kisses her neck.

Elsa giggles, "You hungry? You want dinner? I just went to the grocery store, and ..."

"Right now, the only thing I want is you!" he tells her.

Elsa giggles again, being open to Niall. Promptly, Elsa finds herself undressed, and upon the bed, as Niall rubs her feet, just as he had done for Deirdre. Hastily, Niall makes boisterous love to Elsa, devouring and tasting her, all the while thinking of Deirdre.

Niall has rough sex with Elsa for several hours, making her moan, putting her in as many positions as he can imagine. Though he is with Elsa, he can only think of Deirdre, doing to Elsa what he wants to do to Deirdre. Niall sees Deirdre's face as his body stiffens for ejaculation. His body releases into Elsa, secreting all his sexual frustration, making him holler with fierceness.

Breathless, Niall collapses on top of Elsa, her bosom cushioning his head. He leaves his pulsating member inside of her beautiful body, as she lays with a look of wonderment on her face. She'd never had such heightened pleasure before.

Niall gently holds Elsa in his arms.

"Okay, now I'm hungry. Let's order in."

Chapter Thirty-Four

Two margaritas and a romance novel kept Deirdre together on her flight to Estonia. It isn't until the chauffeur picks her up in the limousine, on the ride to the family castle, that tears begin to flow from her eyes. Already she misses Nicolaus. She wished she had asked Elsa or Francesca; or even Ishani and Maggie to accompany her.

Deirdre is so tired of being sad and emotional. The last few weeks have been very rough. She is very glad she has taken time for herself and stopped working. And she needs to think about whether or not she is going to marry Nicolaus. In her mind, there is no question of whether she wants to marry Nicolaus, as he would always hold her heart. She just really had to figure out if she wants to deal with Ceil.

Deirdre has to decide if she wants to see Ceil and participate with her more than she has, in all the time she has known her, and for the rest of her life. Ceil scares her, and most times makes her feel uncomfortable or awkward.

The castle staff are very happy to see Deirdre. Many curtsy to her as if she is their princess, making her smile and giggle. Deirdre walks the halls of the castle on each floor, going into each room to bide her time until dinner is served. She remembers to text Nicolaus of her arrival. He calls her right away.

"Babe, is all okay?"

Deirdre giggles again, "Yes, my love, all is well. The staff is making something for dinner. I don't know what it is, though it smells really good."

Nicolaus chuckles. "Okay. I wish I was there with you. I miss you already."

Deirdre smiles, as he feels the same way she does. "I know babe. I miss you too."

"How long do you think your soul searching will take?"

"Mmm, I scheduled the flight to be back next weekend."

"Okay. I will be at the airport to pick you up. I hope you get the answers you are searching for."

"Yes, thank you love."

"Although we both know we are going to be married. That's the answer you'll arrive at," he chuckles again.

Deirdre is interrupted by the butler, "Madame, dinner is ready."

"Thank you, I'll be right there," Deirdre tells him in a low voice.

"Well, dinner is ready ..."

"Okay babe. Just remember, it's me that loves you. And I'll do whatever you need me to do for us to be married."

Deirdre nods. "Okay, babe. Thank you for reminding me."

As Nicolaus ends his call with Deirdre, an idea pops into his mind about expanding the children's home project. He jots down his thoughts.

Before joining the staff for her dinner, Deirdre quickly puts in a call to her mother. She used the fact that dinner is ready as an excuse to get off the phone with her. Deirdre decides she was not going to let Nicolaus, nor her mother, talk her into returning home before she's made the decision about marriage. Deirdre wants her decision about when to return home to be based on what she wants, not what Nicolaus' charming, beautiful voice of smooth and sweet cream could talk her into. She already misses both of them, and it wouldn't take much for him or her mother to coax her back home.

After dinner, Deirdre goes into the massive library. Her mind remembers the time she and Nicolaus inventoried everything in every room of the castle, after this ancient place was willed to them from Nicolaus' Great Aunt Clara. Deirdre thought about Aunt Clara, and her words of certainty that she and Nicolaus were destined to be together. She assured them that their love is written in the stars. Deirdre wonders what Aunt Clara would think of her right now. She wonders what advice Great Aunt Clara would give her.

Deirdre sighs, and chokes back the urge to cry as her heart knows darn well what Aunt Clara would tell her. She'd say, 'Nicolaus is already yours, this is undeniable.' She'd probably ask her 'What you doing here in Estonia? Why did you run from Nicolaus?'

The thoughts of Aunt Clara brings a smile to Deirdre's smooth heart-shaped face. She pushes back her thick, dark curly hair. Deirdre touches the books with her fingers, sometimes taking one down to thumb through it. Then she replaces it, her mind finding another book that is of interest, then another. She sets a few aside on the ancient table, with the intent to read while she is on her rest break from everyone in Austin.

Deirdre looks out the large glass windows. It is dark out now. Despite there being no lights on the snow covered property, the icy whiteness of the snow has its own light, making the place look like a dream land. She flings open the huge windows, and is greeted by the crisp, February artic air that flows through Estonia from Sweden.

She breathes the fridged air into her lungs, and lets the wind blow through her curls for a few minutes. Then, with a shiver, Deirdre closes the window. She flees to the lit fireplace in her bedchamber to warm herself again, thinking about how Nicolaus had recently been in Milojastan.

Deirdre looks around the bedchamber. It is the same bedchamber that belonged to Nichols and DeeDee. Again, with fascination, her eyes slowly look at every object in the room, while she warms her body with the fireplace heat.

Nichols and DeeDee are such a mystery to her. She decides that while she is here thinking about everything, she will learn all she can about this destined couple. They were destined, just as she and Nicolaus are destined.

Suddenly, Deirdre wonders if she actually could not marry Nicolaus. If their love is written in the stars, how could she not marry him?

Deirdre sits on the bed, as she tries to stop the tears that fall from her eyes, while she thinks about all the years she and Nicolaus have been together. He loves her so much, he patiently waited to be with her for ten years, twelve years, now, counting his doomed marriage.

Deirdre lays back on the ancient canopy bed and admires the embroidered silk drapes, which are on poster boards of the bed. She hadn't realized how exhausted she is, until just now. She feels tiredness throughout the whole of her body, including the tiredness that is wrapped around her mind. She hadn't slept for the last two weeks, with her worry of Nicolaus' safety while he was on mission, then the loss of Thaddeus, then the loss of Marguerite, all the way to Marguerite's funeral. Sleep falls over Deirdre as she ponders her love for Nicolaus.

Chapter Thirty-Five

Elsa is unusually sick for the last few days. Although she did not have a fever, she has been puking much more than she wanted. And sometimes the aroma of certain foods has her running to avoidance. Elsa buys three different pregnancy tests from the local pharmacy. She uses each of them to test herself all at the same time.

She waits for results of the instructed amount of time. She has slight alarm as each test is positive for pregnancy.

"Oh no! This can't be!" she exclaims with her hand to the side of her aching head.

Elsa immediately calls her gynecologist at the Women's Center for an appointment, fearing she'd have to wait too long to be seen. "Oh thank goodness, there is a cancellation? Yes, yes, I'll take it!"

The appointment opening is in thirty minutes, just enough time for Elsa to drive through the stop and go traffic of Austin. She makes it to the office in exactly thirty minutes.

Elsa is called back soon after she checks in. She explains her symptoms to Dr. Rita Johnston, her physician. They discuss the results of the three over-the-counter pregnancy tests.

"I'm glad you decided to see me. Though you did those tests, sometimes they give people a false positive. The best way to verify a pregnancy is a blood test," Dr. Johnston explains.

Elsa nods. "Yes, I need confirmation before I tell anyone."

The physician touches her shoulder, "I understand."

The medical assistant drew Elsa's blood, and instructed her to remain in the room. "With the advanced technology we have here, we will have the results in ten minutes."

"Well, that is great to know!"

After about ten minutes, the physician returns. "I can confirm for you, that yes, you are pregnant. Now is this a good thing for you, Elsa?"

Elsa smiles, "Oh yes, doctor! I'm very glad. At first I panicked, but now, I am glad."

"The morning sickness and nausea should go away soon. Try using ice chips or crackers to lessen the sickness." Dr. Johnston writes out a prescription and hands it to Elsa. "I want you to get these prenatal vitamins, and begin taking them today." She smiles and touches Elsa's shoulder, knowing this will be her first child. "Congratulations, Elsa!"

"Thank you, Dr. Johnston."

"Let's see you back in about a month. We'll track your progress monthly, and the closer it gets to your due date, I'll have you make weekly appointments. I want you to relax about it, and enjoy being pregnant. You will be bringing someone into the world who hasn't been here before."

Elsa smiles and nods.

"Also, there are quite a few pamphlets in the lobby, be sure to help yourself. And I'm sure you know there is plenty of information online. If you research online, be sure you get information from reputable sources."

"Yes, I'll be studying about pregnancies!" Elsa feels more excited by the minute.

"And Elsa, if you have any questions, feel free to call and speak to one of my nurses."

"Thank you, Dr. Johnston."

Leaving Dr. Johnston's office did not quell the fear Elsa had about telling Niall that she is pregnant. He'd always said he didn't want to get married, though he seems to be going that route with her. And although he loves the babies at the children's home, he'd always said he didn't want children of his own. All of Niall's back and forth made Elsa weary with worry.

Once in her car, Elsa begins to dial Deirdre, as she would know what to do. Remembering Deirdre is in Estonia, Elsa disconnects the call before it can ring. Elsa doesn't want to bother Deirdre with this, as she feels Deirdre has enough to deal with. Elsa starts the car and drives a little slower and more carefully than usual. She smiles at the thought of becoming a mother.

Chapter Thirty-Six

The noon hour arrived before Deirdre awoke the next day. She decides she wants to go horseback riding through the snow, after a lite meal. She wants to go to the brook again. Deirdre is curious to see how the brook looks at this time of year. Is it frozen over? Would it still be flowing? Or is she drawn to the brook because it is the last place she and Nicolaus had a real touching moment without adversity, which had been deprived of them for so long?

The stable manager rode out with Deirdre, to ensure her safety, just as he did last time she and Nicolaus rode the land during their survey. Besides, she couldn't remember the way, and the snow made everything look different. The manager would ensure she did not get lost in these sub-zero temperatures.

Their horses walk majestically through the soft snow, periodically lifting their heads while prancing their feet in the cold slush beneath their hoofs. The snow completely blanketed the massive property. Deirdre chuckles when the manager points out bunny tracks.

Meanwhile, back in Austin, Nicolaus is returning to the mansion from his first day back at work since the funeral. He had a very hard time concentrating, his mind on Deirdre and Thaddeus. He decided to cancel the rest of his meetings, and return home during the lunch hour. In silence, he walks the Ravenell estate, going to the Ravenell cemetery, wishing to visit his son. Nicolaus sits with his back against the backside of the tombstone. He says prayers in Latin for his son. He does not know what else to do. Obviously, there is nothing else he can do. Nicolaus is not sure he would ever get over this loss.

Suddenly, women's shoes are before him. Slowly, he looks up to see the long legs, sexy torso, and lovely shaped bosom of Helena standing before him.

Without asking, Helena plops herself on the ground, next to Nicolaus, extra close, so their arms and legs touch. Nicolaus smiles at her. "What are you doing?"

Helena doesn't miss a beat, "Checking on you!" she tells him in his face, close enough to kiss his gorgeous lips. The lips she kissed once before, and dreams of kissing again. Impulse drives her to go ahead and give him a big ole kiss on his face, close to his lips, making him chuckle. "What's this I hear about you sending my girl away to Estonia?" she made light of his situation.

"Oh, I sent her away?"

"Yep, that's what I hear!" Helena's charming wit could make anyone laugh.

Nicolaus chuckles and looks at her. Helena's beauty seems to always catch his breath. "No, I guess that's what happens when you ask someone to marry you more than once," he jokes.

Helena stands, putting her hand out for Nicolaus. She has no concern if he is finished with whatever he was doing. Nicolaus grabs her hand, and lifts himself up, not to place his weight on her. Helena throws herself to his arms. "Well, that missy better watch out before someone else gets to you."

Nicolaus chuckles again, "No! Never."

Helena leads Nicolaus back towards the mansion. The walk will take a full twenty minutes, as they slowly stroll together. She puts her arm through his, not caring that Joel is with her. "Did I tell you that the children miss you?" Helena speaks of the children at her children's home for foster kids. "I know you've been so busy. If you can find some time, maybe next week, just to read to them, they will be so grateful."

Nicolaus nods. "Sure. I'll be glad to."

Helena stops them walking. "You know, you don't need to worry about Deirdre. You do know she will marry you. Right?"

Nicolaus sighs, imagining that Deirdre has truthfully explained her plight to Helena. After all, they are close friends. Deirdre is very glad to have helped at the children's home, and Nicolaus expanded on what Helena started. He shakes his head, "No, I can't take that for granted. She is concerned about my mother's antics. I can't say I blame her, really. I'm tired of my mother's behavior as well." Nicolaus starts them walking again. "Hey, wait a minute, how did you know where to find me? Is this your first time at our house?"

"Yes, and I'm so excited!" She tightens her latch on his arm, as they walk. "Niall promised to introduce me to your famous mom. He thinks she will set up a fundraiser for us."

Nicolaus nods. "Well, that would be very helpful. She knows lots of important people.

Is Joel with you?"

Helena nods. "Yep, my hubby is asking to see you."

Nicolaus opens the door for Helena to enter, and as he steps in, Joel is immediately in front of them. Joel offers his hand, despite being suspicious of Nicolaus, knowing his wife has a fancy for him. "Mr. Ravenell, very good to see you again, Sir."

"Please, just call me Nicolaus. We're old friends now. You finished the wonderfully impressive job of the commissioned clinics. I hear nothing except praise from each city council where we placed the clinics. Your team did a fantastic job, as I've told you before."

Joel smiles at the compliment. "Yes, and thank you. You know it all begins with the team members. And my team certainly stepped up to the challenge."

"Yes, they really did."

Joel touches Nicolaus on the arm, "I'm very sorry to hear about your losses, Nicolaus. I can't even begin to imagine what you're going through."

Nicolaus nods. "Yes, thank you," he says quietly.

Helena stands between the men to change the subject. "So ...," she looks around Nicolaus' shoulder, "there is your brother! Joel, there is Niall," she says excitedly, with an open palm in the direction from which Niall is arriving.

Niall brings his hand over and connects with Joel's outstretched hand with a smile.

"The children love these brothers, more than anyone I've hired," she says gladly.

Niall then outstretches his arm towards the dining room, "Right this way, please. Mother has the luncheon prepared."

Joel and Helena follow Niall.

Nicolaus makes himself a small drink at the sitting room sidebar. He drinks just enough to take the edge off. Sighing, he sits down to take time for himself, thoughts of Deirdre are heavy on his mind.

Chapter Thirty-Seven

Niall led the couple to the second dining room, which is used for small gatherings. The lunch meal consists of braised beef with vegetable broth, greens and carrots, and corn bread, served with red wine.

"Wow, everything smells delicious," Helena comments as Joel helps her with the chair.

"Yes, it does," Joel agrees.

As the reflective sunlight floods into the bay windows, Nigel notices the faint bruising on Helena's chin and neck. This does not sit well with him.

Niall sits across from the couple, and next to his mother, at the round table. Their meal plates are hot and already placed at each chair, ready for them to begin eating.

"So, Niall tells me you are interested in doing some kind of fundraiser?" Ceil inquires while enjoying the meal. She is grateful for the absence of Nicolaus.

"Well first, I must thank the both of you for your wonderful sons. Both Niall and Nicolaus have assisted me at the children's home."

"Children's home? What is that?" Ceil never heard of such a thing.

"Truth is, it's like an orphanage, only we don't call it that nowadays. The children are all in foster care, either taken from their parents due to abusive situations, orphaned, or abandoned by their parents altogether. So my home gives the children a loving and caring environment, with wonderful care staff."

"My wife does wonderful work," Joel remarks, proud of Helena. They take a moment to smile at each other. Helena appreciates the acknowledgement from her husband.

"Are there many abandoned children?" Ceil asks, actually trying to understand.

"Oh yes, Mrs. Ravenell. Very many. Thanks to help from Nicolaus, he has sponsored us and helped us remodel to make space for more children. And he's helped financially so I could hire more help. And both Nicky and Niall help with care giving, or reading to the children, or playing with them." Helena is excited talking about Ceil's sons, as if they were a godsend to her.

Ceil smiles at the excitement Helena demonstrates. Ceil notices the sparkle in Helena's eyes when she talks about the children.

"I can never thank them enough."

"Mother, Helena has the home set up really great for the children."

"Oh, yes, I remember you, Joel. You presented to the board meeting. Nicolaus hired your architect company to build the new clinics!" Nigel says, "You remember, Ceil."

Joel nods in agreement, and smiles to Helena again. He is remorseful about the argument they had yesterday, when he abused her. He'd gotten so mad at Helena, he'd forgotten how much she did for the both of them. They are now rich because of Nicolaus, because of her relationship with him.

"Oh yes, now that you mention it, Joel is familiar. So you two are the do good couple in Austin?" Ceil chuckles. "That is very good work indeed."

"Yes ma'am. Thank you ma'am," Helena is humbled. "We couldn't have done all this without your sons!"

"Joel, I've seen other structures you've created. The beautiful glass building on Trinity Street downtown," Nigel interjects, trying to get a real feel of Joel.

"Yes, Sir. They wanted a pure glass building."

"Very nice work. I didn't realize you were married to such a beautiful and giving wife," Nigel compliments Helena. She smiles into Nigel's eyes. Joel nods again.

"So you need more funds to keep things going?" Ceil asks warmly, with a smile, continuing the conversation. She seems to like this couple. Though, oddly, she is finding Helena particularly attractive.

"Mother, Nicolaus wrote her a check for three-hundred thousand, the first day he met her!"

"Ah, before he met me!" Helena corrects him with a chuckle.

"Yeah, yeah. Anyway, I told Helena that you could help with a fundraising event, and we could make three times that amount. It's for the kids!"

Ceil sits back in her chair and folds her arms. "Hmm, so this is a competition with your brother? Who can give the most?"

Niall smiles, "Something like that."

"And I have to say, Niall truly is wonderful with babies. He will be a good father one day."

"Really? Babies?" Nigel sounds shocked.

"What can I say? They are drawn to me," Niall has a beaming smile. They all chuckle with him.

"Yes, they really are drawn to you, Niall. They can see right through that tough man facade of yours," Helena tells him.

"Well, since this is in favor of my Niall," Ceil winks at the couple, "I'm sure we can think of something. An exclusive tea party at the country club, three hundred dollars each person, inviting one hundred people, seems easiest. Or maybe a fireman ice cream social, fifty to two hundred fifty each person." Ceil is still thinking off the cuff, calculating dollar amounts. "Yes, I'm sure we can dream up with something. And yes Niall, we will surpass Nicolaus' contributions. Don't you worry about that," Ceil confirms.

"Oh my goodness!" Helena exclaims. "So wonderful!" She looks at her husband, and fans her eyes to keep the tears from forming, "Makes me want to cry!"

Ceil laughs, "Oh heavens, no. No tears around here," she adds seriously. "You and I can start making plans on this tomorrow. Let me check on some things, and I will call you so we can begin planning," Ceil instructs her.

"Thank you so very much Mrs. Ravenell."

"Oh, you can call me Ceil. And my husband is Nigel. We are all adults here."

"Yes, ma'am."

Chapter Thirty-Eight

D eirdre moves out of her comfy zone in the bed to answer her phone, "Hello?!!"

"Hello my love! What are you doing?"

"Ah, sleeping," she lightly chuckles. She sits up at the sexy smooth voice of her beloved Nicolaus. "Hello, my love, what are you doing?" she retorts back to him.

"I'm missing you. Every second of every day. You're at the forefront of my mind. Not one second goes by without me thinking about you."

"Ah, Nicky, that is so sweet."

"It's true. How is your inner search going? You ready to get back home?"

Deirdre yawns loudly, noticing her phone says it is three in the morning in Estonia. "Hmm," she lightly laughs, "Nicky, I literally just got here!" She lays back upon the bed on the cushioned headboard. "Umm, everything is going okay. I went horseback riding over the land. It's so beautiful. Everything is covered in snow out here. Tomorrow I'm going to see the bishop."

"I wish I was there with you, though I do respect your need for time away. I understand."

"Oh darling, I'm so glad you do. I am just starting to feel re-energized."

"That's good to hear."

"How is everyone? Behaving?"

"Yes. Nothing strange. Rumor has it that Niall and Elsa are passionate for each other, everywhere. And Helena and Joel are visiting with my parents and Niall right now."

"Oh really? Niall trying to squeeze money from your mom?"

Nicolaus laughs. "I don't know, I'm not privy to their conversations. I need my own break."

"Ah, you see?" Deirdre makes another uncontrollable yawn and stretch.

"Babe, I'd better let you finish your sleep. I just needed to hear your voice, and wanted to check on you. I love you so much! Never doubt my love for you."

"Thanks darling, I love you too."

"Good night!"

"Good night, darling." Deirdre is so appreciative of how sweet Nicolaus is to her. She does not have to question whether he loves her. Her heart is sad and warm at the same time. She slouches herself back under the covers, her mind fully on Nicolaus now.

Deirdre's phone rings again, just as she had gotten comfortable. She sits up to answer, "Hello?"

"Hey Deirdre, it's Elsa! How are you doing over there?"

Deirdre giggles, and plops herself back onto her pillows, and under the covers. "Well, not bad for it being three in the morning."

"Oh no, I forgot about the twelve hour time difference. I'm so sorry."

Deirdre giggles again, "It's okay, it's an eight hour difference. I just had a call with Nicky, I think he forgot too."

"We can't help it. We miss you."

"Have you noticed Nicky? I mean is he doing okay?"

Elsa laughs. "No! You know he hates being away from you. That man is not on his A- game. He forgets meetings, he daydreams just staring into space, he sent himself home early twice already."

"Oh my God, Elsa. Really?" Deirdre laughs.

"Don't worry, he's okay besides all that stuff. He's been through kind of a lot. He's walking around with a sad face, though."

"Uhm, that's not something I want to hear!"

"I know. He'll be okay. How long are you going to be gone?"

"Just two weeks. My return flight is for next Saturday."

"Oh, okay, not so long. Are you enjoying your time there?"

"Ya' know, I hadn't realized how exhausted I am."

"Dee, you've been through a lot too! It has been difficult for the both of you."

"Yes," Deirdre agreed. "So what's going on with you? How are things in Elsa's world?"

Now Elsa giggles, "Well ... you know Niall and I have been getting busy. Things have been getting hot and heavy."

"Yes, I remember. Did you talk to him about roughing you up, Elsa? Did you follow through after we talked about that?"

"Well, yes, I mentioned it. And ... Dee ... I'm pregnant."

Deirdre sits straight up at the exciting news. "Oh Elsa! That's wonderful! Are you sure?"

Elsa nods, as if Deirdre can see her. "Yes!" Joy is in her voice. "I went to the doctor's office to confirm it. You're the first person I want to share the news with."

"Elsa, that is great! Oh my God, I'm going to be an auntie this time."

Elsa sighs. "Yeah, but ..."

"Oh," Deirdre knew what she was going to say. "You haven't told Niall yet."

"No. Honestly, I'm afraid to tell him."

"You think he would hit you, or something?"

"Not hit me, I ... I don't know how he will react. He loves babies, yet doesn't want one of his own. He acts like he doesn't want to be married." Elsa sighs, "What am I supposed to do, Deirdre? I'm afraid I'll lose him." Elsa's joy melted down to anguish. She began to cry, sniffing back her tears.

"Oh Elsa!"

"What should I do? Wait until I'm showing and then tell him, or maybe don't even bring it up? Once I'm showing he'll figure it out."

"Elsa, you have to tell him. I think you should tell him now, so that when you start showing, it will all have sunk into his brain. You know what I mean?"

"Yes, okay."

"And stand your ground with Niall, Elsa. I imagine he'll try to push back on the announcement. I think you should tell him in the presence of Nicky. At least that way if Niall goes off the deep end, Nicky will be there to protect you."

"Oh, Deirdre, thank you. My mind just told me to call you, that you'd know what I should do."

"Well ... I love you, lady. You should arrange telling him as soon as possible and get that stress off you. If you're stressed, the baby is going to be stressed."

"Right!" Elsa straightens her back with resolve, feeling much better. "Deirdre, thank you. I can't wait until you get home."

"Hey, don't start that baby shopping without me. Uh, I think I'll get the baby some Estonian clothes!" The ladies laugh, and say their goodbyes.

Deirdre lays down, under the covers, determined to get a little more shut eye before making her way to the church.

Chapter Thirty-Nine

In the last moments of Deirdre's sleep for this morning, a dream is upon her. Both she and Nicolaus are dressed in white and standing at their church altar getting married. She is in her wedding dress, and holding white roses in her hands. She and Nicolaus kiss to marry, and then everything falls away into darkness. Only she and Nicolaus stand in the dark, then suddenly, they are ripped apart from each other. Deirdre tries to fight her way back to Nicolaus, against a wind so strong, it lifts her body off the ground, making her float. The same is done to Nicolaus. There is an echo of her shouting his name, as she reaches for him through a black veiled curtain which divides them. Nicolaus is searching for Deirdre, he looks for her and calls for her, yet he cannot see her beyond the darkness. Deirdre stretches her arm to Nicolaus, reaching and reaching as she calls his name.

The dream has Deirdre tossing and turning in bed. She sits up, opening her eyes to see that it is morning. This dream has Deirdre very concerned, as last time she had a dream about herself and Nicolaus, their marriage plans were disrupted.

The sun has just risen across the snow covered ground. The fireplace flame is less than before she went to bed, yet it is still thick enough to warm up the bedchamber. Deirdre jumps out of bed to get ready for the day. She wants some answers from the bishop.

Chapter Forty

Helena is on time without fail, as Ceil asked her to arrive for dinner and fundraising planning afterwards. Nicolaus is home and greets Helena with a kiss after the staff welcome her inside the mansion. He sees that Joel is not with her, as her beauty strikes him again. They are immediately drawn to each other.

Nicolaus shies away from Helena as he notices that her smile for him is beyond a friendly smile. Helena boldly takes his hands. Nicolaus feels confused and muddled, at this something between them, of which he could not name, is so strong, pulling him to her.

He clears his throat, as if to get this thing between them dislodged from his thoughts.

"Very nice to see you again," he tells her, looking into her mesmerizing eyes.

Helena feels Nicolaus' essence. "Ah, yes! Ceil wants me to join in for dinner."

"Planning your fundraiser?"

"Yes, I suppose after dinner."

"Where's Joel?" Nicolaus frowns a little.

"Oh, he had some other work to do, so he's skipping tonight."

Nicolaus nods in understanding, still holding Helena's hands. "Well, right this way," he leads her to the dining room. "Not sure what we're having. I never know until the plate is set before me," he chuckles trying to break the pull between them, as others enter the dining room. "Terrible, isn't it?"

Helena touches his chest, smiling, "Oh, Nicky, I'm so sure you have much bigger things to think about besides what's for dinner."

Nigel approaches Helena and lingeringly kisses the beauty's hand, then her face, "Good to see you again, Helena."

"Thank you, Nigel. I'm always honored to be here."

"You are always welcome here, my dear," Nigel tells her playfully, patting her hand.

Helena can see that Ceil is looking at Nigel with anger. To quench Ceil's jealousy, Helena takes Ceil's hand, and gives her a light hug. Ceil notices that Helena smells of beauty, and her hair is done up in brilliant braids around her head. Ceil pulls Helena to stand next to her, where she would be sitting.

Francesca enters, and grabs Nicolaus into a big hug, planting a kiss on him.

Nicolaus smiles at her. "Francesca, I didn't know you would be here today!"

She smiles at him before releasing her hold on him, "Surprise!" Francesca quickly hugs Helena. She giggles and greets Nigel with a kiss. She then forces Ceil to hug her.

Niall and Elsa walk in, holding hands. They greet everyone.

"Oh, the next couple of the year!" Francesca teases them.

Niall grabs Nicolaus by the arm, and pulls him away, to the sitting room, for discussion.

"Nicolaus, when are you going to give me the rest of the charge cards? You said you'd take care of that issue for me. That you were going to replace them, since they were stolen. You've only given me one card back."

Nicolaus looks at Niall with a frown. "Well ... yeah, that was before I understood what all was going on. You only get the one card."

"What? Are you kidding me? I had ten to twelve cards before. One card is not enough money. I need more."

"You had twelve company cards," Nicolaus corrects him. "And no, we cannot do that anymore, it's actually illegal, and I cannot justify it to our stakeholders. Be glad you have the one card because I labeled it as help with volunteering, since you help out every year at the fundraisers. I cannot go beyond that. No auditor will sign off on you frivolously spending the company's money."

"Oh ... well," Niall is suddenly very frustrated, "that's just bullshit, Nicolaus. Does mother know about this?"

Nicolaus sighs, crossing his arms. "What I remember, you wanted me to keep our parents out of it. You can feel free to complain to mother, though she is not over the funds. I am. You're lucky I had some sympathy for you, and didn't cut you off all together."

"It's bullshit, Nicolaus," he tells him again in an elevated tone, having an immature fit.

"Look, I gave you a two-thousand dollar limit. Once you hit the limit, that's it. If you need more money, why don't you work at the office. I told you we need your help."

"I'm not doing that! I'm not working there."

"Why not? What is your hang up about it?"

Niall looks away from Nicolaus, hating the questioning. Totally hating that Nicolaus is lord over his money. "I don't know. I don't want to do it."

"Well, what kind of work do you think you'd like? What are you good at?"

"Hell ... I don't know," he sulks, sounding aggravated.

"Niall, why don't you take a career assessment test? It will show you the best fields of work according to your likes and dislikes. Then let me know the results, and I'm sure we can find something for you to do. That way, you can make your own money, good money at that, and you won't need to depend on that card. Make your own steady money, doing something you like to do." Nicolaus touches his shoulder, "Men do it every day, Niall."

Niall looks at Nicolaus, taking offense to his last comment, as if Nicolaus is questioning his masculinity.

Before Niall could respond, Nicolaus tugs his arm, "Come on, let's get this meal. The others are waiting for us."

The brothers join everyone in the dining room. The men seat their respective ladies, Nicolaus attending to Helena and then Francesca. Ceil had their chef prepare fire grilled chicken with special spices, handmade potatoes with asparagus and broccoli.

As they begin eating their scrumptious dinner, Ceil starts the conversation. "Helena, who does your hair? It always looks so magnificent. That style is really pretty."

"Thank you, Ceil. You flatter me. I do my own hair. Used to be I didn't have time or extra money for a hair salon, so I'd get creative."

"Perhaps you can do mine sometime. I really like that style." Ceil compliments her.

"I would love to, Ceil!"

Elsa giggles as she feeds Niall as if he were a child, trying to get him out of his foul mood. "Elsa, Niall, that is quite enough," Ceil snaps at them, frowning. "I do not understand why it is so hard for our sons to recognize that they must marry upwardly mobile women. I suppose you have not done your job, Nigel," she scowls at him.

Nigel frowns between bites, wondering what Ceil is blaming him for now.

"Marriage? Who said anything about marriage?" Niall asks sarcastically. He looks at Elsa, her face a frown of anger.

"We'll never have high producing grandchildren at this rate."

Elsa sat straight, deciding to put in play the advice Deirdre gave her. Why not announce her pregnancy now, then she wouldn't have to repeat herself later.

"Oh, Mother Ceil, that's not true. I am pregnant," Elsa happily states.

"What?" Ceil sharply asks.

"What?" Niall asks, shocked, looking at her frowning.

"Hmm, oh!" Nigel frowns.

Elsa half froze at their reactions. "I am with child. I am pregnant," she repeats loudly, to be sure her words were clear.

Niall drops her hand and straightens his spine with stiff resolve. "Well ... do you know who the father is?"

Elsa frowns deeply, "What? Why would you ask me that?"

"Niall," Nicolaus calls to him with authority.

"Well, I am not the only one she has been with."

Elsa gasps at his words, her hand to her chest.

"Is this true, Elsa?" Nigel asks of her. Nigel thought about Elsa's character; he knew Elsa to be a good woman; her work life is stellar; she is a good friend to Deirdre; she even helped at the children's home.

Elsa begins to cry, feeling outraged of the accusation. It seems that Nigel is against her. She doesn't want to cry; however, she cannot stop it happening. She doesn't want to look timid or pathetic. "No, Sir! I swear. Niall is the only one I've been with. This is Niall's child." She feels stupid for having to defend herself in such a way. Quickly, she stops crying. She wipes her face.

"Liar!" Niall tells Elsa, angrily, to her face, trying to run from the truth. "I don't believe you! You have only let me have you because you are loose, like all the other women I know!"

"Niall!" Nicolaus calls to him again.

Niall looks to Francesca and Helena. "I am sorry," he says, "not all the women. She knows what I mean!"

Elsa has hurt written all over her. She is afraid she may cry again, and she does not want to cry. She looks at Niall, "Is that what you think of me Niall? That I'm some floosy, loose woman? That is so disrespectful! You're not going to talk to me like that, Niall."

Francesca became the bridge for Elsa, not holding back. "Frankly, Niall, I think you're full of it right now. You know damn well you've been with Elsa. Hell, we all have heard you, everywhere in this house, inside and out. What the bloody hell, Niall? Now you want to deny the child is yours? You're making yourself look like a damned fool."

Elsa tries to touch Niall. He flings her off him. Elsa's tears are back. "How can you say something like that to me? You know I've only been with you. I love you Niall, I love you."

"Ha!" Niall scoffs.

Helena had enough. She pulls the traumatized Elsa from the table. "Your behavior is very ... disappointing, Niall," she tells him, not caring if Ceil would be offended.

Helena takes Elsa outside to the back patio. Elsa got herself in such a state, she couldn't even talk, so she cried. Though Elsa thought Niall might not be happy with her pregnancy, she never thought Niall would reject her and the baby like that. Helena held her close, as if she were her own daughter. "Shh, now, Elsa, we'll figure something out. Nicolaus will talk to Niall."

"I blame you for this!" Ceil yells at Nigel in the dining room, hitting him across his bicep.

"What did I do?" Nigel frowns, unable to comprehend how Ceil was about to blame him for this.

"It's more about what you didn't do! You have fallen short, Nigel, of your duty as a father. You let your sons run around and do whatever they want. You let them be with whomever they want. You have never been man enough to discipline them, so now this is the result. We shall have bastard grandchildren!" She swipes him again with her cloth napkin, then storms out of the room.

Niall gets up from the table, and leaves the area. Nicolaus follows him. "What the hell is going on with you, Niall? How can you talk to Elsa like that?"

Niall sits on the stair step. He holds his head in his hands. "I don't know." He begins to tear up, as if he were falling apart because nothing is going his way. "This has never happened."

Nicolaus sits next to Niall on the stair step. "Out of all the women you've been with, no one has ever gotten pregnant?"

"No. Never," he sighs.

"Well, perhaps the child you created with Elsa will be special to this world." Niall side-eyed his brother, as he leans towards church talk. "Maybe the child is a gift from ..."

"Don't." Niall tells him, sighing loudly.

Nicolaus takes hold of Niall's shoulder. "Well, it's certainly no secret that you have been with Elsa. We all heard the both of you together. Denying the child seems futile. Look, I believe Elsa, after all, she is a very trustworthy person. Unless she's actually given you reason to think otherwise, and you have proof, you should believe her too, Niall," he explains calmly, getting around the fact that he knows his brother is lying about Elsa. He tries to provide a way out for Niall, without directly blaming him. He wants Niall to do right by Elsa.

Niall turns from his brother, jerking his shoulder away. "What am I going to do?"

"The first thing you are going to do is stop treating Elsa like a stranger, or like some woman you've brought in off the street," he orders his younger brother. "After all, the two of you are engaged. Then Niall, the hardest part is to take responsibility for her and the child." Niall looks to Nicolaus, remembering that he had been through this with Marguerite. "Overall, if you want to be sure the baby is yours, there are DNA tests that can be done once the baby is born. I think the baby is yours, and you should treat Elsa like the baby is yours, until you have proof that says otherwise. You know what I mean, Niall?"

Niall nods. "Yeah."

Nicolaus grabs Niall by the shoulder again, "Niall, I'm always here for you if you ever need anything. Even if just to talk, or ask questions. I'm here for you and Elsa." Nicolaus hugs Niall to him, "It's gonna be all right. It will all work out."

Niall nods without words.

Everyone, except Elsa, arrives back in the dining room.

"Where is Elsa?" Niall asks.

"She left," Helena notifies him. "She is really upset, Niall. She is so happy about the baby, news to be celebrated. Instead you go on some freakish tantrum ..."

"I know. I'm sorry. I shouldn't have done that," Niall interrupts Helena's rant, admitting his folly, Nicolaus' words having influenced his thinking.

"No, you shouldn't have," Helena is upset at Niall. "There are just some things that you don't do to a woman, and for sure, that is one of them, Niall."

"Yeah, Niall, your behavior was just bloody stupid. What happened? You got scared?" Francesca asks him.

Niall frowns, "I don't know. I'll talk to her."

"You took out your fright on Elsa's beautiful spirit?" Francesca pushed. "What's going to happen when you two get married, Niall?"

Niall slouches in his chair, "What's all this talk about marriage? I never said I was going to be married. Engagement and marriage are two different things. Right, Nicolaus?"

Nicolaus scoffs with an eyebrow lift, for Niall pulling on him to back him up on his inaction on marriage. Nicolaus purses his lips, nodding, "Yep. Yep. Two different events, for sure," his voice trails off. He grabs his fork and dives into the dessert plate of chocolate mousse cheesecake, which was placed before him, and served to everyone.

Chapter Forty-One

C eil and Nigel take Helena into the sitting room to work on the fundraising plans after dinner. Nicolaus and Francesca are in the library. The chocolate mousse did not calm her down. "You know, Love, it's days like this that make me want to take your brother to the side and just knock him out. He needs his ass kicked by a woman to make him behave better."

"Oh now, Francesca," Nicolaus chuckles at her.

"I mean it. I've been thinking about it since this evening. It's what he needs."

"Violence doesn't change him." He gives Francesca a kiss to her cheek, and they hug each other. "I had a talk with Niall. I think he'll make things right. The fact that he was able to admit his mistake is a great first step."

They separate, and sit on chairs, opposite each other.

Nicolaus leans forward. "I want to ask a favor of you, Francesca."

"Uh, really?" her mood changes. She is now intrigued instead of angry.

Nicolaus nods. "Well, you know Deirdre is in Estonia. She is thinking over whether she wants to go forward with our marriage."

Francesca shakes her head, "Nicky, you know you don't have to worry about that. The two of you will be married."

"Well, ... it's not a given any longer. Because of what my mother did, you know, regarding Marguerite."

"Oh! I see. She's worried about Auntie Ceil."

Nicolaus nods again. "Yes. She's worried about the future. Now, I respect her need to take time to think this out, I just hate the thought of her being there alone."

"Nicky, you know she is not really all alone with all the staff there. And Bishop Moratey."

"Yes, I know ..."

"So, what's the favor, Love?"

"I want to ask you to go to Estonia and bring Deirdre back."

Francesca chuckles, "Mm-hmm! I think you are bloody miserable without her. Aren't you?"

"I'm not going to lie about how much I hate for us to be apart. And I would feel much better if someone close, someone I can trust, were there with her."

"I've noticed you've been sad, Nicky. You have a sad face when things aren't right with Deirdre. Did you know that?" Francesca teases him a little.

"Just coax her to return this weekend, instead of next weekend. I really would like us to be married on Valentine's Day." Nicolaus pulls out his personal credit card and hands it to Francesca.

"Okay, Love, for you, anything. I can go Thursday afternoon, after my last class, since I do not hold class on Fridays."

"Oh great, that works out really well. Thank you Francesca. I'll owe you, my dear."

"You know I've been going through our ancestry book; the one Auntie Clara gave me. And let me tell you, I'm finding some really interesting facts in our family history." Francesca bounces with excitement. "For example, I'm finding several instances of family names. We of course know there is DeeDee, and Nichols, and I also found the names Olivia, Niall, and Abigail."

Nicolaus frowns at her. "Really? There's even an Abigail?"

"Yes, isn't that Deirdre's middle name?"

Nicolaus nods, "Yes. That ... is kinda strange."

"Oh yeah, and it gets more interesting. DeeDee was not Nichol's first wife. It says she is his *neljas* wife. What is that translation?"

Nicolaus had mastered the Estonian language while in the military. "Fourth."

"Fourth wife! Oh my goodness, I've got to figure out what was going on with Nichols.

I mean if you are on his same path ..."

"Well .... Hmm, ... maybe I'm not on his path at all then. Are you sure that is what it said? Deirdre will be my second wife, and hopefully my last wife." He touches his chest, "She's my heart." He crosses his arms, "Maybe Great Auntie Clara was wrong."

"Nicky, she couldn't have been wrong, because you are going to marry Deirdre, and remember, she told this to Deirdre." Francesca sighs, "This is getting complicated. Why don't you stop by my place and help me with the translation?"

"Okay, maybe next week, after you return with Deirdre."

"I hear you, that maybe Aunt Clara was wrong, Nicky, she seemed very sure of what she was saying."

Nicolaus sighs, "Well, that was also when we had Marguerite. Is it possible that the path changed with her death?"

Francesca narrows her eye in thought, "I suppose. Hey, what if the death of a wife or more than one wife plays into this." Francesca threw her head back onto the couch. "Oh God!

I don't know any more, I'm getting confused."

"We'll figure it out. I'll get on working with you to translate the book."

"Thanks, Love. Why is it I can always count on you, but Niall ..." she shakes her head.

Chapter Forty-Two

Helena is very excited about the planning that is now completed for the fundraiser. She is impressed with all the high society people, donors, philanthropists, and city officials Ceil and Nigel know. It's mind boggling to her. Not only can Ceil get one hundred people to show up, it is as if she could tell them any amount to donate and they will happily do it.

"I'm truly going to make it my dream to be like you when I grow up, Ceil," they both chuckle, leaving the sitting room. "What a power couple you are." Flanked by Ceil on one side, and holding onto Nigel's arm on the other, Helena looks up and sees Nicolaus and Francesca having a conversation.

Helena turns to Ceil, who already offered her to stay the night in one of the guest rooms.

"Would you mind if Nicolaus takes me to the room? I need to ask him something about construction on the children's home."

Ceil sighs, seeing how Helena is eyeing Nicolaus, her actual intent blatantly obvious. "Of course not."

Helena touches Nigel's forearm, then gives Ceil an unreturned hug. "Thank you both so much. The tea is going to be just great."

"I'll have some answers to you by Wednesday. I'm pretty sure we'll have one hundred percent of our guest list attending. You just leave everything to me."

"Ceil, thank you so much. You are so wonderful."

Nigel notices that Ceil seems to be enamored with Helena. He chuckles, not having seen her quite so speechless before. "Nicolaus," he calls to his son. Nicolaus is soon before them. "Please take Helena to the guest room on the far end, the one with the private bathroom."

"Sure."

Ceil notices how Helena excitedly perks up even more by the presence of Nicolaus. Ceil eyes Nicolaus suspiciously, although she says nothing. Ceil can see how Helena looks upon Nicolaus with a childlike fascination, not taking her eyes off him as they climb the stairs.

Nicolaus escorts Helena, as she tucks her arm around his as they ascend the stairs. Helena feels herself uncontrollably giddy and sensual with Nicolaus. She is so glad to have him to herself, even if for this brief moment. The guest room is on the back corner upstairs. It is huge, and nicely decorated. There is a private bathroom inside the room. Nicolaus looks around and sees that everything was made ready.

"Well, here you go! Breakfast is usually around seven. Do you need anything right now, Helena?" Suddenly, they are holding hands again. Nicolaus is strongly pulled to Helena. He doesn't understand what is happening, as surely, his mind is on Deirdre.

With the touch of a lover, he touches her face and her chin, where the light bruising remains. He slightly frowns, suddenly wishing he could kiss her hurt away, so that only her beauty would be seen, instead of the bruises. "Is Joel hurting you again?"

Helena's breathing grew a little heavy, as her body became excited with his every touch. She closed her eyes to meld her face to his gentle touch. She didn't answer him, not wanting to ruin their moment with talk of her husband.

"You deserve so much better," Nicolaus tells her his thoughts.

Helena opens her eyes to Nicolaus' handsome face, which shows concern for her. She could tell by his expression that he wants to make things right. Helena finally figured out that weird feeling she had for Nicolaus as he looks upon her. That feeling she hadn't felt for a very long time. It is ... new love. A giant crush of love, to be exact. Yep, Helena realized, at that very moment, she is in love with Nicolaus Ravenell, the son of a wealthy family, who graciously provided financial aid for the children, and is to marry her best friend. She knew that if the opportunity ever presented itself, she would have this man, without hesitation. She would take him, claim him, and make him hers.

She closes her eyes to his gentle touch. She enjoys the softness of his fingers while she waits, wishing she could have more of him. Patiently, with eyes closed and chin up, she waits. There are only two ways in which this situation will evolve. Either he rebuffs the assumption of the kiss, and she looks like a complete idiot; or he takes the challenge and kisses her. She waits and hopes she is not going to look foolish. How would she ever recover her dignity to him?

Then, what she'd waited and wished for is at hand, as his lips are upon hers with strong intensity. His mouth and tongue seek for that thing that pulls them together. Helena's arms wrap around his muscular frame, embracing and welcoming him, as he also holds her.

Immediately, Nicolaus notices that to kiss Helena is very different than kissing Deirdre. Helena is experienced, and she counters every bit of his kiss with the same measure or beyond what he'd given to her. They part with short, sweet, pecking kisses, finding it hard to pull away from each other.

Helena is over the moon thrilled with joy. This is the best kiss she has had in a very long time. She doesn't want Nicolaus to leave. She wants him to stay with her. She fantasizes about them being intimate together, caught up in ecstasy, and then memorizing the rhythm of his breathing, as he sleeps next to her.

Helena winced at her thoughts, though seeing the look on Nicolaus' face makes her wonder if he is thinking the same thing. She doesn't want her mind to be thinking this about Nicolaus, although the thoughts seem to naturally be there. What would Ceil or Deirdre think of her being in love with Nicolaus, if they ever found out? Joel is already jealous of Nicolaus. Helena finds herself biting her tongue at home to stop herself from talking about Nicolaus, as he seems to always be at the forefront of her mind. The passion of love sometimes makes a person do things they ought not do or think about things they normally wouldn't.

Helena notices everything about Nicolaus, as she gazes upon him. The gentle way his strong and capable hands hold onto her. His manly aura, and the way he smells of sweet cookies. His striking handsomeness, and physically fit and tall body. His elevated mind.

These traits of Nicolaus are all cherished treasures for Helena. What woman on earth wouldn't fall in love with this guy?

With one last, sweet kiss across her lips, "Goodnight," he tells her, feeling electrified and puzzled at the same time.

Nicolaus goes outside, and walks the property grounds, while pondering the enormous confusion occupying his mind of the multiple sins he'd just committed with Helena.

Chapter Forty-Three

C eil overheard Francesca's phone conversation with Rachel last night, about going to Estonia to bring back Deirdre in time for a Valentine's Day wedding. The rest of Francesca's conversation to Rachel is not of interest to Ceil. She heard all she needs to know, which got a scheme against Nicolaus forming in her mind.

It is Ceil's intent to be rid of Nicolaus for all time, and place Niall as their next heir and head of their multi-billion dollar healthcare conglomerate, whether Niall wants the role or not. Niall's childish pushback against stepping into this role does not concern Ceil. Ceil had the realization that for her previous scheme, she'd underestimated Nicolaus' loyalty to Nigel. She was, however, delighted with her back up plan of forcing him to marry Marguerite. She knew he was miserable in the marriage, and she thought he'd eventually run off with Deirdre. To her dismay, that didn't happen at all. He seemed to find his way around any obstacle she created for him.

So, this time, she knew in her mind, the plan had to be more outrageous, with more obstacles. Ceil made sure that Nigel is gone to the office for a meeting with Nicolaus regarding company board business. Niall is away from the mansion with friends at his downtown hangout on Red River Street. Ceil closes the door to her home office before dialing the number of Elsa's father, Jonathan Baird.

Jonathan is known for being eccentric in the circles of Austin's elite. No one knows exactly what he does with his time, though it is known that he has and spends lots of money. He has what one might call a small army of men who accompany him on his retreats abroad. No one is sure whether Jonathan is a spy or a diplomat. His army goes wherever he goes, as he mysteriously meets with high level people, in the nation's capital, as well as in foreign countries.

"Well, well," Jonathan has condemnation in his voice to Ceil over the phone. "I wondered how this might play out. What have you to say about your foolish son, who has made my baby girl, Elsa, cry of a broken heart?" he asks her nastily, not caring if he is being rude. "You know damn well I'm not going to stand for that! He called my daughter a slut after he coaxed her to his bed! Someone needs to teach your boy some manners!"

"Okay, all right," Ceil tells him, trying to get him settled down. "Let's not be so hasty to call my son foolish, when it's really your daughter's foolish behavior with my son."

Baird breathes hard, "The only foolishness is your son's treatment of my daughter, a young, intelligent woman, who is in love with him. Is he so stupid he cannot see that he'd be lucky to have my daughter at his side?"

"Well, why do you think I'm calling you?" Ceil snaps at him. "If you pipe down, we can have a civil conversation about what to do!"

Jonathan clears his throat. "Okay, well ... what do you have?"

Ceil sighs, ready to bring him aboard with her plan. "Well, I want what's best for the both of them. I like your Elsa, she does seem to tame my Niall. I like them together. I think they make a good couple, and ...."

"Yeah, well, I'm more concerned about actions, Ceil. I won't stand for the way your son is treating my daughter. My Elsa does not lie. If she says she is pregnant and your son is the only man she's been with, then he better believe her. And he'd better honor her!"

"Yes, I agree. I'm getting to that if you'd stop interrupting me!" Ceil yells at him. She sighs and continues. "I propose we have a real shotgun wedding ... except without the guns. You get over here this Friday, bring your thugs, and let's get them married."

Jonathan laughs, "You're crazy! Crazier than me!" He takes a moment to think about the offer. "Hmm, I like the idea, I think. But why am I the bad guy here? It's your son that screwed up."

"Well, do you want them married or not? Obviously, I can't be the bad guy, and anyway, it looks better on you. And ...I have another offer for you to sweeten this plan."

"Okay, I'm listening."

"I did some research, and I see that Elsa has a sister. Her half-sister?"

"Yes, Gwen. What of it?"

"Well, I understand that she is in constant recuperation for liking a certain ... substance, shall we say. And she is unmarried, too? Do I have that right?"

Jonathan sighs. His problems with Gwen are well hidden, he wonders how Ceil got ahold of this information. He refuses to confirm her question. "What of it, Ceil? What has Gwen got to do with Elsa marrying .... Oh!" Suddenly, he understands where her thoughts are going, as he knows about Nicolaus, and the death of his wife. "Awh," he laughs, "you are too cunning Ceil Ravenell. What is it you have against Nicolaus? He's your pretty and bright boy, isn't he? Engaged forever to that little virgin tart." He laughs again.

Ceil sighs with relief, feeling he is onboard. "I think you understand where I'm going with this. Elsa for Niall, and Gwen for Nicolaus."

"Hmm! Now why would you want to burden Nicolaus again? The first little scheme you had obviously didn't work. So now you want to try it again, with Gwen?"

"Don't worry about the whys," Ceil snaps at him. "Let's just get this done!"

"And how do you propose to make Nicolaus marry Gwen? He's not going to just do it."

"Well, that's what your goons are for. Right?"

"Hey now! My men are not goons! They are a very talented group of guys, they do me well," he sounds a little offended at her language. Jonathan sits down. "So let me get this straight, you actually want a real shotgun type wedding, for both of your sons to marry both of my daughters."

"Exactly. Bring your goons. Feel free to rough up Nicolaus. In fact, as a bonus, I give you permission to rough up anyone you want, just don't shoot anyone and don't kill anyone, ... leave guns out of it. I do have my limits. Run things the way you want. Don't tell me anything about what or how you will do it. Just make sure it's done this Friday, say around ten in the morning. When you pull up to the first gate, the code is 4297. When you get to the second gate, just tell the guard you have an appointment with me, I'll alert them ahead of time. I'll make sure everyone is here who needs to be. Friday should give you enough time to retrieve Gwen."

"So, you will not interfere in what I want to do?"

"Correct. Makes it a little more fun for you, right?"

Jonathan laughs again. "I think you understand me well, Ceil. Okay then. And I want a real priest, I want Elsa actually married."

"Oh yes, I'll take care of that, no problem."

"Very well, I'll see you on Friday."

Ceil ends the call with Jonathan, satisfied her plan will work. Immediately, she phones the church to schedule the bishop. "Yes Bishop, thank you for taking my call. I want to discuss my will arrangements, and the amount of money Nigel and I want to leave the church. Can you be at our home for brunch at nine thirty on Friday?"

"Well, of course Ceil. Anything for your family," the bishop tells her gladly. After all, the Ravenell family is one of the church's biggest financial doners. And any invitation to the Ravenell's home always involved delightful food. Their chef is one of the best in Austin.

"Wonderful, I'll make sure Nigel, Nicolaus, and Niall are present as well, so that we will all be on the same page."

"Sounds great! I look forward to it."

Ceil is very relieved that her plan is falling into place. She got right to work on obtaining wedding rings and the wedding licenses.

Chapter Forty-Four

D eirdre is happy to go to the beautiful historic Saint Nicholas church, in Tallin, again. The ancient architect structure of the walls and ceilings, which hold carvings of scenes from the Bible, and colorful pane glass windows, brings joy to her heart. Every time she walks in, she feels surprised at its beauty, and her breath is taken away. She can feel her ancestors here, as she walks the length of the middle aisle. Deirdre goes to the front altar, kneels and prays for blessings for a few minutes. She leaves cash by a lit candle, as an offering, before seeking out a pew to sit and think.

This is what she traveled all the way to Estonia to do. Sort out the thoughts in her mind. She knows she is destined to marry Nicolaus, and she imagines their children and what good in the world they would do. Ceil is what is tripping her up now. She just cannot see Ceil being the grandmother to her children.

In Deirdre's mind, Ceil is just too mean. And she has always been against Nicolaus, for which none of them, except Nigel, understand why. Deirdre is fearful this is going to make her children a target as well. What worse type of behavior would Ceil exhibit towards her defenseless children?

After an hour of sitting and thinking, as tears streak down her face, she jolts the pew, and lays down. She is not sure why, it just seems right to lay down and look up at the enormity of the cathedral. The massive wooden rafters form an arch touching the ceiling. "Saint Nicholas church," she says quietly aloud.

Bishop Moratey's face appears before her, blocking her view of the arched ceiling. He offers her a box of tissues.

"Oh! Thank you," Deirdre grabs some tissues and wipes her face with a slight giggle. She sits up properly. "Saving the day ..." she says softly, of his presence.

"May I?" the bishop asks, pointing to the space on the church pew next to her.

"Of course."

As the Bishop sits down, he gives Deirdre a side hug, thinking she probably needs one. With his usual pattern, the bishop pats her arm. "It will be okay, Deirdre." He let another minute pass them, as Deirdre wipes her face. "Are you here alone?"

Deirdre nods. She smiles at the bishop with a slight giggle, "Foolishly, I am here alone. And now I feel like I need my peeps."

The bishop smiles, "Everything okay between you and Nicolaus?"

Deirdre is surprised at the bishop's ability to see her problem. "Well, yes ... I mean no .... Not that I ... I mean no, ... yes." Deirdre stops what she knows is silly babbling. She wipes the tear that drips from her eye.

The bishop helps the conversation along. "Rachel just called me. We had a long conversation. One thing she told me is that Nicolaus' wife had ended her life."

Deirdre looks at him. "Yes, and little Nicky, too! The baby. She named him Thaddeus. I called the baby Little Nicky." The bishop nods in understanding. "She never wanted the baby from the beginning. So, I helped out. Of course, I would take care of Nicolaus' child. I loved him so much. He was so cute. Looked exactly like Nicolaus. I'm pretty sure that bothered her. I just ...." Deirdre stopped talking again.

"It's okay, Deirdre. You obviously need to talk to someone. I don't mind, and I will offer any help I can give you."

Deirdre wipes the tears again. She breathed out some stress. "I will always love Nicolaus. Always! I just don't know about his mother. I just don't know if we should be married. I'm just not sure anymore. Before all this I was so sure we should be married. Even when he was forced to marry Marguerite, I was sure he should be my husband. And now ..."

The bishop nods. "I think you have to focus on what has changed for you. Why do you have doubts now?"

"Nicky wants us to be married next Friday, on Valentine's Day."

The bishop nods again. "I can understand that. Here we call it Friend's Day to celebrate friendships, and in the U.S. the day is for couples to celebrate love."

"Bishop, we literally just buried Marguerite about a week now! It's too soon to marry! And even Ceil is against it."

"Perhaps Nicolaus just wants to move forward quickly and marry you so that nothing else can part you again. And do it on a special day."

Deirdre looks down into her lap. "I don't know."

"What is the thing that's changed for you, about your relationship with Nicolaus?"

"It's his mother. I think I look at her so differently. What she did. The lengths she went through to keep me from Nicolaus. She made sure Nicolaus couldn't do anything about it ... even if he wanted to."

"Oh, don't tell me you are questioning his love for you."

"No, no, Bishop. It's not him ... it's ... complicated."

"Maybe. I think in his first wife's death, the mountain that was placed between the two of you has now been removed. You two are free to marry each other again."

"Yes, I'm grateful, ... though ... his mother ... she did a lot to keep us apart, and ... maybe I don't want her to be my children's grandmother."

"No, Deirdre. Just as you and Nicolaus couldn't choose your parents, you cannot really ..."

"Can't I?" she challenges him. "Am I supposed to just let go of what she did? Sweep it under the rug? She never has to answer for it? How could I ever trust her with my children?"

"Deirdre, this is an excuse. You need to grab hold to that real thing, that true love you both have for each other, and never let go."

Deirdre nods in understanding. She knew that for Nicolaus' sake, she had to find that inner strength to deal with Ceil. And she would find that strength. Because she loved Nicolaus so much, she would do anything for him.

"You know, what happened should tell you that you have something extremely special with Nicolaus. Your love is an example to the world. An example that is badly needed. There are not many Nicolauses or Deirdres we see anymore. And for the two of you to be together? Well, that is just an outstanding and shining example to men and women all over the world. Deirdre, you've got to hold tight to your love. You should know that God will protect your children. You must believe this. Why don't the two of you marry in this church? Walk the same steps of Nichols and DeeDee on your wedding day. You can have cameras and as much press as you'd like. I think that would make the marriage even greater. And what a warning it would give to Ceil's spirit."

Deirdre is wide eyed as she listens to the bishop. What he says does make sense, and his words speak to her heart. Marriage in the Estonian church. The church of Saint Nicholas. Where their ancestors are interred. That really would throw Ceil for a loop. Everything would be out of her control. There is a great peacefulness inside this church. Getting married in the church named for Saint Nicholas just seems so fitting to her.

Perhaps this is why she needed to make this trek. Perhaps she needed to be shown the path of her future with Nicolaus. She had to put the last two years behind her. After all, she did stand by Nicolaus' side, just like she said she would. She had to be ready to face and put up with Ceil. "Maybe Mother Ceil is not as awful as she tries to be," Deirdre ponders aloud.

"Maybe she is not!" Bishop Moratey agrees with her.

The more she thought about it, the more it just seemed fitting that she and Nicolaus get married at Saint Nicholas church in Tallin. She believes this is what is meant to be. After all, their destination to each other is written in the stars of the world and lay in the book that Auntie Clara held in the family annals in Tallin, Estonia.

Deirdre squeezes the bishop's hand with her small dainty hand. She nods. "I like the idea." She imagines DeeDee in her wedding gown. She lauded the bishop's idea on getting married in this church, taking away Ceil's power. Without asking, she hugs him.

The Bishop chuckles, and gently pats her hand. "The other thing Rachel and I discussed, is that she and your mother, and Francesca are on their way here. They were just boarding the plane."

"What? Oh! That's wonderful!"

"They wanted to surprise you. Sorry I ruined the surprise. I think your spirit needs to hear it."

Deirdre stands, hands playfully on her hips, "Well, yes, Bishop. Gosh, thank you for telling me. That does make me very happy!"

She reaches for the bishop's hand and holds it. He pats her hand again. "Nicolaus sent them for you. Said he hated that you were here alone."

Deirdre put her hand over her mouth. "He knows me so well."

"He loves you, Deirdre." He pulls her down to reseat her.

"I know," she says somberly, with eyes closed.

Deirdre spent a little more time with the bishop discussing wedding arrangements. Then she returned to the castle to await her surprise.

Chapter Forty-Five

U nder the beautiful Austin blue sky, Helena arrives at the Ravenell mansion. She is worried about Elsa, and unable to get a hold of her. She thought it better to check on her at the mansion, than down at the VMC business office. She did not want to chance her uninhibited feelings towards Nicolaus to expose him or make him feel uncomfortable. She did not want to be in the way of his love for Deirdre, even though she would snatch him up in an instant if she could.

Helena is announced to Ceil in her office. "Oh," Ceil frowns, "I did not realize we had an appointment." Ceil looks upon Helena, again impressed with her utter attractiveness. She feels herself getting flush.

"I am so sorry Ceil, I'm sure you are busy. We don't have an appointment, I'm just so worried about Elsa. And I can't get a hold of her. I spoke to her yesterday, and she told me that Niall had gone on another tangent about her pregnancy, and that he was extremely rude, and called her ... names. I'm worried, and I thought maybe she was here with you, or maybe you had spoken to her."

"Hmm," Ceil wonders why Helena hadn't picked up the phone to ask her that. "Well, no I have not spoken to her. I wouldn't worry about it. I think it will all be resolved soon," she says.

Helena frowns, "Oh, okay. It's just ... I have never seen Niall behave like this. It does concern me, with him around the children and all."

"Niall will be just fine. So ..." Ceil wants to change the subject, "how are things going at the children's home? I suspect you have someone in charge while you're away, running after my sons and all."

"I'm sorry?" Helena is shocked by the comment.

"Well, don't be sorry. Strong women never apologize!" Ceil tells her, exposing her faulty thinking. "Strong women never cry, and we certainly don't apologize!"

"Ceil ... I ...,"

Ceil waives her hand in the air. "You are in love with Nicolaus, are you not?"

Helena is taken aback. Is she that transparent that Ceil could read right through her? "Uhm, well, I adore everyone in your family, Ceil. The Ravenells are wonderful!" she carefully answers, not sure where this is all going.

Ceil nods. "Decent answer. I've seen it before, you know. You are not the first, and I'm sure you will not be the last. Well, ... my sons opened the door for you, to my home and to my money. I have authority over both. I decide who stays, and I decide how money is spent," she strongly scolds Helena, spurting the half-truth.

"Well yes, I'm always honored for the welcome."

Ceil turns her back to Helena. "Yes, I think I will find you here often. Especially when Nicolaus is here."

Helena felt that she had to get rid of this accusation. She wonders if Ceil saw them kissing. "Ceil, I assure you, there is nothing beyond friendship between me and Nicolaus."

"Really?" she quickly turns around to face Helena. "I wonder ... I wonder what you would do to stay in my graces, to keep close to Nicolaus, Helena. That is what I'm wondering right now."

"I only wish to serve the children, Ceil. Honestly."

"Oh yes, the children," Ceil mocks her. "Come here, Helena," she demands of her.

Helena obeys and stands right in front of Ceil. Ceil looks upon her with widened eyes. She loved Helena's beauty, and her curvy body. "So I ask you, what would you do to stay in my good graces?"

Helena never expected this. She frowns for an answer, "I would do whatever you wish, Ceil. Whatever you want."

Ceil scoffs, "Whatever I wish? Whatever ... I ... wish?" Ceil moves herself forward, close to Helena's face and her lips. "Such beauty." Taking a chance, Ceil touches Helena's face. Then her hand slowly moves down her neck, and her chest, resting there. Ceil waits to see what Helena would do. A wide smile appears over Ceil's face as Helena let her touch her. "Don't you know that matriarchs have desires and fantasies, just as men do?"

"Well ... Ceil, honestly, I never thought about it. I can see that ... yes, you are human. I'm sure you do have fantasies, and a softer side to you."

Ceil drops her hand from Helena. She sighs, "Well, we'll discuss it more later. Right now, you must go."

"Okay, thank you, Ceil." Helena exits the mansion. She had a feeling that Ceil is going to make her do strange things to stay connected to the Ravenells and to their financial support. Helena decided at that very moment that she would do anything to stay close to Nicolaus, and she would do anything to help the children.

Chapter Forty-Six

"I want to be sure the both of you know that I will be gone for at least two weeks," Manfred informs Nicolaus and Nigel in the sitting room.

"Well thanks for letting us know," Nicolaus responds, Nigel agreeing. "Is everything okay? Anything you need from us?"

Manfred frowns at the kindness, "Thank you, I appreciate that. No. I'll be in court. And it's nothing against you or your family. My people, us Navajos, are suing the United States government for land that was stolen from us one hundred fifty years ago. The government reneged on a treaty and stole our land, throwing my people out of their homes and communal habitat. We want that land back to build a school, a hospital, and to provide other things, like maybe a college campus, for our next generation to be successful."

"Manfred, why haven't we spoken about this before? I can definitely help you."

Manfred touches Nicolaus on the shoulder with a smile. He nods. "Yeah, I knew you'd say that Nicolaus. I knew it." He chuckles, "I may take you up on that offer later. Let us get the land back first."

"Manfred, do you need funds for your lawyers? Or even actual high-powered lawyers to help?" Nigel asks him.

Manfred chuckles again, "Nigel, I also knew you would offer to help. We have internal Native American lawyers, who know our treaties. Maybe in the future we will need help."

Nigel nods, "Manfred, you have done so much for my family. You are a stellar security force and if there is ever anyway for us to return the favor, you let us know."

Manfred smiles, shaking both of these men's hands, feeling privileged to know them, and honored to be in their employ. "Your hearts are in the right place."

Chapter Forty-Seven

Francesca, Rachel, and Constance wait in the New York airport, on their Thursday night layover, to get to Riga, then to Estonia. They are each determined to give Deirdre the moral support she needs to face Ceil, and to marry Nicolaus on Valentine's Day.

"We should have brought Elsa with us," Francesca comments. "She really needs a getaway right now."

"Maybe being away is the last thing Elsa needs. She has to deal with Niall," Constance voices. "Just as my Deirdre has to deal with Ceil. It really points out to me how difficult the people in this family are. You know, Nicolaus has been through so much, just to be able to keep his love for Deirdre. Ceil has thought of everything she could to try to run him off."

Francesca laughs, her English accent front and center, "My Auntie Ceil is a damn mess! She's always starting some foolishness!" She giggles.

Rachel leads the ladies to clink their drink glasses at the bar inside the airport lounge. They laugh and take a drink. "Well, we must keep moving forward," Rachel tells them. "Those babies need to get here. I keep saying they are just waiting and waiting to be born."

"Makes me think of poor little Thaddeus," Francesca notes sadly.

"Yes, it does. I think about him often," Constance agrees. "He should have been Deirdre's and Nicolaus' baby. Then he would have been safe."

"I think that is what Nicolaus attempted to do, by having Deirdre take over the mothering of that little one," Rachel comments.

"Deirdre offered to do it. She loves Nicky so much," Francesca points out.

"Yes," both Constance and Rachel say at the same time, agreeing with Francesca.

"Well, we can't dwell on it. I don't want us to be sad when we see Deirdre. Remember, this will be a happy occasion of us bringing her to Nicky to get married. I'm sure he'd marry her right this moment if he could. Let's drink to their eternal happiness." Rachel put her glass in the air.

"Eternal happiness," Constance and Francesca repeat. The three ladies clink glasses again and drink to the happiness and wellbeing of Nicolaus and Deirdre.

Chapter Forty-Eight

Jonathan pulled his team of men together for their planning meeting. Tomorrow is Friday, the morning his daughters are to marry the Ravenell brothers. Jonathan's men are elite henchmen, who never question his motives, or his directives. They are thirty-five strong men of all creeds and sizes. The noise level of the room buzzed loudly as the men went about greeting each other with manly hugs, handshakes, and high fives. They each greet Jonathan with the respect their employer deserved.

Jonathan begins the meeting as if it were a regular office meeting, instead of a sinister meeting to plan illegal activities. "Okay, everyone be sure to grab coffee, juice, and donuts if you'd like. I had my daughter get you breakfast." They met in the elaborate conference room in the basement of his house, which is twenty-five miles west of Lady Bird Lake, in Austin. The exterior of the house is fully bricks, which would protect them if ever a shootout occurred. Jonathan had all ground floor windows removed and replaced with bricks. Windows were in the upstairs rooms and the massive loft.

Elsa had her own town home in Austin, closer to the VMC headquarters office. However, she did dine with her father and stay with him frequently. Jonathan is divorced from Elsa's mother. She'd caught Jonathan in his secret alternative sex life. She was immensely offended that he'd brought his lover man into their home, and into their bed. Once she left, she had very little contact with either Jonathan or their daughters, deciding to make a clean break.

Jonathan sent Elsa on another errand because he did not want her privy to the details of their plan, as she had taken a few days off from work, due to being so upset over Niall. "Okay, so I want everyone here tomorrow morning at nine. And don't be late. We are going to oversee two weddings, my Elsa, and my other daughter Gwen. They will marry the Ravenell brothers, at their estate."

"The Ravenell brothers? Really? That's who Elsa is upset about?" One of his men asked out of curiosity. "Boss, you need to give Elsa my number. I'll treat her right!" This comment got loud laughter and agreement from the men.

Jonathan nods, "Yeah, well, sometimes you can't control who you love." For a moment, he sounds like a caring father. "Anyway, they don't know were arriving."

"Wait! Hold on, Boss," another interrupted. "One of those Ravenell brothers is a special forces dude, isn't he? I saw on television when he was awarded some medal for bravery. There's no way he's going to let us do whatever we want. He's a badass, and ..."

Jonathan interrupts him. "Don't worry about that! Those logistics have already been worked out. They don't know we're arriving, we'll have the element of surprise. And he won't have his gun or anything else on him. We all go in together and overwhelm them. You rough up the men, and leave Niall for me. And now that you mention this about Nicolaus Ravenell, is his name, you stay on him big time. Don't let him wiggle one inch. You take care of him, and I will take my time with Niall. I want us to be in total control of every single situation. We'll force everyone to do things my way."

The men liked the plan and give affirming words and head nods. "And oh yeah," Jonathan continues, "do not, I repeat, do not take any guns or ammo. I don't want anyone to make a stupid move and accidentally kill somebody. They won't know you don't have guns. Just leave it all at home, and bluff them as if you do have it, if necessary. They won't know the difference. This will be an easy task, and we will get it done within an hour."

"Sounds like a piece of cake, boss!" One of his men comments.

Chapter Forty-Nine-TW

"**A**nd cake too!" Bishop Leighton happily drank his tea, after his brunch meal with the Ravenell family. Ceil made sure that Nicolaus and Niall were present as well.

"Both of you, Nicolaus and Niall, do not leave," Ceil commands them. "We have family business to discuss with Bishop Leighton, and I want both of you here, so we are all on the same page. Isn't that right, Nigel?"

Nigel nods in support of his wife. "Of course. It's always best for everyone to get an understanding through their own hearing. And sons, feel free to ask questions as well."

Ceil takes her time about getting the paperwork to discuss how much money they were going to leave to the church in the event of their deaths. She looks out the window and sees the large convoy of black off-road vehicles, large tank-like trucks, and SUVs rolling down the long cobblestone driveway entrance to their home.

Ceil goes into the bathroom to check her makeup and hair, as this is sure to be a long day. The Ravenell men are downstairs when a very loud rapping is heard at the front door. When two staff members open the door to see what is happening, they are quickly overrun by Jonathan and his army of thugs. All thirty-five men pour into the house. Quickly they surround all the men.

Ceil slowly descends the stairs, as innocent as possible. "What is going on here?" she yells.

"Well, you must be Ceil Ravenell. I'm Jonathan Baird, Elsa's father. Get on down here and join the little party."

"What is the meaning of this?"

Nicolaus felt himself in shock, there were so many men who entered their home, unwelcomed, and they each were in a stance ready to fight. Both Nicolaus and Niall were put in the middle of the room, surrounded by the men, who menaced at them, waiting for them to make a move. They were patted down to check for weapons. Immediately Nicolaus knew there would be nothing he could muster to help in this situation. His special forces skills were of no use to him when he is outnumbered by so many men, and his parents are being threatened. It is one thing if he was the only one being threatened, however, under this circumstance, there is no way he would risk harm being placed upon his parents.

Nigel and Bishop Leighton are pulled away from the brothers and forced over to the fireplace. Ceil is grabbed up and forced to stand on the opposite side of the fireplace, away from Nigel.

Elsa is brought in to stand next to Niall. "Dad, what are you doing?" She begins to cry, not understanding what is happening.

"Don't you cry my girl. No more crying," he touches her gently. Then suddenly, he harshly backhands Niall across the face. Niall takes the slap and says nothing. What could he do against all the men? He does not have courage like Nicolaus.

"Oh my God, Niall!" Elsa shrieks and grabs Niall's arm. She stands in front of him, as if she can protect him. "Dad, you have got to stop this!" Jonathan does not respond to his daughter, he only smiles at her, and touches her tears to move them away.

The display of quick violence worries Nicolaus. "What is this about? Why so many people? We can all talk through this."

Baird steps up to Nicolaus. He grabs him by the chin. "Oh, you must be that pretty boy hero, Nicolaus." Jonathan smiles mischievously at Nicolaus, "You need to keep those pretty lips closed, son," he chuckles as Nicolaus frowns and jerks his chin from him, not liking what he said, forcing Jonathan's release of him. This action made Jonathan's men push at Nicolaus and manhandle him harshly.

Nicolaus sees that his father and mother are also both being directly and roughly handled. Several men on each of them. The bishop is between them, also being held. The staff were in the kitchen hiding, and are now being marched into the room, before they had the chance to call for help. They are accosted and cruelly pushed about. The women staff are roughly pushed forward. Everyone is now together, in the same room. The staff are crammed to a corner of the room, and several men guard them, crossing their arms as if waiting for a chance to hurt one of them.

With a nod from Jonathan, Nigel and Nicolaus are harshly punched in the torso, making them both double over in pain. Suddenly, Nicolaus is held by two large men, his arms wrenched behind his back, his legs entangled with theirs so he could not try anything. They know of his strength. On the other side of the room, two men shake Ceil harshly, as if they have no qualms about hurting her.

"Please!" Nicolaus tells them, noticing that Niall says nothing, and does nothing. He understands his brother is ill equipped to handle this mess he's made. No men are next to Niall, as he only watches what is happening. He is afraid to move. "Let my parents go. Don't hurt them. Just let them go. Please!" Nicolaus tells Jonathan. Nicolaus' arms are stretched back, and he is rewarded with another gut punch, as Jonathan grabs up Niall to usher him out of the room.

"No, wait!" Nicolaus calls to Jonathan, ignoring his pained torso, afraid of what Jonathan might do to his brother. Nicolaus struggles against the men to get free. Jonathan ignores Nicolaus and forces Niall into the next room. "Wait, he didn't mean ..." Nicolaus receives another punch to the other side of his rib cage, making his talking cease. The men roughly hold onto him.

"Oh my God, oh my God!" Elsa begins freaking out. "Just stop!" she yells at the men hurting Nicolaus. She doesn't understand what her father is doing, and she is surely afraid he'd go too far.

Suddenly they could all hear Jonathan yelling at Niall. "You dare try to disgrace my princess? You bring her to your bed, and then call her a slut?"

Elsa runs towards the door of the room where her father has taken Niall. She is quickly blocked by two rather large men before she reaches the door. They each stand firm, crossing their arms before their chest. One shakes his head negatively at her. "Let me pass," she orders them.

"No ma'am, sorry. We can't do that. Just stand back over there where you were, before you make us hurt someone."

Elsa breathes hard, then does what she is told. She is afraid she may not be able to stop this awful action of her father.

"I didn't mean ..." Niall attempts to defend his words. Another harsh slap is delivered to Niall's face before he can get his lie out. Niall touches his mouth, blood trickles out.

"And you called her a liar?" Jonathan harshly yells at Niall, as if this were an inconceivable thing, for someone of high stature.

Niall steps back from Jonathan, out of his reach, anticipating another blow. Of course, this doesn't work. Jonathan is upon him, this time a punch is delivered to his mouth, making Niall fall to the floor. More blood flows from his lips.

Angered, Niall jumps to his feet and takes a swing at Elsa's dad. His action is enough for Jonathan to unleash the ass kicking he feels Niall deserves for treating his daughter with contempt.

Elsa cries, knowing her father is hurting Niall, something she would never want to happen. They can hear many punches. Nicolaus struggles to get loose to go to Niall's aid and is unable to. The men increase their hold on him all the more, putting additional pressure on him. Another man who is behind him, kicks the back of his knees, making him fall to a kneeling position. The two men who are holding him, reposition themselves, so he cannot get away. Ceil watches all this with inner excitement, though she tries to remain in her frightened puppy face, especially when the men jostle her.

After several minutes of giving Niall the beating Jonathan felt he deserved, Jonathan then straightens his salt and pepper hair and his clothes, not minding his bloody knuckles. Jonathan jerks Niall up to his feet and shoves him into the room next to Elsa.

"Niall," Elsa cries, as she touches his bleeding facial cuts and his bleeding lip trying to help him. Bruises are already forming.

In rude anger, Niall throws Elsa's hands off him. Embarrassed, he turns from her.

In amusement, Jonathan goes to Nicolaus. "Tsk, tsk, you just couldn't be still, huh? What? You thought you were going to rush over and save your brother? Military man, is that what you thought? Well, as you can see, I have my own army. And I promise you, if Niall ever mistreats my daughter again, there will be hell to pay!"

Nicolaus doesn't understand the point of all this. Is Baird done humiliating and threatening them? Were they going to retreat from their property now, just as they came in?

"Jonathan, hurting my sons is not necessary," Nigel tells him, holding his ribs, in pain.

"Well, I'm in charge right now, Daddy-O-Ravenell. And I say he deserves it. He's lucky my old age tuckered me out, or I would still be in there punching him."

"Jonathan, let's put an end to this already. You've had your fun," Nigel frowns, feeling quite angry not caring if they punch him again. He is also worried about his staff.

"Shut up, man. This party has just started," Jonathan yells at Nigel. "Where is Gwen?" Jonathan asks of his men.

"Gwen?" Elsa questions her father. "Dad, please, it's enough. They understand, they get your message. Please!" Jonathan does not respond to Elsa, he only touches her face, then is back to his men.

"I have her, Sir," says a voice from the front door. Gwen is ushered in, awestruck of what is happening. Jonathan notes that she looks the same since the last time he saw her. She is still thin, dressed as if she were on a beach, in flip flop shoes, baggy thin shorts, and a crochet beach jacket over her hippie crop top. She moves her curly, dirty blond hair out of her grey eyes that sparkle at the sight of her father. Jonathan hugs and kisses her.

"Gwen!" The half-sisters hug each other. "What are you doing here?" Elsa asks, dismayed and confused.

Gwen laughs, displaying her pearly, white, straight teeth, and her sun browned skin.

"I haven't the slightest idea. What am I doing here, dad? Where am I? What's this all about?"

"Did you see that, Niall?" Jonathan tells him. "These ladies love each other. You didn't see them calling each other names or being rude. They are respectful to each other, and that is how I expect you to treat my daughter."

Without words, Niall nods, afraid of bringing up anger from Jonathan. He holds his ribs, as his face is beginning to swell.

"What is the meaning of all of this?" Nigel finally shouts at Baird. "What are you doing, man? Release my family and my staff," he orders him.

"I'll tell you what I'm doing. I'm getting things straight around here, since you two seem incapable to do so. Bishop," Jonathan calls to the religiously cloaked man.

"Let my parents go!" Nicolaus says again. His and Nigel's demands are unheeded.

Bishop Leighton steps forward. "Are you a true Bishop, ordained by the state to marry people?"

"Well," Bishop Leighton wants to find a way out of this for the family. He could clearly see where Jonathan Baird is going, even if the family doesn't understand. "Look, yes, I'm ordained by God to marry people, but you know they have to be registered with the state before they can be married."

"Oh, you don't need to worry about that. I have lots of friends in high places. I will get that taken care of."

Bishop Leighton put his finger to his lip in thought, trying to find another reason not to marry them. "Well, okay, but it is illegal to marry people who are under duress."

"Really? Is that so?" Jonathan roughly grips the bishop around the back of his neck, "For a moment there, I thought you were going to tell me it was impossible to marry them." He steps back and grunt giggles. He swings his hands out as if to dash the thought. "Okay, well, they will not be under duress. Cause you see, I always believe in giving folks choices," Jonathan says loudly for all to hear. "Yes, that's right. So, let's see, Nigel and Ceil, these are your choices, either your sons are going to marry my daughters, or there will be some serious pain, physical as well as mental pain for each of your family members and your staff. Their lives might be shortened, because they will be badly injured. My men are certified in high stakes martial arts. They have assassin hands and feet. And if you think I'm joking, you just try me," he lied, bluffing, as none of this is true, nor do any of his men have any weapons or ammo on them. "I mean I don't mind remedying this situation with violence if that's what you want, and I'll take this house and your land, and whatever else I wish to have." Jonathan could see that his deliberate, empty threats had the wanted effect on the family.

"Father, no! Please, not like this!" Elsa begs him.

Gwen is shocked, she looks at her father with a frown. Her hand to her chest, "Me? Marry?"

Nigel closes his eyes, tight lipped, realizing there is no way out of this. He sighs. "What about money, Jonathan? Do you need money? Isn't that what you're really after? I'll pay you twice what you want, if you just stop all this right now."

Jonathan laughs. "Now why would I want your money, Nigel? I'll tell you what I want. I want your son to be respectful of my daughter and for him to stand up and do what's right. He knows damn well that child is his."

"Okay, okay. We know he made a huge mistake ..."

"A mistake he is going to correct right now! And well, Gwen, she's for your pretty boy here," he outstretched his hand toward Nicolaus. "I want my Gwen married too, so ... why not?"

"I'm to marry Nicolaus Ravenell? Oh, daddy, thank you!" Gwen thanks her father for his twisted deeds with a hug, amongst all the stress and threats. She could never have dreamed of marrying Nicolaus Ravenell. She, as so many other women around the globe, know who Nicolaus is, and knows all about his life and military successes. Also, Elsa has filled her in many times about the happenings of the Ravenell family. And like the public around the globe, Gwen also knows that Nicolaus is to marry Deirdre. For some reason, at this time, that is not important to her. Her thin, weathered, sun tanned, drug laden body embraces her father with excitement.

"No, no," Nicolaus tries to correct this, though he is still in the awkward position on the floor, he is able to partially lift himself. "I'm already engaged, I'm not free to marry ..."

With a nod from Jonathan, his men jerk Nicolaus' arms straight back, and push their knees into his torso, their weight on him, pushing his face close to the floor. This position takes his breath, so he can no longer talk. He can barely breathe, and his shoulder joints are racked with pain, as they are being stretched from the sockets beyond the normal range. It is torture.

"Dad, please! Make them stop! They are hurting Nicolaus!" Elsa advocates for his release. She can hardly believe what she is witnessing.

Nigel wants all of this to stop. He knows they are hurting Nicolaus, most likely, purposefully. "We fully accept your daughters into our family," he tells Baird. "Please, stop hurting my sons. We agree they will be married."

Gwen jumps up and down, clapping with excitement, not really concerned that the man she is about to marry is actually being tortured, right there in front of all of them.

Elsa cries. This is not what she wanted her father to do. Once he got started, there was no stopping him. When he told her she would have Niall's respect, this is not what she thought he was talking about.

With a nod from Baird, the men ease up on Nicolaus, pulling him to his feet.

Nicolaus cannot believe this is happening to him, yet again. "No, please, I am sorry, I cannot ... will not ..." he attempts to reason with Jonathan.

Baird yells at Nicolaus, in his face, "It is not your decision to make, it's your father's decision, and he has spoken. Don't you have any respect for your father? Do you understand that I have no problem ordering my men to hurt your parents to get through to you? I will even let you choose the lethality! What do you want? Poison? A martial arts beating? Bullets? Which do you prefer, Nicolaus Ravenell?"

"Dad, what are you doing?" Elsa asks through her tears. "Please, stop all of this!"

Nicolaus' body is racked with pain as he looks over to his parents who were now being harshly jerked around again by several men, one pulls his mother by her hair. He looks down, and then meets the gaze of Baird. Their eyes lock on each other. Nicolaus is filled with anger, his breathing heavy, as he wants to hurt Elsa's father, his piousness nowhere around.

Nicolaus cannot see that Baird is beaming with joy and nervousness for being next to him, and ordering around the famous Nicolaus Ravenell, one of the bravest men in the country. He wished he had at least two of his men like Nicolaus. Barid wants to torment all that anger out of this handsome young man.

Baird looks over Nicolaus again. Thoughts of what he wants to do to him play on his mind. He grabs Nicolaus' face again, this time there is no resistance. "Get that bishop over here," he tells one of his men. Roughly, he releases Nicolaus.

Gwen, who is as tall as Nicolaus, grabs onto him, moving his eyes from her father. "You're so handsome!" she happily tells him. She touches his pained torso, biting her lip, realizing she could touch him anywhere she wanted because he would be her husband. She met his eyes, with a sparkling smile, which went unreturned. She kisses the side of his face, ready to be his wife, not caring how this is transpiring, only knowing that her father has done well for her. She kisses Nicolaus' face again when he does not resist her, as he is still being restricted by Baird's men.

Chapter Fifty

The staff at the castle are excited that more guests will be arriving. Deirdre asked the chef to prepare Makaroni-Piimasupp, the Estonian milk soup, which is one of Rachel's favorites.

The ladies arrive just before dinner time, and they are famished.

Deirdre hugs and kisses each of them, beginning first with her mother, then Rachel, and then Francesca. "Francesca is this your idea, bringing everyone to see me?"

"Heck no, girl! Nicky was looking all sad, missing you. He asked me to get here to be with you so you wouldn't be by yourself. And I'm like, uhm, she ain't by herself, Nicky. And he whips out his credit card and begs me to bring you home."

Deirdre laughs, believing every word, as it sounded like something her beloved would do. "That is just so sweet of him."

"Yeah, and I brought the whole gang. Why not?"

"I'm so glad y'all are here." Deirdre grabs her mother's hand. "Auntie Rachel, I asked the chef to make your favorite!"

"Oh, that is what I smell. Makaroni-Piimasupp?"

"Yep! Fresh and waiting for us."

Francesca grabs hold of Deirdre's other hand. "Wait a minute! How did you know we were arriving? We wanted to surprise you!"

Deirdre chuckles, "Bishop Moratey told me! He's not very good at keeping secrets!" she chuckles again. "He wanted to cheer me up with the news, and cheer me up it did!"

"Well, let's go eat!" Francesca says, laughing.

The women enter the dining room together, each feeling happy and elated.

Chapter Fifty-One-TW

Meanwhile, back in Austin, the Ravenell brothers reluctantly repeat the marriage vows, while men hold onto and jostle their parents. Bishop Leighton feels bad, however, the serious threats of violence to Nigel and Ceil made him speedily move through the ceremony. The brothers are provided golden rings for their brides, and the same for them. This makes Nicolaus understand that this had actually been planned out. How can they possibly know anything about ring sizes for these four people? Nicolaus becomes more angry, and he wonders if Ceil is behind this. However, as he sees her shriek from being jerked around, it settles his mind that she is not involved.

Once the forced ceremony concludes, Jonathan claps his hands. "Wonderful! Now we shall have consummation! I will not have my daughters tricked or deceived. Let's go boys!" he demands of them, expecting them to instantly obey.

"Hold on here!" Nicolaus eyes Jonathan. "We've cooperated and have done what you wanted. Please, can't your men stop manhandling my parents? Can we be a little more civil and stop threatening my parents and our staff?" he advocates for all of them, trying to be calm in his upset.

The bishop touches Jonathan on the shoulder and nods. "He's right."

Jonathan clicks his mouth and winks at the bishop. "All right, all right. Men, you can relax. Be steadfast," Jonathan directs his men loudly, so everyone can hear him. "Nothing is over until consummation." Jonathan turns on his heel and returns his attention to Nicolaus. He smiles at him mischievously, "Well boys, let's get to it. Strip!"

"You can't expect us to consummate in front of everyone, or our parents!" Nicolaus quickly tells him, frowning, wanting to deck

Jonathan, despite his age and personhood. Immediately, Gwen smiles as she entwines her scrawny arm around Nicolaus' muscular arm. She stares at him, trying to drink him all in. She is very excited that she is about to have sex with this gorgeous specimen of a man. She pulls herself in close to him, and touches his chest.

Nicolaus sighs and closes his eyes to Gwen's reaction of him. He tries not to notice that she is more than willing and ready to jump him.

"Hmm. Quite right! I can see how that could be difficult getting things up, if you know what I mean," Jonathan gives a belly laugh, his men joining in, laughing at his joke. He stops and clears his throat. "Very well, go to the other room. And boys, I want no funny business. Your job is to consummate. Stay on mission so that I don't have to hurt your parents." With a head nod, Jonathan has his men usher the couples into the room, which had Niall's blood on the floor. The men take pillows from the sofas and throw them onto the floor on the opposite sides of the room. Jonathan remains in the room, ordering his men out, wanting some respect for his daughters.

Nicolaus observes that Niall has no trouble getting busy with Elsa. Niall angrily starts in. Quickly, he is on top of her, harshly thrusting himself into her.

Elsa gasps with pain. "Niall, please," she begs him. This is not how she wanted things to go. She knows Niall is angry with her.

He covers her mouth with his so her father would not hear her whining. "There is no stopping. You are my wife now, just like you wanted. Now you will submit to me and do whatever I say," he tells her, sounding as if he will give her no mercy as he punitively plunges inside of her again. He covers her mouth with his lips to hush her cries.

Nicolaus and Gwen gently disrobe themselves. Nicolaus covering himself more than Gwen. He helps her cover up to maintain some dignity.

Nicolaus' mind is in strong man military mode, though he begins to feel himself crumble, as at this moment, he wants to vomit, as he touches the forced wedding band on his finger. The finger he thought he'd be honoring Deirdre within a few days' time. He doesn't understand how this could possibly be happening to him. Again, he is bound to a woman he does not even know and does not want. Again, he is being forced to copulate against his will. He thinks of his parents, and he shoves his thoughts and his feelings away. He has no choice, he must perform.

Jonathan roams back and forth watching the couples. Suddenly, he pulls a leather wrapped crop from his medium length overcoat inside pocket. He walks back and forth, hitting it in his hands, waiting for the opportune moment to use it, on either brother, particularly on Nicolaus, finding his thoughts fascinated with him.

Jonathan sees that Nicolaus and Gwen are sitting next to each other talking. Rudely, he interrupts them. "You can get to know each other later." He strikes his hand with the crop. "Now is the time for consummation," he yells at them. Then more calmly, and a little mischievous, "Nicolaus, you need some help to get going?" he offers.

"No. No!"

Gwen springs into action and sits on Nicolaus' lap. She gently pulls his face to her. "Just focus on me, baby. Don't worry about my dad." Her pretty, curly hair is unruly, against her sun-tanned skin. Gwen's chemical addiction made her thin, although despite being skinny, her body is curvy. Gwen smiles at Nicolaus, then kisses his lips, wantonly. She intends to claim her husband. Her hands are quickly on him. She can feel Nicolaus resisting her, so she kisses him deeper.

Nicolaus pulls away from Gwen, feeling horrid, feeling sold. His mind wonders why it is that he is not in charge of his own destiny. How could he be who he is, and not be in charge of his own life?

The sound of the crop whizzing close by intimidates his attention back to Gwen, as Elsa's moans could be heard with each harsh and punishing thrust Niall gives to her. Jonathan's actions develop into menacing behavior as he quickly walks back and forth, his eyes on the couples, with most of his attention on Nicolaus.

Gwen kisses Nicolaus deeper, finally getting him aroused. "Wow!" she exclaims about his size. She puts herself on him, pushing him in, enjoying every inch of him, moaning with pleasure. Gwen has no apprehensions of moving herself on him. She doesn't care about where she is doing this, as Nicolaus is more than satisfying to her, and she only hoped that he would be the cure for her sex addiction. She believes that having this beautiful man at her side would keep her from straying.

As Gwen works herself wildly, throwing her head back, craving cocaine, she can hear Nicolaus breathe hard at her movements. She knew the drug would really enhance this moment. Her mind fantasized about having the white substance flaking all over her body. This heightened her sexual arousal, making her move crazily over him. For Gwen, one addiction led to the other.

Nicolaus tumbles Gwen onto her back, seeing she needs more than what she is getting. He thinks about his parents as he is flanked with guilt, wanting none of this, trying to be somewhat in control of this little event, wishing to end the horrid situation quickly.

Baird sees his chance and uses the crop to give a hard slap to Nicolaus. Nicolaus does not flinch at the additional torture, he just keeps going with Gwen, though the pain ticks up his anger again.

Jonathan is riled up in sexual excitement, and is unable to resist committing an unspeakable act against Nicolaus. Jonathan grabs Nicolaus, assaulting him, making him stiffen with frenzied ejaculation inside of Gwen.

Just as quickly as Jonathan was upon Nicolaus, he is also gone, leaving the room, re-closing the French doors, knowing that Nicolaus would be furious. Jonathan takes a few seconds to enjoy what he'd just done. He is beside himself with joy for having complete power over Nicolaus Ravenell, the four times decorated military hero. The one guy the president had called on to rescue diplomats out of Milojastan, of which Jonathan was surprised he had not received that call. His actions today made his two time revenge sweeter, forcing Niall to marry Elsa, and partially living out his fantasy of sexually touching Nicolaus.

Jonathan had himself a hardy chuckle. He went to Nigel and Ceil, shewing his men away. "You can leave now," he shouts to his men. "All is well. Leave if you need to leave." Jonathan harshly grabs Nigel by the shoulder, offering his hand to him, "We are family now," he chuckles, holding Nigel's eyes with his own.

Nigel nods and takes his hand to shake it. What else could he do? Not knowing what the hands of Jonathan had just done to Nicolaus, yet fully knowing what Jonathan's hands had done to Niall. He nods, the bishop also nearby.

"No hard feelings, eh?" Jonathan has the nerve to ask for a truce, after having his goons attack and threaten Nigel's family. Jonathan knows Nigel is thinking about all that happened by the look on his face, so he shakes him back and forth by the shoulder, still holding his hand. "No hard feelings, okay?" he asks again, with a tone of demand.

Nigel nervously laughs, not sure what his sons would think of him, however, he knows he has to get his family past this traumatic event. He has to end the situation. He nods, "No hard feelings."

Nigel goes to Ceil. He hugs her tightly. "I'm so sorry. Are you okay?"

Ceil continues to act out her part. She let Nigel hold her, and she pretends to cry a little. "How could you let them ..."

"Shhh!" Nigel rocks her, not wanting her to get started. He holds her tight and brings her away from Jonathan. "Ceil, are you okay, do you need to go to the hospital," he asks her earnestly.

Ceil sniffs, "No, I'm okay."

"You sure?"

"Yes."

Nigel hugs her again, only to be interrupted by Jonathan. "Hey Nigel, you will have some kind of wedding celebration for my girls, right?"

Nigel sighs, nodding. "Yes, it will take us a couple of days, ... yes, we'll get something together."

"Great, and I want announcements in the papers. The whole nine. Let's make it official. We have to restore my Elsa's reputation."

Nigel nods again, "Okay, we'll take care of it."

Jonathan pats Nigel on the back, as the couples emerge from the sitting room, redressed, Elsa's clothes a bit disheveled. Nicolaus looks at Niall with a pained expression though he says nothing. Niall could feel his brother's anger, so he also says nothing, as his own anger is raging inside of him.

Jonathan kisses his girls. He has one last condition, which he announces. "Now, daughters, I want you to hear this. If your husbands do anything, and I mean anything to disrespect you, or upset you, you tell me, and then we will all be back to address the situation. You got me?" Both Elsa and Gwen nod. Gwen looks upon Nicolaus unable to imagine what could go wrong.

Nicolaus is relieved to see the small army of men leaving their property. They release the staff, and Nigel checks on them. Nicolaus also checks on the wellbeing of his parents, swallowing what Jonathan did to him, not wanting to bring it up, or to ever talk about it. He completely avoids Jonathan.

Nigel gives a hug and a kiss to both Elsa and Gwen, welcoming them into the family, Ceil standing next to him.

"Mr. Ravenell ...," Elsa is still tearing.

"Nah-ah!" Nigel holds a finger up, not wanting Elsa to be upset any longer. "We are family now Elsa. You will be bearing my grandchild."

"Yes Sir," she just wants to spew crying all over the place. She can barely hold herself together. Not only is she dying inside from gross embarrassment because of her father, but her clothes are ripped, her marriage seems like a sham, and her own father just forced Nicolaus to marry her sister, when Deirdre would be returning at any moment. "I never intended any of this to happen," she whispers to them, Gwen behind her, "I didn't know what my father was going to do. Please, you must believe me!" Tears pour from her eyes, as she sees her father gather his crew to leave. "He only told me he wanted to talk to you about Niall. He never mentioned any of this." Elsa is now shaking. Gwen's arms wrap around her.

Nigel leads them to be seated, afraid Elsa might faint. This has been trying for all of them. Nigel kneels in front of Elsa and takes her hands. He gently touches her face, "Elsa, I know the type of person you are, I've known you for years, now. I know you are good and kind. I am very sorry that my son has treated you so poorly, that your father felt he had to take extreme action to defend you and your reputation. It would have been much better if Niall had done the right thing by you and asked your father for your hand in marriage." Nigel sighs, trying to bare the weight of all this ugliness.

"I want to believe that everything will be okay from this point forward. At least for you and Niall."

Elsa nods, and hugs Nigel to her, the tears still flowing. He tries his best to comfort her. He pats her back. This reminds him of the time he comforted his love, Rachel, when she had to give up their child for he and Ceil to raise. He hugs Elsa until she stops crying.

Niall stands back, with arms crossed over his chest. He is non-moving, just watching. He doesn't want to deal with anything else today. He is bruised and battered. His ribs hurt, his face hurts, he knows he will need to go to the hospital. He wants Jonathan out of their house. He is doing all he can to keep himself from jumping Jonathan, thinking he might be able to harm him with a surprise attack. However, the number of Jonathan's men stop his actions. Also, he knows he doesn't have great moves, like his brother.

Nicolaus needs a drink. As he pours the whisky, he continually checks to see where Jonathan is in the room. He quickly drinks the shots down, on the third one now. He certainly feels he can take no more today. He has been tortured, forced to marry against his will, again, and sexually assaulted. His shoulders ached from being over stretched. He knows he will be retaining the constant reminders of what Jonathan did to him for some time. How does one get over such actions?

Jonathan walks to Elsa and Gwen. They stand and he kisses each of them with a father's love, ignoring Elsa's tears. Then he and all his men leave the premises of the Ravenell mansion.

Chapter Fifty-Two

D eirdre cannot sleep, as she feels something is wrong. She tries to phone Nicolaus, and he does not answer. She calls again, and again, five minutes apart, and still no answer. She phones Elsa, no answer. She begins to pace the bedroom, with worry in her heart. She tries Nicolaus again, no answer. She dials Nigel's number, no answer. Out of desperation, she does something she'd never do, Deirdre dials Ceil's number, no answer.

Tears flow, as she grabs her prayer beads, and quietly prays for Nicolaus. She sends him a text message, which goes unanswered.

After a few hours, Deirdre puts Ishani and Maggie on a conference line.

"Deirdre, where are you?" Maggie asks.

"I'm in Estonia, at the castle. I just had to get away from everything and everyone."

"I can imagine."

"Yes," Ishani agrees, "it's been very trying for you, Deirdre. I'm so glad you decided to take time for yourself. You really need it."

"Nicky proposed again."

"Oh Deirdre, that's great!" Ishani says happily.

"Well of course he did! I'd be shocked if he didn't," Maggie states. "Oh, so you're taking time out before wedding planning?"

Deirdre sighs. "No, actually, I didn't accept."

"Oh, Deirdre! You told Nicky no?" Maggie asks in disbelief.

"Not exactly. I told him I wanted to think about it. He was so shocked. I felt so bad."

"Oh Deirdre!"

"Well, it's true. After all his mother did to keep us apart, I really have to think about if I want to be part of that family."

"But you'd do anything for Nicky," Maggie reminds her of her previous words.

Deirdre chuckles at her sarcasm. "Shut up! I know it!"

They all laugh.

"Of course, that is the conclusion I decided upon."

"Deirdre, I cannot even see you with anyone other than Nicolaus. You know you two belong together, like milk and cookies," Ishani notes.

"That's what Nicky told me, that we belong to each other."

"You know, really what it is, it's that Nicky needs to stand up to his mother. I mean, Jesus, he's a special forces commander. He needs to get tough with his mother as well."

"Was!" Deirdre corrects her. "He's retired, thank God!"

"Yeah, sure, retired, and yet they still call him back."

"I know. I hate that. And you know he's always had a hard time with his mother."

"I just think you are Deirdre, the Drama Mama." The ladies laugh.

"And yeah, speaking of drama, I'm really worried, because I haven't been able to get ahold of anyone at the house for hours. Nicky is not answering my calls or texts. I'm really worried that something is wrong." Her voice shook with the tears she'd been holding back.

"Oh no! You want us to go over there?" Maggie offers.

"No, no! If something is wrong, I don't want to send you into danger."

"Well, we could call the police, and ask them to do a well check on the house," Ishani suggests.

"Uhh, I hate to send the police over there. You know how they get with people of color in our country."

"Dee, why don't you contact the security? They should know something, or at least go check on the family," Maggie recommends,

"That's a good idea," Deirdre agrees. "Would you mind doing that? And then call me as soon as you know something."

"I'll do it right now, Deirdre."

Chapter Fifty-Three

Nicolaus looks at his phone, as it keeps buzzing, then he puts it down. He cannot fathom the conversation he'd have to have with Deirdre, Constance, and Francesca.

"Nicolaus, I want you to stay overnight," Dr. Emerald Nguyen, the emergency room physician informs him. "I want to be sure you don't have internal bleeding."

Nicolaus covers the top of his mouth with part of his hand, in thought. "No, I don't want to do that. I'll just return tomorrow. I have too much to do."

"No," Dr. Nguyen touches Nicolaus' sore shoulder, "if you are here, we can catch it much faster. If I let you leave, you may not make it back in time before you get into trouble. Internal bleeding can be dangerous ..."

"I know, I know," Nicolaus interrupts the doctor, having had this lecture before.

Gwen had changed into some of her sister's clothes and is right by his side, doing what she believed a wife should do. Nicolaus' phone buzzes again. Quickly, Gwen snatches it before his hand could get to it on the exam table behind him. "It's Deirdre! I'll send her a text for you. Don't worry, hon, I'll leave it to you to fill her in."

Gwen steps aside and types a non-informational text to Deirdre: 'Sorry, can't answer right now. Will ring you later. Love.' Then she turns his phone off and puts it in her purse.

"Okay, well, that is why I think you should stay at least overnight," the physician tells him again.

Gwen returns herself to the conversation, and stands right next to Nicolaus, touching is other shoulder, putting her wifely opinion in, "You should listen to what the doctor is telling you. Anyway, you need rest. You've been through a lot."

The physician smiles, "You should listen to your pretty wife."

Nicolaus looks at Gwen. His brain takes in the fact that she is his wife, which brings his feelings up through the nerves in his gut. Nicolaus lurches off the table just in time for his vomit to land in the trash can. He miserably wretches out what he had earlier forced down. The uncontrollable vomiting multiplies the pain of his rib cage, making it impossible to breathe properly. Nicolaus believes he might faint from the pain and lack of breath.

Dr. Nguyen steps out of the small emergency room for a moment and returns with a few intravenous bags of fluid, one to help control his pain and one to replace fluids for him.

When the vomiting is done, Nicolaus washes his face and mouth, and uses the paper towels Gwen is handing him. Dr. Nguyen looks at Nicolaus as if he'd be crazy to leave now, while placing an oxygen mask on his face. Nicolaus nods, "Okay, then. Just one night."

"Good! And I understand your brother has already been admitted," Dr. Nguyen tells him.

"Okay. I want a private room," Nicolaus demands.

Dr. Nguyen smiles and nods, "I'm sure we can arrange it."

Chapter Fifty-Four

"Your woman's intuition is probably correct," Bishop Moratey tells Deirdre as he pours tea into her cup, followed by tea for Constance, Rachel and then Francesca. "For sure it may be something, or it may be nothing."

"Nothing? Nicky never texts me messages like the one I got after he didn't answer his phone. And he never called me back. And even now, I tried to phone everyone, and no one is answering. It's odd," Deirdre explains. "Francesca, don't you think it's odd that Pops isn't answering his phone or returning my calls?"

"Not like my Uncle Nigel. He didn't answer my calls either. First time in the history of my life!"

"This makes me worried too. It is unusual for Nigel to not respond," Rachel adds.

"I even had my girlfriends send the security over, and they won't tell us anything."

Bishop Moratey sips his tea. "Well, if you needed an excuse to go back home ...."

Deirdre nods. "I decided I do want to marry Nicky. And on the next coming Friday, Valentine's Day, like he wants, only just for us to marry here at St. Nicholas. I don't want to spend time and money flying back home, just to turn around and fly back. I'm sure he won't mind."

"I'm sure he won't!" Bishop Moratey agrees with her.

"Nicky would do anything for you, Dee," Francesca confirms her thoughts.

Deirdre smiles at the truth. She sighs, "I've put up with Mother Ceil my whole life, and I guess we will manage her together. Nicky will just have to be firm with her about our children."

Constance smiles and celebrates her daughter's decision, "Well, that's wonderful, Deirdre. Sounds like it's settled in your mind now."

"I would never want to live my life away from Nicky. I can't. And now it's our time," Deirdre asserts.

"Yep!" Francesca loudly agrees, "even if the timing is a bit off. You've just got to step right on into those moments that change your life forever."

Constance nods. "I agree. You can just get a wedding dress here, and maybe give away the one you have, or keep it for a future rededication ceremony."

Bishop smiles at the wedding conversation. He hands out little plates of ruiskatuts, which are Estonian rye cookies, to go with their tea.

Chapter Fifty-Five

The pain medication is strong and puts Nicolaus to sleep for a few hours. When he awakes he sees Gwen and Elsa sitting and whispering on the loveseat in his hospital room, opposite his bed. He sits up, the intravenous fluids had already been taken out of his arm. He is to be given pain medication by mouth, have blood drawn periodically to check for hemorrhaging, and x-rays, which were already done.

When Gwen notices Nicolaus is awake, she springs into action and is by his side. She smiles at him and runs her fingers through his hair. "How are you feeling? Better?"

Elsa is on the opposite side of his bed. She wants to hug Nicolaus, and isn't sure he will let her. She bites her lip and does it anyway. She pulls him tight to her. "I'm so sorry," she tells him, suddenly wanting to cry again.

Nicolaus returns the hug, they hold each other for a moment, then separate. "It's not your fault, Elsa. Don't ever think I blame you," he tells her, sighing, knowing that she understands he is talking about his forced marriage to her sister. He knew he did not have to say it outright, that she understood him.

He looks to Gwen, and takes her hand, nodding, "Yes, I think, yes, I feel a little better."

Gwen kept her smile going, "The doc said you have no broken bones, just lots of bruising." She pushes at him. "You're my tough man!"

Nicolaus half smiles at her. "How's my brother?" he asks both sisters.

Elsa shakes her head, "He's worse off. He does have two cracked ribs, and his face is all bruised up. Doc says we should start seeing it get better. They want Niall to stay for a couple of days."

Nicolaus sighs, "I want to go see him," he tells Elsa calmly. Nicolaus knows that as the older brother, and because he is the leading brother in the family, it is up to him to make the first move to make things right with Niall.

"Oh, okay!" Elsa is surprised, and glad. "He's actually in the room next to yours. Mother Ceil is with him. And your dad did not need to be admitted. They said he had some slight bruising on his torso."

Nicolaus nods, "I'm glad they did not hurt my father worse than that."

"Yes."

As Nicolaus is dressed in a hospital gown, Gwen looks for and finds the stash of gowns in the room cabinet. She helps her husband into a gown, in reverse, to cover the back opening all hospital gowns have. Nicolaus knows it is probably time for more medication, as he feels sharp pain as he walks to the room where Niall lay, the sisters following him.

Nicolaus lightly knocks on the door, not waiting for an answer before entering. He sees that Niall does have swelling to his face, and he is hooked up to intravenous bags, and medical monitoring devices. Ceil stands as he enters. "Mother," he touches her shoulder, "are you all right?" he asks her softly.

Ceil nods. "Yes. They did not hurt me," she says gently.

"I'm very glad they didn't hurt you." He wants to hug her as the concern on his face shows. He kept hold of her shoulder, hoping she might want a hug.

Ceil looks away from him, "It will all be all right," she says softly. Her concern is for Niall. She feels bad that Niall got hurt in her scheme to be rid of Nicolaus, as she kept to playing her part of the innocent mother.

Nicolaus goes to Niall, who is awake. Niall looks at Nicolaus and doesn't know what to say. He feels this is all his fault, which he is sure Nicolaus feels the same, and he is not sure what Nicolaus is going to say or do. He feels defensive, until Nicolaus sits him up, and hugs him.

Nicolaus holds his younger brother tight, for a long time, realizing things could have been much worse. Although he was previously furious at Niall, as after all, his behavior brought all this on, the violence visited upon the family is not Niall's fault.

Niall tries to end the hug because his emotions are at hand, however, Nicolaus won't let him go. Suddenly, Niall's crying begins, and it is as if he cannot stop crying at all. Nicolaus holds onto his brother, trying to be there for him in the moment, his own eyes welling up and tears falling from him as well, as their anger melts into tears. Elsa hugs onto both of them, her tears flowing. Gwen and Ceil sit down together, not affected by the emotional release at all.

Chapter Fifty-Six

The following day, after being released from the hospital, Nicolaus is home in his father's study, Gwen by his side. Gwen does not know what to do with herself yet, so she hangs onto Nicolaus, every moment. They are discussing the marriage announcements.

Suddenly, Nicolaus stops and reaches into his back pants pocket and takes out his wallet. He gives Gwen his other credit card. "Gwen, why don't you go shopping for yourself? I know you need clothes and things. Have the driver take you wherever you want to go and get whatever you need." He smiles at her, touching her back.

The genuine moment is not lost on Gwen. She wants to kiss her new husband, however, he moves away from her quickly, as if to avoid such an action. She looks at the card. "Okay, honey, what's my limit?"

"No limit. Get whatever you want and whatever you need." He sincerely says to his new wife, for which he has no clue that she is a drug addict.

Gwen looks at him astonished, smiling big at him. "Wow!" She suddenly believes she will be very happy in this family. "What about cash, hon?" she's thinking of her magic powdery substance, unbeknownst to Nicolaus.

"Cash? Ah, you can get cash if you want. The code is 7472. I think there is a five-hundred-dollar limit for cash withdrawals."

Gwen rushes over to Nicolaus and jump hugs him, kissing his face and eventually his lips. She dislodges herself from him, mesmerized by the credit card, and leaves his presence. She is ready to find the driver, ready to go shopping, and ready to satisfy her craving.

Nigel is glad Nicolaus sent her away, as they would be better able to focus on these difficult tasks without Gwen around.

"Father, don't mention me in the announcement. Just announce Niall. I don't want to embarrass Deirdre like that," he tells Nigel as he is typing up the announcement on his laptop.

"Okay, that is true," he agrees with his wise son.

Nigel erases some of his words, and types ferociously, wanting to get the wording correct. "Okay, how does this sound? Announcing newlyweds Niall Ravenell and Elsa Baird, committed to their budding love with baby on the way ..."

"Father, why mention the baby? I wouldn't. I do like the budding love part. Maybe instead of budding, we say promising commitment."

Nigel chuckles, "Okay! I like that!" He erases what he had and places those words.

His phone rings, as it had done so all morning. Nigel looks at it. "It's the ladies again. They must have called a hundred times. I'm going to answer it, I'm sure they are worried. Hello?"

"Oh, thank God! Uncle Nigel! We've been worried sick, not able to get ahold of anyone. Is everything okay?" Francesca asks him, finally getting through. She gestures to Constance and Deirdre to get close to her, Rachel already sitting next to her.

"Ah ... well ..."

"What? Something's happened? Hold on Uncle Nigel, let me put you on speaker phone. We are all here."

"Well, uhm ..."

"Is Nicky there? Is Nicky all right?" Deirdre interrupts Nigel.

Nigel clears his throat. "Yes, yes, Nicolaus is here with me now, he is okay. We did have quite an incident."

"Oh no, what happened?" Francesca asks. The ladies are quiet and listening.

"Elsa's father was furious at Niall because ... he rejected her, and ah, ... well ...." Nigel did not want to panic them.

Nicolaus grabs his father's shoulder. "Don't tell them everything," he whispers to his father. "Please, I'll tell Deirdre ..."

"Nicky, is that you?" Deirdre's extra sensory hearing heard the whispered voice of her love. "Nicky, what's going on? Are you okay? Please don't lie to me."

Nicolaus is surprised, he answers, "Yes, ... I'm here, love. I'm ... okay. Father was just going to tell all of you ..."

"Well ... yes... uhm, ..."

"Niall is still acting crazy towards Elsa?" Francesca asks, as she thought that was done with Niall.

"I'm afraid so. And her father was furious, and ... made him marry her."

"Made him? How's that?" Francesca asks.

"Nigel, we are really worried," Rachel threw in.

"Look, I don't really want to discuss it now, and certainly not over the phone. I think it's better if you all stay there in Estonia for another week or two. We need this to all blow over."

"A week or two?" Francesca frowns at Rachel. "Uncle Nigel, I cannot do that. What's happening?"

"No, no, I want to get back as soon as we can," Deirdre leads the ladies, as Constance and Francesca nod in agreement. "Pops, is everyone okay, what happened? We couldn't get ahold of anyone for days."

Ceil walks in to see what her men are up to.

"Look, the press is going to be all over this, and ..." Nigel tries to explain.

"No. No. That's it. We'll be on our way home. Love you all." Deirdre decides for the group of ladies, then switches the line to call her travel agent to make arrangements for the four of them to leave on the next flight out.

Nicolaus sighs. "Jesus!" He sits on the couch and puts his hands to his head realizing there is just no way any of this is going to be good.

Nigel also sighs. "I'm sorry, son. Look, we'll just announce Niall, and that's all the press will know. I can't imagine they'd find out anything else, unless Jonathan blabs to them."

"Our ladies are going to need security in New York, and once they get to Texas. I don't want the press badgering them and chasing after them. And Elsa will need security to protect her as well, and we'll need to put security detail on Niall to keep him away from the press."

Nigel nods, wide-eyed at Nicolaus' executive function thinking, though seemingly discarding what he'd just said. "Okay. I'll text Francesca and tell her to send me the flight details as soon as they have them."

"I'm working on how you want to do this celebration. A big event or ..." Ceil is interrupted by both men.

"No, small!" Nigel and Nicolaus say loudly, in unison.

"Okay, okay!" Ceil is somewhat surprised at their reaction.

"This is going to be a mess!" Nigel informs his wife.

Chapter Fifty-Seven

Three hours later, Rachel, Francesca and Constance are led into the Estonian airport by Deirdre. Unfortunately, the weather has taken a turn for the worst. They shake the heavy snow flakes out of their hair and off their clothes as they enter the airport lobby doors.

When the four American ladies get to the gate to pick up their tickets they are informed that all flights out are delayed due to the weather. The ladies find seats, and Deirdre sends a text to Nicolaus and Nigel letting them know their status. They did not know when they would be on the next flight, as the storm is just blowing in.

Chapter Fifty-Eight

A s the small party, small in Ravenell terms, began, Nigel thanked the good lord for small miracles. He is actually glad that his ladies are delayed in Estonia. He thought it would help Nicolaus get through this easier. The party is held at their mansion, and only fifty people were invited, half of which are the twenty-five VMC Board Members. Others are people Ceil insisted on attending, such as the mayor and his wife, Bishop Leighton and his wife, elites of the church, and other elites of Austin.

Ceil wants Niall to know these people. She wants him to make a good impression on them. Ceil hired a plastic surgeon, who worked magic to completely lift the swelling from Niall's face. Only light bruising appears on Niall, for which she and Elsa helped him cover with makeup.

Ceil touches her younger son on the chest, gently taking the drink from his hand, "You will not be having any drinks until after this party is over. You can wait for two hours," she tells him softly, smiling, so others would not hear or understand what she is doing. "I need you to be extremely nice to everyone here. Anyway, these guests have all brought gifts for you and Elsa."

Elsa is escorted to Niall by her father. Quickly, Jonathan grabs onto the back of Niall's neck to whisper in his ear, despite them both being nicely dressed. "You do anything to embarrass my Elsa, and I promise you, what I gave you the other day will feel like child's play." He gently lets go of Niall, and helps him straighten his suit, while Niall's eyes are on him. Jonathan is satisfied at the fear and upset he sees about Niall.

Neither Elsa, nor Ceil, are close enough to hear what Jonathan said, however, Elsa could tell by the look on Niall's face, it probably wasn't good. She steps next to Niall, then moves her father away, brushing Niall's nice suit with her fingers. "You are very handsome,

Niall," she offers him, smiling, hoping he is going to behave. Elsa looks glamorous in a black, shining, Italian designer dress, which stops just below her knees. Her hair is done up nicely, and glistening. She resembles a princess.

Ceil smiles at her. "Wow, Elsa, you look lovely!"

"Thank you, Mother Ceil." Elsa understands the importance of this party, she hopes Niall does as well. She knows it will be important to make a good impression on the board members.

Niall looks at Elsa, as Ceil comments to him, "And you especially will be super-duper nice to Elsa." Ceil straightens Niall's blue jacket. He nods.

Niall smiles at Elsa. "Yes, you do look beautiful," he tells her. The nicest thing he has said to her since his fits began weeks ago.

Ceil urges them forward as they are officially announced by Bishop Leighton to the guests.

Next up is Nicolaus and Gwen. Nicolaus takes Gwen's hand, as Ceil approaches them, and Jonathan paces in the background. Nicolaus feels sickly and ignores it. He smiles at Gwen, "You look very beautiful!" he acknowledges what is true, as Gwen actually does look beautiful.

Gwen accepts his compliment with a huge toothy smile. "I can get used to this!" Gwen wore a sequenced blush colored, sheer, expensive Grecian designer dress, which covered her in all the right spots. Her hair is also done up and glistening, similar to Elsa's style. Her makeup is perfect, and her ears hold diamond hoop rings, which match perfectly against her sun-tanned skin.

Gwen entwines her arm with that of her husband, her height matching his. Nicolaus' handsomeness heavily strikes Gwen. He is dressed in his sleek black shirt and gray vest with matching gray pants. His muscular frame evident through his clothes. "I want to be a good wife to you, Nicky. I will be!"

Ceil rolls her eyes at the couples' moment, and gently edges them forward as they are being announced. Though the crowd had clapped in receiving Niall and Elsa, they are whispering and naturally confused about Nicolaus and Gwen. 'Gwen? Who is Gwen? Where is Deirdre? Nicolaus is married to Gwen? Does Deirdre know about this?' So many questions float around the room in whispers.

An hour into the event, which Nigel noted as the half point, Alexander and Dwight, Alexander's father and co-founder of VMC, arrive. They had been preparing for their two-week vacation in Switzerland. Alexander is none the wiser on what is going on, because Nicolaus made up excuses for why he was not in the office for the last three days.

While Gwen had the attention of three elderly ladies who are madly in love with, and lusted over her new, gorgeous husband, Nicolaus sits on a bar stool in the same room, his back to them. Giggling, the elderly ladies have swooped Gwen away to give her some advice on marriage, how to keep a man, how to treat Nicolaus, and of course they answered any questions she had about Deirdre. They are far enough away that Nicolaus cannot make out the words of their chatter.

Alexander grabs onto his best friend's sore shoulders, not knowing anything about the forced events of what had previously happened. "Okay, we finally made it to another Ravenell extravagant party! My dad and I are so psyched about going to Switzerland tomorrow. Glad you're feeling better." Alexander put his attention to the staff behind the bar. "Hey, I'll have a bourbon," he tells them. Upon receiving his drink, he takes a swallow and puts his attention back on Nicolaus, who is also slowly drinking his liquor.

"Switzerland sounds fun. I'm sure you could use the break," Nicolaus replies.

Alexander sits next to Nicolaus facing the same direction. He bumps Nicolaus on the arm. "Yes, and my father wants to show me something about some family heirloom there. First time I've ever heard about it."

Nicolaus chuckles, "Oh, so you've got family secrets too!" He takes another drink. "You are going to have to help me figure out how I explain all this to Deirdre. I'm lucky she is not here right now. I guess, it's lucky. I don't know."

"Explain it? Explain what?" Alexander hadn't been paying attention to understand that Nicolaus seems stressed about something. Alexander doesn't know what Nicolaus is talking about. "Just tell her the truth."

"Well of course I'm going to tell her the truth, but how? It's going to hurt her, and ... now that I'm married again ..." Nicolaus stops talking when he notices Alexander is no longer next to him.

"Oh my God!" Alexander exclaims quietly. "Dear God!"

Nicolaus frowns. Alexander is standing, and leaning on the bar counter. "What?"

"Nicolaus," dramatically Alexander grabs Nicolaus by the arm, "I have never believed in love at first sight. And God knows, I'm not so sure I believe in marriage at all, and I don't understand it, but ... I'm pretty sure I've just found my wife."

Nicolaus frowns as chatter has picked up in the room and several women have joined the corner chair where Gwen and the elderly ladies are talking. The noise level is loud.

Nicolaus chuckles, never having heard Alexander say such a thing. "What are you talking about?"

"My wife ... she's there. Who is that? Do you know who she is?"

Nicolaus glances back in the direction that Alexander is looking. There are several women surrounding Gwen. Nicolaus turns on the bar stool, frowning. "Which one?"

KAMRYNN BELLARY

Alexander nods forward, "That beautiful, half naked goddess, in that rose colored dress. With the stars in her hair."

Nicolaus looks at Alexander and sees a look on his face he'd never seen before. He looks at his drink, then to Alexander. "That's what I've been trying to tell you," he put a hand to Alexander's shoulder. "Her name is Gwen, and she's my new wife."

"Gwen?" he repeats as if mesmerized. "Wait ... what? Your wife? Is that what you said?"

Nicolaus nods, as Alexander finally pays attention to him. Nicolaus turns, facing forward again, feeling defeated. "Yes."

"Oh my God!" Alexander sounds panicked, "She's walking over here."

Gwen had noticed Alexander looking at her from across the room, and she is unable to take her eyes from him. Her mind is tripping, thinking that a mistake has happened of her marrying the wrong man, as she feels herself immediately and uncontrollably drawn to Alexander, unlike the numb, boring feeling she has toward Nicolaus.

By the time Gwen reaches the two men, she is upon Alexander, already taking his hand, putting it close to her. She sees that he is awestruck, and can see that he also feels what she is feeling. "Hello, I'm Gwen," is her introduction to him, that trademark toothy grin present.

Alexander feels himself begin to sweat at her presence. He holds her soft, silky hand. Nicolaus turns and sees how Gwen is looking at Alexander and how Alexander is bemused by Gwen. Alexander's mouth is open, and nothing is happening, as if he is frozen.

Nicolaus frowns. "This is Alexander, my best friend and Vice at the company."

Gwen throws a quick smile glance at her husband, and then her mind is all about Alexander. She steps up closer to him, her toothy smile big for him. "Alexander. Pleased to meet you."

Alexander nods. "Gwen," he repeats again. Nicolaus has never seen Alexander act like this. "Gwen," he says again, tasting her name in his mouth and rolling it around in his mind.

"Yes." Gwen sits to the far side of Alexander at the bar, away from Nicolaus. She is very close to Alexander, touching him. "So ... you work with Nicolaus?"

"Yes ... yes. I'm a lawyer."

"Ooh! Smart and handsome," she laughs with him, flirting.

Nicolaus sighs, not sure if he cares about what is happening between his new wife and his best friend of many years. He finishes his drink. "I'm going to go check on Niall. I'll be right back."

Alexander feels panic again, as Nicolaus quickly leaves him alone with Gwen, no chance for him to object. Gwen picks up Alexander's hand into hers. She looks at him giggling, and flirting. Alexander is not only sweating, he also is suddenly sexually aware of himself. He downs his drink and asks for another. "And you, what would you like?" he asks Gwen.

Gwen winks at him and rubs the inside of his hand. "I'll have whatever you're having." Gwen's mind reasons that it would be okay to drink, as she'd only taken half a snort of cocaine, much less than normal, as she plans to have more later.

Alexander is taken aback at how Gwen stirs him. He'd never felt this with anyone. How could she be married to Nicolaus? "So, you are Nicolaus' wife? How did that happen?"

Gwen laughs. She nods, "Yep, newly wed. How? Well, that's a story! You want to hear all about it?"

They receive their drinks. "I'm all ears!" They both take a drink, and Gwen embellishes the story of becoming Mrs. Nicolaus Ravenell.

Alexander asks Gwen many questions about her home and her family. As Gwen answers those questions, she thinks about how Nicolaus did not ask her anything about herself. Alexander also asked her about her hopes for the future, her dreams, and if she wanted children. Gwen suddenly suspects that Nicolaus has no interest to ask her any of these things. Her long talk with Alexander endeared him to her heart even more.

Chapter Fifty-Nine

A nother day of waiting at the Tallin airport, as the blizzard is expected to continue.

"The best thing is for them to be sure the aircraft is safe for flying. We don't want to go through all this and then get on a plane, only to then have it crash," Constance reminds them.

Both Deirdre and Francesca nod over their breakfast meal on day two of being snowed in.

Rachel notices that Deirdre seems to be the most worried of all of them. Rachel also notices the prayer beads in Deirdre's lap, as one hand works the beads, while the other hand works at eating her breakfast. Rachel touches Deirdre, "Deirdre, if Nigel and Nicky said they are okay, then we should believe them."

"Yes, you're right of course. I guess I'm anxious to get home."

Rachel smiles, "Yes, to get back to your man." The ladies giggle.

Francesca looks up and observes Niall and Elsa on the television. "Geez, it's no joke, the press does not play around, look at that, they are already running the story." As soon as they all look toward the television, the thirty second snippet of entertainment news about Niall is gone.

Chapter Sixty

T hough the party has ended, Gwen and Alexander are still talking, sitting closer to each other. Nicolaus is indifferent to this, and bids everyone a good night, not really caring if Gwen follows him up or not. He is more concerned about Deirdre and Constance.

Nicolaus is physically and emotionally exhausted, his ribs pained him a little. He undresses and gets into the bed of the room he now shares with Gwen. He let Gwen pick which room she wanted in his wing of the mansion. Nicolaus could sleep anywhere, as being in Special Forces trains their best soldiers to do so.

Nicolaus texted his guys and told them he had to be away from their usual four in the morning runs for the next week or two, due to an injury. Though he didn't tell his closest comrades how he received the injury, what the injury is, or that he'd been forced to marry, yet again. He isn't ready to share this with them, as he is still processing it himself. Besides, he hadn't even told Deirdre yet.

Nicolaus calls Deirdre, knowing that hearing her voice will help him be able to sleep.

"Hello, my one and only love, how are you and all my ladies doing?"

Deirdre chuckles, "We are fine, just stuck at the airport because of the weather. They say one more day. So hopefully we will get there soon."

"Why don't you all go back to the castle and wait out the storm there?"

"Well, we thought about that. It's so bad outside, I don't want to ask the driver to take such a risk. You know?"

"Oh yes, I see your point. Well, despite everything, I miss you terribly."

"I miss you too, babe." Deirdre is interrupted by Francesca. Nicolaus could hear background talking, not able to make out what is said. "Oh yeah, Nicky, Francesca wants me to let you know we are seeing reports on Niall and Elsa. The news about their wedding is international. Probably because of you and your international persona, my darling."

Nicolaus chuckles, "Probably because of stocks!"

He hears Deirdre giggle, and then Constance's voice is on the line. "Nicky, this is Constance. Is there anything we should be concerned about once we get back to the states? And is there anything we can do regarding Niall's situation?"

"Mom, thank you for offering. No, there's nothing we can do, not any of us. When you get to New York, we've arranged for you to have security. I am worried about the press once you touch down. So you'll have security in New York to get you to your connecting flight, and then again when you land in Houston, I've arranged for security to meet you. You should recognize the security team as they will have badges and jackets that say, 'private security' and they will have signs with your first names written in purple ink. Be sure those are the only people you go with. The security in Houston will stay with you and will be aboard your plane to Austin. Luckily, I was able to get them on the flight."

"Wow, Nicky, that's great! Thank you, my son." Constance smiles, knowing Nicolaus always looks out for their wellbeing.

"Yeah, I'm pretty sure the press will be trying to get to you. I want to be sure you are all protected. And of course, I'll be at the Austin airport to pick you up. So security will stay with you until they hand you off to me."

"Nicky, that is so thoughtful of you. Thank you so much."

"Of course, Mom, I'd do anything for the four of you."

Deirdre is back on the phone. "So, what did you do today?" she asks in a cheerful voice.

"Ah, well ... I, ah ... visited with many people today. Mother did a small gathering for Niall and Elsa." He didn't want to fully lie to Deirdre. Explaining all this is going to be hard enough.

"Really? And how is Elsa doing through all this? I hate that I'm not there to support her. I've been trying to call her, and I don't get an answer. I'm sure she must be very busy."

"Yes, well ..."

Gwen boisterously enters the bedroom, and plops onto the bed next to Nicolaus, in her elegant gown. "Is that Deirdre on the phone?" Nicolaus tries to hush her, putting his finger to his mouth.

"Who's that?" Deirdre asks, not recognizing the voice.

"I want to talk to Deirdre," Gwen loudly demands, handing for the phone.

Nicolaus frowns at Gwen, moves her hand away, and gets out of bed. He goes to the other side of the large and luxurious bedroom.

"Ah ..., that is Gwen ... Elsa's..."

"Elsa's sister? Wow, so nice she is there for Elsa. My understanding is that she usually does not participate in family activities."

"Yeah, well,... she is here for this one."

Gwen pursed her lips at Nicolaus, and he turns away from her, looking out the bedroom window, onto the estate grounds below. Gwen takes this moment to retrieve a small plastic bag from her jewelry box. She empties the packet onto the expensive dresser furniture piece, and quickly sniffs it into her nose. Since Nicolaus is still preoccupied with Deirdre, she grabs another packet, empties its contents, and quickly sniffs that one too. Any dust left over, she lifts with her fingers and eats it.

"Okay love, I'll talk to you tomorrow." Nicolaus ends the call, then suddenly witnesses Gwen drop her clothes where she stands and jump into bed, naked. It is obvious she has an expectation of him.

Gwen is certain Nicolaus would not know that she'd just sniffed cocaine. She beckons for her new husband to join her in the bed. Nicolaus still has his boxer briefs on, and his torso is bare. Gwen immediately is disappointed when Nicolaus gets into the bed and does not reach for her. Pushing her hurt feelings aside, she grabs onto her handsome husband. He just seems so perfect, despite the fact that she is not attracted to him, as she is to Alexander.

Nicolaus turns off his lamp and wraps his arm around Gwen, which made them be skin on skin. He settles down to sleep, quickly kissing Gwen's forehead, "Good night," he tells her.

Gwen giggles and rubs his taunt chest muscles, "Hey, not so fast, mister! This is our first night sleeping together as a married couple." Nicolaus had been evasive of her the last few nights.

Nicolaus sighs, not wanting to do anything except sleep. "Yep," he says, closing his eyes and taking a deep breath to relax for sleep.

Gwen cannot resist touching this man, her husband. She had her brain fix, now she wants her body fix too. Her hand is immediately on Nicolaus' crotch, startling him. He takes her hand from him. His reaction tickles Gwen, and she laughs heartily in a sweet way.

For her next move, Gwen is right on top of Nicolaus, taking to kissing him on his face, his neck, his chest.

Nicolaus holds her away from him. "Not tonight, please. I'm tired."

"I know you must be," she smiles at him. "I'll do all the work. You just lay back and enjoy, baby. Let me take care of you."

Nicolaus deposits Gwen back to her side of the bed. "I appreciate that, but really, I'm tired, and when I'm tired, nothing is going to happen."

"Oh," Gwen says, feeling another disappointment, not expecting this, although it does sound reasonable. "Okay, well, I'll let you rest. Then maybe in the morning will be better for you."

Gwen gets out of bed, retrieves something from her nightstand, and goes into the bathroom. Nicolaus turns on his side, Deirdre on his mind. He quickly drifts to sleep.

Chapter Sixty-One

The morning hours bring another disappointment to Gwen. She awakens from her most comfortable sleep, ever. Nicolaus is not beside her. She looks at the clock to see it is an early seven in the morning. She wonders where he is. She does take note that he is not in their suite, however, she notices signs that he'd showered and dressed.

Gwen quickly showers herself, dresses, and runs down the stairs and into the main side of the house. Again, as she reaches the breakfast table, Nicolaus is not there. All the other Ravenell family members are present. Gwen is greeted by everyone as she sits down. Not only does she enjoy the delicious breakfast, the conversation with Elsa and Nigel is enjoyable as well.

"You should have Nicolaus show you around the office. Something may even intrigue your interest to work at our VMC, as your sister does," Nigel kindly recommends.

"Don't hang around there too much, because my brother will find all kinds of things for you to do," Niall jokes. He appears to be in a better mood about things this morning. He delighted in being in the spotlight last night, with Elsa on his arm. Niall reminisces about their wedding party event last night in his mind. He looks upon Elsa and smiles, realizing that last night he felt bigger than his brother, for the first time in the history of his life.

As soon as breakfast ends, Gwen takes alone time, in her bedroom, to be on the phone with Alexander. They make future plans to meet up for lunch, and she asks him to show her around the VMC office.

"Of course I'll show you around when I get back in town! Can't wait to see you!" Alexander's ego is stroked as it hadn't been in a long time.

Gwen closes her cell phone and turns around to the stone cold face of her staring mother in-law, who gave her a fright, making her shriek as if caught doing something wrong. She did not know Ceil was in her bedroom. She touches her chest, "Oh, Mother Ceil, you frightened me."

Ceil only smiles at the comment. She slowly walks past Gwen and begins examining the bedroom she now shares with Nicolaus. Ceil picks up items off the dresser, looks at them, then puts them down. She is silent for quite a moment as she examines items that belong to Gwen: nail file, perfume bottles, hairbrush, makeup bag. "So," Ceil says loudly, trying to startle Gwen again, with success. "You are aware that I know everything about everyone in this house. There are no secrets that I don't know about."

Gwen sits down in the armless cushy chair, next to the tall box window. She has a feeling Ceil is going to tell her something.

"For instance, I even know about your dirty little secrets!" Suddenly and with dramatics, Ceil opens the little drawers on Gwen's jewelry chest to reveal the little bags of cocaine.

Gwen is horrified. Quickly, she gazes around the walls and ceilings to see if there are cameras in this room that perhaps she had not noticed before. How else would Ceil know where her stash is? Gwen just looks at Ceil with her big gray colored eyes, not sure what to say. Gwen is embarrassed, and wonders if Nicolaus knows as well.

Ceil put her at ease, "Don't worry, your secret is safe with me." Ceil sits across from her on the footboard bed shelf. "Well, as long as you stay on plan, that is."

Gwen frowns, "Plan? What do you mean?"

Ceil scoffs. "Do you really think it is just luck that you have married Nicolaus?"

Gwen frowns again, feeling confused. "I married Nicolaus at my father's demand. Didn't I?"

Ceil tilts her head to the right, "Well ... maybe ..." she teases Gwen, loving the confusion she caused in Gwen's mind that is showing on her face. "Like I said, I know about everything. And I expect you to do as I say, or little missy, the cops will know all about your little nose sniffing habit. Don't make a mistake you will regret. I know lots and lots of people. And many of those people have power and they owe me favors. I can have you locked away for a very long time, Gwen. Do you understand what I am telling you?"

Gwen touches her hand to her mouth, feeling frightened inside, owning the full throttle threat that Ceil has just given her. She nods. "What do you want me to do?"

Ceil smiles at her. "There we go! You do understand. I know who your dealer is, and I have already paid him a large sum of money to ensure that you do not run out of your little substance. All you have to do is every night when you take your sniff, make sure Nicolaus gets some too. When you start to get low, just text the words 'send more' to his number, and he will have more brought to you."

Gwen is frowning again. Everyone knows that the handsome and physically fit Nicolaus Ravenell does not do drugs. He may drink occasionally, but he is not an outright alcoholic, and he does not consume drugs. "How am I to get him to take it?"

Ceil stands, "Well, you'll have to figure that out, now won't you? And you'd better do it. And you start tonight."

Gwen also stands, her tall, thin body higher than Ceil's. "Mother Ceil, why am I doing this to Nicolaus? I didn't catch that part of the plan."

"You didn't catch it because I didn't tell you. Don't worry about the why, and you are not to discuss this with anyone, not even Elsa. Just stick to your job, or I'll have you locked up."

Ceil uses the dresser mirror to check her beautiful, lush black hair for which not one strand of gray showed, then she quickly exits the bedroom.

Being fully intimidated, Gwen immediately begins working on the plan. She goes online to see how she could administer the drug to Nicolaus.

Chapter Sixty-Two

"Nicolaus, son, where are you?" Nigel's curiosity is heard over the phone. Gwen is driving him crazy trying to figure out when Nicolaus is returning home.

"I'm still at the office, working late, is all."

"Hmm, working late, or working to avoid a certain someone?"

"Well ...," Nicolaus paused his attention on the income reports he is studying, "maybe a little of both. I really do have lots to do and ..."

"And it can wait until tomorrow."

"Just tell her I'll see her ... tomorrow."

Nigel chuckles. "Tomorrow? I said your work can wait until tomorrow, not Gwen!"

"Well ... there is a bathroom shower here, and I have extra clothes for such occasions. I need to get through these finance reports. The board is expecting to know about this at our next meeting."

"Nicolaus, our next meeting is in three weeks," Nigel chuckles again, fully understanding his son's dilemma. "Look, son, you could at least give Gwen a call."

"And actually, I'll be picking up Deirdre and our ladies. Their plane gets in at seven in the morning."

"Oh no. Don't do that! You won't make it back in one piece, the reporters will be all over you. Let the driver get them. If you want to be the one to tell Deirdre what happened, you'd better do it here, or at her house. I'll tell you what, I'll give a call to Francesca. Let me be the fall guy. I'll tell them I sent you on an important errand and you won't be able to meet them at the airport. Those reporters will ..."

"Okay, father, you're right. I hadn't thought about that."

"Okay. Nicolaus, close up shop and get home. Gwen is anxious."

"All right then, I'll be home in a bit."

Home in a bit turned into seven in the morning. Nicolaus is hoping Gwen would be fast asleep. As he enters the bedroom, he is relieved to see that she is still soundly sleeping. He knew Deirdre and the ladies would be at the house in about an hour if their plane is on time.

Nicolaus peels off his clothes and jumps in the shower to ready himself for the day. He is glad he had completed some items that needed tending to at the office for today, because he expects the day to be rough, and he probably would not make it back to work. His brain has been nonstop searching for the words he will use to explain to Deirdre and her mother that he is married again.

Nicolaus quietly completes his morning routine, a total of forty-five minutes, dressing casually. As he exits the bedroom Gwen is still peacefully sleeping.

The noisy hinge of the bedroom door awakens Gwen. She looks at the clock and stretches herself. Seeing the morning sun through the curtains prompts her to yawn and stretch again, which brushed her nostrils with the usual good and clean smell of her husband. "Nicolaus," she calls to an empty room.

Gwen leaps from the bed and runs to the bathroom, expecting to see her husband, only to find evidence that he had arrived home. Excited to see him, Gwen showers, then flawlessly applies her makeup, finishing up with a drag of a comb through her hair.

Downstairs, Nicolaus greets Rachel with a kiss and a sweet full-on hug, then Constance, then Francesca, and then his love – Deirdre. Nicolaus steadfastly embraces Deirdre, never wanting to let her go. He is not sure how upset she will be once she learns the dreadful news. Would he ever be able to hold her again?

Deirdre clings to her man, feeling weak from his love, gladly accepting his kisses on her forehead. She'd missed him so much, she just wants to fill her soul with his presence. She is relieved to see that he is okay.

Nigel flies down the stairs to greet everyone. "Ah, you finally made it back. Welcome home!" he tells them, scooping each woman into a gentle bear hug.

"Nigel, is everyone okay?" Rachel inquires.

"Yes, yes, we all survived. Though it is kind of crazy to be held hostage in one's own home. Nevertheless, we are grateful no one was hurt beyond repair."

"Beyond repair? That does not sound good, Uncle Nigel," Francesca remarks. "So what actually happened? You were held hostage?" Francesca notices the ring on Nicolaus' marriage finger. She lifts his hand off Deirdre to examine the ring. "What gives, Nicky, you started without us?" her keen tongue chides him.

"Elsa's father was not playing around," Nigel starts to explain. "He had several armed men with him. I wasn't sure how far he'd go."

"He had an army with him. Must have been at least twenty-five or thirty men," Nicolaus adds, supporting his father's version of events.

"They were armed, you say?" Constance asks, extremely concerned about those men coming back.

"Yes," Nigel nods, assuming this to be true, though remembering he had not exactly seen any weapons. "They held all of us, even the staff."

"And no one called the police?" Francesca asks.

Nigel shakes his head, "They made sure we didn't call the police. Anyway, I'm not sure what good that would have done. Probably would have made the situation worse."

"So, Niall was forced to marry Elsa?" Francesca wants clarification, knowing this would not be a good thing for Elsa.

Nigel nods again, and then points to Nicolaus, as if to give him the floor.

"I'm so sorry, I ..." Nicolaus struggles to explain. Suddenly, his words are cut off by his new wife.

"Oh my God!" Gwen says loudly with boisterous energy. "Everyone is here? Where is Deirdre? Where is she?"

Deirdre frowns, as she continues to cling to Nicolaus. "Gwen?"

Gwen walks through the crowd of family to the location of Deirdre's voice. "Oh my God!" she says again, with her pearly white toothy grin, her makeup perfect against her tanned skin and dirty blonde curly hair. She walks right up to Deirdre. "My God! You are beautiful, just like all the magazines and everybody says." She takes Deirdre's hand from Nicolaus' torso, to gently shake it. "I'm so happy to finally meet you. My sister talks good things about you all the time," Gwen's smile is big. Gwen's eye caught that of Nicolaus, and she finally sees that he and Deirdre are in a hug. She smiles brighter, figuring he hadn't told her anything yet.

Gwen turns from them, and goes to Constance, feeling star struck. "Oh my God, you must be Deirdre's mother! I see the resemblance. So nice to meet you ma'am," Gwen gently touches her hand with both of hers.

Gwen giggles when she sees Francesca, "And you're that fiery Francesca!" She reaches for and takes Francesca's' hand to shake it. "From England! So wonderful to meet you. I hope we can be friends, Francesca." Francesca smiles at Gwen with no words, not sure what to make of her yet.

Gwen scoots herself to Rachel with open arms for a hug. "And you are the famous Rachel Kiviste!"

"Famous? Well, I wouldn't say that..."

"Loved, and has many secrets," Gwen offers up her knowledge of Rachel.

Rachel frowns, feeling something is way off here. She removes herself from Gwen's embrace and stands next to Nicolaus. "Nicky, you were about to say something?"

"Did you tell them yet, honey?" Gwen asks him.

"Honey?" Francesca quickly repeats.

Gwen places herself to stand next to Nicolaus and Rachel, on the opposite side from Deirdre, still smiling, loving the new family she is inheriting.

"Yes, I ... ah, ... I ..." Nicolaus is having trouble finding words, with all the women frowning at him; all except Gwen.

"Haven't you told them yet?" Nicolaus hears Ceil's voice from the top of the stairs.

An anxiety wave washes over Nicolaus, and he just wants to leave. His grip on Deirdre tightens from fear of losing her, despite Gwen standing right next to him. He feels Gwen's hands on his back and shoulder, she is still smiling.

This whole situation is like a sick movie scene to Nicolaus. He doesn't want to say what has to be said. And now Ceil's presence is making it even more difficult.

Nigel steps in, "Well, ladies," all their eyes and attention shift to Nigel, "what Nicolaus is trying to say, is ... that ... well ... he and Gwen were also forced to marry, at the same time Niall and Elsa married."

"What?" Rachel cannot believe it.

"No!" Deirdre drops her arms from Nicolaus and slowly backs out of his grip. She turns away to process what was just said.

Francesca laughs quietly, though the situation is not funny. She holds up Nicolaus' hand which has the marriage band to examine it. "Are you freakin' kidding me? How can that happen a second time to the same person? Gotta be a world record or something."

Deirdre flings herself around again to face Nicolaus. "Nicolaus, can I please speak to you in private?" she asks him sternly.

"Of course." They go into the library, which is the furthest from everyone. Nicolaus closes the doors. "Deirdre, you've got to know I didn't want this. I would never ..."

"So what happened? I'm still not clear on this," she interrupts him.

Nicolaus sighs, "They broke into the house, here. Elsa's father beat up Niall pretty badly, and several men were holding me down. I couldn't do anything. I tried to refuse to marry, but they had my parents, and threatened their lives. All I could do is what they wanted."

"My God! Did they hurt you, Nicky?"

"Nothing I can't handle. Niall was hurt worse. He was in the hospital for a few days. They roughed up my parents, too."

Deirdre is quickly by his side again, her automatic reaction to him, however, she then pulls back, realizing he is not hers, yet again. "So, you getting the marriage annulled? You were under duress and ..."

"I can't do anything to upset her, or her father will be back threatening the lives of my parents again. He promised us this."

Deirdre takes another step back from her love, frowning. "So ... you're trapped. Again."

Nicolaus sighs, his heart breaking, seeing that Deirdre is continually distancing herself from him. "If we could've just already been married ..."

"What? Are you saying this is my fault?" She is shocked at his words.

Nicolaus sighs again, shaking his head, feeling this is surreal, and still not sure what to do. He still feels like he has no control, and that he can do nothing to fix any of this. "No! I don't know what I'm saying ...."

"We wouldn't have been married yet anyway. I actually wanted you to go to Estonia, so we could be married amongst our ancestors in St. Nicholas Church. It just seemed fitting. Instead ...." She waives her arm in the air and turns from him again, feeling crushed, again.

"Deirdre, I'm so sorry ... I ..."

She turns to face him again, interrupting his empty apology, "No. Something is not right here. Something is blocking us from getting married. Maybe it's not meant to be after all." Deirdre sits herself down, weakened with love for this man. "Maybe I have been completely wrong all these years." Deirdre thought about how many times Nicolaus had proposed to her, and how long she'd put him off, sticking to their engagement of purity for ten long years, and two additional years because of his doomed marriage to Marguerite. Perhaps, maybe, this is her fault, after all.

Deirdre wants to cry and can muster no tears. Perhaps, finally, she has no more tears to cry, or perhaps crying, now, would change nothing. Anyway, no matter how much she cried, if she could cry, Nicolaus Ravenell is not going to be her husband.

Chapter Sixty-Three

Gwen wraps lightly on the library door before entering. She enters and sits down, right next to Deirdre. She gives Deirdre her signature toothy smile, "I'm so sorry about all this. I know it's supposed to be you married to Nicolaus. I mean everybody knows that!

Believe me, this is all a shock for me too. I had no idea my father was going to do all this. Elsa didn't know either. By the way, Elsa loves you so much and she is horribly afraid that you will hate her for the rest of her life.

Please don't be mad at Nicolaus, cause he did try to fight against this. My father made his men shut Nicolaus up, and they hurt him. He was in the hospital for a few days, but he doesn't have any internal bleeding or anything. Deirdre, I just want to say I'm really sorry, and I do hope we can be friends." Finally stopping for air, Gwen looks to Nicolaus, "You do want us to be friends, Nicky, don't you?"

Nicolaus slightly smiles at Gwen and nods.

"Well, anyway, I promise to take good care of him. I want to be a good wife, and be a good friend to you too, Deirdre."

"Yes, well, I appreciate that Gwen," Deirdre tells her, not knowing what else to say.

Deirdre stands, "Well, mother and I are going home. We both need some rest. The last couple of days have been really trying. I guess for all of us." She touches Nicolaus on the chest again. "Nicky, I don't blame you. Gwen is right. I'm very glad you are okay, and not hurt worse than you were. Same for Niall. I love you both, and ...." She frowned, unable to finish her sentence.

Deirdre leaves the married couple and pulls her mother by the hand to go home.

Nicolaus is lost as he watches Deirdre walk out the door with Constance behind her. He fears she hates him. Nothing is to be done right now, as he knows both ladies need their rest. Nicolaus holds on to the frame of the front door to keep himself from running after Deirdre.

Gwen is right behind Nicolaus. She hugs onto her husband. "It will be okay. We'll make it be okay," she whispers to him, then lays her head on Nicolaus' strong shoulder.

Chapter Sixty-Four

"**D**eirdre, I can't believe it!" Maggie hugs Deirdre to her. She and Ishani went right over when Constance called them upset and worried about Deirdre, after the horrid news was dropped on them.

Ishani is really worried, as Deirdre seems despondent, and is not crying. "It's not fair, honey. How much more are you supposed to suffer for Nicolaus? Maybe it's time to cut your ties with him. Deirdre, you deserve so much better."

Deirdre is out of words as well as tears. She sighs, exhausted. She lays her head back onto the couch. "You might be right. Maybe my thinking is faulty. Nicky even had the thought that this is my fault because we should have already been married."

"What? Oh, that's crap!" Maggie defends Deirdre.

"He took it back ,... though ... he's probably right. We could have been married years ago, when he first asked me."

"Dee this is not on you. Don't let him do that to you," Ishani is defiant.

"Oh he doesn't mean it that way. Although he's right. I should have married him years ago. Now I may never get to marry him at all. I hesitated again, and again he has been taken from me."

"Or ..." Maggie tries to logically think this through, "maybe ... just maybe Nicky isn't the one for you. Deirdre, maybe he's not ..."

Deirdre shot up from her laying down position. "Well, I even thought that maybe I'd been wrong all these years. And, then I think ... how can that be?" She sighs again, "Anyway, it's not as if Nicky chose any of this. It's all being forced on him. He's suffering too." Deirdre returned to laying down. "I'm so tired, I can't even think right now." The ladies hug her in support. "I don't even want to think about this right now."

Chapter Sixty-Five

Later that night, as Gwen readies herself for bed, she notices that Nicolaus is about to leave the room. Gwen frowns, "Nicky, where are you going?"

Nicolaus sighs, not wanting to deal with Gwen. "I've got some work I need to review. I'll be to bed in about an hour."

"Nicolaus, it's almost midnight."

In an unusual manner, he snaps at Gwen, frowning, "I know what time it is," turning to leave.

"Hold on there, buster!" Gwen is surprised when he stops at her words. "We're not doing this every night. If it's one thing I learned from Elsa, who is beautiful and smart, is that I need to set the ground rules early in my relationship. So, this is the first rule, ... when I go to bed, you go to bed with me. Nicky, I'm not going to chase you down. Look, I know I'm not Deirdre, but I am your wife and I expect you to respect me as your wife," Gwen tells him sternly, as if determined to make their sham marriage work, for some reason.

Nicolaus has hesitation about what to do. He turns to leave, and her next words stop him in his tracks again.

"No you don't, buster!" Gwen folds her arms. "I wonder how my daddy would feel if I called him right now and told him what you are doing to me."

In anger, Nicolaus turns and glares at Gwen. It is bad enough that the threat is implied and continually hanging over the Ravenell's heads. The action of her pulling the threat into reality brought anger to him. Nicolaus sighs loudly, "Fine!" He closes the door, undresses, and gets into bed with his financial reports and his unwanted wife.

With her wifey smile, Gwen sits on Nicolaus' lap, under the covers. She is dressed in a skimpy negligée. "Rule number two," she grabs the papers from him, and flings them over her shoulder, throwing them onto the floor. "No work until after play!"

Nicolaus cannot believe she'd just thrown fifty pages of his report onto the floor, scattering them everywhere.

Gwen holds his face to hers. "Don't worry about those papers, Nicky. Worry about me! I need you, my sweet husband."

Gwen didn't care much that Nicolaus was not very active or participatory during their love making. She only needed his effective manhood to satisfy herself. She had put cocaine on her lipstick, so when she kissed him, she made sure to rub it off on him, and get it in his mouth.

After several bouts of orgasm, Gwen finally pulls off Nicolaus, leaving him exhausted and feeling weird. His mouth and tongue are numb. Having had her fix, Gwen quickly falls asleep. Nicolaus feels very stressed as he looked at the papers all over the floor. He decides he'll wait until morning to pick them up. For now, he just wants to sleep.

Chapter Sixty-Six

Nicolaus arrived at Deirdre's before going to the office. Constance opens the door, and greets him with the usual kiss and hug, wanting to impress upon him, that despite what has happened, she still loves him as her son. "Strawberry streusel muffins?" he asks, handing her the box of sweets.

"How did you know? We were just making plans to go pick these up."

Nicolaus kisses Constance, the woman who has been his mother figure his whole life. He smiles at her, "I had a hunch!" he chuckles lightly.

"Nicky, are you okay, dear? You don't look well."

Nicolaus enters the kitchen, washes his hands, and retrieves little plates for them to eat the muffins. "You know, actually, I'm not feeling well. Not sure why."

Constance gently touches both sides of his face and feels his forehead. "Hmm, you are not hot at all, hmm, you certainly don't look right."

"I couldn't sleep last night. I have a lot on my mind."

"I can imagine," Deirdre's voice is heard from the stairs. She enters in her pajamas and robe. Nicolaus can't take his loving eyes off her. Deirdre greets her stolen man with a light, quick hug. "Nicky, you look sick or something."

"I was just telling him that. He does not seem to have a fever, though," Constance informs her.

"I've never known you to get sick."

"I think you should go see a doctor. Just get yourself checked. Especially after everything that's happened," Constance suggests.

Nicolaus nods, not sure if he would. "I can't apologize enough for what I've put both of you through. I'm so sorry."

"Nicky, you're sorry for saving your parents? That's nonsense!"

"Deirdre, you're not upset?"

"Well, of course I'm upset, but what good is it going to do? My upset changes nothing! I'm just done with it." Deirdre frowns and takes a bite of muffin to keep herself from crying. Constance touches her hand.

Nicolaus sighs. He knows Deirdre is extremely disappointed, and probably distressed. He is angry. "Next week, Francesca and I are going to translate the Kiviste history and see if we can find some clues about why this is happening."

"Okay, but let's stop talking about it. I don't want you to feel like you need to apologize every time you see us, Nicky. I'm taking that off you right now. Okay?"

Nicolaus nods, "Okay," he says softly, appreciating Deirdre's gesture, but not feeling the weight of the situation being lifted from him at all. He sighs again, "Well, I hate to eat and run, but I've got a meeting this morning." Nicolaus stands and kisses both ladies on the forehead. "I'll see you later."

As Nicolaus leaves the house, Constance takes Deirdre's hand, holding her emotions steady. "Deirdre ..."

"Really, Mom, I'm okay," she tells her in a slow, monotone pitch, as she pretends not to be shaken by this tragedy, for which she and Nicolaus are the main stars. Deirdre grabs another muffin, and sips her coffee, while the forehead kiss sears straight to her heart.

Chapter Sixty-Seven

A few weeks later, one of the male staff members of the Ravenell mansion approaches Gwen, "Mistress Gwen, you have a visitor."

Without hesitating, Gwen's face lights up when she looks at the clock. She motions to the staff member, "Let him on in!"

Gwen lit up even more, if that were possible, when Alexander appears before her in the library, where she was reading a book about marriage. She'd found herself to be terribly bored in her marriage with Nicolaus. She realized he was mostly avoiding her. By the time Nicolaus returned home from work, he seemed exhausted, didn't pay attention to her, and he never took her anywhere. They never had any fun, as Gwen thought they would. Not only is she bored, Nicolaus made it clear to her that he is not happy, since she is not Deirdre. She couldn't imagine how her marriage to Nicolaus would get any better.

Alexander suavely walks over and takes Gwen's hand as she stands. Lovingly, he kisses her soft hand. Their eyes meet and sexual chemistry is popping all over the place. Gwen is completely assured in this moment that her father picked the wrong man for her to marry. At this very moment, she knows it is Alexander who should be her husband. He held her eyes with his as the magic continually played between them. Gwen's heart flutters. Suddenly, she doesn't care that she is Mrs. Ravenell; she has to find a way to deal with this new reality.

They join hands and look deeper into each other's eyes. Gwen giggles like a schoolgirl, knowing that Alexander wants her just as much as she wants him.

Alexander can't believe how moved he is anytime he is near Gwen. He now understands what Nicolaus is going through regarding Deirdre. Alexander concludes that loving Gwen just might cost him everything, however ... for love, it is a chance he is willing to take.

"What kind of wicked spell have you cast on me? I couldn't stop thinking about you my whole trip in Switzerland." Alexander asks Gwen, trembling, wanting to kiss her sweet looking lips.

Gwen chuckles, "It's not a spell. I feel it too! I'm so glad we kept in touch while you were gone."

"You know, I've done a lot of thinking about us. I realize I could lose everything for being in love with you, Gwen. I'd rather take this chance of love with you, even if I lost everything, than to never have loved you at all, Gwen," Alexander tells her romantically, drawing closer to her.

"Oh Alexander! That is so sweet!" Gwen finds her toothy grin hard to put away. Suddenly, she is in his arms, his hands to the small of her back. They are pressed against each other.

"Let's go!" Alexander needs to get her away from the house so he could do the thing he'd been dreaming about for days - kiss her.

Out the door, Alexander steers his convertible sports car along the Austin 360 highway. The day is sunny and bright. He pulls into the parking lot of a popular Mexican restaurant that is just off the highway. He turns to Gwen, going directly for her lips. At first he tastes her soft lips. Then, with hot passion, he pulls her into his arms, fully kissing her, loving her response. Joy courses through Alexander, like he'd never experienced before.

He had to stop himself, as he envisioned pulling this woman to the back seat of his car, and making love to her right there in the open. Instead, he breaks the kiss, jumps out the car, and assists her out. They enter the restaurant for a lunch meal.

Inside the restaurant, Alexander and Gwen sit very close to each other, with non-stop touching in a corner booth. Gwen entangles her arm around Alexander's, her other hand on his thigh. This makes Alexander edgy with excitement.

"Gwen, I know you are Nicolaus' wife, and he may hate me forever for intervening, but ..."

Gwen dives to kiss Alexander's mouth before he can finish his sentence.

"How are we going to do this?" Alexander asks Gwen.

Gwen flashes her signature smile at Alexander. "Uhm, I don't care. Four star hotel, sleazy hotel, no hotel ... whatever you want." Her sexual addiction kicking in strong, as she moves incredibly closer to Alexander, her hand moving up his thigh. She kisses him again. Gwen is certain she's going to have this man one way or the other.

Chapter Sixty-Eight

Alexander guides Gwen through the elevator door to Elsa's desk. "And this is where your sister works," he tells her, as part of the office tour.

Elsa is surprised, and she immediately frowns, seeing how Gwen is looking upon Alexander. She already knew this would spell trouble. "Alexander! And Gwen! What are you doing here? Together!" Elsa gestures her head to the side for Gwen to talk to her privately.

"Oh, Alexander offered to show me around the office," Gwen answers. "Oh, excuse me hon, my sister wants a word," she tells Alexander recognizing Elsa's head gesture.

"Gwen," Elsa whispers, while Alexander went into the conference room, "what are you doing?"

Gwen frowns, "I told you, Alexander offered to show me around the office."

Elsa jerks on Gwen's arm, "Ah-uhn, but what are you doing? I see how you are looking at Alexander." She pulls on her arm again. "Nicolaus is here somewhere."

Gwen takes her arm from her nervous sister. "I don't care that Nicolaus is here. I'm with the man I want to be with." Gwen sighs, "Daddy got it all wrong. He should have made me marry Alexander."

"Gwen, you cannot be serious!"

"Gwen, I didn't know you were here," Nicolaus' voice says from behind them. Both sisters twirl around to see Nicolaus, as Alexander steps out of the conference room. Nicolaus smiles at Alexander, "Hey, Alexander, there you are! I have been looking for you. You still having your two o'clock meeting with the staff? I have a paper for you."

Gwen eases herself back to Alexander and entwines her arm with his. "Alexander is showing me around today," she flashes her now signature smile at her handsome husband.

"Oh. Okay," Nicolaus tells her, his own smile fading away. He notices how Gwen's eyes are lit up as she admires Alexander, not sparing Nicolaus an ounce of mystery.

Alexander remains silent, not sure what to say. He didn't think Gwen would be so open. He knew he'd have to talk to her about that.

"Well, I'll just place it on your desk." Nicolaus turns to leave, "I'll see everyone later," his voice echoes from the hallway.

"Gwen," Elsa whispers, shaking her head in disappointment, as the two carry on like a couple in love. Alexander had another half hour before his meeting.

Chapter Sixty-Nine

That evening, Gwen and Alexander are uncontrollably drawn to each other. In the luxurious hotel room, Gwen places a line of cocaine on the length of her thumb, and snorts it.

"Wait a minute, is that what I think it is?" Alexander asks her. Gwen nods. "You want some?"

Alexander ponders this for a moment. He does not want to seem uncool. He nods, then takes a hit of the illegal substance. Without hesitation, Alexander makes passionate love to Gwen. The cocaine increases the intensity of the sexual experience for both Gwen and Alexander. Gwen is voracious, and Alexander is enjoying every minute.

Nicolaus grew concerned when Gwen did not show up for dinner. She never missed a meal. "Elsa, do you know where Gwen went? She's not answering her phone."

"Oh, so sorry Nicolaus, I really don't know where she is," Elsa answers truthfully, glad he didn't ask her who she is with.

Ceil observes how pale Nicolaus is looking. He seems to be without energy, as she watched in the early morning hours when he couldn't make his usual runs. She had been watching Gwen and Nicolaus through the peep hole she had placed on the wall in the passageway of the mansion, which peered into their bedroom.

Through that peep hole, Ceil saw Gwen rub so much cocaine powder on Nicolaus, it made him droopy, and unable to speak or get up. She watched as Gwen put more of the powder into his mouth while he slept, then take advantage of his incapacitated body. Ceil giggled to herself, wondering when Nicolaus was going to drop.

"What's the matter, Nicolaus? Lose a wife?" Ceil taunts him.

Nicolaus ignores Ceil's tone, "Yes, I'm a little worried. She's not answering her phone."

"Well, hopefully she is all right. Now let's sit down for dinner," Ceil instructs them.

Later, after dinner, when Nicolaus walks into the drawing room, he sees the end of Niall's hard slap across Elsa's face as he manhandles her. The slap twirls Elsa around and knocks her to the floor. Niall starts to grab Elsa up, however, Nicolaus moves him away from her.

"What's wrong with you, Niall?" Nicolaus stoops and helps the defenseless and pregnant Elsa to her feet. She holds the side of her face and cries.

Niall lunges at Nicolaus, shoving him backwards, "Get your hands off my wife!" Niall yells at his brother with obsessive crazy.

Nicolaus frowns at him deeply, "Have you gone mad?"

Immaturely, Niall now turns his unjustified abuse of Elsa onto Nicolaus. Enraged, Niall charges Nicolaus again, plunging his head into Nicolaus' rib cage with all his might, not caring whether or not he hurt his brother. They both fall backwards, knocking over tables and things, until they land onto the floor.

Seeing he had the upper hand, Niall quickly throws a punch to Nicolaus' face, cutting his lip, stunning him. Niall continues his attack, however, Nicolaus employs defensive moves, and Niall is not able to strike him again.

Elsa runs from the room to get help. "Please hurry, they are going to kill each other!" she franticly tells the men of the house, her own mouth bleeding.

By the time Nigel and Manfred rush into the drawing room, Nicolaus has Niall in a restraint hold, on top of him, Niall's face to the floor. Nicolaus used this same maneuver during his military service for unruly people. The restraint is effective without being harmful.

Manfred has to work to get Nicolaus loose of Niall. Ceil rushes in and panics when she sees Niall on the floor. "You brute!" Ceil yells her favorite insult at Nicolaus, her military hero son, not caring what has transpired, not caring that Niall has battered Elsa. "Look what you've done!" She went to her knees beside Niall, who is unhurt, babying him.

Nigel says nothing, he just looks upon Nicolaus with dismay, not understanding what happened. Nicolaus shakes his head and starts to leave, without explaining anything. Elsa catches him by the arm, as she wants to thank him for saving her. However, Nicolaus can't even look at her. He's too angry. When Nigel sees this interaction between Elsa and Nicolaus, and he notices Elsa's bleeding lip, he quickly understands what most likely transpired, however, Nicolaus leaves their presence.

Nicolaus walks out of the house. He walks the grounds, upset with himself. He didn't know how else he could have gotten Niall off Elsa without hurting him. He doesn't understand what happened to his brother, it is as if Niall is regressing somehow. The better man Niall had found, somehow seems to be hidden, and the unpleasant Niall is now front and center.

Nicolaus is overcome with emotion in the pit of his stomach, and vomit is forced up, landing behind the rose bushes, his ribs jarringly painful again. He wonders if painful ribs would be a theme with the Baird family.

It took quite a while before Nicolaus felt that he could face Niall. After cleaning up, Nicolaus found Niall sitting on the west lawn, alone, in a patio chair, watching the sunset. Nicolaus joins him.

Nicolaus sighs. "Hey, I'm sorry for what happened earlier," he apologizes, knowing damn well it is Niall who should be apologizing to him.

"You could've hurt my shoulders," Niall yells at Nicolaus in a childlike manner, rubbing his unhurt shoulder. He moves his right arm in a circle, while Nicolaus' cut lip is swelling.

"I said I'm sorry," he snaps at his brother. "You have to admit, you really pushed me to hit you. I could have returned your punch, but I didn't. And speaking of hitting, why were you hitting Elsa? We don't hit on our wives or girlfriends, you know. That is not what we Ravenells do."

"I have my reasons."

Nicolaus looks at him, frowning, surprised at his words. "Well, you had better not hit Elsa again. If you do, you'll have to contend with me, Niall," Nicolaus sternly warns him, determined to defend Elsa, and to stop Niall's abusive behavior towards her.

Niall stares at his older brother. "Is that all you have to offer me? Empty threats?"

"It's not an empty threat."

"You haven't spoken to me for weeks now, since we left the hospital, and this is all you have to say to me?"

Nicolaus sighs at Niall's complaint, figuring his brother needs to talk about what happened with Elsa's father. "I have not spoken to you because I have been angry at my circumstance. I don't have much to say."

"So you just ignore me?"

"Look, if you had not ..." Nicolaus stopped himself, feeling the anger inside grow, his ribs still aching.

"Say it, Nicolaus," Niall challenges him.

"Forget it!"

"No! Say it! It's all my fault. I know you want to say it."

"Look Niall, I don't think it's all your fault. Maybe if you had just acknowledged Elsa, maybe a little ... things might be different," he sighs, feeling raw emotions emerging again. "I told you to take responsibility for the baby!" Nicolaus half yells at him.

"Damn it, Nicolaus! Do you think I'm happy about any of this?"

"Well, at least you have Elsa. You know Elsa. I had never even met Gwen before, and ...," he stops himself again. He knows that complaining is not going to fix anything. "Let's just leave this matter alone. What's done is done, and it cannot be changed."

Niall frowns at Nicolaus, hating that he always orders him about, telling him what to do. Niall felt the need to stir more uneasiness into Nicolaus' life. "Did Deirdre ever tell you I proposed to her?"

"What?" Nicolaus glares at him, frowning. He can see that Niall wants to get him more upset for some reason. Maybe he actually wants another fight.

"Yeah, when she turned you down, I proposed to her. She was a hot little thing too! Told me she would think about it."

Nicolaus looks at Niall doubtfully, his brain calculating that he is referring to the time he'd just got engaged to Elsa, and Deirdre left the country to think about the consequences of marrying into the Ravenell family. "Deirdre never turned me down. And I'm sure she was extending you a courtesy. I hope you were able to take the hint, Niall. I really hope you will be respectful to Elsa, and honor her as your wife." Nicolaus felt agitated, just as Niall wanted. "And I really do not want to discuss this with you, again." Nicolaus rose from the chair. He left Niall's presence.

As Nicolaus saunters away, he realizes he is getting thrown into a world of domestic violence the same which Helena is living with her own husband. Except, this time, he has no leverage to encourage better behavior from Niall. As usual, there is nothing he can do to change the behaviors of any of his immediate family members.

Feeling very miserable, Nicolaus stays away from everyone.

Chapter Seventy-One

The following day, after the dinner hour, Nicolaus went over to Francesca's so they could get started on the translation. "Nicky! What's wrong with you? You got the flu or something?" Francesca frowns at his sickly appearance, and what seems to be a downtrodden spirit.

"No, I just haven't been feeling well."

"What did the doc say?"

"I haven't been to the doctor, yet. I'll go ..."

"What? Oh hell no, let's go. Right now! You look awful. And you don't feel well either? This is not like you, Love. And what happened to your lip?"

He touches his sore lip. "Niall was acting crazy."

Francesca shakes her head. "Well, you must see a doctor. Let's go, I'm driving."

Francesca takes Nicolaus to an urgent care clinic. When the medical staff see him, they immediately take him to the back to get his vitals. The physician quickly enters the patient room. "Hello, I'm Dr. Gughilmo Patel. And you are Nicolaus Ravenell?"

"Yes," Francesca answers for Nicolaus, ready to give the doctor the full scoop. "Look doc, I'm his cousin. He looks terrible. Right? This ain't our Nicky. Our Nicky is tough and strong, and he runs every morning. Nicky, you've been running?"

"No, I can't make the runs. I try, and then my chest hurts. That's never happened before."

"Well, that's not good. You been abroad? Or in contact with anyone sick?" The doctor asks him.

"No, not that I know of."

"He usually works too hard and too much. I've never seen him like this, doc."

"Okay, well, you do look sickly, and your vitals are not good. What happened to your lip? Looks like you may have been in a scuffle or something."

Nicolaus nods without words, not wanting to explain the ridiculous behavior of his brother.

"Okay. Let me have some blood drawn. We can get the results in about twenty minutes. I want to test you for everything, including sexually transmitted diseases, and drugs, and we'll get an EKG to check your heart. Is that okay with you, Nicolaus?"

Nicolaus nods in agreement with the plan.

"Do you take any illicit drugs, Mr. Ravenell?"

"No. Nothing. I have been having trouble sleeping, though."

"Doc, he's a military hero. He's not on drugs!"

"Well, sometimes our military heroes get into trouble. Okay, I'll have the nurse draw some blood, get the EKG, and some ice and ointment for your lip. You can both stay here in the room until I get the test results."

Chapter Seventy-Two

Alexander brought Gwen to the mansion, though he shouldn't have been driving at all, since he'd taken cocaine earlier. He escorts Gwen up to the door, and passionately kisses her again, making Gwen giggle. Alexander had never experienced anyone like Gwen before. He knows he is smitten and doesn't know what he is going to do about Nicolaus. He departs from Gwen feeling giddy, high, and happy.

"Gwen!" Elsa jerks at her arm again, no one else is around. "What did you do?" She whispers harshly.

"I'm in love, girl!" Gwen shouts loudly, flinging her arms into the air, wanting the whole world to hear.

"Shh! Shut up!" Elsa harshly whispers to her. She whisks Gwen upstairs to the bedroom she shares with Niall, closing the door.

Gwen flings her arms into the air again, with a huge smile on her face, "I'm in love, girl!" she repeats loudly again.

Elsa grabs her arms down, "Stop it! Cut it out!"

"What? Did I do something wrong?" Gwen asks in sarcasm.

"Stop it!" Elsa yells at her, louder than a whisper this time. She shakes her head in disapproval again. "Gwen, you know you cannot do this to Nicky. He had to give up Deirdre, against his will, to marry you!"

Gwen sits down. "Gosh, you sure know how to bust a happy balloon," she tells Elsa, her voice full of disappointment.

"Nicky was looking for you, again. He kept calling you."

"Oh really? I ... I turned my phone off. I didn't want any interruptions while I was with my Alexander." She looks into her little purse. "Oops, actually, I don't even know where my phone is," she says of her eight hundred dollar cell phone, as she rummages through her purse, unable to find it.

Despondent, Elsa sits down, next to her sister. She couldn't believe how bad this had gone so fast for Nicolaus. Just like before.

"Oh Elsa, don't worry. I'll think up a story to tell Nicolaus. I think he barely cares anyway. I'll make up something."

Gwen gets up and exits the room, not even noticing that Elsa has new bruises on her face, or that Elsa seems downhearted.

Gwen bumps right into Niall. She touches his shoulder, "Oh sorry, Niall." Gwen doesn't bother to think if Niall may have heard her conversation or not. She only has two things on her mind, her magic dust, and her new love.

Gwen happily bounces herself to the wing of the mansion she shares with Nicolaus, and goes right to her cocaine stash. One hit isn't enough. She gets more, snorts it, then gets another baggie, and snorts that too. She enjoys her high, and then is fast asleep across the chair in no time.

Chapter Seventy-Three

"So, Nicolaus," Dr. Patel looks at him suspiciously, "how long have you been taking cocaine?"

"Cocaine? What? I don't take cocaine."

Dr. Patel lifts an eyebrow, "Well, that's not what your blood work says." He provides the test results to Nicolaus.

"What the fu ... hell?" Francesca interjects, repressing her more colorful language.

"Are you sure this is mine?" Nicolaus frowns, seeing the result. "Doc, I swear to you, I don't take drugs! Not cocaine, or marijuana, or anything."

"Well, it's getting in your bloodstream somehow."

Nicolaus frowns. "I don't understand. How can that be?"

"You said you haven't been sleeping? Are you waking up and finding yourself somewhere else besides your bed, like down the street, or another room, or the kitchen, in a drug house, or something?"

"No. Nothing like that. I just seem to wake up with the same dream. I can't move, and I see ...."

"Go on!" Francesca demands.

"I see my wife. She seems to be ... having ... relations with me, but I'm not sure. I can't move and I can't wake up. Everything is blurry."

"Hmm, you know, we don't know his new wife very well. Do we Nicolaus? I don't trust her. I didn't get a good vibe when I met her. And everything was so rushed. Doc, could she be doing something to him? Like drugging him? What about that date drug?"

"I don't know," Dr. Patel shakes his head, not wanting to get in the middle of whatever Francesca may think is going on. "I can't answer that without more context, however, what I do see here, in front of me is clear evidence of cocaine ingestion. Look, I'm going to suggest you sleep elsewhere for now. Stop trying to run. This cocaine has got to clear out of your system. It could do serious harm to your heart muscle. Drink plenty of fluids, ten times more than normal, let's get this drug flushed out of you. And I want to see you back here in two days. We'll recheck your vitals and see if there is any improvement. If there is no improvement Nicolaus, I'm going to recommend you to a cardiologist."

"Wow, that sounds really serious."

"Nicolaus, this is serious. Right now, we can see that you have quite a bit of the drug in your body, so let's get it flushed out, and see if you get better. Sleep elsewhere, at least until you are back to see me in two days."

"All right. I'll do it. Thank you, doctor."

"Your bum is staying with me for the rest of this week, cousin. You hear me?"

Nicolaus salutes Francesca, "Yes ma'am!"

Chapter Seventy-Four

Nicolaus finds himself at the church at four in the morning. This is the time he usually goes running through the beautiful scenic nature in Austin. For some reason, he is pulled to the church. He is surprised to find the doors unlocked. He goes right in and follows the blue aisle carpet to the altar.

As soon as his knees hit the floor, tears fall from his eyes. He doesn't understand why he is at the church. He doesn't understand why he is separated from Deirdre again, a situation which heavily baffles him. How is he possibly going to live apart from her again?

Nicolaus realizes his tears are tears of anger, as his mind is full of questions for God. Why was he and Deirdre blocked yet again from getting married? Why is Gwen forced on him? How is he going to undo this? How does he make it right for Deirdre?

"Why?" he cries out loudly, his voice echoing through the church. "What do you want from me? No more lessons! Just show me!" he yells at God. "Make it clear!" His mental anguish transpires through his yells that reach up to the heavens through the church arched roof, from the altar. Nicolaus wonders if Nichols had the same type of questions for God, so many years ago.

Bishop Leighton watches as God's power responds to Nicolaus, wrapping him in holy love. Nicolaus is taken to the floor, speaking words in tongue that others cannot understand. He does not have control of himself, as his body convulses on the floor.

After about five minutes, Nicolaus stops shaking. He remains on the floor and quiet covers him. Bishop Leighton slowly walks toward Nicolaus and can see that he is in a state between sleep and awake. The bishop notices that sweat pours from Nicolaus, as if he'd been close to a fire. The bishop knows it is the fire of God that has touched him.

Bishop Leighton laughs to himself and says praises, as he sits on a pew close to Nicolaus. He now sees why he was stirred so early and led to open the church. The bishop begins to softly sing, with his voice growing in intensity,

"God's eye is on the little ole sparrow,
so, I know, He watches over me.
I sing because I'm happy.
I sing because I'm free.
His eye is on the sparrow.
Oh yes, on the sparrow, on that little ole sparrow,
I know He watches over me."

Chapter Seventy-Five

After about an hour from leaving the church in the still early morning time, as the beautiful sunrise streaks across the Texas sky, Nicolaus finds himself ringing the doorbell at Deirdre's house.

Constance opens the door and greets Nicolaus with the usual genuine hug and kiss. She holds his unshaven chin to examine his face. "Hmm, you look a little better today," she tells him. She frowns at the healing cut on his lip, though she doesn't mention it. "Well, have a seat. I'll make you some pancakes for breakfast."

"Uhm, I'll never say no to your delicious pancakes, Mom!"

Deirdre had been unable to sleep. She tossed and turned all night with pregnant dreams. Her mind is confused, because how could she be having such dreams without a husband? Since Nicolaus is the only man on earth for her, and he is no longer available, she figured she would never be getting pregnant. The sound of Nicolaus' smooth voice and spirited laughter downstairs popped her out of bed. She brushes her teeth, gargles, then quickly combs her hair. She can smell her mother's southern flair pancakes. She gently descends the stairs in her berry-colored sexy satin night gown, which does not reveal much, and her matching robe, which flairs open.

Nicolaus surprises Deirdre, being at the last few stair steps. He gentlemanly takes her hand and helps her down, grabbing onto her waist. Once off the last step, he does not let go of her hand. He hugs her tight, her soft, sweet body against his. Her presence always makes him feel better, no matter what he is going through. He is happy she does not resist him. He does not want this hug to end. Deirdre ends it, with a smile, pulling away.

She thought it odd that Nicolaus would show up just as she was having pregnant dreams. Is this a coincidence? She sighs, wanting to be done with her love for Nicolaus. She is so tired of hurting.

However, when she looks at him, she just wants to meld into him, to never leave his arms, as usual. She wants to kiss him with such a kiss that lasts their lifetimes. Her love for him is just too overwhelming and too big to be put away. It is too huge to ignore. It is too deep to leave behind. What is she going to do?

Constance smiles to herself as she watches the two look upon each other with playful looks of love. She knew that no matter what happened, they would never stop loving each other. Their playful banter made Constance think of her Cecil. She misses him very much. As she flips the pancakes into the air one by one, catching them on her spatula and then placing them on the griddle, she wonders if there is some kind of set misfortune on herself and Deirdre. The kind of misfortune that made them lose their men. Some kind of eternal heartbreak.

Deirdre giggles as Nicolaus' arms go around her again. They have a soft moment, which is natural for them. Nicolaus is relieved that Deirdre is allowing him to hold her. His soul rejoices at the sound of her laughter, while hating his predicament.

"Okay, you two! Breakfast is ready!" Constance set the plates of her special pancakes with bowls of grapes, the butter, the syrup, and juice for the both of them. They sat at the kitchen counter, next to each other.

"You look a little better today, you feeling better?" Deirdre asks Nicolaus. She reaches over and gently touches the healing cut of his lip. She worries that Niall is most likely the cause of this discomfort to her sweet man. She wants to kiss his discomfort away.

Nicolaus nods. "Yes, I'm feeling better. Apparently, someone has been trying to poison me with cocaine."

"What?" Deirdre asks shocked, frowning. "Who ... would do that?"

Nicolaus shakes his head, "Francesca thinks it's Gwen. She says she's the only one with the opportunity to do it." Nicolaus eats down the tasty pancakes. "Thank you, Mom, these are wonderful, as always."

Deirdre frowns, "Gwen?" After taking a bite, she thought it could be possible. After all, why is Gwen always at a drug rehab center? "Oh!" She frowns again, "Why?"

Nicolaus shrugs and sighs, "I don't know. I'm pretty sure Francesca will get to the bottom of it. You know how she just cannot leave things alone."

"Well, hell, in this case, it's better she doesn't leave it alone. Tell her to call me if she needs my help. Nicky, I'm so sorry all this negative stuff keeps happening to you."

Constance gives them both a kiss. "I've got to get ready to meet up with Rachel. We are going shopping and having lunch today. We're excited!" Constance disappears to get dressed.

"Well, it's not all bad. You're back!" He teases her.

"Yeah, back to where we were before."

"Okay, wait a minute now. I've been doing some thinking. Before all this ... stuff happened, I thought about how you and I can continue to make a difference with the foster kids. When I was at the church, I received an idea."

Deirdre smiles at him. She rests her chin on her hand, elbow on the counter. She loves how his eyes light up when he wants to make a difference in the world. "Uhm-hum, I'm listening."

"At first, I thought about us adopting several children, you know once we were married. But ...," he pauses, trying to get past the obvious. "Anyway ... even if we adopted them, this is a finite deal, right? Because there are only so many children the two of us could adopt."

Deirdre smiles at this man she loves so much. The only man on earth who touches her heart. "I'm still with you."

"What if ... and I want you to really think about this, okay?" Deirdre nods. "What if we duplicate Helena's children's home.

Except not just one, ... hordes of them. In every major city in Texas, New Mexico, Nevada, Colorado, ... everywhere we have clinics. And not just one, ... what about at least ten in each major city?"

"Nicky!"

"Now think about it!" His eyes are wide with the same excitement that fills his voice. He spreads his arms out. "Think of how many children we could get out of the foster care system. We'll take care of them ourselves. As a corporation, we could adopt all of them."

She shakes her head, wanting to cry at his sweet heart. "Oh Nicky!"

"What do you think?"

"I think it's brilliant. Expensive, but brilliant!"

"We have the money! And we could do celebrity fundraisers each year to cover more costs. I imagine buying large houses that have at least five or six bedrooms so that we could get at least four to six kids in each room."

"And you'd have to have staff."

"Yes, staff for each home, and professional counseling, whatever the kids need. And I had done some reading about Native American children. Many have been unjustly pulled away from their parents. We should for sure try to especially foster these children and help them reconnect with their families."

Deirdre can't resist touching his face. Tears found their way out of her eyes, as she hadn't cried for days.

She thinks this idea and what Nicolaus wants to do is a beautiful thing. She knows he is trying to do God's work, in his own way. How much more Godly is it to rescue homeless children and provide the support they need to be grown into a healthy adult to contribute to society, than it is to stand behind a pulpit and preach?

Deirdre wipes her face with a napkin, and starts to giggle, knowing he wants her help. "Okay, Nicky, when do we start?"

Nicolaus reaches for her with the look of love he'd always given her. He believed he could see her show up again. He takes her free hand. He looks down, then right into her eyes.

"You know I can't do this without you. I can't do anything without you," he whispers to her. Deirdre nods with a smile. "A lawyer should head up the department. I need a lawyer whose on top of their game and who knows their stuff. Ma'am I would be overjoyed and more than honored if you would please, please, please take the position. I'll give you your own department, a six figure salary, you call all the shots and run it the way you want."

Deirdre is surprised, "Me?"

"My God, who else? And really, I hope you know you don't actually have to work though, because I'll take care of you Deirdre, I will. You can hire someone to run the department the way you want."

Nicolaus sighs relief when Deirdre jumps off the stool, and she puts her arms around his neck. Deirdre hesitates at first, and then as if she cannot resist, which she can't resist any longer, she moves in to kiss him. They kiss, as is natural for them, and there is no way for them to avoid it. They kiss again, more involved this time. Nicolaus does not want this to end.

Chapter Seventy-Six

"I'm sorry, what kind of shoes are you talking about?" Gwen calls from her enormous closet that she filled with clothes and shoes, and matching accessories from her frequent shopping trips.

"The yellow shoes," Francesca calls back to her, having sent Gwen away so she could scope out their bedroom, to find the perfect place to put the teddy bear camera. She sits on the bed to look at the angle from Nicolaus' dresser. Then she stands against the windowed wall, next to his dresser to see the angle across the room to Gwen's dresser. "You know the beautiful ones you wore the other day, when you met Deirdre," she called to her, trying to keep her busy. "Oh, I think this will do," Francesca says to herself. She pulls a sitting chair into the corner by the walled window. She places the bear on top of the back of the chair.

Gwen emerges from the large closet with three pairs of yellow shoes. "I'm not sure which one of these."

Francesca pulls Gwen to the other side of the room, and busies her attention. "Oh my, all of these are so pretty. Which ones do you think would go good with a sea blue sequenced dress?"

"Oh Francesca, that sounds lovely. Are you trying to go for a spring feel?"

"Well, I thought more earth tone."

"Okay, then I think these will work."

"Gosh, Gwen, I didn't know you were such a fashionista! Okay, I'll take these." She grabs the see through box which held the shoes. "Oh hey, you know Nicky is staying with me this week. I'm looking after him. He has been sickly."

"Oh! Well, I should check on my hubby! Would you mind?"

"No, not at all, although Nicky didn't want to bother you about it. He figured you'd be helping my Auntie Ceil with that tea

287

that she and Helena are planning. You know a lot of important people will be there."

"Oh! Well ... you know ... I don't think Mother Ceil likes me very much."

Francesca sat on the bed, knowing the camera is going and recording at her house. "Really? What makes you think that?"

"She's not very nice to me. She says nice things, ... in threatening ways."

Francesca giggles, "My Auntie Ceil is quite a character. You know, the way to crack her is you have to stand up to her, and do something bold that she wouldn't expect you to do, or excel at something she thinks you cannot. I think this tea is just the thing you need."

"What do you mean?"

"Offer to help, out of the blue, and don't take 'no' for an answer. And whatever you get to help with, do an overly awesome job to impress her. That will keep her off your back."

"Oh, I see. But ... if I stay here ... I mean ... what about Nicolaus?"

"Don't worry about Nicky. I've got him. I'll take care of him. He'll be back to your bed next week. He just needs lots of rest. He's been through a lot, Gwen."

Gwen nods. "Okay, sounds good. I will stand up to Mother Ceil in the nicest way possible." They both leave the room together, and continue chatting.

Chapter Seventy-Seven

"All right, Nicky," Francesca takes a big scoop of her ice cream and swallows it down. She and Nicolaus sit on the floor of her townhouse, deciphering the family history book. She struggles with the words written in the Estonian language. "What does 'Nicholsil oli neli naist' mean?"

Nicolaus frowns, translating, "Nichols had four wives. Four wives? Does it say what happened to them? Francesca, let me see that." He put down his bowl of ice cream to carefully handle the big ancient book of their family history. He sits onto the couch and Francesca plops herself next to him.

Nicolaus turns pages and studies them carefully.

"Well, what does it say?" Francesca asks impatiently.

Nicolaus gives a slight laugh and finds something. "Okay, wait, here. Here it says 'abielu vältis Nicholsi', marriage eluded him. Eluded him? What does that mean?" Nicolaus looks over more pages. "Oh my God!" He points to the page, Francesca right next to him, looking as well. "Here it says 'Nichols oli usklik ja tahtis saada preestriks', Nichols was religious and wanted to be a priest". He sighs at this unraveling mystery. "My God, once upon a time, I wanted to be a priest."

"Nicky, are you kidding me?"

"No!"

"Well that explains a lot about you!"

"When I was young, I wanted to be a priest, and mother wasn't having it."

"Auntie Ceil stopped you from becoming a priest? Why?"

Nicolaus shrugs. "I'll never forget how she burned all the books and papers I'd gotten from a church to study scripture. She was happy to burn it."

"Nicky, that sounds awful, and really mean. My Auntie Ceil will have to answer for doing that." They both stopped in thought for a moment. "Nicky, that does seem to put you on the same path as Nichols though. You both wanted to be a priest, and did not. And both were in the military. Hmm, what else does it say?"

Nicolaus returns his attention to the book. "Okay here, 'esimene naine suri oma käte läbi'", Nicolaus frowns as he translates, "first wife died from her own hands, 'teine naine suri õnnetuse tagajärjel', second wife died by accident, 'kolmas naine', hmm,... it's says, third wife, and then it's marked out."

"Let me see that, Nicky." Francesca takes the book and does see that the words are marked out or erased or something. "This word here, Nicky, this word, isn't it 'baby', 'beebi'?"

Nicolaus nods, "Yes, that is baby."

"Now I wonder why that dropped off like that. And then here, it says 'DeeDee õnnelik', what is that? Like?"

"No, happy. 'DeeDee õnnelik'."

"Oh thank goodness, so there is some happiness here."

"Yes, but is that not eerie, about the first wife? And he married four times?"

"Well, shi ... shoot, Nicky, you thought you were only going to marry once."

"Yes, true, so I wonder if Nichols was forced into marriages."

"I know, I wonder too. I've got to put this down so I can think about this without getting a headache." Francesca places a marker in the book and puts it down gently on the table shelf behind the couch. "Nicky ..."

He frowns as he puts ice cream in his mouth, "Yeah, Francesca, what is it?"

"I need to tell you something, and I don't want you to get mad, Love, okay?"

His frown grew deeper. "No way."

Francesca sighs, "I put a hidden camera in your bedroom. I did it today. Hopefully, Gwen won't find it."

"Hidden camera?"

"Well, yeah! We need to know what she's up to. I don't trust her. Do you know I asked her about those yellow shoes she had on the other day, and it took her a long time to emerge out of the closet with three pairs of yellow shoes? Who the hell buys yellow shoes, Nicky? Who?"

Nicolaus chuckles, "Apparently, Gwen does."

"How much shopping is she doing? I didn't go in that closet. I set up the camera while she searched for the shoes."

"Look, to be fair, I did tell her she had no limit on the charge card. She came here with nothing. Not one suitcase. Not even a toothbrush."

"You get the bill yet?"

Nicolaus rolls his eyes without answering her question. "So what is it you think you're going to see?"

"I think I'm going to see her snorting cocaine! We'll see. You're not mad?"

"No. I know you are protecting me, and I appreciate it." He kisses his cousin on the cheek. "So you have to sit and watch it?"

"No, it will record, and we can play it back, even while it records in real time, that way we don't miss anything she does. Technology these days is amazing! Now, I didn't put a camera in the bathroom ...but ..."

"Nor should you. I'll have to draw the line there, Francesca."

"Okay, okay, I was just saying ...."

Chapter Seventy-Eight

Nicolaus and Deirdre enjoyed the quiet time alone at Deirdre's home, while Constance was away with Rachel. They stared into each other's eyes, as Nicolaus gently caresses Deirdre's upper arm and shoulder, while propping himself up on his other arm. He imagined Deirdre as his wife. He imagined their wedding day. He just couldn't believe that all that was ripped from them again.

Deirdre pops up. "You know, we haven't really had the chance to talk about your mission in Milojastan. Was it tough?"

Nicolaus chuckles, wondering why she is bringing that subject up now. "Not as tough as we thought it would be. The best part is we didn't fire one shot. Not one. We got in cautiously. We took out the guards using pressure points and a harmless chemical that rendered them unconscious long enough for us to get the ambassadors out."

"Nicky, did they shoot at you?"

Nicolaus looks in her eyes, reluctant to answer, concerned about where she might be going with her line of questioning. He decides to be honest. "Well ... yes. They did. We could hear the bullets whizzing by us. We were moving so fast, those bullets couldn't reach us!"

"Luck, and the grace of God."

"I'd like to think of it as the grace of God. The ambassadors had been tortured and couldn't run, one of them couldn't walk. So my guys, without a second thought, carried them on their backs. Can you believe that? So awesome, these guys. And I tell you," he lit up talking about the bravery of his team, "they moved fast, as if they had no one to carry. They are really fantastic."

Unable to resist any longer, Deirdre gently touches Nicolaus' face. Touching him, and his gentle caressing, made her longing for him grow one hundred fold. How is she going to get along now?

She went from planning her wedding to the man she loves for a second time, only to have misfortune tear them apart, again. How is she going to deal with this situation? The strong love she has for Nicolaus makes her weak for him.

"Nicky, I want you to promise me something. You've always asked me to make promises, ... now it's my turn to ask a promise of you."

Nicolaus smiles with her. She takes his hand and draws closer to him. He nods, "Okay."

"No more missions," she simply says and then waits for his reply.

Nicolaus sighs, noticing her dainty fingers tightening around his. "Uhm ... that's a tough one. I don't know about that. I mean ... how could I refuse a request from the president?"

"Nicky, you've done more than enough for our country. And ..."

"Deirdre, I ..." he shakes his head, "I ... I don't think I can promise that."

"Look Nicky, you could've been killed. Going into Milojastan with no backup! Why would the President send you with no backup? I was so afraid for you, so worried every day. Every day I prayed for your safety."

Nicolaus gently touches her face. "That one was a delicate mission, it called for a small team. I'm sorry you were so worried."

"No, I don't want you to be sorry. I want you to hear me. No more missions."

Nicolaus smiles at her, loving how she thinks of him. He nods, "I'll do my best is what I promise you," he kisses her hand. "If ever a mission is presented to me, I promise to discuss it with you, and we'll make the decision about me going together."

Deirdre is certain she is not going to get Nicolaus to fully agree to her demand. She is happy with what he offers her. She smiles and sighs, as he kisses her hand again. "Okay, Love," she whispers, "okay."

In a flash, they are closer to each other. With total sweetness, Nicolaus drinks from Deirdre's well of purity, through the kissing of her lips. He kisses her again, and again, and again, pulling her into his arms. He'd missed her so much. His love is overflowing for her.

Deirdre, though unable to resist him, even now, as the love she has for him makes her weak with desire, she breaks the kiss of her sweet love. "Nicky, what are we doing? You're married!"

"I'm not really married."

"Yes, you are. You made vows to that woman."

"Not one that I meant. I know it's ... sickening ... that I'm in this predicament again, but that doesn't change my love for you. Remember what I said? I belong to you, and you belong to me."

Deirdre nods understanding him. "Yes, Mr. Married, you belong to me," she teases him. Deirdre giggles as she pushes at him, separating herself. "All our years together, and you've never seen this room before. I've never wanted to tempt you."

"It's a great room. It's so ... you!" he chuckles, looking around her bedroom. Beyond the lilac colored walls, her room comprised of beautiful Victorian furniture. Bright colors played the window dressings, her bedsheets, and the framed artwork on the walls.

"And certainly, you have never been in my bed!" She notes, as they are fully clothed and on top of her bedcovers.

Playfully, Nicolaus rolls himself off Deirdre's bed, landing with a thud on the rounded pedestal floor, rolling himself down the three short steps that led to her bed, careful not to re-injure his ribs. Deirdre cackles at his theatrics. He raises up laughing with her, "It's good to hear that laugh from you." He brings himself to her for one more kiss, and then gets up. "I'll see you later, okay? I've got a few things to take care of."

"Okay, Nicky. Hey, I know you're married, but I still love you," she calls after him, before he gets to the door of her bedroom.

Nicolaus rushes back over, making her laugh again, and gets another kiss from her. "I still love you, too! Always!"

Deirdre grabs his hand, not wanting him to go. "I want to tell you something." She pulls at him to sit down again. "I have always known that I should be with you. Remember the day you first proposed to me when I was fifteen?"

Nicolaus smiles and nods. "Your mom was so happy, and my mother was furious."

Deirdre smiles with him, "Well, from that day forward, I knew we'd always be in each other's life, and I knew that you were special, Nicky, not like the other boys. And as we've grown, I certainly know you are not like other men. Your heart is sweet, and you are a kind man in every aspect. Just some of the reasons I love you so much. And I know that if we never get a chance to marry, we'll always be in each other's life."

Nicolaus moves in for another kiss, "I promise to never leave your side, Deirdre. Although we may not be married, our relationship remains the same. I will always love you."

They kiss more, because it seems like the natural thing for the two of them to do. Their kissing grew to be the continual symbol of their dedication to each other and the symbol of their love for one another.

Chapter Seventy-Nine

A s Nicolaus leaves Deirdre's house, he thinks about the bad errors he is making with Deirdre, ignoring his marriage to Gwen. He believes that God will understand what he and Deirdre are going through. Surely, their suffering from separation deserves a release from sin.

Nicolaus actually is somewhat refreshed, after having spent time with Deirdre. As he walks to his sports car, he thinks about getting a different kind of vehicle, for the next chapter of his life. Nicolaus drives through the stop and go traffic on the Austin streets, finally getting to the turn off of his parents' home. He drives the mile to the gate, and stops to look at the pictures Francesca is sending to his phone. The photos are camera shots of Gwen, snorting something. It also captured where she had it hidden. "Damn." He'd hoped the opposite would be true.

Nicolaus puts in the code, and drives forward on the mile long cobblestone road. When he arrives at the second guard gate, he notices many cars ahead of him. "What's going on today?" he asks the guard on duty, when he finally reaches the gate arm.

"Mrs. Ravenell's tea. I believe she invited one hundred guests."

"Oh, okay. I forgot that is today."

"Yes Sir, and your father-in-law is here, with several of his ... ah ... friends."

"What? Do you know if they are armed?"

"Yes Sir, I did see a few of them with weapons, and despite me telling your mother this, she told me to let them through. He seemed a bit upset. Something about his daughters called him with complaints."

Nicolaus sighs, his day just now ruined. "Okay." Nicolaus contemplates quickly about this situation, especially with the tea guests present. He knew he'd have to do something to take care of it, so that no one would be threatened or hurt. He figured they were probably hassling Niall, and waiting for him to show up. "Look, I'm going to ask Roddy Strictland to assist me. When he arrives, don't hesitate to let him through." Roddy is his same comrade that assisted him in Milojastan, and is his regular running buddy.

"Yes Sir. Oh and one more thing Sir, Ms. Penelope Drone, from Latvia, is here to see you. She asked specifically for you."

"What? She's here? To see me?"

"Yes Sir, that is what she said. She's been waiting for about two hours now."

"Oh, great," Nicolaus says sarcastically. "Okay. Anything else?"

"Ah, no Sir, I'm sure that is more than enough for you," the guard jokes with him, smiling.

Nicolaus nods. "You got that right."

The guard opens the security arm for Nicolaus to pass. There are several vehicles ahead of him driving the half mile more to the circular driveway in front of the mansion. Nicolaus takes the secret side road to the back of the mansion. He calls Roddy, already knowing that Roddy would do anything for him at a moment's notice. This time Nicolaus had a plan to deal with Jonathan's little army.

"Hey man, how is your day going?" Nicolaus asks Roddy.

"It's good. I'm just running some errands for my wife. No plans for the day. All okay in your camp?"

Nicolaus chuckles, "I wish! One day, I'm going to call you up and ask you to go fishing with me."

Roddy laughs, "Hey, no worries man. We always have each other's back. What you got going on?"

"My father-in-law."

"That weird spy guy with the army, who made you marry Gwen? Is he there?"

"Yes. Unannounced, and has a beef with me and my brother again. And my mother is having a tea party. I've got to contain these guys ...."

"Tea party? Say no more, I'm on my way. I'm only about ten minutes from you."

Nicolaus sighs relief, knowing he can always count on Roddy. Roddy is the only one of his comrades that Nicolaus filled in about what had happened with Gwen. "You're amazing, man!"

"I got you. What are your thoughts on containment, cuz I know you, and I know you're miles ahead on planning already, with those thought wheels turning in your head?" Roddy seriously jokes with Nicolaus.

Nicolaus laughs, then clears his throat for seriousness. "I'm thinking tranquilizing darts."

"Okay, that should do it. We never leave home without 'em."

"Great. Meet me at the secret entrance."

"I'll see you soon, my friend."

Nicolaus is very concerned about Jonathan being here at the same time his mother is having a social event. This is not an ideal situation, and he wished his mother had not let them through the gate. He can't imagine what she was thinking, putting all her guests at risk, knowing how rogue and wild Jonathan can be.

Nicolaus retrieves his gun from the glove box, loads it, and puts it in the back side of his pants. There is no way he is not going to be armed this time. He intends to not have Jonathan, nor one of Jonathan's men touch him. Nicolaus goes into his vehicle trunk, and retrieves the box for which he and each of his comrades keep their military paraphernalia, exactly for moments like this. He gets his tranquilizer darts and the apparatus to propel them ready to go. He loads as many darts as it will hold, and then takes extras. This way he and Roddy can take down Jonathan's men without anyone using guns.

When Roddy arrives, they give each other a manly hug. "If you take the outside, and neutralize anyone you see with a gun, that is obviously Jonathan's militia, I'll take care of everyone inside. And if you can, take their guns from them."

Roddy nods. "Let's do this!"

Nicolaus slips into the house at the side entrance, which takes him into the kitchen. By the time the kitchen staff noticed someone might be there, Nicolaus is already gone, having stealthily passed by them.

Nicolaus quietly scopes out the upstairs, and does not see anyone at the top of the staircase. With a quiet and fast pace, Nicolaus goes upstairs to begin taking out the militia men. Quickly, he uses the tranquilizer darts, hitting the target of a specific area on the neck for each militia man he sees. He descends the stairs, blowing the darts at them, one by one. Nicolaus' high skill and precision accuracy delivers the darts to each man, succinctly, hitting them in the exact area to take them down. Nicolaus mastered this Native American technique while serving in special forces. By the time the men feel something on their neck, similar to a bug bite, they fall to the floor, asleep, under the spell of the tranquilizer.

Nicolaus works quickly and quietly, hoping the guests do not notice him dragging men to the large cleaning closet next to the kitchen, where he locks them inside.

Nicolaus alleviates ten men. Roddy texted him that he'd also taken out ten men, and did not see any others. Roddy locked the men in the pool shed, having removed most of the tools they might be able to use to escape once they awake from their tranquilizer nap.

Nicolaus asked Roddy to enter and be ready, if he should be needed.

"You got it," Roddy replies by text.

Roddy joins Nicolaus in the mansion, and they lock up all the men's guns, knives, and rifles in the gun closet that could only be opened by a code. "Damn militia," Nicolaus mutters under his breath. He can't believe the number of weapons.

Nicolaus then searches the house for Jonathan. On his way to the library, where he hears yelling, he sees Elsa, standing, and crying. Nicolaus takes her hands, "Elsa, where is ..." he stops his words when he sees her black eye and swollen cut lip, which has fresh blood. "What happened?" He hugs her. "Who did this?" He asks her frowning, knowing the answer, while not wanting to assume anything.

Elsa looks down, and then up at him. "Niall," she says sadly.

"Oh Elsa. I'm so sorry." He hugs her again, trying to calm her.

Nicolaus hears the yelling from the library room become elevated. It seems this time Niall is holding his own against Jonathan. Suddenly, the yelling stops, and a scuffle can be heard. Nicolaus touches Elsa on her arms, then goes into the library, not willing to let Jonathan wail on Niall like he'd done before.

When Nicolaus enters, he sees that both men have each other by the throat. With his strength, Nicolaus easily parts them. He flings Jonathan halfway through the room. Jonathan jumps back towards the brothers, going for Niall's throat again. Nicolaus again pushes him across the room. "Stop it!" Nicolaus shouts.

Jonathan has a look fall over him, then he lunges for Nicolaus, slapping him across the face. This was unexpected by Nicolaus, which Jonathan knew it would be. While Nicolaus paused, Jonathan lunges for Niall again.

Nicolaus twirls Jonathan around, returns the slap, and pushes him across the room again. He sees that Roddy has quietly entered the area, and stands guard to let no one into the library.

"You dare slap your father-in-law?" Jonathan yells at Nicolaus, holding his face that is in pain, which stopped his childish actions.

"You dared to slap me, didn't you? Now, both of you stop it! Why are you even here?" Nicolaus asks Jonathan, staying close to Niall, in a protective stance.

"Why? Why? Because that ..." he points at Niall, "that ... fool, there, has been hitting on my Elsa! Hitting my Elsa! What the hell? And Gwen says that you have abandoned her! I told you that if you did not treat my daughters right, I would be back. And ..." Jonathan made a strange whistle noise. Nicolaus presumes he is calling to his armed men. When no one rushes to help him, he whistles again and gets the same result. Jonathan looks sheepishly at Nicolaus. "What have you done? Where are my men?"

"Your men are fine. They are just a little tied up right now."

"What did you do?"

At this moment, Niall is very glad Nicolaus is his brother. Niall finally realizes how it is Nicolaus who seems to always be the one to save them. He feels that his brother is beyond courageous. He didn't understand how Nicolaus could have dealt with all Jonathan's men, although, somehow, in this moment, he is sure that is what happened.

"Why can't you be civil about these matters? It's okay to be upset, but we are sick of your threats. Who the hell do you think you are anyway, bringing guns into my parent's home? What's wrong with you? What kind of father are you?" Nicolaus yells at him.

"What ... I ... how..."

Nigel arrives at the doorway, shaking Roddy's hands, "Roddy, thank you for being here," he tells him. Then he goes to Elsa, who is shaking and crying again, "Oh Elsa, I'm so sorry. It will be okay," he hugs Elsa to him, not sure what else to say. He has no excuses to give her for Niall's monstrous behaviors toward her. He doesn't understand it, himself. He kisses her head, sorry that Niall has abused her.

"You can be upset, but guns?" Nicolaus walks up to Jonathan, right into his face, "Don't you ever, I mean not ever, bring your militia or guns in this house again. Not ever!" Nicolaus shouts, ready to lose it.

Elsa and Nigel are watching the exchange just outside the door. Niall also watches.

Nicolaus harshly pushes Jonathan again. He shoves the old man backwards several times, until he falls into a chair, Nicolaus showing that he is in charge.

Jonathan is speechless. "Well, I .... I ....," he looks up at Nicolaus.

Nicolaus sighs, and keeps speaking. "We are not perfect!" he motions his hand between himself and Niall. "God knows I have lots of faults. If you want to talk to us, you're going to do it the right way. All this militia crap, that goes away, as of now. Never again do you bring those men or those weapons to this house."

Jonathan starts to laugh. He laughs heartily at Nicolaus.

In an instant, Nicolaus snatches the old man up by his collar, hoping he doesn't have a gun. "I didn't say anything funny, Baird. Not one thing!" Jonathan stops laughing, and Nicolaus harshly releases him.

Jonathan smiles up at Nicolaus and starts to get up. Nicolaus stops him, not letting him stand. Jonathan holds his hands in the air. "Okay, okay. I'm just amused at your courage. No one has ever spoken to me like that. Not once. And I want you to know, I hear what you say. And ... I agree with you. No more guns or threats." Jonathan offers his hand to Nicolaus. "We're family now."

Nicolaus takes his hand, and helps Jonathan to his feet. Nicolaus beckons for Niall, not taking his eyes off Jonathan, because he does not trust him, and isn't sure if he is lying. Niall stands next to Nicolaus. "Niall, let us agree right now, there will be no more hitting of Elsa. She deserves to be treated better," Nicolaus says, then puts his hand to the back of Niall's neck. If he tried to resist or go negative, Nicolaus was going to squeeze that neck until he relented.

Niall nods. "You're right. I'm sorry."

Nigel and Elsa enter the library, and join the men.

While on the other side of the mansion, in the enormous formal dining room, many guests are sitting at the round tables, as it is time to play the game of bingo.

Ceil turns the tiles to call the numbers when Gwen, who is sharply dressed in a sparkly blue, v-neck halter topped, pant suit, moves Ceil's hand away from the turner. "I've got this, Mother Ceil." She takes the game device from Ceil, without asking. "Hello everyone, I'm Gwen Ravenell, and I will be calling the numbers tonight. Everyone ready?" Gwen doesn't begin until she receives a positive response from the players. "All right! First square, ... B5. Next square, ... E2. Next ..."

Helena chuckles, as Gwen has taken the best part of the night away from Ceil. She whispers to Ceil, "Well, look at your new daughter-in-law, trying to impress you!" Elsa had filled her in on all that happened. Helena hoped she would see Deirdre today.

"G5," Gwen calls out.

"Yes, yes, I suppose so."

"If she does a good job, you've got to give her a break, Ceil."

Ceil looks at Helena. "Yes, I suppose," she says again.

Nigel and Jonathan are sitting and talking, properly. Nicolaus hugs Elsa, as he gives her to Niall, who kisses her split lip. Nicolaus watches as Niall takes Elsa upstairs.

"Finally! There you are!" Penelope says loudly at Nicolaus, grabbing his arm to twirl him around to her. "I been waiting and waiting for you! For hours!"

"Penelope! What are you even doing here?"

"I here, all the way from Latvia to talk about my sister. You no answer my letters," she says in broken English.

"Letters? I haven't received any letters from you."

Penelope goes into her purse and pulls out a bundle of letters that are bound with a pink ribbon. "See?"

Nicolaus looks at her, his eyebrow up, "Well ... I didn't get them."

"No, no! Your mother tell me you were going to burn each one, and she snatch it from you and save them. She say she beg and beg you to read my letters."

Nicolaus frowns and crosses his arms at such a fabrication, shaking his head no. He touches Penelope, and she jerks away from him. "Look, Penelope, I'm sorry. I didn't get any letters. What do you need to talk about? You could have called me."

"My sister! Marguerite!"

Nicolaus backs away from her. "No, I'm not discussing Marguerite with you. The matter is closed."

"No, it's no closed, Nicolaus. I want answers."

Nicolaus sighs, "Penelope, I don't have any answers. I know what you know."

"No! You lie to me, Nicolaus! How you lie to me, right in my face, Nicolaus?" Penelope wants to cry, and it shows.

Nicolaus sighs again. He needs a drink.

Chapter Eighty

H elena leaves the Bingo game, since Ceil and Gwen have everything under control.

She wants to explore the mansion to get a feel for the magnificent rooms.

Suddenly, Helena stops in the great room, when across the way, she spots Nicolaus being badgered by Penelope, whom she recognized. Helena gets flush as she watches Nicolaus across the room. She understands what affect he has on Deirdre, as her innermost being aches for him. She actively imagines what being close with him would be like. She tries to imagine what it would be like for Nicolaus to intimately touch her. Her want for him multiplies immensely, her body reacting to the very sight of him. Her thoughts are making her feel lightheaded. Helena almost couldn't stand it, she desperately wants to act upon these feelings.

Niall left Elsa, as she wants to rest. He happens upon Helena, where she stands, fantasizing about Nicolaus. Niall sees that familiar look on Helena's face as her eyes follow his brother. He'd seen that look on the faces of many women who wanted his brother, for which not one of those women succeeded in wooing Nicolaus to their bed.

Niall touches Helena's shoulder, and they greet each other. He frowns at her, knowing what she wants – his brother.

Just then, Deirdre enters the house. When Niall sees Deirdre, he quickly moves for her, and is stopped by Helena's arm, as Nicolaus looks up and sees his beautiful love.

Nicolaus' attention rudely leaves the nagging Penelope, and he is the first to float over to greet Deirdre. Her appearance bedazzles him, striking him in his man brain.

Deirdre wears a lovely, opal colored, satin flowy dress, which has diamond spaghetti straps. This dress actually reveals her figure.

Matching diamond hair clips adorn both sides of her head, pulling her thick, wavy hair back.

Deirdre wraps her dainty arms around Nicolaus' large, muscular frame, as he smiles upon her, holding back from what he wants to do most - kiss her.

Niall circumvents Helena's hold on him, and throws himself in this game, and is also upon Deirdre, hugging her. Helena walks over and boldly separates the men from Deirdre, bringing her into the dining room, with the rest of the guests.

Gwen trips up on the square letters when she, as everyone else in the room, looks upon Deirdre with a pleasantness. The pure beauty of Deirdre interrupts Gwen's thoughts, interrupting her pace, suddenly, making her doubt herself.

Quietly, Deirdre sits herself on a bar stool, close to the door, and waives at everyone with a smile, trying not to distract from the game.

Helena is a quick rescue to Gwen, as well, going to her, and touching her hands, bringing her attention from Deirdre back to the game. As the participants are waiting for the next square to be called, Gwen resumes, though now she feels nervous with Deirdre present.

Out in the other room, Penelope continues to follow and nag Nicolaus. "Nicolaus, you will not escape me. You will not escape your punishment. I promise you!"

Nicolaus sighs, already tired of Penelope Drone. He grabs her by the shoulders. "Penelope, please, just cut it out!" He knows she has trouble controlling her tangents. He sighs, and pours her a drink, and hands her the glass, expecting her to take it.

With pouty lips, Penelope takes the glass, and drinks from it.

"Is your father here with you?" Nicolaus asks her, seating himself on the sofa, already feeling mentally exhausted from the day.

"No, I arrive alone to speak with you, Nicolaus," she tells him much more calm.

Nicolaus nods. "Where are you staying?"

"Staying? Oh, here, at the house!"

"Okay, well, it's not a good time to discuss this. As you can see, my mother has a party going on. And there are other issues I have to deal with. Maybe we can talk later tonight, or even tomorrow, after we both have some rest. Okay?"

Penelope is mesmerized by his eyes. She frowns, hating that he is charming her. She nods, and swallows down the drink. In silence, he leads her to the large dining room where the bingo game is taking place. As soon as Penelope sees Deirdre, she hugs her, and sits next to her.

Chapter Eighty-One

R oddy, Nigel, Niall, and Nicolaus escort Jonathan and his men out of the house.

"Hey, what about our weapons?" Jonathan asks, frowning.

"Weapons? What weapons?" Nicolaus throws back at him loudly, hoping to alleviate them of some of their dangerous armaments.

Jonathan wags his finger at Nicolaus, and laughs, "Ha, ha, ha! All right, my man," he tells him, not wanting to push farther, knowing Nicolaus has the upper hand today.

The Ravenell men watch them leave the property. Roddy goes to the upstairs balcony. Using his binoculars, he watches them completely leave out the gate, and go onto the nearest highway entrance ramp. "Yep, they're gone!" he tells them.

Nicolaus sighs, "You know what father, I'm thinking we need to gate up the whole of our property boundaries. I don't want them to be able to get in here again. It's a real vulnerability that could really be detrimental in the future."

Nigel crosses his arms. "Hmm, I'll have to think that through."

"Does thinking it through mean consulting mother? 'Cuz I really don't think it matters what she wants. We need to consider the safety of everyone."

Nigel looks at his son, knowing what he is saying is wise, though not convinced he wants to gate the family in, away from the rest of the world.

"I'm changing that security gate system tomorrow," Nicolaus informs them.

Chapter Eighty-Two

"You are absolutely stunning," Nicolaus smiles at Deirdre as he puts her in her car, as the tea is over, and everyone is leaving.

"Did I stun you?" she playfully asks him.

"Yes, ma'am, you sure did!"

Deirdre gazes into his eyes. "Good! That's the intention!" she giggles.

He leans in for a kiss before she drives off.

Nigel walks Helena to her vehicle. "I'll tell Ceil to call you tomorrow with a tally of the funds. I'm sure she got you a good amount," he says, holding her by the waist. Helena's beauty does not escape Nigel's eyes.

Helena looks at Nigel, stopping in her tracks, turning in his arm. She notices his arm does not fall from her waist. "Nigel," she frowns, wanting to know his thoughts, "what do you think about Nicky and Gwen? Nicky should be with Deirdre."

Nigel nods. "Yes, Nicolaus and Deirdre are fated for each other. Other events seem to force them apart."

"It is very sad. They love each other very much."

"And what of you and your husband? Are you fated to be together?"

Helena smirks, not liking his question. "Fated? Perhaps not."

"Does he think he owns you?"

"Owns? Nigel, what do you mean?"

"Your bruises do not escape my aging eyes. In a marriage, bruises are either caused by passion, or hatred from a tearing apart."

Helena looks down, frowning. "My husband does not love me. He never did."

Nigel hears the sadness in her voice. Helena's sad beauty reminds him of Rachel, whom he once intended to marry.

However, his circumstances, similar to that of Nicolaus, led him to be intimate with her outside of his own marriage. For some reason, Helena's presence brings calmness to Nigel's spirit, again, reminding him of Rachel.

"Oh now," he pats her shoulder, "I'm sure Joel has loved you. The two of you may have grown apart."

Helena nods, "Perhaps."

"Would you like me to have Nicolaus speak with him?"

Helena chuckles, "Nicky already did that! It did help for a little while." Helena sighs, "I just need to leave him. And I will ... before he hurts me again."

Nigel offers unlimited support. "Helena, any help you ever need from us, you know we are always here for you. Anything you need at all. And you are always welcomed to stay with us."

Helena hugs onto Nigel, the man from which the seed generated to create Nicolaus. She is very grateful to him. "Nigel, thank you so much. Your whole family has been so wonderful to me."

"Of course!" Nigel kisses Helena's face, then her neck, and then her face again.

Helena thinks the neck kiss is a little much, she looks at him but says nothing of it. Nigel loads her into her vehicle, and she drives off. Nigel sighs, feeling like he wants more from Helena, maybe because she very much reminds him of Rachel.

Chapter Eighty-Three

Nicolaus remembers to follow Francesca's instructions, and places his phone on the nightstand next to the bed, as he got under the covers. He knows Francesca will be watching the camera to see what mischief Gwen is up to.

Truly exhausted, Nicolaus does not notice that Gwen is shaken from Deirdre's presence at the party, and from the excitement surrounding her sister. As Gwen eases herself into bed, she isn't even sure she had impressed Ceil, and this worries her greatly.

"Look Gwen, I dealt with your father today. If you have complaints, you are not to go to him anymore. I made that very clear to him. You talk to me, and we'll work it out. Okay?"

Feeling confused, Gwen nods in agreement without words.

Nicolaus quickly kisses Gwen on the side of her face. "Goodnight," he tells her as he settles down to sleep, turning his back to her. He's had a stressful day. His mind is on Deirdre. Images of her in that pretty opal dress play upon his mind as he drifts to sleep.

Later that night, after several phone rings, Gwen finally turns Nicolaus' phone off, before it can wake him. She already placed cocaine powder in his mouth a few times, in his nose, and now she is rubbing it on the intimate parts of his body. She found this so much easier to do when he is in exhausted sleep, as he had been most nights lately.

Nicolaus stirs, waking himself up, remembering the plan. The cocaine hadn't taken it's full effect yet. He sits up, only to find Gwen helping herself to him, just as he'd previously seen in his supposed dream. "Wait ... wait ... stop, ... stop." She finally stops. "Gwen, why didn't you wake me?"

She scoffs, "I don't need to."

"What? No, Gwen, if you want to be with me, then be with me."

"It's not a big deal hon, I do this all the time."

"What?"

She put her hand to his chest to lay him back onto the pillow. "Relax, Nicky. Go back to sleep."

"Are you kidding?" Nicolaus is offended. Turning from her, he frees himself from her hands. As Nicolaus gets out of bed, he falls onto the floor, his nervous system not working properly.

Just then, Francesca frantically bangs on their bedroom door. "Gwen, it's Francesca, open up!" Banging on the door again, she yells, "Gwen! Open the door." Francesca had a mind to just bust into the room, not caring who was dressed.

Gwen throws on her robe and opens the door.

Francesca rushes in. She sees Nicolaus on the floor, "Oh my God!" Francesca drops on her knees where Nicolaus lays. She lifts his head off the floor onto her lap. His weight is heavy due to his muscular frame. "Get me a towel or something to cover him up," she demands of Gwen. Gwen gives her a nearby towel, and Francesca covers Nicolaus.

Nigel descends the stairs, having been alerted by the staff, and after hearing some commotion coming from Nicolaus' side of the mansion. When he arrives to the bedroom, he sees Nicolaus on the floor, with eyes rolling back as he goes into unconsciousness. "What's happened?"

"She's drugged him again. Uncle Nigel, I think we need an ambulance." Francesca pats Nicolaus' face, trying to wake him. "Nicky!" she calls to him, and he does not respond. "My God, how much did you give him, Gwen?"

Gwen begins to panic. She shakes her head. "I don't know! I didn't!" She tries to lie her way out of the situation.

"Don't freakin' lie about it, Gwen! I saw you. Tell me how much you gave him, so we can tell the doctors," Francesca yells at her.

Gwen twirls around, crying, "I don't know! I don't know!"

Nigel rushes out of the room to a phone to call for an ambulance. Nigel is just remembering that he'd seen Nicolaus drinking earlier, as well. Suddenly, he is very worried.

The sound of the approaching ambulance riles everyone out of bed. It has been at least fifteen minutes and Nicolaus is still unresponsive. The emergency workers place an oxygen mask on his face, and quickly lift Nicolaus onto the gurney. Francesca jumps into the ambulance and stays by Nicolaus' side, as it speeds off to the nearest hospital.

Gwen clings onto Elsa and Niall, afraid of what is to happen. Ceil is the only one who did not get out of bed. Nigel enters their bedroom, rushing around to get dressed to get himself to the hospital.

"What's happening? Is he dead?" Ceil inquires, a little too wishfully, sitting up on one arm, her eye mask pulled up.

Nigel frowns at her. "No, thank God. He's still breathing." Nigel can see that Ceil is not getting out of the bed. "Aren't you going to the hospital with us?"

Ceil lays back down, and replaces her eye mask to shut out the light. "Just call me when you have news, dear. No need for all of us to be down there at this hour." She snuggles herself under the covers, knowing there may be hope that Nicolaus might slip away, or into a coma or something. Ceil sighs gleefully at her artful work and goes back to sleep.

Chapter Eighty-Four

"Gwen, what happened?" Elsa hugs her sister to her, and leads her to sit down on the couch in the room she shares with Niall. Niall had sought out Ceil, to speak to her about what happened.

Gwen wrings her hands. "I don't know! Oh my God! Oh my God! What if I killed him? Elsa, what if he's dead?" Gwen covers her face with her hands, realizing that she may have killed the famous Nicolaus Ravenell, of whom everyone knew, and if so, she would indeed be going to jail.

Elsa became alarmed by Gwen's words. Her face and lip still pained her, and she tries to put that aside for now. "Gwen, what are you talking about? What did you do?" Elsa takes her sister's hands and holds them. "Now, slow down. Just tell me what happened."

Gwen sighs, knowing she'd better tell Elsa the truth. She knows Elsa would be keen about what to do. She could always count on her younger sister. "I only did what Mother Ceil told me to do. I gave Nicky some of my coke. I don't know, maybe I gave him too much. I don't know!" Gwen stands away from Elsa, waiting for the barrage of judgmental questions.

Elsa frowns deeply, "Gwen, you're still doing coke? Here? In this house?"

Gwen nods. "Yes, and somehow Mother Ceil knows. I don't know how, but she does. And she told me that she knows many people who owe her favors, and that if I didn't give Nicky coke too, that she'd have me locked up. She scares me Elsa. I didn't know what else to do, so I gave it to him."

"Oh my God, Gwen, you've been giving Nicky coke? How?"

Gwen shrugs. "I just wait until he goes to sleep. Then I give it to him. It was hard at first, then it just got easier, 'cause he goes to bed very tired. He's never had a reaction like he did tonight. I don't understand what went wrong."

"What went wrong? Gwen, you shouldn't have been doing this at all!" Elsa stands in thought, "Oh my God, Nicky wasn't feeling well, and he looked awful. Gwen you'd been giving him drugs then? All this time?"

Gwen looks sheepish and then nods.

"Oh, ..." Elsa is trying to piece all this together. "why did Mother Ceil want you to drug Nicky? She wants to kill him?"

Gwen throws her arms in the air, as she is filled with panic again. "I don't know! I did ask her why she wanted me to do this, and she wouldn't tell. Just threatened to lock me up if I didn't." Gwen sits down and begins to cry again. She knows she is in big trouble. "Oh my God! What am I going to do? I don't want to go to jail, Elsa. Please, you have to help me."

Elsa hugs Gwen to her. "Okay, okay, now, hush. It will be okay." She held Gwen tightly to her, knowing her sister is scared. Elsa then stands with resolve. "This is what we are going to do. You are going to bring me all the drugs you have here in the house, and I'll hide them away, until I can get rid of them. Then, we are going to go to the hospital and check on Nicky. If he is awake, you are going to tell him the whole truth. Everything!"

"Elsa, I can't. I'm scared!"

"Gwen, if it's one thing I know about Nicky, it's that he is fair. He always does the right thing. We'll put our trust in him. We'll go down there, and you'll tell him everything. Don't say anything to Niall. We'll wait until we are before Nicky, and then we'll tell everything."

Gwen nods, still feeling very scared, hoping Elsa is right, as Elsa has known Nicolaus longer than she has known him. "Elsa, ... what if I killed him?" she asks in near panic again.

Elsa shakes her head. "Let's try to stay positive. Go get dressed. And Gwen, make sure you cover your body. We'll sit with Nicky for as long as it takes."

Chapter Eighty-Five

"Mother, why aren't you going to the hospital to see about Nicolaus? They carried him out of here unconscious."

"Niall, you can check on him for me, and report back. I don't need to be there."

"Please don't tell me you're not concerned."

"I'm concerned. Just know this, Niall, ... if Nicolaus should happen to go into a coma, or ... expire, you will take his place at the company. So I want you to be ready."

Niall scoffs, "No thank you, Mother. You'll have to find someone else."

"Niall, don't be a jackass!" Ceil sits up, annoyed at her younger son's attitude. "The company must pass into the hands of a Ravenell. If things work out as I hope they will, you'll be in that VP chair. You'll be making decisions for the company, and then soon, you'll be head of this family, which is your rightful place. So don't be snarky about this! It's time for you to grow up and be ready to replace Nicolaus. Anyway, I'm so sure you will do a much better job than he has ever done."

Niall looks at Ceil very doubtful, and made no comment to what she is alluding to. "Well, first things first. I'm going to check on my brother."

Chapter Eighty-Six

D r. Patel, who happened to be working in the emergency room tonight, speaks with Nigel and Francesca. "I see that Nicolaus is back, worse than before when I saw him at the urgent care clinic. You swore to me that Nicolaus does not take drugs. And here he is ... with an overdose!"

"Doc, it's not his fault," Francesca explains. "You remember I told you I didn't trust his wife. I hid a camera in their room, and I saw her put drugs in him while he was sleeping. She put it in his mouth, and his nose, and on his ... well, let's just say his privates. And I tried to call him to wake him up as soon as I saw her begin to do it, but Nicky was asleep, and the phone didn't wake him. So you see, he didn't do this. He's been drugged. Again!"

Dr. Patel sighs. "And drinking! He's very lucky. He could have died from the combination mix of alcohol and cocaine. I cannot tell you how many of these cases we see on a daily basis, and many people just don't make it."

Nigel nods, crossing his arms. "Dr. Patel, we are very grateful for any assistance you give my son. Will Nicolaus actually be all right?"

"Yes. He is very lucky. What happened is that his blood pressure spiked extremely high. He could have had a stroke, as his blood pressure was beyond stroke level. That's why his body shut down, as a protective measure. We were able to get his blood pressure down, and he is stable now. Well, except for the drugs in his system."

Nigel touches Dr. Patel's arm, and is relieved that a worse fate did not happen to Nicolaus. "Thank you, doctor. Thank you."

Dr. Patel nods. "He will need to stay for a few days so we can detox him. We'll need to clear all that cocaine out of him."

"Yes, doctor. Whatever needs to be done."

Chapter Eighty-Seven

E lsa, Gwen, and Niall enter the hospital room where Nicolaus lay in the bed. Nicolaus is hooked up to many monitoring machines and an intravenous bag. The bed alarm is also set, as he's now considered a fall risk in his weakened state.

Deirdre and Francesca are on each side of Nicolaus, Deirdre sitting on the bed, Francesca in the chair. Rachel and Constance are present as well. Rachel runs her fingers through Nicolaus' soft hair, in a soothing motion. She appears very worried.

No one is more relieved to see Nicolaus awake and breathing than Niall. He heaves a sigh of relief. Niall is not ready and does not want to replace his brother at the company. He goes to Nicolaus and touches his shoulder. "You gave us all a scare! You okay?"

Nicolaus nods. "Yeah, I'll be all right. I have a terrible headache, though."

Gwen and Elsa both go to him, touching him. Gwen sits herself on the opposite side of the bed from Deirdre. "I'm so sorry, Nicky," she begins in earnest. She cries, knowing she could have killed him. She is so relieved to see him alive and up, as if nothing major happened.

Nicolaus touches her hand, to calm her. "Take it easy," he tells her. "Luckily, there's no permanent damage. Doc says my blood pressure went so high it knocked me out. They got it down, closer to normal, it's still a little high though. We have to flush the drugs out of my system again. I think it will normalize when ..."

"Oh my God!" Gwen blurts out before everyone, she can't contain herself, "I could've killed you! I'm so sorry, Nicky. I'm so sorry!"

"You really could have," Rachel scolds Gwen, remaining very upset about all of this.

Nicolaus tightens his hold on her hand, as he is tethered and cannot move to give her a hug, though he sees she needs one. Elsa quickly provides the hug to her sister, and Nicolaus nods. Gwen removes herself from Elsa, and throws herself to lay on Nicolaus' lap, as he is partially sitting up, the bed supporting his back.

Nicolaus chuckles, moved by her tears, "I think you gave me a little too much."

Francesca jumps in, wanting answers to the questions Nicolaus is avoiding asking. "Gwen, why were you giving Nicky drugs, anyway? What makes you think that is something you should do to a person?"

"Yeah, Gwen, why would you do such a despicable thing?" Rachel badgers her.

Just then Nigel returns to the room, having placed a quick call to Alexander, letting him know what is happening.

Elsa touches Gwen's back, and she sits up. Elsa nods to Gwen, signaling now is the time to tell everything.

"Well ... I'm so sorry Nicky," she apologizes again, "... Mother Ceil told me I had to do it. She said she would have me locked up if I didn't."

"What?" Niall frowns, shocked.

"That's ludicrous," Rachel grew more upset, not doubting Ceil would perpetrate such an ugly act against her Nicolaus.

Nicolaus scoffs, "She told you to drug me? Why? To kill me?"

"She told me to drug you. That every time I had some, I had to make sure you got some too. I'm sorry, I was scared. I don't want to be locked up!"

The hospital room is very quiet as Nicolaus thinks about what Gwen said. Finally, he responds. "Well ... you're going to rehab, to kick this thing, or ..., *I'll* have you locked up! How about that?"

Deirdre touches his chest, "Nicky!" She looks at him disapprovingly.

"What? Well, obviously, she needs rehab. I mean it, Gwen."

Gwen peers at Elsa, who is nodding at her. "Okay, I'll do what you want."

"I'll make arrangements for you to go tomorrow. I'll probably be hooked up to less contraptions."

Francesca gives strong voice, "No. I'll make the arrangements for you to go now! You're not leaving my sight, Gwen! No more drugs for you!"

Rachel agrees with Francesca's actions. "It's best not to let Ceil know where she is. And afterwards, she can stay with us, unless Nicolaus finds another solution."

Gwen bursts out in tears. She knows she should be grateful for the help the family is offering, however, she did want one more taste of her cocaine before she had to give it up. She'd been to rehab so many times in her life that she'd never been serious about it. Gwen thought about the fact that she could have killed a perfectly healthy, handsome, and caring man, and these thoughts triggered her into wanting to do things right this time.

Gwen certainly knew that if Nicolaus made a complaint to the legal authorities, she'd be arrested. She understood he is offering her a path to a better road, an offer she had to take, or she would be facing heavy consequences. Elsa hugs her sister to her, feeling indebted to Nicolaus. She guides Gwen to a nearby family room. Francesca follows them, already on the phone, making calls.

"Father, is mother here with you? I'd like to speak to her," Nicolaus asks.

"Nicolaus, I don't want you to confront your mother about this. I'll do it."

Nicolaus looks at his father, not trusting he'd follow through. "And ... will you ... actually ... do that, Father? I want to know why."

Rachel steps up to defend Nicolaus. "I want answers too. Why would she do something like this?"

Nigel cut off both Rachel and Nicolaus. "We all want answers. Nicolaus, right now, you need to focus on getting better. Let me worry about your mother. And that goes for all of you. Let me deal with Ceil."

Chapter Eighty-Eight

Alexander is surprised to get a call from Francesca.

"Hey Alexander, look, Nicky is in the hospital for a few days, and ..."

"Is he all right? Nigel didn't give me many details."

"Not really. He was drugged again. Overdosed, by Gwen."

"What?"

"Yeah, she's done this before. This time she gave him too much. Nicky will be okay. The docs want him admitted for a few days to ..."

"What about Gwen? Where is she?"

Francesca is surprised at his questions. "Oh, she is not near him. At Nicky's insistence, she's in rehab, I just dropped her off. It's a long story. Nicky wants me to tell you he has a meeting with ..."

"Where is she, Francesca? Where is Gwen?"

"Alex, what's with all the questions about Gwen?" She paused and waited for his answer.

"I ... ah ... well ... we've become ... friends. And I know she's been having issues.

I just want to be sure she is okay."

"Hmm! What kind of friends?"

"Francesca, please! Just tell me where she is."

"You seem more worried about Gwen than you are about Nicky. Nicky could have died, you know, Alexander."

"What?"

Francesca sighed, trying to decide if she should give him the information on Gwen.

"But he's all right? I mean you said he's okay,"

"You know what? Let me just give you what you need, and you can decide on whether or not you want to contact Nicky. Okay?

Will that work for you, Alexander?" Her tone is that of upset. "Gwen is at Elk's Crest Rehab Center, just outside of Austin."

"I know that place. Thanks Francesca. And hey, for the record, I am concerned about Nicolaus. I'll go by and check on him later. I promise."

"Whatever, Alexander." In frustration, Francesca ends the call. She went home to discuss the happenings with her mother.

Chapter Eighty-Nine

N igel finally found the opportunity to confront Ceil, before Nicolaus returned home from the hospital. He sat her down next to him in the sitting space of their gigantic, luxurious bedroom. Nigel held onto Ceil's hands, as he looks her in the eye. "Ceil, please tell me you did not have anything to do with making Nicolaus so ill, having him drugged. Please tell me you did not put Gwen up to such a terrible thing."

Ceil took her hands from her husband and pretends to be shocked at his accusation. "What? You want me to repeat what you said word for word? How could you even ask me such a thing, Nigel? How could you accuse me of something like that?"

"Ceil ..."

"Did you even defend my honor to whoever is spreading such vicious gossip?"

"Your ... honor?"

"Aren't you my husband? After all these years do I still have to school you on what to do? How to protect me and the reputation of our family?"

"Ceil, be reasonable," Nigel breathed out stress. Ceil's reaction of denial is not unexpected.

"What do you want, Nigel?"

"The truth, Ceil, the truth."

"Are you saying that you believe someone else, or ... that druggie ... tramp of a girl over me? That you would take their word over mine?" She frowns at Nigel with the drama of classic theater.

Nigel shakes his head realizing Ceil is not going to admit to what she'd done. He knew he would have no answers for Nicolaus, or Rachel, or anyone else. Pressing the issue is not worth the fight or the foolhardiness Ceil would surely bring about. However, Nigel is hopeful that perhaps now Ceil would back off Nicolaus, at least a little, since the spotlight of suspicion is on her.

Chapter Ninety

Three days later, Nicolaus contacts a security company before he leaves home for work. His priority is getting their security gate changed.

"What makes you think you have the right to make any kind of changes around here without discussing it with us first?" Ceil hassled Nicolaus, as he was leaving out the door.

Nicolaus sighs, feelings still raw for what she'd put Gwen up to. He looks upon his mother who is harshly glaring at him. "Mother, I don't care if you like it or not. I'm making changes for the security of all of us. I'm not checking with you on anything. We will all have scan cards, which will be specifically programmed for each person. You will not be allowed to lend your card to others, or to just buzz anyone in. So ... you'll either abide by the new technology, or you'll be locked out of the house. Easy as that. Now, if you'll excuse me..."

"Who the hell do you think you are, speaking to me like that?" she chides him.

Nicolaus smirks at her, "I'm your son, Nicolaus Ravenell!" He smiles and leaves his mother with a dismayed look on her face. Ceil didn't have a response, which surprised him.

Chapter Ninety-One

Nicolaus had a meeting scheduled with a popular car company. He hoped they wanted to donate to the foundation for foster children. "Please won't you sit down?" Nicolaus offers the two men seats on the opposite side of his desk.

"Well ... thank you for meeting with us."

"Of course!" Elsa provides water bottles, and snacks of cookies, as it is three in the afternoon. "So, tell me, what's on your mind?" Nicolaus asks, not knowing the topic of the meeting.

"Well, Nicolaus, we have been following you and the company. We see that VMC is doing very well. Congratulations!"

"Yes, thank you. We have lots of brilliant and talented people working for us," Nicolaus tells them humbly, not taking full credit for the success of the company. He knew he'd be a fool to do so.

"We think you might be able to use some good publicity about now."

"Good publicity?"

"Yes. We would like to offer you the opportunity to represent our brand. By that I mean, endorse our brand. We have the studios and everything available to make the commercials."

"Wait a minute ... you want me to make commercials for your cars?"

Both men nod with excitement. "You're the perfect demographic: successful, young, good looking, even a veteran. And you drive a sports car!"

"Wow! Thank you for the offer ... hmm ... however ... I don't do endorsements. I think, maybe ... my brother. My brother might be willing to work with you. He already drives one of your cars."

"Your brother ... Benjamin?"

"Yes, he goes by his middle name now, Niall. Niall Ravenell. He's looking for an opportunity. Let me give him your information and I'll ask him to get in touch with you. Also, any corporate donations to our children's foundation will get free advertising in our annual stockholder's report."

"Well, that is wonderful, Nicolaus. We are always open to support such good causes."

The men stand and they all shake hands in new partnership.

Chapter Ninety-Two

N iall was quick to jump on the car commercial opportunity, as it is easy and fun work, with a double benefit of paying well. Part of the arrangement is for Niall to do some media interviews.

Today, Niall is in the studio with a race car magazine interviewer. A yellow sports car is in the background, its doors and hatch open for interesting flair. The backdrop of the studio has black walls, which makes the yellow sports car really pop to the eyes. Niall and the interviewer are sitting to the side of the car, the car behind them.

"We are glad to have Niall Ravenell at this year's car show. Niall is the son of Nigel Ravenell of the Villamae Medical Corporation, a most successful healthcare company in our nation. Niall, we understand you have owned this brand before. Tell us what you like about the specifications."

The makeup artist made Niall look very handsome. His hair is just right. A little makeup on his eyes lightened the dark circles from too much drink and not enough sleep.

"Well, the motor in this model is great, it goes from zero to one hundred in less than sixty seconds."

"Zero to one hundred?"

"Yes, and it handles very easily."

"So you've been driving for a while. And endorsing?"

"Yes, I've owned this model for a few years now. As far as endorsing, I'm new to this. My brother hooked me up!"

"Well, we'd love to talk to you more about endorsing our brand as well." Niall nods with a smile, feeling his endorsement career may really be taking off. "You mentioned your brother ... would that be the famous Nicolaus Ravenell?" The media interviewer jumps right onto that subject. Every good journalist, no matter their field, wants the scoop on the relationship woes of Nicolaus and Deirdre.

"That's right."

"Well what's up with his marriage trap? Everyone wants to know why he continues to abandon Deirdre Omari? Why he keeps marrying someone else?"

Niall laughs lightly, not sure what to answer, not having anticipated this topic to be brought up. He put his hands in the air. "Your guess is as good as mine! I can tell you his current wife is no match to Deirdre."

"Not as good, huh?"

"Not even! She's a floozy! Right now she's involved with our company lawyer, my brother's best friend."

"Oh, what? Heavens! Well, that's quite hot info, right there."

Niall put his hands in the air again, "I've probably said too much. Oops!" he says pretentiously. "Anyway, my fav color on these vehicles is silver. Silver looks really cool when you are going really fast."

"And I presume you recommend this model?"

"Hell yeah! Everyone, go out and buy one. You'll look cool, just like me."

With a few more questions, the interview ends.

"Hey Niall, you think I can get an interview with your brother?" the interviewer asks. Niall shrugs, still feeling very cocky from being in the limelight. "I don't see why not. Here, I'll give you his personal number, and you can call him directly." Niall writes Nicolaus' private cell number on the interviewer's note pad.

He stands to leave, looking for a drink, feeling great.

Chapter Ninety-Three

Immediately, Nicolaus began receiving calls on his cell phone from numbers he didn't recognize. However, seeing unknown numbers on his phone is not unusual, as he did sometimes receive calls from celebrities wanting to donate to the foundation.

"Hello," he answers with a slight frown.

"Nicolaus Ravenell? This is Walter, a sports reporter, asking for a response before we print this article about your relationship with your current wife, Gwen."

"What article?" He did not contain his surprise, even though he knew that eventually the press would want to know about Gwen.

"The one that quotes your brother as stating she is, quote, a floozy, unquote, and quote, involved with your company lawyer, unquote."

"My brother said that?" Nicolaus sounds shocked.

"Sorry Nicolaus, it's what he said. Your comment?"

Nicolaus sighs loudly, "No comment." He ends the call. His phone immediately rings again. "Hello."

"This is local news for Mr. Nicolaus Ravenell."

"This is Nicolaus."

"Nicolaus, your brother, Niall Ravenell, has just aired an interview, calling your wife a floozy and states she is romantically involved with a senior member of your company. Can we get a comment from you?"

"No. No comment." Nicolaus ends the call, and the phone rings again. Nicolaus places his phone on the do not disturb mode, so it would stop ringing. He opens his laptop computer and looks for the interview. He finds it listed among several news stories of what Niall said about Gwen. Nicolaus immediately grows angry.

He clicks on the interview to listen. He hears the exact words the reporter told him, then the interview ends.

Nicolaus replays it again, this time noticing the callous and reckless way Niall threw this information into the public sphere. He didn't seem to have a care of how this would affect Gwen, Alexander, him, or the company.

Nicolaus slams shut the laptop, breathes a hard sigh, and sits back with eyes closed. This is going to be another storm he'd have to navigate. He breathes several deep breaths to control his anger.

Chapter Ninety-Four

When Nicolaus returned home he ran right into Niall. He shakes his head and glares at his brother, taking a breath before speaking. "Why did you say those things about Gwen in that interview today?" he asks evenly.

"Oh, you saw my interview?"

"The whole damn world saw your interview." Nicolaus shakes his head again. "What the hell is wrong with you?" he asks, trying not to explode on Niall.

"What's wrong with me? I just told the truth."

"You don't have to answer every question a reporter asks you, Niall," Nicolaus explains to his brother with hand gestures. "And you sure don't have to give them your twisted version of what you claim to be the truth."

"So you are going to deny that Gwen is sleeping with Alexander?"

Nicolaus frowns at the coldness of his brother. "It's nobody's business, Niall. And it sure isn't for you to tell the world. What's wrong with you?"

"What's wrong with me? What's wrong with you? Gwen is no angel."

"Well neither are you! The least you can do is protect her dignity!" Nicolaus yells at him, suddenly realizing that Niall probably doesn't understand what his words mean. "Why would you even do that?"

"Why do you keep hurting Deirdre?" Niall threw at him.

Nicolaus frowned deeper at his brother, again feeling shocked. "I know ... you are not standing there ... trying to accuse me ... of purposefully marrying Gwen. I know you're not doing that."

The brothers step up to each other, their chests bumping.

Nigel appears and separates his sons. He'd heard the commotion between them, and felt another fight coming on. "Okay. Okay. Stop. Fighting gets us nowhere."

Nicolaus shakes his head at Niall again, unable to believe his actions. "Sometimes you don't even act like my brother, Niall."

"You know, mother has been trying to get rid of you for some time now. Why don't you just leave!" Niall yells at his brother, thinking he could do the impossible - dislodge Nicolaus from the family. "Take the hint, Nicolaus! Just get the hell out!"

Nigel pushes Niall out of the room, away from Nicolaus, seeing the brothers are still very heated and upset.

Chapter Ninety-Five

At the end of the week, Nicolaus and Alexander hold the monthly board meeting. Nicolaus feels that the board members are unusually resistant to him throughout the whole meeting. This struggle seems to go with the tough week he's been having.

"The last item on the agenda is the funding for the new position of Director of Philanthropy for the foundation," Alexander announces.

"Ah yes, Nicolaus and Alexander, several of us have questions about this item," one of the board members notes. "We thank you for laying out the plans for the children's homes. However, we don't think this is a good idea. It's too risky."

"Liability will be too high," another board member chimes in.

"Nicolaus, we are not trying to be critical, as we know you and Alexander are doing a really good job of running the company. I mean my goodness, we are at record profits!" one of the members commends them.

"Yes, we have devised long term investment tools to keep the company solidified," Nicolaus explains. "And we will have a five hundred thousand dollar investment coming to us at the end of today, and we will have a one point two million dollar investment next week. Our goal is to try for three million in long term investment dollars each month." Nicolaus nods at Alexander who is agreeing with him. "If we can reach this goal each year, it will shore us up for at least three years into the future, perpetually."

Nigel touches Nicolaus' arm. He is smiling wide and beaming with pride at his son. "The way you and Alexander are taking care of the company is really amazing. Impressive, even! Thank you, son! Thank you, Alexander."

"This company is definitely in better shape than when we handed it over to the two of you. We are very proud of you," Dwight adds.

Nicolaus and Alexander smile and nod a thanks to each other and their father's.

"Yes, we agree, that is wonderful and impressive planning. We just can't save all the children from foster care. It's a noble idea, but we just don't think it will work."

Nicolaus frowns at them. "You're forgetting, it's within the foundation, a non-profit, so the liabilities will be covered. It's our give back to the communities, and these children do need our assistance. It goes with our mission. I agree that we cannot save them all, although we must, and should, and can try to save as many children as possible. We can get them out of the foster care system, get them graduated from high school and into trade school or college. We can even hire some of them in our clinics, regardless, we'd be giving them a career path for independent living. So you see, it's a long term social investment in the communities. Who knows, it may even be possible for us to help to develop a physician or two; for sure some nurses!" He advocates for the children, laying out the vision.

"Nicolaus, we think it's noble, only that ..."

"Ten homes in every city where we have clinics? That is just too much. It's too big."

"Well ... we can cut it back," Nicolaus tries to appease them. "We can do five houses instead of ten."

"And anyway, rumor has it you plan on giving this position to Deirdre, your former fiancée," another board member challenges him.

Nicolaus nods. "It's not a rumor, it's true. We need an effective and intelligent lawyer in this position, and Deirdre helped to create the plans. This all started with her ideas. She will either be in the roles of lawyer and director, or will hire someone to manage the program after fully developing it out. Once this position is created, the rest of the funding will be generated through the foundation."

"I don't know, Mr. Nicolaus," they continue to argue against him, "isn't that a conflict of interest for you? How would there be accountability?"

Nicolaus lets out a long sigh. "Look, it's not a conflict of interest, because I will not be handling the funds. Our accounting department keeps all this separated. Look everyone, I only need you to provide the initial funds for the position. The foundation, and the board members of the foundation will take care of the rest."

"And you want two-hundred forty-five thousand dollars a year? That's a hefty salary."

"Well, it's not too much for the dual roles of lawyer and director. We need to make the salary fair and competitive."

"We are sorry, Mr. Nicolaus, we feel you are too close to this. We will not be voting on this item today."

"Wait ... what? Are you saying ... no?" Nicolaus is astonished, never having heard this from the board members before. Normally, they go along with his proposals, and approve them after their questions are answered.

Ceil stands. "We are clearly telling you that we are not going to be funding your side chick." She turns to the board, "This meeting is adjourned!" As Ceil leaves, the other board members follow her out the room.

Nicolaus frowns, still astonished, "Did ... she ... just ... insult me?" he asks Alexander and his father.

Nigel sighs, "Sorry son, I believe she did. If it helps you though, I would have voted to bring Deirdre on. I think you've created a wonderful position for her, where she will clearly flourish and do great work for our company, and for those children."

"Yes, I agree," Dwight adds his approval. "You will need someone you can trust in this position. And anyway, like you said, she's already in on the planning."

"Don't listen to what they said about this being too big. This is indeed a noble cause, and I think you should find a way to move forward," Nigel encourages him.

Nicolaus nods. "Thank you, father. Thank you, Dwight."

Nigel stands and leaves the conference room with Dwight. Only Nicolaus and Alexander remain seated at the large, high grain wood table.

Nicolaus gathers his documents, his mind already on his next move. "Alexander, just split my salary and give half for Deirdre."

Alexander chuckles, "Well, that still leaves you eighty-five grand short, though."

"Yeah," Nicolaus sighs, "I'll get with accounting, and we'll find that money." He shakes his head. "I can't believe they refused to fund the position."

"Nicolaus, how's Gwen?" Alexander asks him, changing the subject.

Nicolaus sighs again, realizing he is full of sighs today. "You know, I'm not really sure. I haven't been able to get myself to go see about her after what she did." He looks at Alexander, having finished gathering all the documents. "I suppose I'll hear from the rehab center if anything bad happens. Right?"

Alexander chuckles again. "Well ... I've been to see her, and she is doing all right. This seems a little tough on her though. It may actually be the first time she's serious about getting clean."

Nicolaus eyes Alexander with curiosity. "You went to see her?"

"Of course!"

There is silence between them, which makes Alexander uneasy. "Nicolaus, isn't there anything you want to ask me?" He opens the door for discussion with his friend of many decades. Alexander could not imagine what this scenario of discussion about Gwen with Nicolaus would be like, though he knows it must be done. Now is as good a time as any.

Nicolaus thinks for a moment. He didn't want to mention the Niall fiasco, as it did not seem to reach Alexander or the company as of yet. Additionally, he is not sure how to broach the obvious subject. "Not really. Is there anything you want to tell me?"

Alexander touches the arm of his closest friend. "Look, Nicolaus, I'm going to be straight with you. I love Gwen. I love her, I'm in love with her, I want to marry her. She's my 'the one.'" He stops talking to wait for Nicolaus' reaction. Alexander is surprised when Nicolaus smiles brightly at him. "Nicolaus ... did you hear me?"

Nicolaus nods and chuckles. "Wow! I'm really happy for you. I have never heard you say anything like that about any woman, Alexander. You're in love!"

"Yes, ... with Gwen."

Nicolaus playfully nods again, "With Gwen," he repeats, with a great smile, wide eyed, honestly happy for Alexander.

"Nicolaus? You're not mad?"

"How can I be mad? I think it's great!"

"Nicolaus ... I'm in love with ... your wife."

"You're in love with Gwen. I'm in love with Deirdre. It's a mixed up world, isn't it?" Nicolaus chuckles. "You just have to be careful, you know the media would go after all of us over this."

Alexander grabs Nicolaus' arm. "Look ... would you be very offended if Gwen wanted to annul your marriage to her?" He got right down to his plan of action for receiving Gwen.

"God no! Where do I sign? You have the papers drawn up already?"

"No! I'd have to have someone else do it. But seriously, Nicolaus ..."

"I am being serious. Alexander, I owe you. I haven't forgotten what you've done for me. How you helped me save our family, our company, and our money. I will never forget that. You treated me like a brother ... better than my own brother has ever treated me. You are my brother Alexander, and I will do anything for you. I can see that if you could marry Gwen, it would make you happy. Just tell me what to sign, and I'll sign it."

"Wow! Great! Thank you, Nicolaus." Alexander's hold on Nicolaus tightens with gratitude. "Only, you'll have to tell her to do it. She won't listen to me. She's scared. Nicolaus, if you tell her to get the annulment papers drawn up, she'll do it."

"Okay, no problem." Nicolaus pulls Alexander into a brotherly hug. "No problem at all. I want to see you happy!"

"Thank you, Nicolaus."

Chapter Ninety-Six

Nicolaus and Deirdre walk with Penelope through the airport. "Hey, let's stop here for lunch," he offers, as they still had plenty of time before Penelope had to board the plane for Latvia. Nicolaus sits them down at a round table, Deirdre between them. Nicolaus retrieves menus, for each of them, which were placed in the container on the fancy table.

After looking over the lunch menu, Nicolaus points out an item to Penelope. "Penelope, you've got to try this burger. I think you'll like it."

Deirdre nods, "Yes, I think I'll have that one."

"Why you being so nice to me, Nicolaus?" she asks, in a calm tone. "You glad to see me leave. First you help me to respect my sister at her grave, and then you drive me to the airport, and now you buying me lunch."

Nicolaus smiles at her. "I'm sorry I haven't spent more time with you, it's just been very busy this week. I haven't seen Deirdre either."

Deirdre nods with a smile. "It's true. Sometimes Nicky does get very busy, Penelope."

The waiter approaches their table, and after some small talk, takes their orders, and then replaces the menus for them.

"So you no intend to answer questions, then?" she asks him.

Nicolaus waives his hand through the air. "What do you want to know?"

Penelope livens up at his response, having expected a fight. "What is the last thing you talk about with my sister?"

Nicolaus clenches his jaw, and frowns. The memories still vivid for him. "I remember that she happily admitted to killing my son. I told her we couldn't live together anymore, and that she would go home with you and your father. She said I would disgrace her, and I told her she had already disgraced herself, and that my decision was final. Then ... I told her I forgave her." Deirdre touches Nicolaus' hand, seeing the pain on his face. "Penelope, that is the last I said to her. I left the room, and the next thing I knew ...."

Penelope releases emotion through tears. "No wonder." She opens her purse and pulls out tissues to wipe her eyes. "She was right you know. Sending her home is to disgrace her, Nicolaus." Penelope gets a hold of herself. She wipes her face.

"Look, it was the most logical thing to do. She wasn't happy here. She took it out on my son. In the most ... horrific way."

"Nicolaus, you played a part in it. You have to be punished as well," Penelope declared.

"Punished? You keep saying that."

Deirdre touches Penelope's shoulder, trying to calm her unreasonable talk.

Nicolaus frowns at her comment. "Don't you think I'm already being punished? Every morning I think about the harm that was brought upon my baby son. How he is in his little coffin, buried in the ground. I can never hold him again, or kiss his head, or see him grow.

I'll never have him back."

Deirdre pivots to touch Nicolaus' shoulder, to try to comfort him.

Nicolaus continues, "I have to take solace that my faith in God tells me that my son is actually not in that coffin, only his body, and that his spirit is already in heaven. I believe he lives with angels now. And maybe someday I'll see him again. The tearing away of him is hard to bear, and I think that is what you feel about your sister, Penelope. You probably miss her." He reaches across the table and touches Penelope's hand.

She looks at him in his eyes. "Yes, thank you for that, Nicolaus." She sighs, some of her anger melting away.

"What does your religious faith tell you? Will you see Marguerite again?" he asks her, his thoughts of his former wife softening for the first time since her death.

"I believe so, because she was sad and distressed."

Both Nicolaus and Deirdre silently nod, agreeing with her.

Penelope felt a little better by the time their food arrived. Nicolaus orders them drinks as well. He hoped to settle Penelope down for her flight home.

"How is your father doing? How's the business?" he asks her, changing the subject.

"Father has let me do more. He is teaching me the finances," she tells them.

Nicolaus smiles at her. "That is really good, Penelope! Really great!"

"I'm a strong believer in women in power," Deirdre states. "And then, Penelope, when we get that power, we use it to do great things, and to help others along the way."

Nicolaus is very glad, and relieved that Penelope changed her tone and talked about normal things. He and Deirdre spent time with her, up to thirty minutes before her boarding time. They walk her to the security gate, and bid her goodbye, wishing her well. Deirdre giving her a hug, as one would a family member.

Penelope is not so sure she is satisfied with the day, however she is glad that Nicolaus actually wanted to spend time with her. She knew she had to consider her situation carefully, as earlier in the week, Ceil had taught her about strategic planning, and how to plan to get the results she wants. She is very sure she can use this same advice in her personal life as well. During the week, Penelope had also bonded with Elsa, a friendship she knew would pay off in the future.

Chapter Ninety-Seven

L eaving the airport was not as easy for Nicolaus and Deirdre as when they arrived with Penelope. After dropping Penelope off at her gate, when they turned, they were suddenly swarmed by a mob of news media people. They hadn't even noticed they were around them until it was too late. Photos are snapped, and microphones are thrown into their faces.

"Nicolaus, aren't you married to Gwen Baird? Where is she?"

"Nicolaus, we understand your wife is in a rehab center, and yet you are here with Deirdre. Any comment?"

"Where are you and Deirdre returning from? A rendezvous?"

"Deirdre, what do you think of Gwen taking Nicolaus from you?"

"Deirdre, how can you be with Nicolaus after he's jilted you so many times?"

"Nicolaus why did you jilt Deirdre? Don't you want to clear this up for the public?"

Nicolaus shields Deirdre from the mob of reporters and cameras that were in their faces. The reporters are trying their best to get a glimpse of Nicolaus and Deirdre; to get a photo in just the right light, with just the right facial expressions; trying to get a phrase or a comment, for their millions of readers and television viewers.

Of course, neither Nicolaus nor Deirdre answered any questions. Nicolaus just tried to navigate them away from the media people. Difficult to see where they are going, they get cornered.

"No comment!" Nicolaus says loudly, so they could hear him over the loud flashing of cameras. "Please, let us pass!" The reporters and journalists do not abide by his demand.

"Why another marriage to someone other than Deirdre?"

"Deirdre, what happened?"

"Deirdre, are you heartbroken again?"

"Please, let us pass!" Nicolaus says again, fully shielding Deirdre, protecting her with the whole of his body.

After about thirty minutes, the airport security finally came to their rescue, making a path for them to get away from the press. However, they are followed and harassed all the way to the vehicle in the parking garage. The press peppers them with non-stop questions.

As Nicolaus finally drives away, he notices the press are still following them. Deirdre is definitely traumatized by the event, and she mostly remains quiet, wondering if she is going to have to need security again.

Unbeknownst to Nicolaus, Gwen is also being hassled by the press. They want this story, and some of them will do anything to get answers.

One particular press member visited Gwen for three consecutive days, having discovered her whereabouts. Gwen had a feeling she shouldn't talk to the press, and she didn't understand why they kept appearing after she told them to go away.

"Gwen, I brought something for you!" Pete with the 'National Tell It Right Gazette' teases her with an item wrapped in a towel.

Gwen smiles, as she could only guess what is inside the towel. She let Pete into her private room, and led him into the bathroom, to avoid the rehab center cameras. She locks the door.

"Uh-uhn! I have a little something you want, and you have a ... little something I want. Fair is fair, Gwen." He teases her with the towel wrapped item.

Gwen begins to sweat. Her saliva glands are activated. She nods, "Okay, okay. Let me see it." She wants to make sure it's her sweet magic dust he is offering.

With a smile, knowing this story would be big enough to get him a promotion, Pete gives her the towel.

Gwen opens the towel and sees a large bag of cocaine. She smiles, calculating in her mind that if she is careful, and only snorts small amounts sparingly, it might last her until she is released. She tastes it, and her mouth goes wild with desire to snort it. She looks at Pete with a smile. "What do you want to know?"

Chapter Ninety-Eight

Nicolaus pulls his car over at Lady Bird Lake, to call Alexander. "Alexander, when is the last time you saw Gwen?"

Alexander frowns with concern. "Why? Is everything okay?"

"Well, I hope so. Deirdre and I are being pursued by the press. We were at the airport dropping off Penelope, and they came out of nowhere. I'm hoping she's okay, because they know she is in rehab."

"Oh no! Do they know where she is?"

"I don't know, they didn't say."

"You know what? I'm going over there to go check on her right now."

"Okay. Call me."

Chapter Ninety-Nine

F rancesca used her links to the Estonian castle staff to try to fill in the blanks about Nicohls and DeeDee. She is a little worried about the pattern she thought she saw emerging in the family history book writings. "Okay, so Nicolaus and I got as far as the third wife. We want to know if Nicohls was forced into the marriages, and what happened to the third wife."

"Well, Mistress Francesca, you are asking very poignant questions, indeed," Butler Brown informs her. "As you know, DeeDee is Nicohls' one and only true love, and ..."

"Wait .... Hello? Hello? Are you there?" static fills the phone line, cutting off the butler's explanation.

"And then once Nicohls went to war ..."

"Brown? Are you there? Hello?" Francesca grew frustrated. "Can you even hear me?

I think the connection went bad again."

"And so when Nicohls ...," the butler, keeps talking through the bad connection, because it sounds fine on his end, and he isn't aware that Francesca is having trouble hearing him. Then suddenly, the line just leaves, and a high-pitched tone resonates from the receiver.

"Oh, hello?" Francesca ends the call on her end. She thought it odd, that this is the third time this has happened. She'd phoned before and the lines were just fine. Somehow, when she asked about Nicohls and DeeDee, the lines would go bad. This worries her even more.

Chapter One Hundred

Gwen is very happy to see Alexander, even though she'd seen him as recently as two days ago. She hugs him to her, and begins kissing on his neck and chest, her addictions in full force again. "Baby ...," she is unable to conceal her want for him, "get over here sweety!" She pulls him into her private room, locking the door.

Immediately, she is upon Alexander, all over him. Alexander holds her at arms length to look at her, and notices her mood and her eyes are different than when he'd seen her a few days ago. "Gwen, are you on something?"

Gwen frowns and turns from him, not answering. She doesn't want to be interrogated. She just wants him. She turns around and tries again, moving quick for a kiss.

Alexander doesn't want to upset her. "Gwen, tell me, has the press been here, talking to you, trying to get a story?"

"Yes," she nods. "Please don't tell Nicky. I don't want him to be mad."

Alexander shakes his head. "He won't be mad. We've got to get you out of here. You're no longer safe." Alexander kisses Gwen again, his heart beating double time. "Let's get you packed up, and out of here!"

Chapter One Hundred One

A few hours later, Nigel saw the stories were breaking on the evening news about Nicolaus, Deirdre, and Gwen. The airport footage is accompanied by the mysterious story of who Gwen Baird is, their guess at how she happened to marry Nicolaus, and how she is put away.

As Nicolaus and Deirdre walk into the mansion, Nigel's cell phone and the house phone begin to ring at the same time. Nigel answers one call, and it is a reporter. As soon as that call is ended, the phone rings again.

Nicolaus walks up to his father, "Sorry, father. They barraged us at the airport."

Nigel sighs. "Why are they asking about Gwen? Oh, right ..." he realizes the answer to his own question.

"Alexander is actually bringing Gwen now. They got ahold of her at the rehab center."

"What? They breached security at the center?"

Nicolaus nods, "Whatever that security might be," he chuckles, knowing many of these facilities have lapse security.

"Gwen should already know not to talk to the press," Nigel comments frowning.

After another hour, Alexander escorts Gwen into the mansion. He man hugs Nicolaus briefly. "These gate cards work wonders. The gate closed so fast after we got in, it kept the press from tailgating behind us."

"Great! That's the intention. Hello Gwen." Both Nicolaus and Deirdre give her a hug. Nicolaus notices that Gwen seems giddy for someone who is detoxing off drugs.

Nigel greets them as well, and he hugs Gwen. "Gwen, are you all right?" he pats her shoulder.

"Yes, Sir. I'm just fine," her toothy grin and wide-eyed smile is back.

"You talk to any reporters?"

"Well ... no," she lies, afraid of any repercussions.

Elsa sprints into the room and hugs her sister. "Gwen, you all right?"

Gwen nods.

"There are news reports about the family, ... including you," Elsa informs her.

"Oh."

Alexander grabs onto Gwen, seeing that she is getting anxious. She doesn't know what may happen to her.

"I've been trying to get ahold of dad, and I cannot seem to reach him. I've been trying to call him for over a week. Did he tell you where he was going?" Elsa inquired.

Gwen shakes her head, and frowns. "No, he didn't tell me. I didn't even know he was gone again. He didn't call me."

Sometimes Jonathan would disappear for a while, and his daughters did not know where he was. Elsa is worried, because he would usually respond within a day or two of her trying to reach him, whether by call or text.

"Well, if you don't mind, father, I'd like to speak with Gwen. Elsa and Alexander, please join us," Nicolaus says.

Nicolaus leads them into the drawing room, and he closes the door, as he continues to hear the non-stop ringing of his father's phone. He'd already turned his phone off, not to be continually bothered by the press. Deirdre and Elsa sit together.

"Well," Nicolaus starts off slow, not wanting to scare Gwen, though happy to help Alexander's relationship along. "There is great love in this room," he looks around, his eyes first landing on Deirdre, then on Gwen. "Great love! And great love cannot be squashed, or diminished, or ignored. I've found that it's impossible to ignore love that is burning in your heart for someone. Gwen, just as you knew about me and Deirdre, before you and I were forced together, I now know about you and Alexander."

Gwen jumps with fright, afraid of what consequence she may face.

Alexander quickly takes her hands. "It's okay, Gwen. It's all right."

"Yes, I couldn't be happier for both of you," Nicolaus chuckles. "I support your love for each other."

"Nicolaus, thank you," Alexander simply replies.

"Yes, and Gwen, if you want to be with Alexander, to marry him, as he wants, all you have to do is give me annulment papers and I'll sign them. An annulment will dissolve our marriage, and you'll be free to be with Alexander."

Gwen gasps, as Alexander had mentioned this to her. "Nicky, are you sure?"

"Yes, of course. If it's what you want ..."

Gwen shakes her head with enthusiasm, "Yes, yes, please."

Nicolaus smiles, as Alexander and Gwen are very hopeful as they look into each other's eyes, while Alexander clings to her. Nicolaus looks to Deirdre, she is shocked, not having expected this. Deirdre puts her hand to her mouth, and begins to silently pray for this to happen, because it would mean that, in the future, she and Nicolaus could marry.

"Nicolaus, we talked about this on the way over. We want to leave. I want to take Gwen away from the press swirl. I'll have my office draw up the annulment papers, and bring them over tomorrow. You can sign and hand it right back to my staff, and he'll fax it to us.

We're going to take our time and drive to Las Vegas. We'll probably stop and spend some time in Albuquerque on the way there. Once the papers are filed in the court, which should only take a few days, we will get married." Alexander said all this without taking his eyes off Gwen.

Nicolaus frowns at him. "Vegas? What about your dad? He'd want to see you get married, Alexander."

Alexander looks at Nicolaus, sighs, shaking his head. "I'm not worried about that. I just want us married, so I can take care of Gwen."

"Wow! Okay, well ... at least let me help you with the expenses." Nicolaus immediately pulls his check book out of his suit pocket. "Consider it my wedding gift to both of you." He sits down and writes out a generous check. He hands it to both of them, however, Gwen snatches it up quick to look at it.

"Nicky, are you serious?" Gwen asks her husband, remembering how sweet he can be.

Nicolaus nods with a smile. "Alexander, maybe you should have your dad go with you. Or at least fly him there to be your witness."

Alexander stands and hugs Nicolaus to him in gratitude. "I hear you my friend. I'll have to think about it."

Chapter One Hundred Two

Nicolaus and Deirdre did not speak about their impending marriage plans for outright fear of jinxing their future. Nothing is to be done until his marriage is annulled. However, Nicolaus did already feel the unjust weight of his second unwanted marriage lifted off his shoulders.

The following morning, Deirdre reported to her new position at Villamae Medical Corporation. She is sharply dressed in a designer pant suit. She is amazed when Nicolaus leads her to her new office, right next to his.

Nicolaus and Alexander had moved into the executive office suites on the top floor of the building, which is part of VMC, once they officially took over the company for their fathers. They adopted offices on opposite sides of the floor, as Alexander needed a few additional offices for his legal staff as well.

With heart felt gladness, Nicolaus opens the door to Deirdre's office. The sun beams into the glass wall, which presents a tremendous view of downtown, overlooking Lady Bird Lake, and had elegant furniture, which he'd personally selected for her.

"Nicky, are you sure you want me in this office?" She enters and twirls in the large space. It is large enough to place other people. There is a conference table, and an additional small desk. Her large, glossy, redwood desk played against the window, giving her a side view outdoors, and a side view to her large office door.

"Of course!" He briefly hugs Deirdre. "You'll be doing very important work. And you are an executive now. You deserve this, and more. I'm so grateful you agreed to help me with this project! And ... I'll be right next door if you need anything.

Deirdre, you may want an administrative staff person to help you out, I didn't want to assume anything. And as we discussed, you'll have funds to hire the staff needed through the foundation.

I scheduled us to meet with the VMC board next week, to give you time to draw up some preliminary plans, since they acted like they didn't want to fund the position. I think once you speak to them, and maybe show them some pictures of the children we'll be helping, that will convince them differently. Then we'll meet with the foundation board the following week."

"Right!" She says, still in shock over her grand office.

Nicolaus looks at his watch. He touches her shoulder. "I've got a meeting in fifteen minutes, and I need to pull some notes and some figures. Company orientation will be at nine, and I've instructed Elsa to get you where you need to be. We can share Elsa until you decide if you need an assistant of your own. I'll see you later."

Nicolaus rushes off to get ready for his meeting. Deirdre is impressed with how professional Nicolaus is towards her. She hopes this trend will continue.

Slowly, Deirdre sits down in the cushy, ergonomically correct desk chair, in awe. Suddenly, she realizes this is all a blessing from God, providing her another chance for a new beginning of her new life with Nicolaus.

Together, they are going to help hundreds of children. They will be extending the strong love they have for each other to children who have little to no love at all. She grabs a tissue, and wipes the tears of joy from her eyes. Deirdre knows that she and Nicolaus are going to have a massive impact on many people, on many children.

Chapter One Hundred Three

The next day, Nicolaus escorts Deirdre to the office café for lunch. Nicolaus and Alexander often had lunch in the café with the other staff, wanting them to know they see them as people, and they appreciate their work.

As expected, many eyes are upon the couple. Nicolaus wants his staff to get used to seeing he and Deirdre together, as it would be more so once they are married.

A courier from Alexander's office tracked down Nicolaus, during the lunch hour. He has the annulment papers ready for his signature. Nicolaus quickly looks over the papers, signs them, and gives them back to the courier, who dashes away. Nicolaus' mind and his heart are relieved, as he smiles at Deirdre. Now it is only a matter of days, maybe a week, and his marriage to Gwen will be dissolved.

Chapter One Hundred Four

"Mum!" Francesca calls. Something doesn't seem right. She'd been unable to reach Rachel on the phone for the needed items at the grocery store. Francesca puts the grocery bags down in the kitchen. "Mum!" she calls again.

Rachel answers Francesca in a weak voice, "Over here. Over here."

Francesca hears her mother's faint voice coming from the guest bathroom. "Mum!" Francesca frantically goes to Rachel, who is on the floor crying and holding her head due to the excruciating pain that is radiating from her brain. "Mum!" Francesca had never seen this before. "What's wrong? What's happened?"

"My meds," Rachel can hardly speak. "My meds, in my room, on the stand." Rachel cries out in pain, cradling her head while laying onto the floor.

Francesca rushes to her mother's bedroom. There are two bottles of medication on the nightstand; one is Dilantin for seizures, and the other is Morphine for pain. Francesca grabs the morphine and runs back to her mother. "This?" she shows Rachel the bottle. Rachel nods. Francesca quickly reads the recommended dosage. She provides water and one pill, for which Rachel gestures for her to provide her another. Not arguing the point, Francesca gives her another pill, and watches her mother swallow them down.

Tears well Francesca's eyes. She slumps onto the floor, next to her mother, taking her hand, already understanding what is wrong.

"You cannot tell anybody," Rachel vows her daughter to secrecy, in her weakened state.

"How long, Mum? How long did they give you?"

Rachel closes her eyes to the pain, and shakes her head negatively.

"Oh!" Francesca exclaims. It's unthinkable! She is going to lose her mother to brain cancer.

Chapter One Hundred Five

The following day, Nicolaus is in the middle of a meeting with the accounting team, when, unusually, he is interrupted by Elsa, who is followed by deputies from the sheriff's department. Elsa gestures to him that it is important. Nicolaus dismisses his staff, letting them know he will reconvene the meeting at a later time.

The deputies remove their hats. "Mr. Nicolaus Ravenell?"

"Yes. Won't you have a seat?"

"Ah, no Sir," one of the deputies answers. "And we need Mrs. Elsa Ravenell."

Elsa frowns. "That is me!"

Nicolaus also frowns. "What is this about?"

"I am very sorry to inform you, Sir, that your wife, and your sister, Ma'am, Mrs. Gwen Ravenell, was involved in a car accident. Your partner, Mr. Alexander Collins, was in the vehicle with her."

"Jesus! Where are they? We'll go to them immediately."

"Well ..., I'm very sorry to tell you this, Sir, ... they were hit head on by an eighteen wheeler freight truck. It had a full load. We believe the driver suffered some kind of medical crisis at the time of the accident. No one ... survived, Sir."

"Oh no!" Elsa cries out, feeling like she might faint. Nicolaus catches Elsa in his arms, and helps her to a chair.

"Are you sure?" Nicolaus asks, frowning, while trying to tend to Elsa.

"I know this is very difficult, Sir, I am very sorry. We are sure. No one survived."

Nicolaus slightly shakes his head, unable to believe what is being told to him. "Where did this happen?"

"On the highway, in Albuquerque, about four hours ago now, Sir."

Nicolaus sits down, shock befalling him as he tries to comprehend this unbelievable news. Alexander and Gwen had only been gone for two days. If they were in Albuquerque, that means they had not even made it to Las Vegas yet.

"My God!" Nicolaus is suddenly overcome with emotion, as Elsa begins to cry. "My God!" He hugs Elsa, unable to comfort her, unable to comfort himself.

Chapter One Hundred Six

When Nicolaus returns home, Elsa with him, Deirdre and Helena are there for them, having heard the news. Deirdre had spent the afternoon with Helena, preparing for her board meeting presentation. During this time with Deirdre, Helena, more so, receives an understanding of how both Nicolaus and Deirdre are utilizing their full potential as wealthy human beings with good hearts, to do good for others.

Nicolaus finds that he cannot go into the room he shared with Gwen. He couldn't open the door, nor stand to enter and see her things. Surely, she had expected to return. Nicolaus' mind does not want to accept that he will never get to speak to either Alexander or Gwen again. He slides down the wall, and seats himself outside the bedroom door for a while, tears spilling from his eyes as he mourns both Gwen and Alexander.

Suddenly Helena is next to Nicolaus, on the floor, as Deirdre remains with Elsa to comfort her. Helena grabs onto Nicolaus and holds him tight. Immediately, he leans into her, accepting the comfort. He wants to be angry, however, somehow, Helena vanishes that feeling from him. Helena grips him tighter, as if he were hers. "Shh! It's all right, Nicky," she whispers to him, stroking his hair. She consoles him as best she can, realizing this is a difficult time. She revels in his acceptance of her as she reassures him.

Helena rubs Nicolaus' back as she can tell he is calming down a little. She kisses his head and strokes his hair, something she didn't think she'd ever get to do. "It's going to be all right."

"No," he tells her. "I have done this. Oh God, Helena, what have I done?"

"Nicky, you had no way of knowing this would happen," she tries to logically explain to him, not exactly sure what he is talking about. "This is not your fault."

"No, you don't understand," he explains softly, with emotion.

He attempts to pull away from her, and she won't let him. "You rest here with me, at least for a little while." She rubs his back again. She fully takes his muscular torso into her arms. Her heart is glad she is able to be here for him at this particular time. Something she knows he will never forget. Something to intimately remember of her.

Niall takes over the comforting of Elsa. When Deirdre sees that he behaved properly, she seeks out Nicolaus. Deirdre finds Nicolaus on the floor, outside the bedroom he shared with Gwen, in Helena's arms. Thinking nothing of the scene, she joins them. Nicolaus quickly takes her in his arms, pulling her close to him.

Nicolaus continues painfully explaining, taking their deaths fully on his shoulders. "I was too lenient with them. I should have insisted Gwen live up to her end of our marriage, just as she demanded of me. Instead, I saw an easy way out and I took it. I celebrated their love, even though it was a sin. Now, they've died with that sin on them. I should have saved them from it. I knew better, and I ignored what should have been done to honor God, ... for my own selfish reasons."

Deirdre hugs up closer to Nicolaus, feeling this is partly her fault as well. "I'm just as guilty as you, my love, 'cause I didn't speak up, or speak against the idea, either. I was just happy for a pathway for us to be together," she cries against him.

The religious countenance of the couple gave Helena a quick perspective and drew her away from her lusty want of Nicolaus. Helena is shocked that Nicolaus thinks of this situation in this way. She realizes she doesn't understand his mind as well as she'd thought she did.

Tears now fall from Helena's eyes too, "You ... are both ... so different from the others ...." She is not even sure if she is referring to the Ravenell family members or people in general.

"What have I done?" Nicolaus whispers aloud. "Their souls could be condemned."

"Nicky, we have to pray for their souls. You have to pray for them," Deirdre directs him, knowing his prayers are powerful. "And ... we must seek forgiveness as well," Deirdre whispers, sharing the shame of this burden with her beloved.

The three of them stay in a heap on the floor for a while, hugged up and crying. Helena witnesses the prayerful side of Nicolaus, as he starts off praying as usual in the Latin language, and then converts the prayers to English. She is awestruck. In humility, Nicolaus realizes he'd have a lot of praying to do just to try to make a small transformation on this tragedy, if God or the angels would even acknowledge his prayers.

After a while, Nicolaus goes to Nigel, and they phone Dwight together. Overcome with emotion again, "Father, we need to go be with Dwight."

When they arrive, Dwight tries to be strong, however, neither he nor Nicolaus can hardly hold themselves together.

"Nicolaus, I want you to know that Alexander called me this morning before getting on the road. He told me he'd planned on marrying Gwen, once your marriage to her was to be annulled in a few days. He wanted to marry that girl, and he said you insisted I should be there." Nicolaus nods in silence, the pain raw on him. "He was going to send me a ticket once they arrived in Vegas." Dwight sheds tears for his only son, his only child. "I want you to know that I appreciate that you wanted me to be there for him and told him to have me there." Dwight wipes his eyes, and clears his throat. "Of course I wanted to see my son marry. You were absolutely right about that Nicolaus."

Nicolaus hugs Dwight tightly, "I'm so sorry," Nicolaus whispers to him, still plagued with guilt. Nicolaus feels for Dwight, having lost his own son, he partially understands Dwight's pain. Except now, Nicolaus is experiencing the loss of a brother as well, at the same time as the loss of another wife.

Chapter One Hundred Seven

Nicolaus had a restless sleep. He is exhausted and wasn't even aware that he'd fallen asleep on the drawing room sofa. Sleep found him sitting up, his head back, Deirdre next to him. Ceil actually felt pity for Nicolaus, and covered the couple with some throw blankets in the early morning hours.

Nicolaus opens his eyes to Deirdre, looking upon him, holding his hand, her beauty evident. She slightly smiles at him. He wonders if she slept at all.

"I want to go to the church," Nicolaus tells her.

Deirdre nods. "Then I'll go with you."

Nicolaus showered and changed clothes, while Deirdre freshened up. They left for the church together. They didn't worry about breakfast, as it's early, and the house is still quiet.

They walk hand in hand into the large church. The pews are empty, however, having heard about what happened, the priest and the bishop are present, as if they almost expected the arrival of Nicolaus.

The bishop outstretches a welcoming arm to them. "Are you here to pray?" He asks.

Nicolaus nods. He releases Deirdre's hand and goes to the altar. He falls onto his knees at the praying stand. Immediately, tears pour from his eyes, as in his mind, he has work to do regarding Gwen and Alexander. He bows his head, indeed his whole body.

"And you, child?" the bishop reaches for Deirdre. She kneels next to Nicolaus, closes her eyes, and bows her head as well. In her own heart, she prays for Nicolaus, that his words and prayers be heeded. She prays for Gwen, remembering that toothy smile. She prays for Alexander, that he be at peace. The priest prays over the two of them.

Nicolaus whispers his sorrowful prayers in Latin. Bishop Leighton looks upon Nicolaus, with knowing eyes, always amazed at him. Bishop Leighton can see that God has placed a destiny upon Nicolaus, and he can see that he is emerging into that role, outside of his family.

Bishop Leighton watches as Nicolaus' prayers grow stronger, and he cries uncontrollably, as more and more words of prayer flow from his mouth.

Feeling that something is about to happen, Deirdre opens her eyes to watch. Suddenly a force grips Nicolaus. The bishop could see the Holy Spirit of love upon Nicolaus. He takes the anointing oil, blesses it, and with his thumb, he spreads some on Nicolaus' forehead, sealing the vision and the appropriation God put upon this young man. When Bishop Leighton removes his thumb, Nicolaus falls backwards, wrapped in holy power.

"Nicky," Deirdre whispers his name, hoping this is the sign of his prayers being answered, that he is also being healed.

The bishop gently pulls Deirdre to her feet and into his loving arms, as they both keep their eyes on Nicolaus. "God is touching him. It is not every day that we see young men like Nicolaus being touched by the holy spirit. He will be a stronger man for it." Bishop Leighton pats Deirdre's arm, pulling her to him, his usual way of hugging his congregants. "Have some tea with me. Let us leave him in peace. He will be all right. My priest will be here to watch over him."

Reluctantly, Deirdre leaves Nicolaus and walks with the bishop.

Bishop Leighton leads Deirdre to the back rooms of the church. They enter the kitchen.

He hands her some tea leaves and the grinder, and he puts the large teapot of water on the stove to boil. "You truly love Nicolaus, don't you?"

"Yes, Sir, I do," Deirdre chuckles at the bishop's insight and question, as she grinds the tea leaves.

"I always see you with him, for years now, no matter what. Even through his previous marriages. Always by his side, devoted to him. Even willing to raise his child, which was not yours."

"Yes, Sir," she says humbly. "I love Nicolaus, I'd do anything for him."

"That kind of devotion is usually reserved for service to God. Perhaps you should have been a sister of God inside the church."

Deirdre chuckles again. She kisses the bishop's cheek. "You are very sweet." She returns her attention to grinding the tea leaves. She sighs, "Bishop, if God grants my prayer, will you ..."

"Yes daughter. You will be the next wife. A true wife to him," he answers her question. Deirdre looks at him shocked that he knew what she was going to ask. However, the bishop also sees the cloud that looms over this innocent woman. "God does not give us forever to live." He takes the ground up leaves from her, puts some in a cup, and using a ladle, pours hot water over them. "It is what we do with the time He does give us that matters. Do you understand, daughter?"

Deirdre nods, frowning. "Yes."

The bishop continues his explanation. "Parties, and gatherings, and dances do not matter, daughter. What does matter are the poor, the fatherless, the hungry, the sick, and the beggars. This is whom God wishes us to look after."

Deirdre nods, fully understanding his intent. "Yes, Nicky and I are starting a project to help children, Bishop. The exact children you have just named."

The bishop smiles at her, touching her arm. "This is very good. Although, Deirdre, it must be bigger. You and Nicolaus have international influence. You must use this influence that you have been blessed with wisely. When you become the next wife to

Nicolaus, it will be as if you are a princess. You must remember these things I am saying, as it will be easy to lose sight once the marriage happens. You cannot look to his mother for guidance, as she has a heart of stone, and she does not care of these matters." Deirdre's eyes grow wide at his words, surprised that he knows about the real Ceil Ravenell.

The bishop makes another cup of tea for himself, and then another for Nicolaus. "Nicolaus' father, though he has done very good work with medical care for children and the underprivileged, he is afraid of his wife. It is up to you and Nicolaus to make changes, and to bring improvements to people's lives. You'd be very surprised how minor changes make a huge difference to very many people." The bishop led Deirdre to a round table. They both sit down.

"Doesn't Nicolaus need this information, since he ..."

"Nicolaus already knows these things. When he was a child, he used to study scripture. He was insatiable about it."

"Yes, I remember."

Bishop Leighton clasps his hands to his mouth. "And I see that Nicolaus has not forgotten these things, ... though he has not been fully practicing them, either. That is probably why God is upon him. He must remember his purpose." The bishop takes a slurp of his hot tea. "Nicolaus has been struggling about what to do, and how to go about things. However, with you by his side, it will all be clear. You are the devoted woman that will bring his purpose about."

Deirdre humbly nods, hoping the bishop is correct. She sips her tea and looks at the direction of the door. "Should we go check on him?"

The bishop smiles, knowing she is worried about the man she loves, as a good wife should be. "Yes, let us."

They re-enter the inner sanctuary of the church together and find Nicolaus sitting on the floor at the altar. He'd removed his shirt to dry the sweat and tears from his face and body, his bare muscular torso exposed. The priest hands him a towel to dry himself.

"See daughter? I told you he would be all right."

They walk over to Nicolaus, and the bishop helps him up. Deirdre grabs onto his arm, touching his chest, and they lead him back into the kitchen. Nicolaus replaces his wet shirt, and they all sit at the round table. Deirdre hands Nicolaus his tea.

In silence, he sips the tea slowly, noticing it is bitter and has bits of leaves floating in the cup. Nicolaus looks at the bishop. "What does God want of me?" he asks softly, almost in a whisper.

The bishop chuckles. "Perhaps He wants of you what He wants of all men: your soul."

"He has that. He has my soul."

"Then perhaps He wants more of your time. More devotion. More service. Perhaps He wants you to remember your purpose, Nicolaus Ravenell!" The bishop smirks. "Deirdre and I were just talking about that very thing."

Nicolaus looks to Deirdre, her beauty striking him, right there in the church. His heart pines for her, while at the same time aches with mourning for Gwen and Alexander. Quietly, he drinks his bitter tea, a reminder of how blessed his life is, despite his sorrows.

Chapter One Hundred Eight

B reakfast time at the Ravenell mansion feels extremely awkward. Gwen's chair is empty, and neither Nicolaus nor Deirdre are present, as they are at the church.

Now it is Niall who cries uncontrollably. He cannot believe Alexander, whom he cares about, and had known for years, though he had not always treated with kindness, has died. His crying made Elsa cry, she hugs Niall quickly, and then she runs out from the breakfast room, unable to endure his sadness.

Lady Helena pulls a chair next to Niall, and she does what Ceil and Nigel were totally incapable of doing, she consoles him. She holds him to her, and he cries like a child. "Alexander is gone," he says it as if saying it made it more impossible to believe. "I shouldn't have done what I did! I shouldn't have talked bad about them to the media." Niall seems to finally understand the weight of his actions. He feels shameful, and his crying intensifies.

"Shh!" Helena frowns, tears welling in her eyes. "It's going to be all right." Helena holds him tight.

Looking upon Niall, Ceil begins to sob. She recognizes the tragedy of these young people being taken from them. She'd made up her mind to like Gwen, and to use her for her revenge against Nicolaus. She hated Nicolaus the more so because of it.

Nigel observes Ceil as her sobs become loud mourning, into her napkin. He didn't know what to do for her. He takes her hand, and then finds himself crying as well.

Ceil stands up and also runs away from the table, out of the breakfast room.

"Our family cannot go on like this," Nigel cries. "We are so hateful to each other. We are no examples to anyone! Only Nicolaus and Deirdre. They try to live right and good." Nigel feels the sting that anyone of them could die at any time for any reason.

"We have to make changes in our lives. We all must, or all will be lost." In despair, Nigel slowly leaves the room.

Chapter One Hundred Nine

The funerals were held one day after the next, Gwen is memorialized first. Helena assists Nicolaus, while Deirdre, Ishani and Maggie support Elsa. Elsa has been furiously fussing that she is unable to reach her father. She wondered if something bad had happened to him as well.

Then, on the day of the funeral, Elsa heard her father's voice behind her, and she turns to see him. "Dad!" Elsa runs to him and hugs him. "Oh my God, I've been trying to get a hold of you! Where have you been?"

Jonathan smiles at Elsa, then frowns at her bruised lip, and eye, and says nothing of it, as Gwen's funeral service is about to begin. "Taking care of business. When I heard the news about Gwen, I took a first plane over."

The family, guests, and press settle down in the church. Elsa eulogizes her sister. She acknowledges Nicolaus as a good husband. Elsa remembers their time as children, Gwen's likes and dislikes, and she talks about Gwen's unmet dream of becoming a stage dancer in New York. Then she talks about how much she loves and will miss her sister. No one in the church has dry eyes.

Nicolaus stands before the coffin, for one last look at Gwen before it was closed. He is plagued with guilt again, feeling her death is his fault for encouraging her to run off with Alexander. If he'd opposed them, perhaps they would have never left at all, and they'd both be alive.

Deirdre went right to his side, realizing he is feeling guilty. She hugs onto Nicolaus, lifting herself on her toes, kissing his face. "Honey, I just know, God will forgive all," she whispers to him. "Gwen was sweet, and kind to everyone she came across. We'll always remember her smile." Nicolaus looks down, stepping back from the coffin. With Deirdre's help, he finds his way back to the church pew. He needs to sit. He is having a hard time understanding why this is all happening.

Nicolaus observed that neither Gwen nor Alexander suffered bodily damage from the wreck, as they both look as if they are sleeping. He prayed that they did not suffer at all, if it was God's will for them not to suffer.

As the minister began to end the service, Nicolaus begins his silent prayers again, hoping that Alexander is finding a wonderful journey to the heavens in his afterlife. Nicolaus begs for forgiveness for both Gwen and Alexander, requesting for their love of each other to be highlighted over their sin of adultery; for their love of each other to be honored.

Deirdre holds onto Nicolaus hand and arm, as he tightens his hold on her hand, his prayers growing more intense. The choir sings as the coffin is being prepared to be taken out of the church, and onto the family burial grounds, at the Ravenell mansion.

Gwen will be laid to rest next to the other Ravenells, specifically next to Marguerite.

Nigel grips Nicolaus' shoulder as they are to lead the people out of the church. There are quite a few people in support of Nicolaus, Nigel, and Ceil. Nicolaus ends his prayers, and leads the family out, Deirdre by his side holding onto his arm, he clutches onto Elsa's hand, not caring what Niall wants. As they leave the church, paparazzi, international news media, and several reporters follow the family in droves, snapping photos, and trying to get comments.

The funeral procession winds its way through the Austin streets. In the limo which carries the young Ravenells, Deirdre, Ishani, and Maggie, Niall apologizes to Nicolaus.

"I'm sorry for what I did regarding the press. I was wrong," he tells Nicolaus, as he grips onto Elsa's hand.

Nicolaus touches Niall's other hand and nods, fully accepting the apology.

The parents ride in the first limousine. Both vehicles reach the circle driveway of the Ravenell mansion. Paw bearers remove the coffin from the hearse vehicle, and carry it to Gwen's final resting place. The family follow the coffin the quarter mile trek to the gravesite, where Bishop Leighton conducts the burial service, reminding the family, and the guests to remember God in all they do, in all their actions.

The family gathers around the coffin, as it is lowered into the ground. Niall stands next to Nicolaus, not sure what to expect. Nicolaus hugs his younger brother to him, in forgiveness and solidarity. The ladies notice that Francesca is missing, and think this odd.

Elsa and her father stand before the grave. Elsa is distraught, crying tears for her sister. Niall steps up and actually holds onto Elsa, hugging her to him, as he should. Niall did a good job of trying to console Elsa, even though he did not have much interaction with Gwen.

Deirdre and Helena keep their eyes on Nicolaus, as it is Rachel who is next to him now, holding onto his hand and his arm, being his support, steadying him, comforting him.

Chapter One Hundred Ten

At the end of the burial service, Elsa takes her father and Niall inside the mansion, into the sitting room, and locks the door for privacy from the guests and the press.

Elsa tells her father that she is considering leaving with him. "Dad, I'm thinking of permanently leaving here. Perhaps I should leave with you now."

This does not sit well with Jonathan. He jerks Niall by the neck. "Why does my only remaining daughter talk about leaving you? Look at her! She is in tears. Her lip is cut. Her eye is bruised. What have you done to her?"

Fear strikes Niall as Jonathan's grip on him tightens. No one is around to help him, as all the family is still outside. "I have been a good husband. Tell him Elsa. Tell him!"

Elsa drew courage from her father. She shoves at Niall's chest. "Tell him what? How you hit me, and slap me around? How Nicolaus had to save me from you? How you hate me, and think I tricked you into marrying me?" She shoves him again, and decides to tell all. "How you have no respect for me? How you never let me sleep, and never let me rest?" She collapses to the floor in tears. This is all too much for her.

"Oh, so now, you need a lesson in how to treat a woman, especially my princess. You will take your lesson like a man," he orders Niall.

No one really knows what exactly happened behind those locked doors, except the two men who were in the room. Nicolaus and Deirdre happen upon Elsa crying, sitting on the bench outside the sitting room door. Nicolaus and Deirdre comfort her.

When Jonathan reappears out the sitting room door, he grips Nicolaus around the neck, surprising him. "You must help your brother learn how to treat his wife." He briefly and roughly hugs Nicolaus to him, "I bid you goodbye, Nicolaus Ravenell."

Jonathan turns to his daughter, lightly kissing her face, "I want a weekly report on your husband, Elsa. Ready yourself for the birth of my grandchild." Jonathan leaves her to offer Ceil and Nigel his goodbyes.

Nicolaus enters the sitting room to find Niall, who had fainted and is on the floor. Worried, Nicolaus taps Niall on the face, trying to wake him. He seems to have similar bruises to what he'd given to Elsa, his eye already swollen shut, his lip bleeding, and his other eye bruised. Niall regains consciousness, moaning. He grabs at his crotch in pain, and Nicolaus can only guess that Jonathan hurt him there. Nicolaus hoists his brother over his shoulder, and carries him up to his bed.

Chapter One Hundred Eleven

The following day, Alexander's funeral is even more difficult for Nicolaus. All the Ravenells attended, except Francesca, again. Deirdre and Rachel flank Nicolaus, Deirdre not letting go of his hand. The loss of Alexander also hit Deirdre hard, as she cries tears of sadness. She can't believe he is gone.

Nicolaus notices there is less press than at Gwen's funeral. He, Nigel, Rachel, and Deirdre sit up front with the rest of Dwight's family. Alexander's grandmother, and plenty of cousins attend, as well as several friends, his law firm staff, and others from the community.

After the funeral and burial service, Nicolaus and Deirdre drive Rachel home, as he is worried about Francesca. At the sight of Nicolaus, Francesca runs to him, and holds him tight, her tears unstoppable. Rachel pulls Deirdre with her into the kitchen, giving them some privacy.

"How was it? I'm so sorry I couldn't be there."

Nicolaus wipes Francesca's tears, frowning at her. He shakes his head, having trouble finding words. They sit down. "Are you okay?"

"I just ... I just couldn't do the funerals. Oh Nicky, I'm sorry."

"Don't be sorry. As long as you're okay."

Francesca sighs, "Who can be okay with all this going on?" She touches Nicolaus' shoulder. "Nicky, this has got to be so hard for you."

Nicolaus nods again, words muting him.

They hug each other again. Francesca so wants to tell Nicolaus about Rachel, hating to keep this magnitude of a secret from him.

Rachel and Deirdre reappear with tea and cakes.

Chapter One Hundred Twelve

Nicolaus takes time for himself and does not return to the office right away. A week has gone by since Gwen's death. Rachel noticed that Nicolaus is very sad, and maybe a bit distraught. She fears he may get lost in a funk, and not find himself again. She is concerned that he may not take the next step that everyone expects him to take. Most of all, Rachel worries that Nicolaus might lose sight of his greater purpose of running the company and controlling the family interests for the future.

However, Rachel is overjoyed that Nicolaus is spending much time with her and Francesca, even sleeping over, despite her being sure he is mostly avoiding his parents and Niall. Rachel touches Nicolaus. She knows what he is thinking. She knows she has to get him to move forward. "What are you waiting for?" she gently asks him, nodding towards Deirdre, who is sitting across the room from them in conversation with Helena.

Nicolaus bites his lip. He looks down, still feeling very solemn.

"Stop blaming yourself. It's not your fault."

He crosses his arms, his hand to his mouth. He isn't sure what to say. Nicolaus slightly smiles, "How do you know what I'm thinking?"

"I know you, Nicolaus. I know you, my love. You couldn't have changed anything that happened."

He sighs. "I encouraged them when I should have chastised them. I sent them to ..."

"You sent them off with your blessing to be happy." Rachel touches his shoulder. "You encouraged their gift of love, Nicky. The measure of a man ..."

"Yeah, and now ..."

"So you think you have some kind of power to send people to their damnation or something?" She frowns at him to get her point across. "They are grown people, Nicolaus.

Do you think they needed your blessing? They could have run off to be together, regardless."

Nicolaus tries to let Rachel's words comfort him, and is finding it hard to do so, although he knows she is right. He understands he is no lord or king to grant anyone anything or to place judgement on anyone.

Rachel grabs both of his arms in a hug. "It's time for you to claim your true bride, Nicky. The angels have kept your children long enough. Life is too short." She kisses his face. "Don't waste any more time. None of us know how many days we are given here on earth. Love your bride with all your heart, and give her more than your best." Rachel kisses him again. "You couldn't have prevented Gwen's death, anyway. Remember the family book?"

"The family book?"

"Yes. The second wife dies by accident."

Nicolaus looks at Rachel in awe and worry. He does remember this. He frowns. "What of the third wife? What's to happen?" His eyes look right upon his beloved Deirdre. He loves her so much, yet his heart aches for Alexander. He doesn't understand why he is now gone.

Rachel shakes her head, "I don't know. You and Deirdre must write that chapter." She kisses him a third time. "Make it a good one, Nicolaus." She leaves him, hoping she has given him the push he needs.

Chapter One Hundred Thirteen

Deirdre noticed that Nicolaus had not removed his marriage band that bonded him to Gwen. This troubles her greatly, because she didn't know what it meant. She also noticed the depression that had set about him. She stepped in and took over some of his meetings, and today, she presented to the VMC board without him.

Deirdre felt confident as she went through her presentation slides that were on the large monitor for all to see. Her figures and case studies demonstrated why her future plans for the foundation are solid. For her last demonstration to the board, she had a youngster, who is a resident at Helena's children's home, give an account of their brief history.

"Well," the young lady starts, "it's hard to say my story. I was in foster care, and I was in many homes. I ran away a lot, because those people didn't care about me. And they were mean. When Ms. Helena took me in, I was cold and hungry, and I've been with her two years now. I just graduated high school, and am studying to be a medical assistant. I hope to work in one of your clinics. Papa Nicky promised me that if I got my medical assistant certification, he would get me a job, so that I could make money, and even have a career. Papa Nicky is helping me study and will pay for the certification test. It's all been so nice. I feel like I can really make it now. That I can have a nice future."

The board members boisterously clap for the young lady, and some of them giggle at the expression of 'Papa Nicky', a name the children came up with for Nicolaus. Many board members give her words of encouragement.

Even Ceil seems impressed. "Deirdre, I think we've heard enough. You did a very good job in presenting your case," Ceil happily states. "All right everyone, let's take a vote. I move we approve the position of Director of Philanthropy for the foundation, to be paid a salary of three hundred thousand per year."

"Ah, excuse me, Ceil. Mr. Nicolaus had proposed two hundred forty-five thousand a year for the salary."

"Yes, I know. I believe we need to throw in extra for Deirdre's administrative assistant, as she will immediately need one. The foundation can enter on the backend to continue that funding. We, the VMC board, can and should approve both positions. I move we do so. Now let's have a vote!"

Without further discussion, the board votes unanimously to approve both positions.

Deirdre is very surprised. After the meeting adjournment, Deirdre kisses and hugs Nigel, and hugs Ceil. She talks to each board member, shaking their hands and thanking them personally.

"I hadn't understood this project before your presentation. Now, I'm very glad we are doing this, and I'm glad that Nicolaus has chosen you to be the Director. I do think this is wise of him," a board member tells her.

"Thank you. We are very excited for the work we will be doing for the children," Deirdre responds.

Deirdre and the young lady enter her office to share the news with Nicolaus. However, he is not there. Deirdre drives the young lady back to the children's home, and discusses her worries with Helena.

Chapter One Hundred Fourteen

When Deirdre returns home, she happily discusses her observations of the board meeting with Constance, and Ishani and Maggie, who are present, visiting for support. "After I presented all my facts and figures, I had Lily tell her story. You know, Lily is one of the star children, she has a bright future ahead of her because of Helena and Nicolaus. Can you believe that it was Mother Ceil who told the board to vote and to give me additional money for an administrative assistant? She was so authoritarian, they did what she told them without argument."

"Your presentation was probably striking. How could they turn you down, especially having that young lady there to tell her story?" Maggie comments.

"Yes, that probably sealed the money right there," Ishani agrees.

However, when Deirdre thought about Nicolaus, she is quickly in a panic. The excitement of her accomplishment dissipates, and she puts her hands to her forehead. "I'm so worried about Nicky, though. I don't even know where he is right now." She sighs. "Why hasn't he taken Gwen's wedding ring from his finger? And he's said nothing of our marriage. What if he no longer wants me? Oh God," she sits on the first step of the stairs, "why did I ever turn down his proposal? I was so stupid! What if he doesn't ask me again?"

The ladies rush to Deirdre, Constance sitting next to her daughter. "Deirdre, dear, you must not do this. You are just being impatient. Nicolaus has to work through all that's happened. I'm sure he probably feels bad about it all. Two losses at once is a lot for anyone. And this is his second round of two losses at once. I'm sure this is hard for him, honey. Just give him some time. He will come to you. He always does. And he will ask you again. You know this. The bishop even told you so."

"It has been two weeks. He has not been here to see about me. He's just all sad, even at the office. I cannot do anything for him."

"Don't' say that Deirdre," Maggie feels bad for her.

"Deirdre, you've already done what you were supposed to do for Nicolaus. This is impatience talking. A Ravenell wife must have patience. In your new role as Nicolaus' wife, you must demonstrate perfection and patience. Are you forgetting that your love for Nicolaus is destined?"

"No, mother. I have not forgotten." Deirdre sighs, feeling she needs to do more.

"Deirdre, your mom is right, just give Nicky some time," Ishani agrees.

"Now you will stop this foolish talk, and this needless worrying. Let the man have time to mourn his losses."

"Yes, Mother."

Chapter One Hundred Fifteen

The next day, Maggie takes it upon herself to check on Nicolaus. She wants to do so as a friend. She is led to Nicolaus' sitting room in his wing of the mansion. Photos of him with Deirdre seem to be everywhere. Maggie notices right away that Nicolaus looks like his usual handsome self, only solemn and sad.

"Maggie!" They hug, and he lightly kisses her cheek. "Can I get you anything?"

"Oh no thanks."

Nicolaus leads her to have a seat in a chair opposite of his. He is unable to muster a smile for her. "Deirdre sent you?"

"No, she actually doesn't even know I'm here. I just want to check on you. How are you doing, Nicky?"

Nicolaus looks down with a grimaced frown. He shakes his head, no words.

Maggie draws closer, sitting herself on the arm of his chair. She touches his shoulder. "This all must be really hard." His frown grows deeper at her words. At first Maggie isn't sure what else to say. "I hope you aren't blaming yourself for any of this, Nicky."

"I do blame myself." His eyes meet hers. "It is my fault. And I can't fix it."

"Nicky, it's not your fault. You have no control over someone having a medical crisis. The truth is, that driver could have hit any of us. He could have hit anyone, it just happened to be Alexander and Gwen."

He slightly nods, not accepting her notion. He put his hand to his mouth, and changes the subject. "How are you doing? How's ... Fred?" he asks of her boyfriend.

"Pete," she tells him with a smile.

"Oh, Pete. How's that going?"

Maggie goes back to her seat. "No, not so great. He gets on my nerves every day. I think I'm going to have to kick him to the curb."

Maggie's comment brought a surprise change of expression about Nicolaus. "Hmm. You strike me as a tough woman, Maggie. Someone who is hard to please."

Maggie chuckles. "Yeah, I guess my expectations are pretty high." She cocks her head to the side. "Don't you know anyone, ... army of one fine unit, ... quite a few good-looking men, ... quite a few well to do and proud, ... who could be on my level?" She jokes with him in sarcasm, changing up all the military slogans she could think of.

Nicolaus gives her a slight smile, "I might know a fella or two." He nods, "Sure, let me make some calls."

Chapter One Hundred Sixteen

"Don't be mad Deirdre, I went to check on Nicky."

Deirdre smirks at her friend, wondering what she is up to. "I wouldn't be mad for that. How's my baby?"

"He's really down. He's kicking himself. He seems to feel responsible for what happened."

Deirdre nods with a frown, her heart aching for her love. "So I was right, he may not get over this. He might not ask me again."

"Now don't go there, Deirdre. I just said he is really down. Nicky loves you, you've always been his constant."

Deirdre pouts. She wants to cry ... no tears are present. "What else did he say?"

"Ah nothing, just that he would look at setting me up with one of his friends."

"What?" This made Deirdre chuckle. "You managed to broach that subject, huh?"

"Well ... I ... it just came up!"

Deirdre laughs at Maggie, who is hardly ever speechless. "Well, that could be a good thing. Nicky knows a lot of great guys, in and out of the military. He knows celebrities too! Your set up will be a real surprise." The ladies giggle.

Maggie hugs Deirdre to her. "Really, it's going to be okay."

Chapter One Hundred Seventeen

A few days later, in her despair for not having seen or heard from Nicolaus, Deirdre decides to go to the church to pray, remembering the words of the bishop. As Deirdre enters the church she is greatly surprised to see Nicolaus on his knees, at the altar. Immediately, she thanks God. She remembers what her mother said, and knows that she mustn't appear desperate to Nicolaus, and greater yet, she must remember why she came to the church in the first place. Quietly, Deirdre gracefully walks the long aisle, goes to the altar, kneels beside Nicolaus, closes her eyes and prays.

Of course, Nicolaus recognizes the beautiful aroma of his love. He smiles, his heart glad, taking her presence as the sign that he'd been praying for. Without stopping his prayers, he touches Deirdre's hand. Overjoyed, Deirdre takes his hand, and together, they pray.

The priest and the bishop watch over them, well pleased, knowing God will bless them in union very soon.

After an hour of praying, still on their knees, they embrace each other.

Nicolaus removes the marriage band that bound him to Gwen. He leaves it at the altar. Hand in hand, he and Deirdre walk out of the church.

Chapter One Hundred Eighteen

Having just left the church, and no longer able to be apart, whatsoever, Nicolaus and Deirdre hold on to each other's hands, the symbol of their eternal connection. They hold their breath under the beautiful blue water, as the inspiring sunset, with streaked colors of purple and orange, highlights the sky and reflects onto the calm waves of the cove. Nicolaus and Deirdre emerge from the water together, coming up for air, at their secluded spot at Hippie Hollow. They are clad only in their under garments, as is their routine. Nicolaus encircles himself over Deirdre to shield her, as usual.

Nicolaus grasps Deirdre's lips passionately with relief and exaggerated excitement. He is still sad and grieving at the loss of Gwen and Alexander, but also finally feels free. Only to hold Deirdre in his arms brings some sense of solace. As he kisses her beautiful, soft, puffy lips, every fiber of his being wants to make love to her, right here and now. However, he calms himself, releasing her lips.

Nicolaus holds Deirdre tightly to him, her bosom against his chest, fitting perfectly in his body space, which is made specifically for her. "You will marry me tomorrow," he half orders her, not willing to let anything ever creep between them again.

Deirdre's heart rejoices. She chuckles at his demanding tone. "Yes, darling," she tells him, looking into his mesmerizing eyes. She wants him so badly, she can hardly stand it. The feel of his hands on her skin melt her. His loving embrace makes her weak, as always. It has been so long since they'd been able to be intimate like this. Deirdre's love for Nicolaus is bursting from her eyes and from her heart. She treasures this man.

Deirdre knows she can no longer let her fear of Ceil, nor anything else keep her from Nicolaus. They have been through too much. It is daunting to think about all their sorrows and sadness, trials and tribulations, yet through it all, Nicolaus never let go of her hand. Not once.

"Tomorrow, Deirdre," Nicolaus strongly reiterates, as if to let her know he is not ever going to let her get away from him again. He is determined that she be his wife, no one else, no matter what. Their time to be together is now.

"Yes darling!" She holds tightly to her man ... her husband to be ... her only true love.

Chapter One Hundred Nineteen

Rachel is always so happy to see Nicolaus and Deirdre. She is stunned to see them dripping wet, clinging tightly to each other. "You two okay?" She asks with concern. She knows Nicolaus has been seriously struggling over the loss of Gwen and Alexander. As she pulls them inside, she can tell that something has changed and is so glad that he appears to have pulled himself through the tragedy.

Nicolaus sighs, not letting go of Deirdre. Though he is taller than she, Deirdre fits right into the side of his body, tucked under his arm. She is his perfect fit. "We're good. We're getting married tomorrow, Auntie Rachel. We wanted you to be the first to know."

Rachel gasps, nodding, "Oh my God! Wonderful, wonderful!"

"Well, just a small gathering," Deirdre interjects, "you know, just family. That's all. I think we can do something big later, right babe?"

Nicolaus looks at her and pecks her lips. "If that's what you want, babe."

"Okay, okay, wait .. so Ceil and Nigel don't know?"

Deirdre clings tight to her man, "You're the first."

Rachel breathes out, wanting to cry. They have no idea how much this means to her. She hugs them both, and sweetly kisses them. "What can I do to help? What do you need? Where do we start?"

Nicolaus and Deirdre look at each other and chuckle, realizing they really hadn't thought this through. "We have everything, don't we?"

Deirdre nods with a smile.

"Okay, let's see, you have the dress ... the rings ... the license ... the place ... the minister ...," Rachel lists, realizing that everything is basically in place.

"Oh wait, I'd better call the bishop."

Deirdre giggles. "Auntie Rachel, we don't care about any of the traditional things right now, you know. We just need to be married."

Nicolaus dials the bishop on his cell phone using one hand, the other remaining on Deirdre. "Hello Bishop! This is Nicolaus. Hope I'm not disturbing anything. Good, good. Well, I'd like to ask you to clear your calendar in the morning to officiate my marriage to Deirdre. Can you do that?" Nicolaus kisses Deirdre's precious head as he waits for the bishop to rummage his desk to find his calendar, not expecting them to want marriage this soon. Nicolaus smiles when he is given a resounding affirmation. "Wonderful! Yes, Bishop, we'll see you at ten, then. Okay, thank you. Goodbye."

Nicolaus looks at Deirdre, then lifts her in the air, and twirls her with joy, something he had not been able to do for some time. "It's official! Tomorrow at ten in the morning."

"Oh Nicky!" Deirdre is gently brought down from the air, into a kiss.

Rachel is in awe of her son and Deirdre as a couple. She is so happy that everything turned around for them. She notices the previous ring has been removed from Nicolaus' finger. Rachel claps her hands in joy, just knowing that heaven is lit up in celebration. Her arms go around them again. Their love is just so inspiring.

Even though it is going to be a small gathering, rather than the huge celebration their kind of love deserves, Rachel still wants it to be special for them. As they made their way to the door to leave for Deirdre's house to inform Constance, Rachel tells them that she and Francesca will make the arrangements for their special first night as husband and wife.

When they enter Deirdre's home, still connected together, words were not needed. Constance gasps, clasping her hands with the sweet smile of a bride's mother, "When is it?" She knew right away, and hopes they had not already eloped.

They both smile at her reaction, and together, they hug Constance. "Tomorrow, Mother, at ten in the morning," Deirdre informs her. Nicolaus kisses Constance on the forehead.

Constance is overjoyed. Like Rachel, she recounts the things they have in preparation for the marriage, and realizes they already have everything they need, except a cake.

"We'll need a cake! You must have something! I'll take care of it." With a kiss to the couple, Constance disappears to the back of the house, and makes a call to the mansion chef, asking him to remain quiet about the good news, until Nigel is notified. She asks him to make some kind of little cake to celebrate their love. She also thought about contacting her hair stylist, for herself and for Deirdre.

Nicolaus gently kisses Deirdre's lips. "I'm going to go tell my family, grab a few things, then I'll be back here in about an hour."

"Hon, is that wise? I mean ... you're not supposed to see me in my dress, and ..." her words and worry were hushed with another kiss from him.

"We're not going to be apart anymore, ever again. I don't even want you to go anywhere until I get back. Okay? Promise me."

Deirdre chuckles at his insistence.

"We're not taking any chances."

"Okay, babe, be careful. I promise, I won't go a-n-y-w-h-e-r-e!" She chuckles again, hoping she doesn't spontaneously combust or something crazy, for the next hour. She calls Ishani and Maggie with overflowing excitement.

Nicolaus feels a little apprehensive as he pulls his car into his garage space at the Ravenell mansion. It seems irrational to him that he is apprehensive about how his parents may react to the news that he is going to finally marry Deirdre tomorrow. He is certain the act of marrying Deirdre should have been done over a decade ago. However, he is more hesitant about his mother's reaction, than that of his father, nonetheless, he is concerned.

Nicolaus gathers the items he will need before telling his parents. He figures this way, if things get heated, he can make a quick exit. He grabs his suit and shoes that have been waiting for over two years, since he'd worn a different suit to his first wedding. He places them in a suit bag. Then he grabs an overnight case and packs his toiletries and accessories. He isn't concerned about forgetting anything, as he knows whatever he might need will be at Deirdre's house.

Deirdre's ring and his matching gold and diamond band has been kept in Constance's secret space, as he'd asked her to hold them for him years ago. He'd bought that special ring for Deirdre over five years ago, hoping every day that she'd change her mind and give him a wedding date.

So now, everything is ready, and packed in his sports car. Nicolaus decides to only tell his parents, and will ask Nigel to tell Niall, Elsa, and Dwight, and anyone else close to the family his father wants at the wedding. Nicolaus wants to be about the business of getting back to Deirdre's side. He wants to be there to protect her, protect their time, and protect their future.

As he seats both Ceil and Nigel opposite of him in the sitting room, all Nicolaus can think about is getting back to Deirdre's side.

"I just want you both to know that I am marrying Deirdre tomorrow, at the church, at ten in the morning, and it will be an honor to me if you both were there."

"Oh son! That's great! That's great! Ahh ... Nicolaus,... isn't this hasty? We won't have time to invite anyone or to make preparations." Nigel is shocked at this quick turnaround.

"It's just going to be small. We just want to be married. We can do that other stuff later, if that's what Deirdre wants."

Nigel frowns, and sighs, "Son, you're going to be offending many people. Insulting others."

"Father, didn't you hear me? We don't care about that right now."

Nigel sighs again, not liking how hastily this is being thrown together. "Okay, of course we will be there."

"No, I'm not going," Ceil states nastily. Her attitude completely different than when she was recently in the board room, supporting Deirdre.

"Mother," Nicolaus frowns, "your presence would mean a lot to both of us, and ..."

"I'm not your mother," she interrupts, dropping this bomb of information on him.

Nicolaus' frown grows deeper, thinking she is insulting him, because of course she would insult him at a time like this. Except he doesn't understand the insult. "You're not my mother," he repeats, hands in the air at the assumed cryptic message, shaking his head, "what do you mean?"

"Ceil," Nigel reprimands her.

"I'm not your mother," she says clearly, staring him in the eyes. She enjoys seeing the confusion on Nicolaus' face as he thinks through what she is saying. "Go ask Rachel." Ceil stands and leaves the room.

Nicolaus watches her leave, as if in shock, then his frowning eyes go to his father. His thumb points in the direction Ceil had left the room. "So ... what is she talking about now? She's not my mother," he repeats as if trying to figure out a coded message.

"Nope, we're not even going to let her spoil your good news." Nigel stands, almost glad that Nicolaus doesn't get what Ceil is saying, bringing Nicolaus up with him, placing his hand on his shoulder. "I'm very proud of you son. I don't think I say that enough to you."

Nicolaus is humbled by his father's words. "Thank you, father. Will you be there tomorrow?"

"Of course, son."

"What's happening tomorrow?" Niall interrupts their conversation.

Nicolaus smiles at his brother, not sure how he will receive the news. "Deirdre and I are getting married in the morning at ten, at the church. Please, you and Elsa be there."

"Oh, it's finally happening, huh?" Niall nods. "Of course, we'll be there." Niall goes to Nicolaus and hugs him. "I'm happy for you, brother. Really, I am," he says rather flatly, mostly trying to convince himself as jealousy prangs him again. Niall feels rather irritated that Nicolaus will be the first to have Deirdre, despite the ten year wait.

"Thank you, Niall, I appreciate that."

"I'll go let Elsa know." Niall leaves them, and goes up the stairs to notify Elsa, who immediately calls Deirdre.

Nigel put his hand to Nicolaus' shoulder again. "Anyway, son, it may be to your advantage if your mother does not attend. Please do not let that get into your psyche. Tomorrow will be a wonderful day."

Chapter One Hundred Twenty

I ndeed, the following day is a wonderful day. The Austin sky is clear blue, no clouds in sight. The weather is just right, not too hot nor too cool.

Bishop Leighton is more than happy to marry Nicolaus and Deirdre. He is not only very grateful of their financial support of the church over the many years, he is also grateful of their support of the ministries. Anyway, the bishop, like everyone else in the country, knows that for whatever reason, these two people are destined to be together. He envisions that out of their love for each other, more blessings for others are surely to follow.

Neither Nicolaus nor Deirdre care that their wedding is small. All they care about is being married. They are determined that no one is going to stop them this time around. Francesca and Rachel worked quickly to arrange the honeymoon. She kisses Nicolaus on the cheek, tucking the airline tickets to Estonia into his jacket pocket before he walks up to the altar to wait for Deirdre's entrance. Then Francesca goes to assist Deirdre.

The small number of guests are mostly family, and Dwight with his wife. Elsa stands next to Niall, and Helena, now part of the family, quietly walks in. She blows a kiss to Nicolaus as she sits on the church pew, next to Constance and Rachel. Helena notices that Nigel is gently holding onto Rachel's hand, and that Ceil is not present. A few of Constance's cousins, and her uncle, as well as Maggie and Ishani are present.

Everyone stands as the woman church piano player begins to play the music to *"The Blood Will Never Lose Its Power"*, a gospel classic. Lowly and gently, she sings the words to the song.

The church deacons, one on each side of the wooden French doors to the chapel entrance, open the doors, and there stands

Deirdre, in a beautiful white dress, not the actual wedding dress that she'd bought so long ago. Her hair is beautifully curly.

As the doors open, she sees Nicolaus at the altar, looking fine, dressed in his classy French tailored blue suit, waiting for her at the altar. She sees his emotion as her beauty takes his breath away.

His Deirdre is wrapped in beautiful white lace and flowers, and she is just for him. His dream, finally becoming reality.

Deirdre begins to move down the aisle towards Nicolaus, as if she floats on air. Francesca walks before her, placing the flower petals on the aisle for the bride walk. Nicolaus has to stop himself from running and bringing her up. He knows she'd want to make the walk to him herself, in her independent spirit.

Tears of joy trickle out of Deirdre's eyes as she draws nearer to her love, her Nicolaus. This is finally happening! She is finally going to marry Nicolaus Ravenell, the only man she is destined to be with for eternity. Her eyes stay on him as she gently moves down the aisle, careful not to trip. She feels the absence of her father, and knows if he were there, he'd be gladly walking her down the aisle. Deirdre reaches Nicolaus' outstretched hand, as he helps her up the steps to the altar.

"You are amazingly beautiful," Nicolaus has not taken his eyes off Deirdre. She blushes at his comment, feeling very humble and full of love. Their hands quickly join, and they are then inseparable as they turn to listen to the Bishop perform their ceremony.

Bishop Leighton reads through passages from the bible and does his diligence as he would for every couple he marries. He gives them simple marriage advice.

When it is time for their vows, Deirdre goes first. "Nicky, you are my heart. I have loved you for so long, and I promise to love you forever, ... to eternity. You are everything I have ever wanted in a man, and more. I promise to be what you need in a wife, and to always, always love you, and respect you." Her tears are on automatic, falling from her eyes, her heart so full of love for her Nicolaus, their hands never leaving each other.

Nicolaus feels the same, his heart bursting with love for this woman. "Deirdre, I have loved you since before I was born," he smiles, "as Auntie Clara would say, our love is written in the stars. You've been by my side before we even understood what love is, and you loved me then. Thank you. I could have never made it through this life without you." He sighs, emotion choking him, "I love you so much. I always have and I always will. Thank you for staying by my side, through all my troubles. I promise to always, always, love you, and respect you, and to be by your side. We'll walk through each day together. Forever."

The bishop then has them exchange rings. Nicolaus gently kisses Deirdre's hand, before softly placing that ring he'd bought years ago upon her finger. She is surprised, as she had never seen the beautifully sculpted diamond ring. Rachel cries at the romantic sweetness of her son. Nigel side hugs Rachel, his hand rubbing her arm. Then Deirdre places the diamond encased gold band ring upon Nicolaus finger. Their hands lock together. The Bishop puts a blessing upon their rings, and then upon the couple. Next they light the unity candle, which is again in Deirdre's favorite color of dark berry, their eyes of love staying on each other.

Then the couple kneel to receive the Eucharist. It is at this time of receiving that Eucharist when both Nicolaus and Deirdre, with joined hands, just after the bishop anoints both of their foreheads with holy oil, are both wrapped in the love of God, that universe power, the holy spirit. Together, as a couple, hands still intertwined, they are on the floor feeling this divine intervention.

Nigel and Niall bolt from their seats to assist, not understanding what is happening, as this is the first time they'd witnessed this. They are stopped by the bishop.

"It's all right," he assures them. "They are being touched by God. Everyone sit down, and remain quiet," he instructs them. Without question, they do as the bishop says. As Bishop Leighton begins to emotionally pray over the couple, Nigel gets an understanding of Nicolaus' love for God, that he may be special, beyond what he'd ever thought of his son before.

The holy visitation is short as both Nicolaus and Deirdre open their eyes after a few minutes of time. Nicolaus wipes the tears from his face and is honored that God would touch he and Deirdre on their wedding day. Nicolaus lifts Deirdre, as she is completely amazed at what she'd just experienced. Still, their hands never having parted, they are both perfectly put together, not a hair out of place, despite being touched by God's power.

The bishop wipes the tears from his own eyes, and the wedding ceremony continues.

"Nicolaus and Deirdre, you have both taken this business of holy matrimony to another level, and I ask blessings on you as God has truly blessed your union. As such a blessed couple, may you be fruitful and bring forth many children to assist in this world of ours. It gives me great pleasure to pronounce you as husband and wife. Nicolaus, you may kiss your beautiful bride."

With a smile, and without hesitation, Nicolaus draws Deirdre into his arms and kisses her sweet lips, dipping her back, then bringing her up, only then ending the kiss. The family and guests are happily laughing and clapping. They smile at everyone.

The bishop sweeps his arms before the couple, "I give to all present, Mr. and Mrs. Nicolaus Ravenell."

Nicolaus swoops Deirdre, and all her dress, into his arms, his eyes only on her. He carries her out of the church, to the claps of everyone present. With elation, he gently places Deirdre into the waiting limousine, and the couple head back to the mansion for a quick celebration.

"How do you feel, Mrs. Ravenell?" Nicolaus asks Deirdre, unable to stop smiling.

Deirdre shakes her head, her hand to her chest, "We finally did it! We're married!"

She is ecstatic. "Do you think God was blessing us? Blessing our union? That was so wonderful. And unexpected. I didn't know how being touched by God would feel."

"Yes, I think so. It's the only thing I can imagine," he holds Deirdre as close as he possibly can. "Our love is not only written in the stars, it is also publicly blessed by God." Nicolaus kisses her sweet lips again, and again, and again, just like he wants. He is so glad they do not have to push the love they have for each other into that invisible closet anymore.

Chapter One Hundred Twenty-One

D eirdre, Rachel and Francesca fiercely and quickly plan the religious fairytale wedding to be held at the Tallin historic St. Nicholas church, which will take place the day after the night they arrive for their honeymoon.

Deirdre is so happy she cannot stop smiling. Rachel hugs her with an overflowing heart of joy for both Deirdre and Nicolaus. "I'll talk to Ceil."

Deirdre touches Rachel on the shoulder. "No, I have to do it."

"Deirdre, I don't think that's a good idea. She was not very open to Nicolaus. She's in a foul mood."

Deirdre nods, "I know. I have to do it. For Nicky, I have to."

Francesca and Rachel watch Deirdre in awe, as she elegantly leaves them, her beautiful aroma adrift behind her. They could already see the self-assured change illuminating from her.

Deirdre is escorted to Ceil by the mansion staff. Ceil is in her bedroom, in the large sitting area, looking over some fashion magazines, interested in new clothes. Deirdre knocks on the door, and enters. "Mother Ceil, may I speak with you?"

Ceil looks up from the magazine. She eyes Deirdre with a crooked smile, observing her wedding dress. "What do you want? Is this the part where you ask me for Nicolaus' hand in marriage?"

Deirdre giggles, then sits across from Ceil, her official mother-in-law. "No! This is the part where I ask you to dress dashingly for our Estonian wedding. I really missed you at our little wedding today. Nicky and I will be married again at the St. Nicholas historic church in two days, and I want to see you front and center," she boldly tells Ceil.

Ceil tries to hide her shock of such a wonderful event. She clears her throat to get rid of any excitement that may be present. "Now, why would I do that?" she asks flatly.

Deirdre stands, hands behind her back, slowly pacing. "Well ... I don't know. Perhaps because there will be people from all over the world there. Perhaps because media from everywhere on the globe will be there. Perhaps because of the goodwill you could offer to many businesses who may now be interested in VMC. Perhaps just to support Nicolaus. Or perhaps ..." dramatically, Deirdre flings herself to her knee, at Ceil's lap, grabbing her hands, "because, as the future grandmother to my children, I'd really like for you to be there." Deirdre stands, "Besides, if you don't go, you'll be the only one not there." Deirdre places her hands on her hips with a big smile to Ceil, and waits for her response.

Ceil shakes her head in agreement, sighing. She knows Deirdre is right. How could she not attend? She would be the only family member not there, and the press would have a field day with such a happening. Ceil nods. "Okay, I'll be there," she breathed, having let Deirdre break through her coldness. "What's our theme?"

"Oh, Mother Ceil!" Deirdre is so excited. She hugs up Ceil and kisses her face. She takes Ceil's hands. "You can wear whatever you want, though I'd love to see you in something gold. I think that would suit you so well. Gold for our regal mom!"

Ceil chuckles at her comment. She receives another kiss from Deirdre, who happily leaves her presence. The beautiful aroma of Deirdre, again, adrift in the air.

Chapter One Hundred Twenty-Two

While Deirdre was off seeing about Ceil, Rachel corners Nigel in his home office, closing and locking the door, for fear of being rudely interrupted and wrongfully accused of something by Ceil.

This man still has such an effect on her. He'd held her through most of the wedding ceremony, and she enjoyed being so close to him, them touching, and being in his arms. Rachel wants to throw him down on his desk and kiss him. Instead, she touches his shoulder. "Nigel, Nicolaus told me you were very upset with him about the small wedding ceremony. Honey, you know good and well he needed to marry Deirdre as quickly as possible before some other tragedy happened to stop them from being together."

Nigel frowns. "I realize that. This is so thrown together. And no one was invited. No preparations were made. No press releases. Many people,... many important people, are going to be offended."

"Well, not anymore! You are going to open your coffers and offer to fly at least one hundred folks, that you think should have been here today, to Estonia for the real wedding."

"What?"

"It's Deirdre's dream. And Nicky knows nothing about it. She wants to surprise him."

Slowly Nigel nods in understanding. "At the St. Nicholas church?"

"Exactly."

"That's going to cost a lot."

"Nigel, I don't care how much it's going to cost. We're going to do this for Nicolaus!

Our son. Our baby. My baby." Suddenly, Rachel feels as though she wants to cry. Her sickness zapped her strength, as she'd been doing a lot today. Tears stream down her face.

Nigel takes Rachel into his arms, comforting her.

She wipes her tears. "And for God's sake, Nigel, please don't let Ceil ruin anything.

Not this time. I want everything to be perfect for them. Let's please give this to them. Don't they deserve it?"

"Yes, yes, of course, you're right. Okay. I'll get right on this."

"Thank you, Nigel. Anyway, I think you may find that most people will pay their own way. We can just offer if we really want them to be there. I already have the hotels alerted, and I'll give you all that information. This is going to be so great!"

Nigel hugs Rachel, and smiles at her. He couldn't resist planting a kiss on her beautiful lips. Rachel eagerly responds to Nigel. It has been so long since he kissed her. She is glad for it. Sadly, she realizes it may be the last kiss she will ever receive from Nigel, who is the only man she has ever loved.

Chapter One Hundred Twenty-Three

The newlyweds only have about forty-five minutes before they leave for the airport. Francesca purposefully wants them to make a quick exit, for less chance of Ceil ruining things for them. The mansion chef made a light lunch, and a small wedding cake.

Francesca busied herself snapping photos, and taking videos, getting comments from the family for the Kiviste/Ravenell family archives. Fifteen minutes to go! Francesca has the couple cutting the small cake. Nicolaus lovingly holds Deirdre's hand, standing behind her, as they slice the cake together. They cut a piece and with intertwined arms, feed each other, then kiss the mix of the frosting and the cake into each other's mouths. Deirdre giggles, and then they kiss more. She is very sure she'd never tire of Nicolaus kissing her.

Deirdre goes upstairs and quickly changes into her white jumpsuit, keeping with the theme of the day. She knows they are of course going to Estonia. She pretends like she doesn't know their destination, to keep the wedding surprise for Nicolaus. She is so excited about it, she can barely contain herself. However, no matter where they went in the world, even if it were just to her room, she didn't care, as she only wants to be with her love, her Nicky.

As they leave the mansion, they are hugged and kissed by everyone, except Ceil, who is still absent. The family pelts them with white rose petals as they walk to the waiting limousine.

Since it is a mid-weekday, the first class section of the plane is sparsely populated with passengers. Nicolaus is very glad they had not drawn attention by any press people, as they were mainly left alone and treated as regular passengers through the airport and onto the plane.

Nicolaus is still holding Deirdre's hand, only separating when necessary, then quickly rejoining hands again.

"So babe, are you going to tell me where we're going?"

Nicolaus chuckles, "Nope! It's a surprise."

Deirdre laughs, knowing it is she who is going to surprise him. Excitement bubbles up out of her, as the plane begins to taxi the runway.

Once their plane lands in New York for a transfer, they have little time to get to their connecting flight. Deirdre balks with glee, hugging her husband tight. "Yes, yes!" she pretends more excitement at the destination of their connecting flight, making Nicolaus chuckle at her reaction. Anyway, Deirdre is very happy at the idea of spending their wedding night at the castle. It only seems fitting.

Once they finally land in Estonia, the castle staff picks them up at the airport. Suddenly, the Estonian sky opens up, pouring rain over the city. The sound of rain on the cobblestone streets makes a hush romantic sound.

Just getting from the car to the castle door drenches the couple. As Deirdre steps out of the car, Nicolaus again swoops her into his arms, to carry her over the threshold of the castle, following his own dream of doing this for her.

As they enter the drafty castle, they are greeted by all the staff who clap the couple in, happy that they were able to finally marry. Once the Estonian people throughout the country learned about their love story, it seemed that everyone was rooting for them.

Nicolaus gently places Deirdre on her feet, giving her a sweet kiss, then he greets the staff with handshakes, and thanks them for the reception and for waiting up for them. Deirdre looks for Butler Brown, as he is in on the planning for tomorrow. She sees him, and winks at him. Brown smiles, and bows his head to her, reassuring her all is in order.

The kitchen staff have prepared a meal for the Ravenells, and made them a small cake to celebrate their union. Deirdre thought this very sweet and certainly would not arouse Nicolaus' suspicions for tomorrow's occasion.

The newlyweds are seated in the small dining room, close to the toasty fire, which is lit in the giant fireplace. They sit close to each other, their backs to the fire for warmth.

Though they try to eat the food that is placed before them, their minds are just preoccupied with other matters. Consummation matters.

Deirdre is worried about what she knows is soon to occur. She is worried that she isn't actually sure what to do. She is very concerned that she might disappoint Nicolaus.

Nicolaus' thoughts are racing of what he'd learn in the medical journals about sex, and the technical aspects of the act. He is thinking about what Deirdre might like, wanting his time with Deirdre to be completely different from that of his other two wives.

The chef understands what is going on between the couple, as they hadn't taken their eyes off each other since arriving, and Deirdre appears nervous. Nicolaus touches her back with a smile, trying to reassure her.

The chef decides to help the couple. "Ah, Mr. Nicolaus, perhaps you'd like us to show you to your room. You must be ready to retire, Sir. We can save everything until later, Sir."

With a smile, Nicolaus nods. "Yes, please!"

Nicolaus stands, hugging Deirdre to him. The chef nods, and hands them off to the head butler, who guides them to their room. "I had the staff prepare this suite especially for you," he tells them before opening the door. "This room was that of Nicohls and DeeDee, Sir. I'm very sure they'd have it no other way, than for you to spend your wedding night here."

As the butler opens the door, the magic of time past is before the couple. Nicolaus again, swoops Deirdre into his arms, making her cackle with joy, loving how his strong and muscular arms lifts her as if she weighs nothing. He carries her over the bedroom threshold.

"Wow!" Nicolaus exclaims at the sight of the room. The room has been transformed, since the last time they were both there, and even since Deirdre's most recent visit. The room has a spirit of elegant romance, as if it is transposed from a time of the past.

The staff added items that were used back from the time of Nicohls and DeeDee's life, including some of the items that actually belonged to Nicohls and DeeDee. The newlyweds can see an old hairbrush on the vanity stand, with an antique stool; silk robes, each with initials, N for Nicohls and D for DeeDee; a wash bowl next to golden rings on the hand carved dresser; and a shaving blade. Ancient Kiviste family stationary lay on both nightstands, with a feather and ink for writing, and an ink pad with a stamp that held the family crest lay next to it.

The original headboard of the bed is engraved with the Kiviste family crest. The bed is adorned with golden lace curtains that flowingly drape from the four sides of the poster rods of the bed. The bedcovers are not familiar from their previous inventory, and are covered in red rose petals. Chilled wine sits on the dresser.

The historic room is warmly romantic, only lit by candles all around, and the fireplace which has a roaring fire. The large fire does not drown out the raindrops that lightly tap on the castle bricks, making a soft rhythm.

The butler nods, feeling Nicolaus is satisfied with how they prepared the room for them. He closes the door, leaving the couple to themselves.

Everything about this moment is different for Nicolaus than anything he'd ever experienced with the other women. His heart is leaping with nervousness and deep desire at the same time, for the only woman he has truly ever loved. Nicolaus, the military hero, trembles with love and the highest height of desire he's ever felt, as he looks upon Deirdre, something he'd never endured before.

"Let's get out of these wet clothes," Nicolaus sweetly tells Deirdre, gently placing her on her feet.

Nicolaus quickly undresses down to his underwear, and then with a smile from inner peace and gladness, one by one, he gently removes Deirdre's clothes. She lets him undress her. As she steps out of her jumpsuit, she stands before him in her undergarments.

Nicolaus softly sighs, ready to see this woman he loves in her full beauty of nakedness. He kneels, and gently removes her silk panties, revealing her womanness. Without hesitation, he kisses her there, making her gasp in surprise. As he arises from kneeling, Deirdre places her hands on his strong, muscular chest, feeling very nervous, and a little afraid. Smiling, Nicolaus removes his briefs. Then, he removes the last thing that separates their nakedness, her brassiere. Deirdre suddenly feels self-conscious and wants to cover herself, when suddenly Nicolaus swoops her off her feet again, and gently lays her onto the bed.

Nicolaus wants Deirdre to be his to the end of time. His mouth quickly covers hers, and she can tell that he is anxiously excited. He kisses her neck, and licks her erogenous zones, tasting her, making her moan. Nicolaus wants to kiss and taste every inch of her body, knowing if he can kiss it, he can claim it.

It is his intention to kiss and taste her and even tease her a little, from her shapely breasts to her womanly valley, and the path his children would travel out of her body. He wants to kiss the birthing path and bless it before entering her.

"Nicky," she whispers his name, already feeling herself aroused, not sure what to do. Deirdre's virgin body is electrified, giving heightened intensity to her nerve endings, making her jump and shutter at his stimulating touch and kisses. She closes her eyes as her man, her love, her husband, kisses every part of her body.

She gasps and sighs when he kisses her breasts. "Nicky," escapes her mouth again, as he kisses her stomach, her belly, and then gently kisses her womanness again. Nicolaus reigns kisses on her inner thighs, the power grid of women, from her knee, inward on one leg, then switching to the other. Deirdre gasps at the sensation, as she had never thought of anyone kissing her inner thighs.

She reaches for her love, as she feels her legs part, and he brings her sensations she'd never known before. Deirdre shrieks, and gasps, and moans, as Nicolaus relentlessly pleasures her. Her body uncontrollably arches. She can hear him moan as he continues to work her, while his hands caress her. Deirdre arches again, quivering with pleasure she'd never known before.

She feels the sensation of his mouth riding up her belly, her stomach, and her breasts.

Her arms go around Nicolaus, as he lay on top of her, claiming her sweet mouth, indulging her.

The fireplace fire warms their skin and smoothly flickers without disruption, while their own inside fires make them hot with desire for each other. Nicolaus keeps his attention on Deirdre, kissing her delectable lips.

Deirdre breaks their scorching kiss and places her face against that of her husband, loving the feel of him on top of her, loving their full nakedness together.

Nicolaus smiles, knowing their love is special. He looks upon his beautiful wife. He could never imagine them ever being apart again. "Are you all right, babe? You feel comfortable?"

Deirdre smiles, pulling him into a kiss, thinking about their ancestors. "I love you so much," she tells him with a smile. They peck kiss several times.

"I love you, woman." Nicolaus again endlessly kisses her, as is finally time for him to claim his Deirdre, his love, his true wife, the only one on earth for him. He'd been dreaming of all of this for so long. Placing himself inside of his wife, the virgin barrier hinders him momentarily. Nicolaus, fully aroused, easily glides into Deirdre. Her vagina tight, hot, wet velvet, just for him. The feel of her inner ridges makes Nicolaus groan, bringing emotion to him for finally being inside Deirdre.

He begins slow and easy at first, feeling every inch of her against his member. And then led by his body and the wonderful feel of Deirdre, he is drawn in. He wants to get as deep and as close to her as heavenly possible. Deirdre moans, and winces beneath him, holding him close, tears of joy and tears of pain fall from her eyes, happy her man is finally inside of her.

Deirdre understands they are being bound together in the best way possible. This spiritual bind is so strong and so natural, touching each other's souls in their lovemaking. Deirdre never wants to be with any other man. Not ever. She can see she feels good to Nicolaus, and that is all that matters to her. His mouth covers hers in passionate kisses as he keeps the momentum going inside of her sweet vaginal walls. They breathe heavily together as one entity.

They are entangled with each other for a long while, Nicolaus only stopping once his body releases itself inside of her, causing a moan to escape his mouth as he thinks of the children he prayed to bring forth. He does not break his hold on Deirdre, remaining inside of his love, the feel of her body incomprehensible to him. "My angel," he tells her, still reigning kisses on her.

Gently, Nicolaus turns Deirdre onto her side, remaining inside of her, supporting her leg, and with all his weight, he thrust in her, making her moan with ecstasy. The feeling of her sweet walls surrounding his flesh perplexes him beyond understanding. Nicolaus has not experienced sex in this manner. This is so different than what he learned from both of his previous wives. Deirdre moans with pleasure as he gently goes deeper, moaning with each movement.

"My God ... my love, ... so good, so right," the words from his mouth sound like poetry to Deirdre's ears as he continually loves her, bringing her immense pleasure.

Deirdre enjoys the full length of her man, as he gently pounds her with passion, uncontrolled moans escaping her mouth. After much time has passed, she hears Nicolaus let out another moan, then he shudders, releasing his pulsating love inside of her, fulfilling the dream he's held for years. His mouth is all over hers. Soon, Deirdre feels her vagina spasm, and she moans at the feeling, realizing what is happening.

Nicolaus keeps Deirdre close to him, in the special space of his chest, as they drift to ecstasy sleep. Deirdre lay warm in her love's arms, feeling the most loved she'd ever felt her whole life. She can feel Nicolaus' heartbeat against her back. She is so satisfied and so happy that she'd never given herself to anyone else. She only belongs to Nicolaus Ravenell. She does not want this night to end.

Chapter One Hundred Twenty-Four

The following morning, after their joint bubble bath, Deirdre disappears to get dressed, and Nicolaus dresses in his white suit as instructed by Francesca. Nicolaus waits for Deirdre downstairs, as it takes her a little longer to prepare. Nicolaus is amused by the staff, of which the women straighten his clothes without asking, one adjusts his hair, and a few young ladies giggle with joy when they see him. The young staff girls are shewed away by an older staff woman, for fear of spoiling the surprise.

Deirdre finally slowly descends the stairs in a huge hooded blue cape coat, which completely covers her and drags the floor. The coat covers the wedding dress she had picked out a few years ago. The hood on her head hides the tiara which holds the beaded veil.

Nicolaus meets her halfway up the stairs to help her down, fearing she will fall for not being able to see her own feet, or the steps. He chuckles, "Deirdre, it's not that cold out. You sure you want this big coat?"

"Well, I'm cold," Deirdre tells him, in a tone to get him to stop asking questions.

"Okay, okay," he says, her tone working on him. They complete the steps together, and they go to the waiting limousine. "Now, where are we going again?"

"Oh! Yes, to the church. Bishop Moratey wants to see us. He wants us to take some pictures."

"Oh, okay," Nicolaus smiles and does not seem surprised or suspicious. "That's why we need to dress in white." This makes sense to him.

Deirdre smiles, as she isn't exactly lying. Bishop Moratey is going to marry them, and they will be taking pictures. "By the way darling, you look very handsome, as always." Deirdre reassures him.

Nicolaus smiles at her comment. "And you ...my dear ... look like a fashionable Eskimo," he laughs, teasing her. Deirdre hits at him, making him laugh more.

The limousine coasts down the streets of Tallin. As it turns onto the street of the church, crowds of people line both sides of the street. Nicolaus notices that most people are also wearing white. They wore white because the church asked them to, in keeping with the traditional American wedding colors. The crowds of people get thicker the closer they are to the church.

"Hmm, some kind of festival is going on," Nicolaus comments. Deirdre smiles at him.

Decorations of streamers and balloons in the colors of white, gold, and blue; as well as white and gold flowers of different variations seemed to be everywhere.

"Hmm," Nicolaus comments again, as he notices there certainly is a color scheme going on. He sees even more people dressed in white. "Some kind of white party."

As the limousine pulls to the church, the thick crowd of people begin to clap and cheer for the couple, some yelling their names. When the door is opened, Nicolaus exits the vehicle, and the cheering grows louder. He smiles, not understanding, and waves to the crowd. He helps Deirdre out, and as she exits the limo, she sheds her blue coat, revealing her beautiful wedding dress and veil. People in the crowd cheer louder and clap for the couple.

"What's all this?" Nicolaus asks with happiness, thinking about the pictures they would be taking.

"This is all for you, babe. It's for us. It's our wedding!"

Nicolaus looks around, smiling, understanding revealed to him. "It's beautiful."

He hugs Deirdre tightly. He pulls back to look at her, "You're so beautiful!" He twirls her around for the crowd, and the crowd cheers again, even louder, some ladies scream out Deirdre's name, as if she were a star. He hugs her again. "I'd marry you a million times," he tells her, kissing her. Every move they make seems to stir the crowd to a joyful response.

As the limo drives off, people surround the couple. The city mayor steps forward and stands between them, with a microphone in his hands. He shakes their hands, introducing himself, before speaking.

"As our wonderful city choir gets in place to serenade the two of you, I want to personally thank you, Deirdre and Nicolaus, for this wonderful opportunity to host your beautiful and much anticipated wedding in our wonderful city of Tallin!" Thousands in the crowd respond positively, clapping in agreement. "You have put our city on the worldwide map for wedding destinations. Thank you! We know the Kiviste and Ravenell family heritage runs deep in Tallin. Today, we honor you and your love! Our wonderful city choir will now lift their voices in song, in honor of your love."

The mayor disappears, heading towards the church, as the choir, which surrounds the couple, lifts them up with a popular song of 'Endless Loving'. Their voices are heavenly, and indeed, seem to be singing up to the heavens to celebrate Deirdre and Nicolaus, who are fully embracing each other. The first stanza and chorus of the song is sung in English, and the second stanza and chorus is sung in Estonian, finishing the song in English. This really delights Nicolaus, as it is done beautifully.

Suddenly, a full orchestra, which is placed just inside the church, begins to play a sweet love song, 'This Moment'. A local Estonian singer sings the sweet words of the song for the couple to walk the sparkling white carpet leading to the church vestibule.

Nicolaus takes Deirdre's hand and the rest of her, gathering her close, holding her tight. The crowd claps for them as they walk to the church. The words of the song are delightful and perfect to their situation of being destined to each other, same as the previous song.

Emotion grips both of them, especially as they walk paced with the orchestra and the singer. Both Deirdre and Nicolaus notice that women and young girls shed tears of joy for them, for the bond of their love as they walk by. Deirdre is moved by seeing women she doesn't even know, in a country she does not even live in, shed tears of joy at the love she shares with Nicolaus. Tears also stream from her eyes, as her love, her man, her Nicolaus, holds tight to her as they walk in unison towards the historic church doors. She knows she is finally living her dream of life with Nicolaus.

When they reach the front of the church, the press who'd been taking pictures, are now in their view, then also they see their extended Omari, Kiviste and Ravenell families. Nicolaus' aunties, Ceil's sisters, and their husbands, hug and kiss both of them. They are greeted by their many cousins on both sides of the families as well, including Ned, Cato, and Bobby, and their wives.

As Nicolaus and Deirdre enter the beautiful historic church through the huge door frames, and large, beautiful rafters, Francesca appears, then Constance, Rachel, Nigel, Elsa, Niall, and Ceil. Deirdre holds onto Nicolaus as he is overcome with emotion for having everyone here to celebrate their love. Deirdre kisses him, and wipes his tears away, as well as wiping away her own tears. She is very glad for the joy this has brought to him, knowing he so much deserves it.

The family enters the church, escorting Nicolaus to the altar, to wait for his bride, as Francesca stays with Deirdre.

"You did it! You did great! He's so surprised!" Deirdre happily tells Francesca.

Francesca chuckles. "Oh my God, Bishop Moratey is so happy for this. That man is stoked. He can't believe he is finally going to get to marry you to Nicky. And my God, that walk to the church was freakin' romantic. Deirdre, I'm not sure anyone can top that. I saw all kinds of people in the crowd crying! Even some men!"

Francesca helps Deirdre with her veil, pulling it over her face, then kisses her cheek with the love of a sister.

Francesca walks behind Deirdre, holding her long train, so that it doesn't drag the floor.

A unison gasp fills the church as the lovely bride sets her foot inside the door to the main chamber, where all the wedding guests await.

The look on Nicolaus' face is priceless as their eyes meet. Even Niall cannot take his eyes off Deirdre. Deirdre touches her hand to her veil, feeling nervous, as everyone smiles at her. From the altar, Bishop Moratey reaches out his hand towards Deirdre. Slowly, Deirdre gracefully walks the long isle, again, careful not to trip on her dress. Francesca signals Deirdre to walk towards Nigel.

"You are very beautiful, Deirdre. And I am so happy that you are officially my daughter!" Nigel is very proud as Deirdre wraps her arm around his, and they walk down the aisle as the love song continues. Truly Deirdre is a picturesque vision.

The flashing of cameras is non-stop as Deirdre walks the aisle of the beautiful medieval church, with Nigel standing in for Cecil, her father and his past friend, in the tradition of bringing the bride to the groom, in this case, his son. The inside of the church is beautiful, with huge white bricked arches that line both sides of the aisle. Sunlight flows in through the numerous large glass windows. There are two very large, golden chandeliers which suspend from the arched ceiling.

An overabundance of people arrived to witness their wedding, as it is opened to the public, and their love story is known worldwide. The church is packed with people, and there is standing room only. People are actually standing around the walls of the church, next to the several members of the press.

Deirdre notices that many people from the United States are in attendance, including celebrities and foundation donors. This surprises her. She waives at so many of those she knows.

Niall, who stands in the first row, closest to Nicolaus, watches the romanticism of his brother, as Nicolaus' eyes follow Deirdre's beautiful smile and happy countenance the full walk to him, her husband.

Deirdre lives in the moment. This is what she'd imagine marrying Nicolaus in this historic church would be like. She knows, without a doubt, that she is walking the same footsteps as DeeDee when she married Nicohls, so long ago. She can feel it. She believes Auntie Clara is smiling down from heaven on them, being very pleased with them.

As Deirdre and Nigel reach the last stretch of the walk of the aisle to Nicolaus, the songs switch off and the Estonian church choir began to sing 'O Perfect Love'. The beautiful rhythm of their acapella voices fill the church up to and through the ceiling arches.

When they reach Nicolaus, Nigel hugs his son, then places Deirdre's hand in his.

Both Nicolaus and Deirdre greet the Bishop with dueling unstoppable smiles.

Francesca places the train of the dress in a spiral pattern at Deirdre's feet, then lifts her veil, revealing her face, and moving it behind her head. Gently she kisses Deirdre, taking her bride's flowers, then kisses Nicolaus, and joins the family in the audience.

Bishop Moratey is very thrilled this marriage is happening, right here in Estonia, and that he gets to officiate. He gives reverence to God for the wonderful example of love to the world. He hadn't seen the church this filled in a very long time.

The bishop begins the ceremony. "Welcome to all! We have all drawn together, seemingly, from all over the world, to celebrate the enormously cherished and captivating love between Nicolaus

Ravenell and Deirdre Abigail Omari. Their love is predestined, similar to that of their not so distant ancestors."

The wedding ceremony takes about thirty minutes, for which Nicolaus and Deirdre are happy to take the holy communion, and restate their vows, while touching each other's rings, for the world to see and hear. Nicolaus gives Deirdre a romantic dive kiss, leaning her backwards, his strength holding her, to the heightened delight of the crowd.

Then as he'd always pictured in his mind, when the bishop pronounces them officially, Nicolaus again swoops Deirdre off her feet as if she weighs nothing, and carries her the length of the aisle, the huge crowd happily cheering, and pelting them with rose pedals for their walk all the way from the altar to the outside of the church.

The reception is held at the Royal Celebration Hall, which is owned by the Kiviste family, and located on the other side of the city. The hall is enormous, large enough to hold all who attended the wedding inside the church, and those who were outside as well. People are provided traditional Estonian treats to choose from, including small plates of Semla- traditional sweet bread with berries; sliced baked apples with ice cream; small slices of Estonian layered honey cake; and Estonian bread soup. The orchestra was moved to the hall, so dancing and celebrations could continue.

Nicolaus is very happy to see Roddy and his wife, Washington, his comrade, with his wife, and even Manfred and his wife in attendance. "My guys! Wow! So glad you are here. Can you believe all this?"

"Someone in your family knows how to throw a wedding!" Washington comments.

"This is really great. Congratulations, man!" Roddy hugs Nicolaus to him, shaking him with a gigantic smile on his face.

Manfred gives Nicolaus a pickup hug. "You finally got the correct girl this time!"

They laugh.

Nicolaus looks over and sees one of his military friends accompanying Maggie. Giancarlo is strong, dark, and of a happy nature. Ishani is close by as well. Nicolaus goes over to Giancarlo. They clasp hands in a brotherly handshake, and bump chests. "G! I can't believe you're here!" They men hug briefly.

"What are you trying to do to a brotha?" he asks jokingly and laughing, head nodding towards Maggie. "And now all this? You putting the pressure on all of us, man!"

Nicolaus laughs at Giancarlo's words, then gives a quick kiss to Maggie and Ishani. "So glad you're both here."

Nicolaus returns his attention to Giancarlo, all smiles. "Well, what'd I tell ya'?" he throws a quick glance and a head tilt towards Maggie.

Giancarlo laughs, "Man, you were right!"

"She's a tough one."

"Yeah, just the way I like my women."

"Good! Glad you're here."

"Oh yeah, your pops paid for us to be here. He must really love you to spend this kind of money to fly folks over. Wouldn't want to miss this fairytale wedding."

Nicolaus smiles, pointing to Deirdre, who is being hugged and kissed by Ishani and Maggie. "It's all her!"

Deirdre is so happy she can't stop smiling. She basked in the moments with everyone, completely enjoying being in her exquisite wedding dress. She obliges everyone who wants a selfie with her, sometimes getting Nicolaus in the photo, sometimes Maggie and Ishani, sometimes other family members.

She grabs her man, and her friends, and brings them to the dance floor. Nicolaus and Deirdre dance to many songs. The family joins in dancing with them. Then magically a line dance forms, and it seems as though hundreds of people join in to dance with the family, including Bishop Moratey. Nicolaus pulls Constance by both hands, to dance between he and Deirdre. Constance is thrilled and very happy for her daughter.

After a long time of line dancing, Deirdre goes to Rachel, and hugs her tightly. "My God, Auntie, this is the best! I could never thank you enough…"

"You don't need to thank me. I know you love my Nicky, and that he loves you. That is all that matters to me. Finally, you two are married! You both must take care of each other, and bring those children into the world."

Deirdre kisses Rachel. Nigel is nearby. Deirdre grabs him up, and kisses him as well. "Thank you so much, Pops, for this wonderful celebration. I know you helped with the wedding, I cannot thank you enough."

Nigel smiles upon Deirdre. "You are both deservedly happy. It's in the stars, remember? I have no doubt that you'll grow old together."

Time now to cut the wedding cake, which neither Nicolaus nor Deirdre had seen. The cake is wheeled out on a steel kitchen cart. It is a beautiful six-tiered cake, with white frosting and blue flowers. The topper on the cake is the letter 'R' with the Ravenell name spelled out in gold letters underneath. Nicolaus is very surprised by this. On the side of the cake the letter 'N' is just diagonally placed above the letter 'D', also in the color blue. Blue flowers encircle the bottom tier of the cake, which is the largest.

Nigel and Ceil have the Kiviste family heirloom cake spatula. Together, they hold onto it, and hand it to Nicolaus and Deirdre. With joy, the new couple accept the specially carved spatula, as if there is some kind of passing a torch tradition.

Nicolaus takes Deirdre in both his arms, and together, both their hands cut the cake. They both feed each other a small piece of cake, the photo cameras flashing excessively, as Nicolaus kisses Deirdre. Then he kisses her again, and again, to the delight of the ladies in the crowd, who blurt out noisy fanfare at the romantic charm of the couple.

The server takes over the cutting of the cake for them.

Nicolaus steps up to his parents, with Deirdre connected to him, his arm around her waist, holding her close. "Thank you so much, this is really all beautiful." He pulls Ceil into a hug, not caring if she wants it or if it is returned. "Thank you," he whispers in her ear. "Thank you for being here. It means a lot to me."

When Ceil doesn't pull away from him, even though he is nervous about Ceil's reaction, Nicolaus continues with his thoughts. He feels that his mother is behaving herself fairly good enough before all the cameras, the people, and the dignitaries. He wants to confront her because he just cannot have his mother rejecting Deirdre every day, and making her life miserable, as she has done to him.

With Deirdre still in his arm, Nicolaus bends his tall frame down, in a humble stance before his mother, and he speaks gently. "Mother, I know you have given your best for me and Niall, and I understand and it's okay if you don't care much for me, and that you prefer Niall. Please, I ask you ... I implore you ... I beg you ... please ... respect Deirdre. She is now my wife, and I love her with my whole life. Please," he begs her. Deirdre is very surprised at Nicolaus' words and actions. His voice is low enough so that only they could hear him with all the partying, chatter, and music going in the background. "I am not saying you have to honor her on a pedestal, just please treat her with decency. She deserves that much, to be treated decent."

Ceil is caught off guard by Nicolaus, as his eyes warmly wait for her reply. He is unmoving, still holding onto Deirdre, who is also looking at Ceil with a sweet expression, waiting for her answer. Ceil stares at him, frozen coldly, in time. A slight smile appears on her face, and she is unmoving under Nicolaus' hand to her shoulder.

Nicolaus nudged Ceil, almost bowing his head, as if he were addressing a queen.

"Please, I hardly ask much of you. And I only ask this one thing, that you treat Deirdre with the decency she deserves." Again, Nicolaus is still, and waits for her answer.

Ceil sighs, unable to deny what he said. He has hardly ever asked anything of her.

And it does seem very fitting for him to ask this of her at this moment in time, in the manner of which he is asking. Ceil decides she could manage the request, her mind thinking about Helena, and knowing she would want Ceil to be affirming towards Deirdre and Nicolaus as well.

"Very well," she simply answers with a nod, a slight smile, and a gentle patting to Nicolaus' back.

Nicolaus is relieved and astonished at the same time, as he looks upon his mother. "Thank you!"

With the rustle of her wedding dress, Deirdre is upon Ceil and hugs her tightly. "Thank you Mother Ceil, thank you." She kisses Ceil's face, overjoyed for the day, feeling this would open a new chapter for the whole family. "If it were not for you, there would be no Nicolaus Ravenell. Thank you so much!"

Nicolaus then hugs his father again. He feels this is the most authentic love he's ever received from his parents.

Elsa and Niall are close by. Niall is quick to grab Deirdre, and kiss her face, close to her mouth. Deirdre just smiles at him, and holds onto the very pregnant Elsa. She is six months along now.

Nicolaus grabs Niall by the shoulder, "Thank you for being here." The brothers hug.

Nicolaus and Deirdre talk to their other family members, whom they hadn't seen since Clara's funeral. "Please have lunch with us tomorrow. You are always welcome at the castle," Nicolaus tells them.

The celebration of love continues into the night. The press made live news reports about the Ravenell wedding, which were already flying all over the globe.

Deirdre's dream wedding became a reality, and it is more than she could have asked for. Together, she and Nicolaus, holden tight to each other every moment, mingle with the guests, the famous people, as well as the unknown local folks.

Chapter One Hundred Twenty-Five

D eirdre's dream continues into the night as she and Nicolaus again settle into the historic castle bedroom, which they now claim as theirs. She loves that his hands had rarely left her body in one way or the other, since they'd cut their wedding cake.

All of the Ravenell family decided to stay at the castle, as there are plenty of rooms for everyone. Once they arrived, Nicolaus wasted no time in swooping Deirdre off her feet, into his arms, and up the spiral staircase, to the claps and bursting laughter of the family members.

He locks the door to the historical bedchamber, which held the historical bed, where he'd made love to his precious wife the previous night. The staff had tidied up the room and already had the fire going for them.

Nicolaus helps Deirdre out of her beautiful wedding dress, sweetly kissing her neck as he did so. Then he kisses her arms, and the sensual areas of her body, until she is fully undressed. Suddenly, in Nicolaus fashion, he swoops her off her feet again, which he loves to do, and gently lays her upon the bed.

No nervousness or hesitation tonight, as Nicolaus is already fully inside his wife, gently making love to her. He is completely convinced that if he doesn't hear love moans released from Deirdre, that he is not doing his husbandry duty of pleasing his wife and working to bring his children about.

He loves the new feel of their naked bodies together. It is as if she is the only woman on the earth who was created specifically for him.

Deirdre does not fight the moans that escape her mouth, as Nicolaus gently, at first, pounds her with love, then the pounding intensifies, taking her breath away, and putting her mind in a frenzy with hot pleasure. Her body grips Nicolaus, causing him to cease up and moan with ejaculation. His all-enveloping and loving embrace puts her at ease, as he grasps her lips with his, in non-stop kissing. Deirdre let Nicolaus hold her. She let Nicolaus love her. She enjoyed the moment of being one flesh with her man, her eternal love. She relaxed in the complete safety and overwhelming comfort of his arms.

Together, they drift to ecstasy sleep.

In the morning, the family gathers for breakfast. Nicolaus and Deirdre join everyone in the late morning hours. Rachel and Francesca are absent. Nicolaus' Aunt Janelle and Aunt Zoe take he and Deirdre out to the gardens, away from the house so they can talk. Both Nicolaus and Deirdre bring their morning breakfast of black rye bread, cheese, and sausage with them.

They sit in the gazebo. "Thank goodness," Zoe clasps her elderly hands together. "You two should have been married long ago ... if it weren't for Ceil's meddling ..."

Deirdre chuckles, almost sitting in Nicolaus' lap, she is so close to him. "Oh well, now, some of that is my doing ..."

Nicolaus' arms wrap around his wife, holding her tightly, not wanting to ever miss a moment to hold her, ever again. "No ... I was away a lot with the military."

They each try to take the blame.

"Well, now the angels are singing over you two," Janelle says. "Nicolaus, how's life been, though? How's my sister been treating you? Why haven't we heard from you before all these events?"

Nicolaus chuckles and shakes his head. "I'm so sorry, I just ... didn't know about you. My mother never mentioned you," he frowns, now thinking it odd that Ceil never let them meet her sisters. "Well, even our other cousins on my father's side, Cato and them, we hadn't seen them since we were kids."

"That's because Ceil knows we know things she don't want other folks to know. And she's mean and spiteful, so folks don't want to be around her."

"Things?"

Janelle nods. "Yep! She likes to keep secrets, you know. How's she been treating you?" she asks him again, knowing the secret of his birth parents.

Nicolaus glances at Deirdre, and they both chuckle, Nicolaus laughing to himself. He shakes his head again, with a slight frown. "She doesn't like us very much," he half whispers.

Zoe, who looks the spitting image of her sister Ceil, only older, touches Nicolaus on the knee, and nods. "I know sweety. I figured."

"I'm sure it's something I've done that I can't remember, like when I was a kid or something. I tried to get my father to tell me what happened, and he only tells me it's something he did. I can't really get a straight answer from him."

"Well ... and you probably won't," Zoe confirms for him. She touches his knee again, "If Nigel won't tell you, you need to ask Rachel."

Nicolaus frowned at her. "That's what mother told me." Nicolaus looked at Deirdre to explain, as he hadn't mention it to her. "Before our ceremony in Austin, she said something about not being my mother, and told me to go ask Rachel. I don't know what that is supposed to mean, and father wouldn't tell me."

"She says she's not your mother?" Deirdre's lawyer mind discerned the direct words that he didn't pick up on. "Well, then Nicky ..."

"I think you should wait until you're back from your honeymoon. Don't spoil things now with all this. Just wait. When you return, then you talk to Rachel," Janelle advises them.

They both nod in agreement.

"What are you doing for your honeymoon, anyway?" Janelle asks them.

"Well, since we are already over here, I figure we can take two weeks to enjoy the European landscape, go to different countries, maybe spend a day or two in each one. I would love to see some historic churches."

"Oh that's a wonderful idea. My son, Claude, in his work, he knows many leaders of all the countries. He can give them a heads up and you can meet with them."

"Meet with them?" Nicolaus is not sure what she was getting at.

"Well, of course! You two are international celebrities. Did you see how much press was at your wedding? They think you're some kind of royalty with influence and power. And you should use that to your advantage. You're cause celebs now!"

"Cause celebs?" Deirdre is amazed at her new auntie's comment. She has never thought of herself and Nicolaus in such a manner. "Hmm, I don't think we are."

"Oh yes you are!" Janelle would not be dissuaded. "And I understand that you are doing something for children back home. Well, do you think all children here are happy and have a home? You'll find that many are in the same situation or worse. Think what you can accomplish if you expand your thinking and try to help children on a larger scale. The good thing is there is actually a safety net in most of the European countries. Getting the homeless children into that safety net is the issue."

Deirdre grabs Nicolaus around his arm, "Babe, she's right! My God, this idea had not even dawned on us. We could go to where the children are in the streets, have the press follow us, then meet with leaders and pressure them to do something to help those children."

Janelle slaps her own leg, "Exactly!"

"Okay, I like that. We can make a difference, while taking a vacation."

"Yes, and you both deserve time. So make sure you get into that European water, breathe the European air, and enjoy yourselves too," Zoe reiterates with light laughter.

Janelle stands, "Let's go talk to Claude!"

Chapter One Hundred Twenty-Six

As Deirdre and Nicolaus begin their honeymoon, Deirdre feels as though she is still dreaming. Every place they go is more beautiful than she could have ever imagined. And it only seems right that she should be in such beautiful places with the man she loves.

Being who they are, their love story internationally known, VMC also internationally known, and their fundraising efforts internationally known, opened many doors to them.

Before their plane landed, Nicolaus received celebrity calls to host them, and even assist and escort them when he explained their private efforts about the children.

Their first stop is Helsinki, Finland. Nicolaus is astonished when they are offered to stay with a high ranking official, and to dine with the Prime Minister. Suddenly, Nicolaus understands the pull his cousin, Claude, has. He is impressed.

Deirdre is ready to make demands on the driver, before things get underway, especially as the press is already following them around. She is shocked to count at least twenty press cameras, and several reporters, men and women, running to set up near their limousine.

Deirdre is standing halfway out the limo, Nicolaus next to her. "So do you know where street children are?"

"Street children, Madame?" The driver scowls at her, not fully getting her meaning. "Yes, you know ... children running about, not in school, perhaps unruly, perhaps being where they shouldn't."

"The homeless children?"

"Yes! Homeless children." The driver nods. "Great! That's where we need to go. Oh, and first we need to stop by a few stores." She seems to be announcing this to the press, while pretending to ignore them.

"Deirdre ... what ...?" Nicolaus doesn't understand what she wants to do.

Deirdre baulks at her love, "Well, we can't go empty handed! Those kids need things, clothes, shoes, socks, toys, books, ... you know."

Nicolaus looks at his wife wide-eyed. This little undertaking appears to be getting beyond what he thought they would be doing. He nods in agreement with her.

Deirdre reaches up for a kiss from him, and he relents to her, the press cameras flashing excessively. "Don't worry, babe, I already called Ms. Winfree before our flight. She is delighted to help. Anyway, aren't we meeting with Tobias? We should take him with us to buy some items. Let's have him meet us at the store," she says loudly for the press to hear. Tobias is a larger than life sports figure in Finland. He's tall, handsome, and a bachelor.

They get into the limo and Deirdre makes the call to Tobias. He is more than happy to meet them at the store to help them supply items to the street children.

Once they arrive at the store, the couple greet Tobias with a hug. The large department store is filled with patrons who grow very excited at the presence of Nicolaus and Deirdre, and especially Tobias.

The media is immediately upon them, wanting to know more about the visit. Nicolaus stands in the background out of the cameras, as the press focus in on Tobias, while he explains what they are doing.

Nicolaus talks with Tobias after the segment. "This is going to go on beyond us once we leave," he tells his friend, "best have a place for people to donate."

Tobias agrees. He has the press take another segment, and asks people to continue to support homeless children through the local Finish Children's Services.

Deirdre is already off gathering items, wasting no time. Suddenly crowds of women surround her, watching, wanting to help. "We need pants for girls and boys of all sizes, shirts, and tops, and jackets. Sox, and ...." Before she can finish her sentence, the helpful and proud Finish women are doing the gathering for her. They fill several shopping carts with hundreds of items.

Deirdre touches Tobias' shoulder, "How are we going to distribute this? Oh my, this feels a little haphazard."

Tobias smiles, "Don't worry Deirdre, after this press coverage, I think the next places you go it will be done up and ready for the two of you." He looks around, amazed at all the shoppers helping them. "How about backpacks? Since you grabbed books, we can put sets of items in the backpacks."

"Great idea."

Both Nicolaus and Tobias purchase all the items, enough for one hundred fifty children.

In the parking lot, as the three scurry to get the sets of items into the backpacks, the women who were in the store helping them shop, now help them pack the backpacks, loving being close to Tobias.

As the limousine drives slowly, it is followed by several press vans. When they enter the area where the street children roam, children pour out seemingly from everywhere. The children immediately surround the limousine, the vehicle itself being a sign that the people inside have money.

When the vehicle door opens, Nicolaus and Tobias step out, then Deirdre.

"Tobias! Tobias!" Several children recognize him, yelling his name.

"Ooh,... you're pretty!" a little girl tells Deirdre.

The children are upon them, happy to have visitors. It's not every day that people visit street children.

Several children are surprised that gifts were brought to them. Some even cry, as they look inside their given backpack.

"A kampa! (A comb!)"

"Vaatteet! (Clothes!)"

"Kengät! (Shoes!)"

"Omenats! (Apples!)"

"Karkkia! (Candy!)"

"Kirjats! (Books!)"

The children are amazed at the contents of their backpacks. The hardest part is trying to match the best size clothes and shoes to the size of the child.

Deirdre gladly receives the hugs and kisses from the children who are very needy, and dirty. Many have torn clothes, some no shoes. The ruckus and excitement of the children is loud, and the noise level outmatches the press reporters.

Tobias is again interviewed, as all the backpacks were handed out after about twenty minutes. The children remain gathered around Nicolaus and Deirdre, as the couple help some of the children put on the socks and shoes they'd brought to them.

Deirdre has tears in her eyes when it is time to go. She does not want to leave the children out on the streets. Nicolaus feels emotional as well. Tobias is the last to climb into the limo for their departure. "Well, now you take this raw emotion to the Prime Minister. Make him feel what you feel." Tobias clears his throat to stop his own tears, feeling the same emotion the couple is feeling, watching them hugged up to each other. "This is really a good thing you are doing. May you both be very blessed."

Nicolaus smiles at his dear friend. "Thank you for helping us today."

"It is my pleasure! Giving me some ideas on how further I can help, too! This is my country. I should be more involved! And I will be from now on! Thank you for showing what needs to be done.

Your small acts of love has shown all of us what we need to do to secure the future for these children."

Later that day, the Prime Minister's wife served an extravagant evening meal for the Ravenells and had invited additional guests. Nicolaus and Deirdre found it hard to eat as they thought about the street children. The Prime Minister's wife notices their low appetite.

"Deirdre, tell us about the children you met today," she got right to the matter at hand, thinking it better that she bring up the subject, instead of the Ravenells pointing out their problem to their eyes.

Deirdre lit up, "You're children ... they are so wonderful! They were so sweet, each of them. Very respectful."

"Perhaps because you had gifts for them," one of the dinner guests rudely snarks.

"Possibly, but that is what the spirit of giving is supposed to do, isn't it?" Nicolaus reasoned. "Helps bring calm and all manner of kindness and respect."

"I hope there is something that can be done to help get those children off the street and into homes," Deirdre continues. "Please tell us if there is anything we can do. In our own country, Nicky and I are working on launching a chain of children's homes across part of the nation, to help such children. We are going to adopt them outright, through our company."

"Through your company?"

"Yes. It's allowable in our country because of the way the corporation is set up," Nicolaus explains. "Deirdre and I would love to partner with you and assist in any way needed. It would be our honor."

Both the Prime Minister and his wife smile at the charming couple. "What you did today is actually very sweet. I'll have my

Minister of Children's Services follow up with you. Please be sure to leave us your cards."

Everyone turned in close to midnight. Nicolaus and Deirdre are both physically and emotionally exhausted. They rest, Deirdre in Nicolaus' arms.

The plan is for sight-seeing tomorrow, then heading off to the next country to highlight the plight of street children. The next stop – Stockholm, Sweden.

Chapter One Hundred Twenty-Seven

The international media coverage on the fairytale wedding of the beautiful American lawyer, Deirdre Omari, to the handsome American military hero, and Vice President of VMC, Nicolaus Ravenell, is splashed on all newspapers, on live television reports, on celebrity entertainment shows, and on talk shows everywhere, in every major country. Even the papers in South Africa carry the story of the romantic fairytale wedding.

Abigail's colleague throws the paper on her desk at the straight-laced media company, where Abigail hones her craft of journalistic writing. The paper lands on top of the story she is editing. Abigail had just gotten back to work, after getting over the death of her fiancé, Jacque. They'd been together for two years. He'd fallen ill just after he proposed, then died shortly thereafter. She'd been gone for twelve weeks.

"See? I told you! She's your dobbleganger. You cannot deny it now."

Abigail picks up the paper. There is a large, glossy, colorful photo of the couple. Abigail is immediately struck by Nicolaus, finding him very good-looking, with heavily inviting eyes, even in print. She frowns when she sees Deirdre. "Deirdre Omari? Omari?" Abigail feels as though she is looking at herself.

"She even has your name! Uncanny, isn't it?"

"Or is it?" Abigail shot back at her longtime colleague, Shanice, who always wanted to find something to tease her about.

Abigail quickly reads the story, then sits back in her chair in thought. She remembers that her father had some dealings in Austin, Texas, a long time ago, something he never spoke about. It was a time before they moved to South Africa.

"You are missing something very important!" From across the desk, Shanice points to the paper. Walking to Abigail, her fingertips tap the wedding dress in the photo. "Look here. Do you see it?"

Abigail looks at the dress. She is taken aback. "Oh, that's impossible!" Abigail says of the wedding dress that looks identical to her own. She'd bought it on a whim when Jacque wanted them to try to wed before his sickness grew worse. He wanted Abigail to be his widow, however, it was just too late for them. His illness came on fast and furious and took him quickly.

"I tell you, it's eerie down to the details." Shanice sighs, "Well, I've got to go, a story awaits my investigative skills. I'll see you later." She is off in a rush.

Quickly, Abigail takes a magnifying glass from her desk, and she views the wedding dress in the photo. She is shocked that the pattern looks exactly the same as her own dress. "That's impossible!" she whispers to herself.

As tenured staff, Abigail has much freedom. She left the office and found her father at home in his usual hobby of building model trains. He's been retired from working for some time now, and uses this hobby to keep his mind occupied. His model train set is elaborate.

Abigail places the newspaper before his eyes. She sits down, sighs, and gently asks of him, "Father, is there something you haven't told me?"

Cecil glances at the paper. He also sighs. He knew this day would be happening soon when he'd seen all the media coverage on the Ravenell wedding. He is very pleased for Deirdre, as she looks happy and seems to be very much in love with Nicolaus, who he thinks is a great man, much like Nigel, his father, whom Cecil knows from their history together. A history that is very distant to him now. What father wouldn't want his daughter to marry an intelligent and kind military hero? Knowing his secret daughter is happy, makes his heart glad. He only wished he could know more about her mother. There is nothing about Constance online that he could find.

Cecil tries to ignore the question of his present daughter, and continues fiddling with the model train.

Abigail touches his hand, to interrupt him. "Deirdre Abigail Omari," she notes Deirdre's full name, the reverse of her own name.

Cecil stops what he is doing, and looks at his daughter tight lipped. He frowns and nods, "Yes, we need to talk."

Chapter One Hundred Twenty-Eight

C eil is not sure what to make of the news coverage Nicolaus and Deirdre are receiving on their honeymoon. She does think that too much is being made of the couple. While Nicolaus is away from his post at VMC, and everyone is still rather sad about Alexander, Ceil decides to give Niall a go, and she decides to announce this last minute unilateral decision at breakfast.

"Niall, today I want you to go to the office in your brother's absence."

"Me?" he asks surprised, almost shocked that Ceil would even suggest such a thing. "What would I do?"

"Mother Ceil, perhaps you'd like Niall to accompany me today. After all, the Chief Operating Officer is in charge while Nicolaus is away," Elsa reminds her, trying to ease back her expectations.

Nigel nods. "Yes, Elsa is correct."

"No. I want Niall to stand in for Nicolaus. Anyway, you never know if something could happen to them while they are away. Niall needs to prepare for succession. He can review the Chief Operating Officer, and what he is doing. Niall can confirm decisions."

Niall chuckles, "Mother, I don't know what to do! I wouldn't even know what I am looking at. Anyway, that is not my focus. My focus is on endorsements now."

Ceil sighs loudly, irritated at Niall's attitude. "I keep telling you, stop being a jackass! Many of our family have paved the way for your future. I want you to get a taste of that."

"Your mother is right. You do need to be more involved, just as Nicolaus is," Nigel provides his support to Ceil, agreeing with her this time. "You should go and learn what to do, just as Nicolaus did. Actually, you need to go to college and learn about finance, just as Nicolaus did. He has a master's degree in business administration and finance; and he obtained it while leading troops. It's past time for you to get a college degree, which would help you a great deal, as well, Niall. Your endorsement gig is okay, although ... it's not part of our business. Endorsements will not sustain your future, and I want you to be more serious about your future. You need to understand the business world and how finance works. And maybe then we can even find a position for you next to your brother."

Ceil smiles, pleased at Nigel's response. She lovingly touches his arm.

Niall does not respond. He thought despairingly, hating how much they are literally comparing him to Nicolaus and trying to place him in the same path as his brother. He is really hating the demands they are trying to place on him. He'd never set his foot on a college campus. He sighed with mouth closed, as he couldn't think of an excuse to get out of the request to go to the office, or of the demand to better himself through education.

"Going to the office now will be good practice for you, Niall," Ceil adds sweetly. "After all, one day, you might be the one running everything."

"God help us all," Nigel mutters.

Chapter One Hundred Twenty-Nine

More news stories hit the print media, as well as the television entertainment news regarding the Ravenell wedding. The press is working this human-interest story for as long as possible. They now sent out and discussed the list of countries Nicolaus and Deirdre planned to visit, which the couple released for their advantage.

The list is extensive: Stockholm, Sweden; Oslo, Norway; Copenhagen, Denmark; Dublin, Ireland; London, England; Paris, France; Belgium, Brussels; Amsterdam, Netherlands; Hanover, Germany, and back to Tallin, Estonia. They note that the couple plans to meet with leaders of each country to discuss the conditions of street children, and request for changes to be made to meet the needs of these children.

Talking heads and political pundits discuss the audaciousness of the American couple, who have European ancestry, and whether they were trying to force their westernized values on these European leaders. Discussing the background of the couple, including Deirdre's work and Nicolaus' military status and commendations, the Kiviste family castle and historic family influence in Estonia, and their connection to the St. Nicholas Church, as well as Nigel's family history, were all now lively topics as well.

Chapter One Hundred Thirty

I t is noon when Niall finally appears at the VMC headquarters. He'd refused to ride in the limo with Ceil earlier, and he refused to go with his wife. He told them he'd make his own way to the office. When he enters the board room, he is dressed appropriately, and looking handsome, however he does smell as though he'd fallen into a large vat of liquor.

"Ah, Niall, there you are! Here, take your brother's chair," Ceil tells him with a smile, masking her embarrassment.

Niall sits down in the chair that belongs to Nicolaus, which is immediately to the left of Nigel. He slouches back, pushing the awaiting stack of papers on the table away from him, not even looking at them.

The board members are looking at Niall in awe, quickly sizing him up as the lesser half of the Ravenell brothers. Immediately, they are not sure he could be trusted with the billions of dollars their corporation made from investments and medical care insurance payments. They are not sure he could be trusted in Nicolaus' place or leadership role.

"Well, the last item on the agenda for today is the hiring of new physicians for our New Mexico clinic. Ceil, I believe that is your item."

Ceil sits taller and straighter, trying to be a silent example for her son. "Yes, thank you. It was brought to my attention that our New Mexico clinics are having a hard time attracting pediatric physicians. I have made an analysis on this, if you turn to the page attached to the report, you'll see that our pay is too low for the specialty."

"Um, excuse me," Niall interrupts Ceil. "What is pediatric?"

"That is a physician for children."

"Oh. Sorry, please continue."

Ceil nods and continues, "So, I propose we increase that pay by no less than fifty thousand dollars."

"Fifty thousand?" Niall blurts aloud, feeling this is a lot of money. "Fifty thousand?" he asks again.

Ceil gives him a narrowed glance. "Yes, well, if you look at the analysis ... go ahead and get the paper, Niall, we'll wait ..." she says trying to be patient.

Niall begrudgingly grabs the stack of papers that he'd earlier pushed away. He fumbles through them, not finding what he needs. Nigel helps him get to the paper. He looks it over.

"Now, as I was saying, there Niall, the analysis shows that we are offering too low of pay for that specialty, and ..."

"This is already good pay we are offering. Can't we just find someone who is willing to take this pay?" he asks, not understanding what he is discussing, trying to seem important. Thinking he is acting as his brother might.

"The problem is that other clinics are offering more. As you see on the report ..."

"Who cares about the other clinics? We should stick to our price," he argues abrasively, believing he looks smart, while actually showing his ignorance.

Nigel touches his arm. "Let Ceil complete her explanation, then we can voice our opinions."

Niall nods. "Sorry, go ahead, Ceil," he tells her rudely, never having addressed his mother as such.

Ceil eyes Niall and sighs. "We have to offer a competitive wage, or we will not get these positions filled. We currently need four pediatric physicians. We don't want to have to turn away our patients." Ceil folds her hands before her, having finished her comments.

"I offer that we table this discussion until we hear from the recruiting team. They have a meeting today and can bring us up to speed on their plan," the board Secretary notes.

The board members vote to table the item.

Nigel closes the meeting. "This concludes our meeting. Thank you all for being here."

As the board members quickly exit the conference room, they eye Niall with distrust. Some already knew they would never allow Niall to replace Nicolaus.

Nigel touches his son's hand. "Your mother should have given you the rules of the meeting, so you'd know how to conduct yourself."

"She did tell me something about it this morning, ... I wasn't really paying attention. This seems really boring to me, father."

Nigel chuckles, "Well, it's not boring when you are the one who has to provide the information or be on top of everything to know what is going on." Nigel could see that in this short amount of time of his short explanation, he'd lost Niall's attention. "Hmm," he wonders to himself.

As the board members leave the room, Ceil stands next to Niall, and she touches his shoulders. "Next time be on time for the meeting please. And you will learn to follow the rules I told you about this morning. No interrupting!" she chides him. "Now, take your wife to lunch downstairs in the café, and meet me back at Nicolaus' office at half past one to prepare for that recruitment meeting. You shall attend, and bring me up to speed." Niall nods, not sure this is a good idea.

Chapter One Hundred Thirty-One-TW

After lunch with Elsa in the downstairs café, Elsa takes Niall to Nicolaus' office.

"Mother Ceil said she will be here just about now. I have some work to do, so you can wait for her in here." Elsa smiles at her husband, and they peck kiss before she departs.

Immediately, Niall sits down in Nicolaus' desk chair, to get a feel for it. He looks out at the wall of windows, in the top floor office, opposite the desk, which has a clear, unobstructed view of the Texas sky. One could see the street below, that runs parallel to Lady Bird Lake, which cuts through the center of the city.

Niall sits back, wondering if he really could take Nicolaus' place. He notices that the office is adorned with many framed snapshot photos of Nicolaus and Deirdre, looking happy, showing her engagement ring. Niall picks up the eight by ten framed photo on the corner of Nicolaus' desk, of the couple at a prior year performing arts center celebrity fundraiser.

Niall thinks about how he doesn't have any photos of himself and Elsa, as surely he should have some.

"One day this will be your office," Ceil's voice interrupts his thoughts.

Niall smirks at her comment, gently replacing the picture onto Nicolaus' desk. He sits up straight in the chair. "Mother, what am I doing here? I have no idea what is going on."

"You think Nicolaus knew anything before he was placed in the role where you should be? No. He knew nothing. Your father trained him. And if you bring yourself here every day, I will train you, your father will train you, the lawyers will train you ... hell ... I'll even make Nicolaus train you. Get some college under your belt, as your father suggested this morning. Then you'll know exactly what to do. But son, you actually do have to put in the effort."

Niall nods, as if what his mother is saying was actually beginning to sink in. "Okay, I'll think about it. I'm just not sure I'm cut out for this."

"And just what is it you think you are cut out for? Babysitting?"

Niall frowns and clears his throat at his mother's insult of his efforts to assist at Helena's children's home. "We raised a lot of money for the children's home," he reminds her.

Ceil nods, "Yes, and that is a good thing. A one-time thing. Now Niall, I want you to start preparing to replace Nicolaus."

Niall looks around the office again. He notices how it is clean and tidy. There are no papers laying around, nothing in the inbox. He sees wall shelves that contain many large binders full of papers, which he assumes are reports. The filing cabinets are dusted and orderly. The conference table holds a box of tissues and a pump bottle of hand sanitizer. On top of Nicolaus' desk is a flat calendar for which he sees his brother's neat handwriting of scheduled meetings and reminders. The essence of his brother is everywhere in the pristine office.

Ceil notices that Niall seems to be getting uncomfortable. She sits on the edge of the desk opposite of him. "Now, pay attention. I want you to look smart at this meeting. They will be discussing recruitment strategies for what we just talked about in the board meeting. The team knows you will be attending, I have already alerted them. I want you to mostly listen, take notes, and then you can fill me in on what is said." Ceil stands. She sighs nervously, as this is her first real test for Niall. "You ready?"

Niall stands and nods, "Yeah, sure. I'm ready."

Ceil folds her arms and looks at him with a mother's head tilt. "Really? Aren't you forgetting something in order to take notes?"

Niall smirks at her again, "I don't need that. I'll use my noggin."

Ceil looks at her son disapprovingly, then lets it go. She led him to the meeting. "Good afternoon everyone, this is Niall, my younger son, who will be standing in for Nicolaus today."

"I'm Daniel Araceli, the Chief Operating Officer." Daniel put his hand out to Niall, who takes his hand, nodding. The men shake hands. "It's a pleasure for you to join us. Please have a seat." Ceil exits the room. After several more introductions of the team members, the meeting begins.

"So the issue with the New Mexico pediatric docs is that the pay is too low."

"I heard this argument earlier. That pay is set well. Why do I keep hearing the pay is low?" Niall immediately and ignorantly argues. He has already forgotten his mother's instructions of mostly listening.

"Nicolaus set the pay based on the regional market for pediatric physicians. However, I think a mistake may have been made in that the market research is for first year physicians."

"What? My brother made a mistake?" Niall immaturely scoffs at this bit of information.

Daniel frowns at his reaction, and then corrects him. "Well, the research team made the error." Daniel passes out some papers with figures and diagrams. "When I looked over the research, this is what stood out to me. You can see that the amount is based on first year physicians."

"The research team may have forgotten to go back and update the figures," another team member offered.

"Possible."

"This pay is pretty good, don't you think? I mean this is annual pay. Why should my family dole out more money? I say we wait for someone to take this pay."

Daniel has a slight smile, with a head shake, "Well, it's not that easy. No physician will accept this amount when the competitors are paying more."

"Yeah, but there are only so many slots for physicians in one city. Once the high paying slots are gone, then they will have to accept our figure."

"Usually they won't. We have been unable to fill these vacancies. Recruiters are not having luck, and we feel it's because of the pay amount."

"So, throwing fifty thousand more dollars of my parents' money on this, makes it all better?" he asks sarcastically.

Daniel pauses the meeting with a hand in the air. "Just to clarify for you, Niall, this money is from insurance payments, not straight from your parents. Additionally, there is foundation money, which is built up by donors, which your brother, actually, has done an excellent job in increasing donations."

"Oh yeah, my brother. Yeah. Yeah." Niall's attitude turns negative relatively quickly, at the mention of Nicolaus' accomplishments.

Daniel continues, "I suggest that we recommend increasing the salary by fifty thousand dollars, and adding ten days off with pay, which is not offered by the competitors."

"More money?" Niall complains. "You just throw money at everything, or what?"

Daniel chuckles, "Oh, I'm sorry, did you have a strategy you'd like to propose?"

Immediately, Daniel's nature reminds Niall of Nicolaus. He sighs, starting to feel impatient and inadequate for being placed on the spot. He has no clue what strategy he'd offer. Niall is ready to leave. "No, what you have said is fine."

Daniel nods, "Oh, okay, thank you. Now, let's discuss ..."

"Wait, we're not done with this meeting?" Niall asks, his frustration showing.

"Oh no Sir, we have this conference room for an hour and a half. We still need to discuss advertising and marketing budgets for recruitment. Also, a few recruitment members will be along if you'd care to meet with them privately."

"Ah, no." Niall stands. He is done. "You are doing a good job. Carry on." Niall swiftly exits the conference room, closing the door. He wants to run out of the building, as he feels trapped and frustrated. He feels the weight of his ignorance.

He looks up and happens to see Elsa approaching from the other end of the hall.

Elsa sees that Niall looks distraught. She goes to her husband with a frown of concern. "Niall, are you all right? Is everything okay?"

"No," he snaps at her. "Where's my mother?"

"She's in a meeting, ..."

"Another damn meeting?" he says rather loudly.

Elsa put her hand to Niall's chest to try to calm him. "Honey, maybe you should just go home. It's okay. First days are always rough for everyone."

Niall does not like that Elsa is trying to tell him what to do. He harshly grabs her by the wrist, making her shriek. Without words, Niall forces Elsa to a nearby closet. As he opens the unlocked closet door, he harshly throws Elsa inside the supply room, locking the door. Niall needs to get rid of his frustration, because he feels it growing. He doesn't know of another way to deal with his inadequacies.

"Niall, what are you doing?"

Elsa receives a back-handed slap across the face, making her six-month pregnant self, unsteady on her feet and almost falling. This gives Niall enough time to force her over the stack of boxed copy paper, get her clothes down, and shove himself into her. He roughly holds her so she cannot move or get away from him.

Without words, Elsa silently takes what her husband harshly forces upon her. He finishes with a muzzled moan against her shoulder. Breathless, Niall releases his wife.

Through her tears and astonished humiliation, Elsa straightens her clothes and quickly leaves the closet, hoping no one has seen them. Unfortunately, when she opens the door, Ceil is right before her. Without words, the mascara running tear tracks down her face, and blood trickling from her cut lip, Elsa leaves the area.

Ceil enters the supply closet to find her Niall disheveled, pulling his clothes together. Ceil is abounded in disappointment beyond words. "Go home," she tells him sternly. "We'll talk later." She leaves the closet not sure what to do.

Niall now feels himself in a rage. The embarrassment of his mother finding him in such a state is too much for him. He suddenly has an inkling, for the first time in his life, that perhaps he has trouble controlling himself. "Why did you insist I be here today, mother? Why?" he yells at Ceil. "To show me that I add up to nothing?"

"Now you know better than that!" Ceil yells back at him. "You know I love you, and I want you to be ready. But what are you doing?" she shouts at him, not caring who heard.

"No, it's the opposite," he hardily believes. "Well, I get your message loud and clear,"

he shouts. Niall points a finger at his mother. "Do not expect me to step into his place if something happens. I am not Nicolaus. And I never will be." Niall storms out of the closet, for which now they have an audience of concerned staff, security, and even Daniel.

The commotion brings Nigel about. He sighs and side hugs Ceil to him, feeling her disappointment. "Okay everyone, it's all right. It's over. Please get back to work." Nigel nods at security to acknowledge their presence.

Chapter One Hundred Thirty-Two

The Swedish Minister of Health Services met Nicolaus and Deirdre at the airport. The couple is stunned, not having expected such action.

"We are so honored to meet you," the gray haired, male Minister tells them, earnestly shaking their hands, his whole team behind him. "Please follow this way. We have prepared to meet the children with you. Do not worry, we are providing all the provisions."

Deirdre looks at Nicolaus with wide eyes. They get into the first limousine of a line of vehicles and are driven to where the street children stay. One of the vans that followed them is filled with backpacks of clothes, lunch boxes with food, and toys for the children.

The children swarm the limousine, and when the couple step out, the children understand what is happening, as it is Deirdre and Nicolaus they hug and kiss on, not the Minister. The press take pictures, and highlight in their reports that although the children are greasy and very dirty, neither Nicolaus nor Deirdre shy away from the little scrawny arms of hugs, or dirty faced kisses.

As would be normal, the children are elated to be given anything, especially food, fruit, candy, and toys. The cheers, and laughter of the children is on a high noise level. The Minister watches, as if he is learning from the couple.

Deirdre goes to him, with a little girl in her arms. The little one hugs her tight around the neck, while Nicolaus helps several little boys put on socks and shoes.

"This is wonderful, thank you for helping us!" she tells the Minister over the loud chatter of the children. He nods to her with a smile. "Will they have to remain here? Will they still sleep out here tonight?"

"Well ...ah ... well ... ah ..." he stammers, "we had not planned beyond this, Lady Deirdre."

Deirdre hugs the little one to her, who now had her dirty thumb in her mouth. She couldn't have been over the age of six. Deirdre pats her on the back, looking upon her. Her clothes are mangled and dirty. Her hair unruly and tangled. Deirdre cannot imagine leaving this baby out here on her own, not now that she directly knows about her.

The Minister observes Deirdre comforting the child in silence. Deirdre isn't sure what to say, she only hopes her actions are speaking louder than her words ever could.

Suddenly, she sees the minister call over several of his staff, who appear to be social workers. She remains silent and focuses on the little girl. Deirdre also sees that some of the very young boys begin to grab onto Nicolaus as well, even though he is helping others. She fears these children have been left alone to fend on their own for far too long. Nicolaus is very good about paying attention to each boy that approaches him. The press is frenzied around Nicolaus.

"Lady Deirdre, we have now made plans to have a shelter for these children, and I promise you, we will find them homes."

Deirdre's heart is delighted. She hugs the minister to her, and the little girl hugs him too. "Please, let us know what we can do to help. We'll do anything," she offers.

The minister chuckles and nods. The social workers arrange to bring more vans, and to set up a shelter at a community gym, until they figure out the details for the children.

Within two hours, the minister and his workers have all the children off the street. They set up cots and eating areas for the children. Today they are provided warm soup and bread, with cookies. Deirdre and Nicolaus help to serve the children. The staff set up showers for the children, and they are able to get out of those dirty clothes. After lunch, Nicolaus plays ball with many kids, while Deirdre helps to comb the girls hair.

When it is time to serve the children dinner, the Minister takes Nicolaus and Deirdre out to eat at his favorite restaurant. At the entrance, the Minister dismisses the last of the press that are following them around. Both Nicolaus and Deirdre are very glad to have a relaxing moment with the Minister. Nicolaus understands the key to these relationships is getting to know the leaders, which opens doors.

Later at their very fancy hotel, Deirdre phones Elsa, while Nicolaus sweetly massages her aching feet. "Elsa, I wish you were here with us! I need your excellent coordinating skills," Deirdre tells her. "This thing is getting bigger than the both of us."

Elsa sniffs, unable to stop herself from bawling. "I'm so glad for you," she manages in a raspy voice, the result of crying most of the day.

"Elsa," Deirdre sits up, taking her feet from the soft grip of her honey. "What's the matter? What's wrong?"

"Nothing, Deirdre. I want you to enjoy yourself. You don't need to hear about my troubles right now."

"Elsa, I'm always open to you."

"I know," she whispers, feeling stupid and weak.

"Elsa," Deirdre could tell something is terribly wrong.

"How's my niece?" Nicolaus blurts into the phone. He hears Elsa giggle.

"She's fine!" Elsa put her hand on her belly, already loving her yet to be born daughter.

"Elsa, you promise me you'll get some rest. We'll be home in a few weeks."

"Yes, I promise."

As soon as Deirdre ends the call with Elsa, she phones Ishani, and conferences in Maggie. She asks them to promise they will go check on Elsa. In the midst of her conversation, Deirdre emits squeak noises when Nicolaus grabs her and tickles her off the phone. Then he makes sweet love to her.

Chapter One Hundred Thirty-Three

Not to be outdone by the couple, the Oslo Minister of Children's Services meets Nicolaus and Deirdre at the airport and transports them to the shelter where they had already brought the street children, the day before. The children are fed and cleaned up. When the children see the couple, they drop whatever they are doing, and run to them with happy banter. Deirdre thinks it odd that the children seem to know who they are. She doesn't understand how this is happening everywhere they go.

Nicolaus throws his expensive sports coat on the ground outside, and plays soccer with the children. They love that he doesn't care if he gets muddy.

After the first round of the game, Nicolaus stops and makes a conference phone call to some of his celebrity soccer friends. "Hey, guys, what are you doing?"

"Hey, we heard you were going to be in town. You here?"

"Yeah, I'm at the children's shelter. Can you help me out? I don't know much about soccer, and these little kids are kicking my butt." They all laugh.

"You know what, for you, I'll be there."

"Yeah man, I'm on my way."

Deirdre stays inside with other children and does arts and crafts with them, and then eventually reads to them.

The celebrity soccer players arrive with their wives. The wives assist inside with Deirdre, and the men play soccer outside with the boys.

They all stay with the children for about four hours, and then the Minister takes them all to eat, dismissing the press. They all offer their help for the children. Deirdre notices a pattern starting to form amongst these Ministers, and she is not sure she likes it. She isn't sure it is a good thing or a bad thing. She decides not to worry about it for now, as it seems too early to tell if all these efforts are sincere, and would continue once they'd returned home. The hope and most important part is getting them to pay attention to the children in the streets and to take some actions towards helping securing their futures.

After lunch, the Minister escorts the couple to the Oslo Royal Palace, and leaves them to tour with the other tourists, offering to drop their luggage at their hotel. Both Nicolaus and Deirdre are taken aback by the enormity and the beauty of the Royal Palace. Their favorite room has the bird painted ceiling. Some of the other tourists ask to take selfies with the couple, for which they oblige them.

The following day, they visit the Oslo Cathedral. They walk hand in hand along the cobblestone walkway to the cathedral entrance. Nicolaus cannot resist touching the mastery artwork on the steel entrance doors. They enter to see the historic beauty of the church, the unique chandeliers, and the immaculately painted ceiling. They sit on a front pew and give reverence to God. Nicolaus is so grateful for their public standing and their small influence. He knows that if he and Deirdre can help even just a few children, they are doing what he thinks God expects of them.

Nicolaus holds Deirdre's hand and arm tightly as he whispers prayers of thanksgiving, peace on the children, and blessings upon their marriage. Several people, both men and women, approach the couple, even as Nicolaus is praying. The friendly people either hug them, or kindly touch them. Deirdre is amazed that they are recognized by everyday people in a European land.

After about two hours at the cathedral, Nicolaus and Deirdre take a taxi to the cultural museum, where they spend several hours enjoying the cultural exhibits and learning about the Norwegian people.

By the end of the day, both Nicolaus and Deirdre are worn out. They take another taxi to their hotel, have dinner in the hotel restaurant, and then retire for the evening, Nicolaus holding Deirdre close as they sleep. They want to be ready for the next leg of their trip - Copenhagen.

Chapter One Hundred Thirty-Four

T he following day, after arriving in Copenhagen, Nicolaus and Deirdre spend a couple of hours with children at a shelter. They are escorted by the Minister of Public Affairs. They join the children for lunch, serving them, playing board games and charades with them, and listening to whatever they wanted to tell them. They notice the children are not as clingy as the others, however, they still did seem to know who they are, having clapped them in when they arrived.

Later that day, while touring one of the famous royal castles in Copenhagen, Nicolaus has an odd experience. They enter the castle with many other tourists. The day is busy for the castle touring staff.

Nicolaus and Deirdre get separated as Nicolaus looks upon the exquisitely painted ceilings in the king's office room. The beauty and detail of the historic paintings have his attention when he loses track of Deirdre.

Nicolaus looks up and observes Deirdre, across the room, only she is grabbing onto his arm, pulling him into a hug. Nicolaus frowns at her, the woman across the room disappearing from his sight. "How did you do that?"

"Do what?"

"You were just across the room. I .... I just literally saw you ... across the room."

"Oh nonsense, I've been right here."

"No, Deirdre, really," he's adamant, "I just saw you across the room."

Deirdre glances across the room, her eyes searching for someone. She can see no one who resembles herself, through the many people who are present. "Well, is she wearing the same ..."

"Yes," Nicolaus answers quickly, making Deirdre frown, finding this mystery a little troubling. Someone who looks like her, wearing the same clothes?

"Hmm, maybe we'll see her again." They continue the tour of the beautiful castle. They move into the room that retains the crown jewels. Deirdre's imagination leaps with inspiration as she gazes upon the king's and queen's crowns. She kisses Nicolaus on the face and holds tightly to his arm, so very glad he is finally her husband. She feels so happy and blessed they are officially a couple. The crown jewels bringing romanticism to her mind.

Abigail and Dominique peek around the corner at Deirdre and Nicolaus, watching them, as they observe the royal jewels. "She's wearing the same clothes as me! And her hair!" Abigail touches her hair, "It's the same as mine!"

"Okay, okay, don't freak out," Dominique calmly tells her. "There has to be an explanation for this."

"An explanation that my father won't tell me. Who is this woman?" she whispers.

Nicolaus thought he heard something and looks back in the direction of the ladies. Abigail and Dominique jump back out of his view. They can barely see him around the corner, and watch as his attention returns to Deirdre, as he hadn't spotted them.

"Okay, this is getting weird. Get the pictures to show your father, and let's get out of here before we bump into them."

Abigail uses her phone to snap pictures of the couple. "Maybe I want to bump into them."

"No, Abigail, remember we said it would be too awkward! Let's get the facts from your father first."

As Dominique and Abigail leave the castle, Nicolaus happens to be looking out the window, and he sees the back of who appears to be Deirdre, though she is clearly next to him, holding his hand. He points out the window at the ladies. "Look … look! See?"

Deirdre peers out and sees a young woman with curly black hair, her similar physique, dressed in the same blue dress she wore today, running away from the castle with a woman beside her. Nicolaus pulls Deirdre along as he takes off running after the women.

Abigail glances over her shoulder and sees that Nicolaus and Deirdre are running after them, and trying to get their attention. Abigail and Dominique are quite a length away from the couple. They get to their car, jump in, and drive off. Abigail hides her face as Dominique speeds away before the couple can get near them.

"Oh my God, that was close!" Dominique says, as she puts distance between them and the couple, speeding down the road.

Chapter One Hundred Thirty-Five

The Ravenell mansion is quiet as everyone is gone.

Niall took Elsa out for a night of fun and to apologize for how he had been treating her. Nicolaus and Deirdre are still in Europe and continue to receive massive coverage over every media channel, including the national entertainment shows.

Nigel is off at the country club, golfing with Dwight and some celebrity friends.

Ceil no longer wants to pretend about her feelings for Helena. When Helena arrives alone, with no husband, as Ceil had invited them both to dinner, she pulls Helena inside.

"Where is Joel?" Ceil inquires.

"He's at a meeting he could not get out of." Helena informs her.

"Good!" Ceil chuckles. "I'll have you all to myself!"

Helena looks at Ceil with a smirk, not sure what to make of her comment.

Ceil has the staff serve them dinner, then she dismisses them, having them leave the wine bottle for them both to drink. Ceil sits at the head of the dining table, her usual spot, and has Helena right next to her. She touches Helena's face, as she eats her salad. "Such beauty," she comments.

"Thank you, Ceil." They begin to eat the main course. "So Ceil, tell me, what are you really after? What really drives you?"

"Well now, you are awfully direct, aren't you?"

Helena nods. "I've been told so. I want to learn from you. I want to be successful like you. Powerful."

"Hmm. Success is in here," Ceil points to her head. "Even a fool can think of themselves as successful."

"Oh that is true. And power?"

"Power arises from collecting cards, so to speak. From what you have to offer."

"Money?"

Ceil shakes her head. "Not necessarily. Take our marriages. In a marriage, it is early decided who has the power. In all our relationships really."

"And the power of this family lies with you?"

"I have the power in all my relationships, Helena. Even with you, dear." She touches her hand. Ceil can see that the touch makes Helena nervous. This excites her.

"Oh, you mean we are equals."

"No, Helena, we are not equals. I hold the purse strings for your little child home. Now don't I? I decide if you can walk through my front door. I even decide if you can see Nicolaus," she threw in for good measure, knowing that Helena is attracted to Nicolaus.

"Oh, I see," Helena stops eating. Suddenly, she has the impression that she has stepped into a carefully planned trap.

"You could even say, because I know so many people, I could even decide if your little child home remains open."

"Oh now, Ceil."

"I'm just saying ...."

Helena takes a drink of the vintage wine. She then voices what she knows is imminent in Ceil's actions anyway. "So, because you hold the purse strings on me, there is something you want me to do."

Ceil smiles at Helena, then touches her face again. She nods. "Yes."

Helena looks at the mother of the man she is in love with, whom she often fantasizes about, whom she'd do anything for, who has just married her best friend. She sighs, as Ceil's hand gently slides down her smooth face. "And what is it you want me to do?"

Ceil drops her hand and stands. "Be my companion."

Helena frowns at Ceil, expecting an odd request. "Ah, I don't understand."

"Be my companion. Play tennis with me. Go on trips with me. Hang out. Go to the country club. Go shopping. Have gal pal time."

"Gal pal time? Ceil, are you serious?" Helena looks at Ceil Ravenell as if she might be ill or something, perhaps out of her mind.

Ceil shrugs her shoulders, "I really like you, Helena. And I want to spend time with you. Real time. Friend time."

Helena stands, and looks upon Ceil with concern, not sure what to make of what she has just said. Then, she hugs Ceil to her. At first the hug is unreturned due to Ceil's normal cold nature. So Helena hugs her again, and Ceil returns the hug. "Now that's better! I always hug my friends, and I always expect the hug to be returned." They both sit down to finish their meal.

"So, what do you think about Nicolaus' and Deirdre's honeymoon?"

The coldness quickly returns to Ceil. "I don't ever want to talk to you about Nicolaus. Not ever," she says sternly.

Helena looks at Ceil with a frown, nodding, "Okay. Let's talk sports. I didn't even know that you like to play tennis."

Chapter One Hundred Thirty-Six

Niall gentlemanly helps Elsa into his small, low to the ground, Italian sports car after their meal at the high priced, exclusive restaurant.

Niall jumps into the driver's seat, and he feels sheepish as he sees Elsa with her pregnant belly, struggling to sit in the small vehicle. "Look Elsa, I just want you to know I'm sorry for what I did to you at the office. You didn't deserve that. I just want to make it up to you."

Elsa looks at her husband, who she feels is trying to be sincere. "Niall, the only way you can make it up to me, is to stop hitting me. Stop humiliating me! I'm your wife! Your Ravenell wife! Doesn't that mean anything to you?"

"Of course!"

"What are you going to do when the baby gets here? Hit me while I'm holding the baby? Hit me during childbirth? Kick me when I'm down?"

"Elsa, I'm sorry! Okay? I'm sorry!"

Elsa begins to cry. "I can't keep doing this, Niall. I love you so much until it hurts. You know what? I can't let you hit me anymore, Niall! I'll leave, and once I leave I'm never coming back to you." Her crying and upset took her into hyperventilation. Suddenly she has a sharp pain on the side of her belly. "Ouch!" She put her hand where the pain is, her crying subsiding to the pain. Then it hit again. "Ouch!"

"What is it? You can't go into labor yet, it's too early."

The pain happens again. "Ouch!" Elsa begins to laugh. The joy of the baby momentarily replacing her emotional pain. She takes Niall's hand and puts it where the pain occurred. "It's our little one. She's kicking."

The baby put her foot out again, this time gentler, and Niall could feel the little foot. "Oh my God! That's amazing!" They both giggle together. Niall kisses Elsa, his hand on her belly. "I don't want you to leave. I love you. I promise I'll do better. I'm so sorry." He kisses his wife again.

Chapter One Hundred Thirty-Seven

Nicolaus made different arrangements for when they arrive in Dublin. He wants to spend time with Deirdre before seeing the children, as he'd read about many homeless families in the Dublin streets, not unlike the same situation in the United States. He also has a feeling that since these would be families, their presence is going to be highly anticipated.

Once their plane lands, they are able to sneak away from the press. Nicolaus has them take a private romantic horse drawn carriage ride across many miles of the Irish moors, outside of the city, to avoid the main streets. Soft wind whisks through the carriage on the warm day. Nicolaus embraces Deirdre close to him the whole of the ride. Neither of them can keep their hands off each other, intimately touching and passionately kissing. Within an hour, they arrive at the famous Irish castle where they will be staying.

The staff treat the couple like royalty. They are provided warm Irish vegetable soup, with warm bread and fixings. Nicolaus pulls Deirdre's dining chair as close to his as possible. The backdrop to their romantic dinner are the artistically, beautiful mural painted castle walls. Period pieces of relics, jewelry, armor, and other items are placed throughout the castle. Though the castle is open to the public, it seems as though Nicolaus and Deirdre are the only guests.

Deirdre giggles as Nicolaus spoon feeds her, and she feeds him as well. They kiss away any soup drizzle or breadcrumbs that may have landed outside their mouths. It is not long before Nicolaus swoops Deirdre in his arms and carries her up the castle stairs to their room, the staff in awe of their love, everyone already having known their story.

Deirdre is amazed at how fast she is void of her clothes, and Nicolaus' excited breathing is upon her, grasping her lips. His loving arms encircle her. She feels so happy. She doesn't understand how she can possibly be so happy when there is so much misery in the world around them. Deirdre basks in the loving sphere Nicolaus created for her, remembering he is a direct gift from God, their destined love binding them together in the sweetest heaven on earth.

Nicolaus put his loving techniques to work, all over her body, making her moan with each loving motion. Suddenly, a rush of energy overwhelms both Nicolaus and Deirdre, and for the first time, they climax together, as one flesh – as heavenly close as possible to each other, locked in the pulsating gift of ecstasy.

Nicolaus finds himself momentarily suspended in time, inside the warmth explosion of his wife. He appreciates that when he is back to himself, it is Deirdre's delicate and compassionate arms he collapses into, his body against hers, her beautiful soft bosom against his strong muscular chest.

Deirdre experiences a sudden blazing hot burst of energy inside of her womb. She clutches onto Nicolaus - her love; the only man on earth for her. She perceives that he is out of sorts with orgasm, as is she. Deirdre grips tightly to Nicolaus, keeping him in place, as she realizes she may be getting impregnated. The energy burst lasts for about two minutes, then subsides.

Nicolaus' mouth covers hers passionately. Deirdre never dreamed their love could be so wonderful as this. She tightly clings onto Nicolaus, never wanting to let him go.

Chapter One Hundred Thirty-Eight

The Minister of Housing for Dublin accompanies Nicolaus and Deirdre in the limousine ride to the place in the streets where the homeless families are staying. Many children and elderly people are present among the homeless. The couple was not sure how to prepare for this visit and they did not bring anything, as they know the department is already doing what it can to help, and they are notified that hot meals will be arriving soon.

Once Nicolaus helps Deirdre out of the limousine, the children approach them, first the girls, then the boys. Soon the moms follow.

"Ooh, ... you're so pretty!" The usual compliment from one of the children is given to Deirdre.

"Can I stay with you?" the little voice of a little girl says, as she hands herself up to Deirdre. With a smile, Deirdre gently lifts the little one into her arms.

"Where's your mommy, honey?" Deirdre asks her. The little girl points to a woman who is hanging onto additional children. Deirdre nods to Nicolaus for them to draw near the mother. Deirdre hands her daughter to her. "Hello, ma'am."

"Well, you're Deirdre Omari. From the U.S. Aren't you?"

Deirdre nods with a smile. "Yes ma'am, Deirdre Ravenell now! Just here to see how we can help."

"Uh, and you're that handsome Nicolaus!" she comments with her Irish accent.

Nicolaus nods, "Thank you. How long has it been for you?" he gently tousles one of her small son's hair.

"Oh, you're about to make me cry now. It's been a while since we've been out here. Five years. Ever since my husband died. It's been really hard." Her tears begin to flow. Nicolaus frowns at her obvious pain. All he could do is offer her a shoulder. Immediately, she latches onto Nicolaus. Suddenly other mothers gather around them to voice their situation. The press is already taking photos, gathering recordings, and videoing the event.

Nicolaus steps back while Deirdre listens to the mothers, shedding tears with them at some of their heartbreaking stories. Nicolaus quickly phone conferences about four celebrities he knew would be nearby and asks them to meet these families with them. Two of them arrive within thirty minutes, to the cheer of the crowd and the children, who rush them.

The Housing Minister points out that many of these families are already housed in hotels. "That is really great, really good!" Nicolaus encourages him, careful not to ruffle feathers. "What can we do to help?" he offers.

"I'm on the streets!" A mother throws her words at the men.

"My brother is lost," another little girl shouts, so they could hear her.

"I'm cold! I sleep in the gutter," another little boy notes aloud.

"Is there capacity in the city?" Nicolaus asks, advocating for the families.

"Well ..."

"Any place, that you could make a shelter. Like a community center, a large gym, ... something. We'd be glad to help out."

A celebrity soccer player pulls the media cameras. "As this is our community, those of us who are able must step up and do more." He grabs Nicolaus to him, his arm playfully around his neck, and then he kisses Nicolaus' face. "This beautiful man here, and his beautiful wife, are leading the way, showing us that we must not leave any children behind." He releases Nicolaus. Laughing, the men chest bump before the cameras. They are suddenly rushed by many boys, who are laughing and want to play soccer with them.

One of the celebrity wives hugs Deirdre, "You two have pulled the lid off what has been covered in many countries for so long. We must all take action now!"

KAMRYNN BELLARY

The Housing Minister decided to use three community centers throughout Dublin to house the families until he could figure out housing for them. The Ravenells and the celebrity couples pledge to help with finances towards ending childhood homelessness in Dublin.

The following day, the couple make their way to London, England, and find similar conditions as in Dublin. The Housing Minister and other city leaders collaborate future plans with the Ravenells and celebrities whom Nicolaus called in to help.

The next day, Nicolaus and Deirdre are in Paris, France. They complete the usual pattern of meeting with human services and city leaders with local celebrities to develop a collaborative plan to assist the children. The city has a huge turnout of people who want to not only meet Nicolaus and Deirdre, they also want to help the children.

After a day of playing field games with the children, listening to families, serving food, and handing out toys, Nicolaus and Deirdre are surprised with a grand ball in their honor.

The grand ball is open to the public.

"You need a call to action," one of the celebrity actors tells Nicolaus.

Nicolaus looks at him as if he were a genius. "Oh yes! You are so right! Look at all these people here to help!"

At the grand ball, Nicolaus and Deirdre are called forward by the city mayor. Humbly, they stand next to him, in the enormous, historical ballroom, which can hold hundreds of people. There are hundreds more people outside. Deirdre wraps herself around Nicolaus' arm, as he holds her tight around the waist.

"We wanted to give you this grand ball to celebrate the unique love the two of you have. You provide us an excellent example of the spirit of true love. And not only that, you have extended your love to others, across the globe, amazingly. You not only touch the hearts of people everywhere you go, you also touch the lives of children. We must learn from you. And we have learned that we must do better by all our children. None of them should be left behind." The crowd of people in attendance clap for the young couple in agreement with the mayor.

"My wish for you is that your story and what you are trying to do is known throughout the world, and that your story is an inspiration to generations of children not yet born." The mayor hands the microphone to the couple for their comments.

Nicolaus takes the microphone. With a huge smile, he put his hand to his heart, "Wow! We are so incredibly touched by all this, was not expected at all. Look, we just want to do all we can to help alleviate some suffering of children. Deirdre and I, we are only two people. So much more work needs to be done. We haven't even touched on help to children in countries of Africa or South America, or cities in Australia, and even more cities. I challenge my colleagues to help us. And you say well who are my colleagues? If you are wealthy, and you are in your 20s, 30s, or 40s, you are my colleague, no matter where you live. I challenge you to use just one percent of your annual wealth, just one percent, in the cause to help get children off the streets, and help them have a productive and beneficial future in society. Many of these children are cold, and hungry, some don't have clothes or shoes. They need to be in school. We, the wealthy, and anyone else who'd like to help, we need to show these children the love of God. We need to directly demonstrate that love to them. Many of these children are literally living on the streets, alone, with no parents. They are lonely and cold, and have no one to turn to. So let us be the ones they can count on. Will you accept my challenge?"

The roar of cheers from the crowd and thunderous clapping is ear shattering and earth shaking. The reaction touches Nicolaus, almost moving him to tears. He put his hand to his heart again, giving Deirdre the microphone.

Deirdre waits a few minutes for the crowd of people to calm down. Their enthusiasm to help touches her heart, also moving her to tears. "We just love all of you and cannot thank you enough for showing up for the children. We want you to continue to show up for them long after we are gone." Again, explosive cheering and clapping erupts from the crowd. Their enthusiasm is amazing to the couple. They look at each other, with excited joy. When the crowd quiets down, she finishes her thoughts. "And please, any food left over from this grand ball should of course go to the families who need it most." Deirdre gives the microphone back to the mayor, and she is in Nicolaus' arms. He swirl hugs her.

The grand ball with festive food, live music, and charitable talk continues on into the night. Nicolaus and Deirdre stay until the very end.

Chapter One Hundred Thirty-Nine

An unprecedented rainstorm flows through Austin. Ceil and Helena are caught off guard as they play tennis in the outdoor courts at the country club. They are more than drenched by the time they get inside the doors of the country club. The thunder roars with magnified majesty across the Texas sky.

Helena giggles as she and Ceil race from the limousine to the inside of the Ravenell mansion. Immediately, they go up to Ceil's luxurious bedroom to change clothes.

"Oh, I'm sure I have something to fit you, and something you'd like, Helena," Ceil yells to her from her enormous closet.

"Okay, sure." Helena peels off her wet clothes, not thinking. She is naked, looking for a towel to dry off when she notices Ceil behind her. She turns, "Well, I ...."

Her words are cut off by Ceil's kiss. Shock courses through Helena, when Ceil's soft lips kiss her again, this time with force and meaning, taking her into her arms.

When Ceil breaks the kiss, Helena looks to her, searching her eyes, without words. She is trying to see if Ceil is serious. Helena immediately knows Ceil is serious when she kisses her again. The towel is no longer needed.

Chapter One Hundred Forty

Before leaving Paris, Nicolaus and Deirdre, of course, visit the world renown Notre Dame Cathedral. The exterior architecture and artwork of the cathedral is breath taking. The length of the church stands alongside the River Seine, capturing romanticism as well as a Godly nature appreciation. The immense church entrance seems to reach up to the sky.

Nicolaus holds tightly to Deirdre as they enter. They are taken aback by the enormous mosque like arches that line both sides of the interior aisle, holding what appears to be an upstairs floor, and beautiful stone pillars. Windows are placed above the upstairs floor, through the whole of the cathedral. The gigantic rafters are beyond one's imagination, bringing wonderment of the architecture leaps and bounds for such an accomplishment.

Nicolaus and Deirdre take their time walking and observing the beautiful cathedral. Nicolaus feels a holy presence throughout the enormity of the space. He is awestruck, and senses himself very small in the eyes of God in this space. Eventually, they make it to the front of the church, where they both sit on a pew. Silently, holding hands, they both say prayers about modern day problems in this historic church.

The rest of Nicolaus' and Deirdre's whirlwind mission honeymoon brings them additional honors. They receive the keys to the city in Belgium, and are honored with a dinner, at one of the elegant castles by the lower royals. Nicolaus announces that they will receive all honors in the name of the children and the families they are attempting to bring assistance to.

In Amsterdam, Nicolaus and Deirdre experience the Renaissance Centraal Station along with other tourists. In speaking with the city leaders, Nicolaus and Deirdre want to learn about their human services system, as it seems different from the other countries they visited, ensuring most families are not homeless. Nicolaus believes their system could be a basis strategy for utilization by others.

In Hanover, Deirdre and Nicolaus are honored with a music concert, for which the proceeds will go to assist children and families off the streets. At Deirdre's hedging, the couple receive assurances that children are being moved off the streets and into shelters at this very moment. Nicolaus again put his challenge in the media. The couple are very happy with the reception they receive from the crowd and from the celebrities who attend to perform the concert. The following day, they visit the royal gardens, and the fairytale castle near the city of Pattensen. They are both in shock at the excessively fantastic beauty of both places.

The next day, the couple returns to Estonia. Before returning to their castle home, they are met at the airport by the mayor of Tallin to discuss their homeless family issues. Nicolaus is encouraged to know that Tallin has low numbers because of the efforts to increase housing. Again, he discusses the lessons learned that they feel can be emphasized in the collaborative effort. Nicolaus offers for he and Deirdre to be of help, and he promises to get some big name celebrities to assist in the cause.

Very happy to be back at their own castle home, both Nicolaus and Deirdre are overjoyed with their accomplishments of the last two weeks. The castle staff treat them to traditional Estonian cuisine for dinner, which they enjoy in the dining room before the large fireplace.

With excitement, they rehash specific wonderful memories, think about all the children and families they have met and helped, and are excited to continue the work of assisting children around the world.

Having retired to their bedchamber, laying in each other's arms, Nicolaus ponders how much his life has changed in the few weeks that he's been married to Deirdre. Their marriage brings out the best of each other. He kisses her forehead, distinctly recognizing that their marriage is truly defined by their love for each other. He can clearly see how their love, blessed by God, is causing them to bring others to the cause of blessing children and families. Their love seems to have a positive effect on others.

"You know, all this help for the children across the world has all happened because of you," he tells her, kissing her again.

Deirdre twists herself up, her hand to his chest. "No, Love, it's because of you."

Nicolaus shakes his head, "No babe, it's you. Your heart. Your sweetness. Your goodness. You're an angel. You have made a huge difference in the world."

"No, we, together, have made a difference. I couldn't have even thought of half of this without you, babe. Your challenge to the world is amazing!" She kisses his chin, then his mouth.

Exhausted and happy, they drift to sleep in each other's arms.

Chapter One Hundred Forty-One

Dominique and Abigail watch the live entertainment news coverage of what the media named 'Nicolaus' and Deirdre's diplomatic honeymoon'. The press followed the couple to each city they visited, and highlighted the grand ball given for them in Paris, and the charity concert in Hanover. And now that they have returned home to Austin, the press is with them there as well.

"Nicolaus, would you like to repeat the pledge challenge for folks here in the United States?"

Nicolaus has Deirdre close to him, his arm wrapped around her, protecting her from the crush of press cameras, press microphones, and press people. He does not release her as he speaks. "Yes, thank you. Deirdre and I are just two people, and there is so much work that needs to be done. Here at home, we are working to rescue children from foster care, in the hopes of providing them a future, a career.

I challenge all my colleagues, those being wealthy, like us, in their 20s, 30s, or 40s, no matter where in the world you live, to pledge at least one percent of your annual income to the cause of helping homeless children into housing, and help to secure their future. We, who have resources, and anyone else who wants to help, we need to show these children the love of God by helping them. We can show them the power of God's love by showing mercy, getting them off the streets, and back in school where they should be, so they can work on their future. If we all pitch in together, we can assist with this crisis. We can help children all over the world."

"Very well said, my man, very well said." The reporter offers his hand, and Nicolaus shakes it hardily.

"Thank you for providing me the opportunity to voice our challenge."

Deirdre, dressed elegantly, with her hair pulled back, smiles and waves to the cameras. She and Nicolaus continue their way through the throngs of cameras and press, out of the airport, to the waiting limousine, to bring them home to the Ravenell mansion.

Abigail is astonished to see that Deirdre is wearing the same color of clothes that she is wearing today. She is very upset that her father is not being honest with her. She turns to him, as he is sitting and watching the news coverage with them.

"She cannot be a coincidence, father. I want to know who she is."

Chapter One Hundred Forty-Two

Nicolaus gave Deirdre the task of choosing the bedroom they'd be sharing in their wing of the mansion, the same courtesy he'd given his previous wives. This is literally the first time the couple has been home since first exchanging nuptials in the local church. Their side of the mansion has seven bedrooms, two of which are now off limits to anyone.

Deirdre opens the door to a semi -Victorian decorated room, which is the most inner of all the bedchambers, with no access to the secret passageway. The color theme of the room is earth toned, just as she thought Nicolaus would like. She stands with her hands on her hips and observes the furnishings. She thinks some of the pieces are a little outdated, though exquisite, and looks new and unused.

The European style bed, hints of royalty with four thick, intricately carved wooden posts with detailed engraving. Transparent golden sheer panels drape from the top rods flowing down to the mattress, giving it a romantic feel. Matching bedroom set pieces are strategically placed throughout the extensively large room. The bed is covered in matching brown and gold comforter and sheet sets. The sitting area on the far side of the room has matching furniture. On the way opposite side from the sitting area is a carved out space, with a box window for sitting, and a large red wood desk set, including a heavy chair.

The two windows of the room are adorned in golden curtains.

Nicolaus grabs onto Deirdre, kissing her neck, making her giggle, as he speaks to his Aunt Janelle on the phone.

"You did a marvelous job! The both of you! You had news coverage from all the major stations and reporters out here. The challenge is a great idea! You found your voice. See? I told you."

"Yes, thank you Auntie Janelle for your great inspiration. We worked together, and it just all fell in place. By the grace of God."

"Of course it did! And look how many children you got off the streets."

"I'm sure we'll be getting more calls for collaborations. We are very grateful for the opportunity to serve the children."

"Spoken like a true humanitarian!"

"When will you see about a visit with us here in Austin?"

"Uhh! Ceil hasn't invited us."

"Well ... I'm inviting you! If you want, I'll get your tickets."

Janelle chuckles, "Now you are trying to open a can of worms."

"No! You have to visit us. You can see the work we are doing here as well."

"Okay, Nicolaus, I'd be glad to see you. Let me check on some things and I'll get back to you. I want to spend some time with Rachel anyway."

"Okay, sounds great!"

Deirdre twirls herself in her husband's arms to face him, as he ends the call with Janelle. "How about this room, babe? You like?"

Nicolaus is all smiles. "Yes, I like." He looks around the room, having hoped she'd pick this one. "This is actually my favorite room."

Deirdre chuckles, "Awh ... babe! Why didn't you tell me?"

"Cuz I wanted you to pick the room. I want you to feel comfortable. And hey, you can pick another room for yourself if you want, you know like for reading or creating, or whatever." He pecks her lips, holding her close. "You can do whatever you want. Make any changes you want to any place here. Make it your home." He pecks her lips again. "It is your home now. Unless you want us to find another place, or stay at your house."

Deirdre smiles at his generousness, "Nicky." They kiss passionately, Nicolaus holds her in his arms. "I want to be right here with you. Everyone is already here. Officially my family now."

Nicolaus smiles at her. "All right then. Let's tell the staff this will be our main room, and we'll go see Mom."

Chapter One Hundred Forty-Three

Constance holds her daughter tight, as she'd missed her over the past two weeks. She looks upon Deirdre, touches her face, and hugs her again. Happy tears streak from her eyes. She is more than certain that Nicolaus will not only make her daughter happy, she knows that he will take care of her in all aspects of her life.

Deirdre giggles, touched that her mother is happy for her. "Oh Mom!"

Nicolaus hugs both of his ladies to him, kissing Constance on her face.

Constance relinquishes them, wiping her eyes, laughing. "I'm pretty sure I was able to follow each leg of your journey," she tells them. "And look!" She shows them the many reputable magazines she bought, which carry their story.

"Oh wow!" Deirdre looks at all the magazines. "I can't believe these companies covered us. This is astounding!"

"Mom, did Deirdre tell you I saw her look-a-like?"

"Look-a-like?"

"Yes, in Copenhagen. We got separated in the castle museum. I looked up and could swear I saw Deirdre across the room, and then she was right next to me. The woman looked exactly like her and was wearing the same outfit."

Constance frowns with concern. She breathed out, "Did you talk to her?"

"No. She was elusive. I saw her and another woman leaving. We tried to catch up to them. They ran away from us, jumped in a car, and took off."

Constance breathed again, and touches her chest, frowning. She looks at Nicolaus. "Her hair? Was it ..."?

Nicolaus nods. "Exactly the same. When I saw her across the room, I literally thought she was Deirdre."

Constance sits herself down with a frown. "It's her twin sister."

Nicolaus looks at Deirdre frowning. "You have a sister?"

Deirdre is now frowning. "Mom?"

Constance looks up at both of them. "Abigail, your sister."

Deirdre steps next to her mother, having never heard about this. She sits on the arm of the large chair, while Nicolaus gets Constance a drink of sherry, as she looks like she needs something. He hands her the drink and kneels before her. Constance takes a sip and places the glass on the nearby end table.

Nicolaus takes hold of one hand of Constance, and in the other, Deirdre's. "Mom ... what is it?"

"Did she look well?"

Nicolaus straight answers her. "Yes. She looks exactly like Deirdre. Hair, body, face."

Constance breathed out again, and nods. "It's her. It's my Abigail. Lost to me all these years."

"Mom, what happened?"

"Cecil took her when he left me."

"Why did my father leave us? You know, you have never explained this to me. I don't even know what happened."

"I wonder if Cecil is well," Constance questions aloud, seemingly lost in thought.

"Mother," Deirdre calls to her, annoyed.

"Mom, I'll look for them."

"No!" she tells him, grabbing his arm.

Nicolaus frowns at her, shaking his head.

"Ceil has made them unsafe. From the very beginning. She tried to ..." her words fall off. She does not want to discuss it.

"My mother has something to do with this?" Nicolaus asks her shocked. Immediately, it made him sad for Deirdre. Nicolaus was going to stand, as if to jump into action.

Constance knew Nicolaus would want to be vigilant about taking action. "No, Nicolaus. Leave it alone," she pats him on the chest, stopping him from standing.

He is shocked by Constance's calmness. "No!" He stands, frowning with resolve.

"I will find them for you! For the both of you! I'll make right whatever my mother did."

Constance stands, and latches onto Nicolaus. "Nicolaus, you mustn't. They will not be safe if Ceil discovers them."

Nicolaus looks at Constance in disbelief. "What did my mother do? What has she done? Why have you never told me about this?" he is full of questions now.

Constance chuckles at him. "You were just a boy; trying to survive Ceil, yourself. I have watched you grow into a courageous, smart young man, who has never given up your destined love for my daughter. And, even as a grown man, Ceil is still after you." She pauses her thoughts. "Oh Nicky, there are many things you don't know about Ceil. What could you have done about any of it?" She touches his face. "Nothing," she answers her own question to him.

"Mother," Deirdre hugs her mother to her, very worried.

"The less you know, the better, my dear. You don't need this worry on you."

Deirdre frowns at Constance, with questioning eyes. "I have a sister? A twin! That woman is my twin?"

"Yes, most likely. I named her Abigail Deirdre, as you are named Deirdre Abigail."

"She lives in Copenhagen?"

"Oh, I don't know that. Best we don't know where they are. It is enough for me to know she is alive and doing well."

"Don't you want to see her?" Nicolaus questions Constance. "Talk to her?"

"Of course I do! It's the sacrifice I have to make to keep her safe, I must stay away. It is the best we can do for them. Keep them away from any detection. If you go poking around about them, it will get back to Ceil, and it will compromise their safety. We must not speak about it. Please Nicky, I beg you, just leave it be."

"You don't have to beg me, Mom. You never have to beg me." He thought for a moment, feeling very perturbed about all this. "I do promise you, if ever the opportunity presents itself for me to bring her to you, that I will do." He pulls Constance into a hug and kisses her head. Then he grabs Deirdre to him, sighing, frowning, and feeling very unsettled about all of this.

Still frowning, "Mom, Deirdre wants to move some of her things to the house on Saturday. Would you like your things to be moved as well?"

Deirdre hugs Nicolaus to her, loving that he has always been very respectful and loving to her mother. Their mother son bond is so touching to her.

Constance smiles at Nicolaus, and touches his face. "Very sweet of you to ask, but no ..."

"I want you to live with us!" he quickly tells her, still frowning. "You shouldn't be here by yourself."

"In this beautiful home Deirdre bought? My goodness, I love this house. Anyway, I'm sure Ceil would want you to clear that with her."

"I don't care what my mother thinks."

"Nicky," Deirdre touches his chest to calm him.

"Perhaps even you and Deirdre need to get your own place, so you can have some breathing room."

Nicolaus looks at Deirdre with an eyebrow up, "See babe, I told you."

Deirdre touches his chest again, feeling he is worked up, still upset over her sister. "No babe, I'm a Ravenell now. We should live with the family. I want to live with the family."

Nicolaus sighs. "At our wedding in Estonia, I asked my mother to be respectful of Deirdre. She agreed, and so far so good."

Constance laughs lightly, "Well ... you know your mother, Nicolaus. Do not let your guard down where Ceil is concerned. And Deirdre, if you are going to be at the house, you will have to watch out for Niall. Just because you are married is not going to change his behavior. In fact, you'll be closer to him now. He'll have more chances to make an advance towards you."

"He better not!" Nicolaus inserts. "Thank you Mom, we will keep our eyes open. Won't we darling?"

Deirdre nods in agreement.

"And Deirdre, I want you to promise me, right here and now, before your mother, that if Niall says anything inappropriate, or if he does anything, or even hints at doing something inappropriate, that you'll tell me immediately." He grabs onto Deirdre around the waist, making sure she is taking him seriously.

Deirdre nods. "Yes."

"You promise me," he chides her.

"Yes, yes, I promise."

Nicolaus sighs, irritated that he had to ask such a thing of her. "Just know we can always move to another place, or move back here at any time. I don't want you stressed out. Especially not once you are carrying my son." He gently touches her belly, as if the baby is already there.

Deirdre giggles. "I won't be. Anyway, I'll be with you at the office most days now, and we'll be together in the evenings. It should be fine."

"Mom, really, I want you to live with us. No matter where we are."

Constance touches Nicolaus' face again, she smiles, "Ceil doesn't deserve you."

"Mom, I'm serious."

"I know, honey. Not now, perhaps later," she says of living with them.

Chapter One Hundred Forty-Four

Constance, Nicolaus, and Deirdre join Rachel, Francesca, and Helena at the mansion for dinner. Because it is somewhat of a welcome home dinner, Ishani and Maggie join everyone, as well. Everyone met in the library to chat before dinner. Elsa and Niall are the last to arrive.

Nicolaus and Deirdre greet everyone with hugs and kisses. Nicolaus hugs Elsa to him, as he is not so sure she is okay, though she pretends to be. He touches her pregnant tummy. "How's my little niece?" he asks her with a smile.

Elsa always appreciates Nicolaus. She loves him for all he'd done for her. She smiles at him. "She is still doing great. I can't wait to meet her."

"Me too!"

Niall is quick to awkwardly step next to Elsa, as if he needs to protect what is his from Nicolaus. He and Nicolaus side hug, Nicolaus more than Niall. Nicolaus pulls his brother into a full hug, which is not returned.

"You get enough of the press following you around?"

Nicolaus nods. "For sure. I think we did pretty good to use it to our advantage though. Hopefully, all will subside."

Helena steps right up to Nicolaus. She is so very happy to receive his full embrace. They peck kiss as a greeting. Ceil does not like their interaction.

"How have you been?" Nicolaus asks her. "All okay with the kids and at home?"

"I just missed the two of you like crazy." Helena goes in for and receives another hug.

The young ladies chat on the far side of the room, at the grand piano, while Nicolaus, Niall, Constance, Rachel, Ceil and Nigel are across the room, most of them sitting. The old piano is hardly ever used. The staff provide them drinks all around.

It is in this very room, where Niall assaulted Deirdre. Right now Deirdre feels she is able to claim her power back. She feels very strong and resolved whenever Nicolaus is near. He makes her feel as if she can accomplish anything.

The ladies sit on the extended piano bench, squishing Deirdre and Elsa in the middle. Ishani plunks on the keys in a rhythmic melody, as she knows how to play, having learned as a child. They giggle and whisper like young girls at a slumber party. They make observations and comments about Deirdre's husband, nonchalantly watching him from across the room. He is standing and chatting, while sipping his drink. They notice his physique, his masculinity, and comment on his most likely capabilities. Helena finds this very amusing and is happy to be included in their group.

"So how was the whirlwind honeymoon?" Francesca asks in a loud whisper.

"Oh my God, the honeymoon was a dream! We went to so many wonderful places, and saw so many things, and beautiful churches. We met so many people. And the children, they are precious. We even road in a horse drawn carriage in Ireland, it was very romantic! Everything was exciting, and more than I could have ever imagined!"

"Um-hm, that sounds wonderful, Deirdre. So ... how is he? Get to the nitty gritty, girl." Maggie asks, more to the point, making the ladies giggle.

Deirdre's bashfulness is on full display. She nods with an eyebrow lift and no words. The ladies giggle, and bump her, making her silently nod again, watching his natural graceful movements from across the room.

On the other side of the room, Nigel chuckles at the ladies, imagining their conversation. "While you were gone, Ceil had Niall fill in for you at the office." Nigel nods to Niall.

Niall frowns, as he'd hoped his father wouldn't mention it. "We don't need to discuss anything about that!"

Nicolaus finally sits himself down next to Rachel. He kisses her, and worries that she does not look herself, thinking she may be sick or something. The idea of Niall filling in for him is comical. Nicolaus quashes his laughter and tries to remain serious. "How did it go?" he asks of his father. "You find everything okay, Niall?"

Nigel chuckles again. "No, it did not go very well."

"It was his first day," Ceil defends her most loved son. "I threw him to the wolves without preparing him. It's my fault it didn't go well."

Nigel shakes his head, "Something about the supply closet."

Nicolaus frowns with closed lips, not wanting details. "Oh, well, I'm sorry Niall." He sits back. "Well, let's have a do over. I'd be glad to show you the ropes," he offers, knowing Niall would never accept.

Deirdre's silent head nodding is not enough for the ladies. Ishani, with her beautiful and shiny east Indian hair, plays some additional notes on the other end of the piano, to throw the folks across the room off their intentions. She whispers to the group of ladies at Deirdre, "We want details!" The ladies boisterously laugh.

"How is he during the tumble?" Maggie whispers, pushing for information.

"Oh he's ..." Deirdre pauses, reflecting in her mind, "wonderful! Truly!"

The expected cooing is aroused from the ladies.

"Is he satisfying?" Maggie wants to know more without being rude.

Deirdre laughs, "Oh yes, ladies. Very!" Boisterous laughter breaks out from the ladies again. Helena bites her lip and sighs, her fantasies about Nicolaus being fed.

Niall looks over at the ladies who were scrunched together, giggling and whispering. He knows they are talking about Nicolaus, while Nicolaus thinks nothing of it.. Their actions make him jealous. Niall puts his hand out. "No, I think I'm done with any of that. I want to stay with the endorsements."

"Nonsense!" Ceil starts in on Niall. "Nicolaus has offered to show you what to do, so the next time you will be ready. You will accept his offer." Suddenly, Ceil notices that Nicolaus is looking at her strangely. She immediately confronts him. "Why are you looking at me like that? You are the one who offered."

Constance grabs at Nicolaus' leg. She knows why he is looking at Ceil, he is wondering what she'd done to Deirdre's father. "Nicolaus, you and Deirdre must be famished by now." She moves his gaze onto her, and off Ceil. Her touch reminding him to remain silent about their earlier conversation.

He nods, "Yes." Nicolaus finishes his drink.

Just then, dinner is announced by the staff.

Nicolaus retrieves Deirdre from the ladies, and Helena falls into step with them, grabbing Nicolaus about the waist. Ceil sees this, and does not like it one bit. However, dinner is quiet and uneventful. Everyone mainly disburses afterwards. Elsa and Niall go straight to their bedroom. Constance, Rachel and Francesca take leave to go to their respective homes. Nigel and Ceil off to their side of the mansion to their luxurious bedroom.

Ishani, Maggie, and Helena continue to entertain Deirdre and Nicolaus, as they play a word board game in the sitting room. Conversation, laughter and drinks are still flowing.

No one is sure if it is the alcohol taking effect on Deirdre, as suddenly, she is very forward about claiming Nicolaus. After the first round of the game, Deirdre, at first, sits herself on his lap, and they kiss here and there. However, eventually, their stance grows hotter by the moment. Suddenly, Deirdre twists herself on Nicolaus, facing him, kissing him. Their kissing immediately went to the hot passionate ten mark, making them both breathe heavy, to the amusement of the ladies, who egg them on.

Maggie jumps to her feet. "I'll get the staff to make you a bath!" She rushes out the room to get this done for them.

Maggie's actions break Deirdre's concentration on Nicolaus, making her remember others are present. Deirdre grows shy. She moves herself to face their friends again, smoothing her hair. She returns her attention to the game, except Nicolaus' hands are now respectfully roaming her body, and he is sweetly nuzzling her neck, making her giggle, turning her onto him again. He seeks another kiss from her. Deirdre laughs nervously and gives into him, knowing what surely will be happening for them in the very near future.

Now it is Helena's turn to feel prangs of jealousy. She is so happy for Deirdre, however her desire for Nicolaus grows as she watches them. She'd never had this kind of love with Joel, not even when they were first married. She knows it is too late for her and Joel, as Joel does not respect her, and probably never did. Helena can only imagine what it would be like for Nicolaus to touch her intimately. She wants to know what it would be like. How would she ever know?

Maggie returns, rushing into the sitting room. "They say your bath will be ready by the time you go up the stairs."

Deirdre smiles at her friend. "Maggie, thank you so much, so kind of you," she nervously laughs again, wondering how she and Nicolaus are going to make their exit without feeling weird about it.

Deirdre's wondering is resolved immediately, as Nicolaus stands, lifting her into his arms, her feet never even touching the floor. "Well ladies, no sense in letting that wonderful bath get cold." He gracefully exits the room as if he were a romantic lover in a novel.

The eyes of the ladies watch as Nicolaus effortlessly carries Deirdre, his eyes never leaving hers, her arms around him. Nicolaus walks them to their side of the mansion, and swiftly climbs the stairs with his wife in his arms. At the top of the stairs, their passionate kissing begins again.

The three ladies swoon for their friend, joyous about her happiness. Maggie leaves to meet up with Giancarlo, having called him abruptly, wanting to make a space for him after experiencing the heart felt love between Deirdre and Nicolaus. Ishani goes home for ice cream and a movie. And Helena, who is now largely a fixture at the Ravenell mansion, goes to her room and indulges her fantasies about Nicolaus.

Deirdre giggles as Nicolaus sweetly washes her, this not being their first joint bath since being married. They cherish this intimate act of love for each other. Nicolaus loves to dry Deirdre, gently massaging and kissing her body along the way.

"You know we've got to christen this bed?" he teases her.

"We do?" she kids him.

Not only had the staff made their bath for them while they were entertained downstairs, the staff also placed white roses in several places in the bedroom. They placed red rose petals on the floor leading to the large bed, with more rose petals in the shape of a heart on the bedcovers.

"Oh, they are so sweet!" Deirdre comments on the staff's actions.

Nicolaus gently lifts Deirdre, pulling the covers back, he places her on the bed. Without hesitation, he is passionate on her womanness, bringing her hot, immeasurable pleasure. Her love torrent and uncontrolled moaning signifying to him that he is doing his duty and doing right by his wife.

Deirdre shakes with pleasure, "Nicky," she calls to him.

Nicolaus lovingly gathers his wife into his arms, and gently makes love to her, fully and deeply filling her sweet love walls, bringing her more pleasure.

Deirdre matures in lovemaking with Nicolaus, as she alternates between gasps and moans of pleasure, and calling out her husband's name. Their lovemaking is rhythmic and passionate.

Creepily, Niall watches his brother with Deirdre through the bedroom door he'd boldly cracked open, disregarding their dignity and privacy. Niall couldn't resist opening that door, as he had been looking for Nicolaus, when instead he heard sounds of lovemaking and soft noises that sounded like Deirdre. He is only sorry that he cannot see much, as the couple is covered by the bed sheets, and the sheer golden bed curtains obscure their image.

Niall watches as Nicolaus is careful and gentle with Deirdre, something he knows he'd never be able to manage. Niall is actually surprised that Nicolaus is sexually exuberant, feeling himself superior to his brother in this matter. He continues watching and grows obnoxiously jealous of Nicolaus for having Deirdre, while yet becoming sexually stirred himself. The couple climax together, moaning together, holding on to each other. Nicolaus passionately reigns kisses on Deirdre.

Quietly, Niall closes the door, and slinks away to find Elsa, to get rid of his sexual arousal for Deirdre.

Chapter One Hundred Forty-Five

The next day is Saturday, and much activity is happening at the Ravenell mansion. Nicolaus oversees the movers bringing Deirdre's items into their home. Ceil is racing around preparing for a dinner party to honor Niall this evening. After all the good publicity that Nicolaus and Deirdre drummed up, she wants to even out Niall's fail at the office. She must find a way to shore up his reputation, as talk has gotten out about his behavior. The only thing she can think of to help is a dinner party in Niall's honor, to highlight his accomplishments with the endorsements, and his future training to assist Nicolaus.

Nigel shakes his head, pulling Ceil aside, "Ceil, I don't think this is a good idea. A party is not going to help Niall. Putting your son on display will only agitate him more. What he needs is education. You should be forcing him into college instead of throwing him a party."

"Nigel, you are in my way," she tries to move past him to continue her frenzied actions, trying to completely ignore his wisdom. Nigel catches her by the arm to get her attention. "Just let me do what I do," Ceil tells him.

Nigel sighs and lets her go. It is too late anyway, the invitations have already gone out.

Helena is perturbed at Niall's behavior towards Elsa. It is disturbing to her, as she has lived through domestic violence with Joel most of her marriage. She feels a strong need to do something about this situation. In her mind, she feels if she could talk to Niall, maybe show him some tough love, perhaps he would change his ways. Already, she has barred him from the children's home, for the safety of the children.

Helena happens upon Elsa and Deirdre in the kitchen. Deirdre is assisting Elsa in applying some witch hazel ointment to her face to ease the bruising.

"I think we will be pregnant during the same time. Isn't that wonderful?" Deirdre whispers to Elsa excitedly, while she carefully applies the ointment.

Elsa smiles at Deirdre, taking her free hand. "Already? How do you know?"

"Well, I'm not positive yet, although, the other day, while I was with Nicky, I had a wonderful feeling inside of me. It felt like moving energy," she whispers. "You feel anything like that?"

Elsa giggles. "Nope. Just morning sickness."

Suddenly, Niall appears. He carries one rose in his hand. The rose had been trimmed of thorns and cut to a small stem. "Here," he tells Deirdre, "this is for you." He proceeds to place the rose into her hair. Helena fully enters the kitchen, to witness the scene.

Deirdre is astonished. How could Niall be so rude to Elsa? She pulls the rose from her hair. "Niall, I can't accept this from you." Deirdre places the rose in Elsa's hair. "There! Now, this is where your rose goes, to your beautiful wife. You are like my brother, nothing more."

"As it should be." Nicolaus' voice is loudly heard, as he walks upon them. Immediately, he is next to Deirdre, his arm around her waist. "Everything okay here?" he asks with concern.

Deirdre touches his muscular chest. "Yes, babe."

"You sure?" he asks, eyeing Niall. Deirdre nods. "Okay. I need you to check something with me."

"Okay."

Nicolaus escorts Deirdre from the kitchen to their side of the wing to attend to the moving activity.

"Niall, can I speak with you?" Helena asks.

"Of course," Niall follows Helena to the library.

Helena closes the door. "What the hell was that? Why would you insult Elsa?"

Niall looks at Helena with no words, not having realized she was going to yell at him. He knew he couldn't explain his lust for Deirdre to her, and didn't want to try.

"And why do you keep hitting Elsa? You know, I don't want you to be that guy, like my husband. Is that who you want to be? The guy no one likes? You're breaking my heart, Niall. Did you know that your fists don't make you a man?" She held onto his hand, for demonstration. "No Niall, they don't." She is upon him, straightening his shirt.

She continues. "Your fists don't make you a man. Your cock doesn't make you a man, either. You know what does make you a man?" She continues to straighten his clothes, and periodically looks into his eyes. "Being honest and trustworthy, a person of your word. Respecting and protecting your family. Supporting your family and providing for their needs. Loving and caring for your family. Being a leader, an example in your community, caring for others. Those are the things that make you a man, Niall. The childish shit you've been living for the last few weeks, all that ... makes you less of a man. I know you can do better. We all expect you to do better, Niall. I want to be able to have love for you, Niall, not loath you. I want to be happy to see you, not roll my eyes when I see you. I want to be proud of you and proud to know you."

Helena ends her spiel, feeling she told him her full thoughts. Niall seemed to be listening. He hugs her, accepting what she said, nodding to her. Helena returns the hug, strongly, as a friend wishing things were different. Without words again, he leaves the library.

Chapter One Hundred Forty-Six

The dinner party was not as successful as Ceil had hoped it would be. Niall sabotaged her intentions to repair his reputation by having slipped away, saying nothing to her, so she has no idea of his location. Surprisingly, for Ceil, she again finds herself agitated with Niall.

Ceil inquires of the staff of his whereabouts, and no one knows where he is. Ceil is unsure what to do. She knows if she keeps everyone waiting to eat, they will know something unpleasant is going on. However, on the other hand, if they sit to dine without the guest of honor, they will know something strange is happening. Ceil decides it's easier to make excuses, than to have growling, hungry guests.

Nicolaus and Deirdre are nearby, chatting with some of the guests. Ceil grabs Nicolaus to the side. "Go find your brother!" she half yells at the military hero in a whisper. "I will not have this family disgraced any further." Ceil turns with a smile on her face, and urges the guests to the dining room table.

Sighing, Nicolaus goes to look for Niall. He searches all the rooms of the mansion, including the kitchen. When he doesn't find Niall, he realizes he must have left the premises, or he just really doesn't want to be found. Nicolaus decides to look no further, and to leave Niall be.

Alone in his Italian sports car, Niall speeds down the highway, breaking the speed limit rules entirely. This is the only way he can think, while driving alone. Niall wants to get clear in his head. He thinks about what Helena told him, and of course, he knows she is right. So now he'd gotten a talking to from Helena, and a threat from Elsa. Niall certainly doesn't like that what Helena described to him as a man, seeming to be describing his brother. Again, the universe is putting in his face how he falls short, even of being a man. Emotion chokes him, as he realizes he can never measure up to Nicolaus.

Niall has a keen realization that Elsa is a good woman, and he feels undeserving of her love. Having a family with her scares him, as he does not see himself as a family man, and he doesn't know what would change that. And then there is the question of Deirdre. Niall exits the highway and runs a red light through the intersection, not slowing down. No matter how much he indulged himself with Elsa, he cannot get Deirdre out of his mind.

Niall scoffs at the idea that Elsa cannot measure up to Deirdre, while he cannot measure up to Nicolaus. Perhaps they really are a good match. His mind plays fantasies of being with Deirdre. He remembers when he had her cornered in the library. He fantasizes about doing this again, and maybe even taking it farther. He is stimulated at the thought of her, then quickly grows angry about her being married to Nicolaus. Why is Deirdre in love with Nicolaus, but not him? He wants Deirdre so desperately.

Suddenly, Niall slams on his brakes, screeching his tires with brake smoke, to get to a complete stop before hitting a mother in the crosswalk with her children. The mother jumps with startle, jerking her children towards her when she realizes the car might not stop.

"Sorry!" Niall yells out the window. "Sorry," he waives to the mother.

She eyes Niall with contempt, then continues her slow trek across the street, only going as fast as her toddler's legs can stretch, while carrying a baby and pushing a stroller.

Niall looks up and around to see where he is. He is near a school and a local library. "Damn!" he mutters under his breath, realizing he almost ran over this woman and her children. Once she clears the road, he slowly drives off, slowing the vehicle for the continuation of his drive, as the dinner party in his honor goes on without him, to Ceil's embarrassment.

Chapter One Hundred Forty-Seven

Niall has been gone for a long time. When he returns to the mansion, it is after midnight. He enters quietly through the back door, hoping to avoid his mother or anyone else. He decides to sleep in a guest room, where he would be undisturbed and not questioned, and then he can leave again in the morning.

As he passes by the library, his nostrils recognize the beautiful aroma of Deirdre, and he sees the intertwined couple in the romantic moonlight that beams in through the nine-foot windows. Niall stops and watches as Nicolaus lovingly embraces Deirdre from behind, wrapping her in his arms. He wonders if Nicolaus is going to throw Deirdre on the table and have her, as he'd done to Elsa.

Nicolaus nuzzles Deirdre's neck and sweetly kisses her. "I love you, baby, I love you so much," he whispers. Kissing her again, "You're the only woman in the world for me." Deirdre giggles, and returns the sentiment. "You are so beautiful," he whispers with another kiss.

Deirdre's breathing grows heavy, as Nicolaus' hands respectfully roam her body, and she stretches herself up to kiss his mouth. Gently, he kisses her. Deirdre giggles again, as Nicolaus effortlessly swoops her into his arms to carry her to their love den.

Quickly, Niall flees the area, as the couple had not noticed his presence. From the opposite end of the hallway, Niall watches Nicolaus as he carries Deirdre, never taking his eyes from her, as she lays against his strong shoulder.

Suddenly, it dawns on Niall that he does not feel the way he can clearly see Nicolaus demonstrating his love for Deirdre. He does not feel this way about Elsa, having no understanding of himself, that perhaps his mind might not express his love for Elsa the same as Nicolaus expresses his love for Deirdre. Niall's jealousy grows ten-fold as he watches the couple disappear.

Chapter One Hundred Forty-Eight

The following morning, Niall changes his mind and decides not to leave the mansion. He is still bothered about Deirdre, as he appears at breakfast with everyone.

"Oh, so now you show up," Ceil chides him immediately, feeling very displeased with her most beloved son.

"I know, I know, I'm sorry mother."

"I hope you are happy knowing you greatly embarrassed me last night," she snaps at Niall, who is sitting to her immediate right.

"That you are all right is all that matters," Nicolaus loudly states, for Niall's benefit, to quelch Ceil's tantrum that he knows is about to be present. It is obvious to Nicolaus that Niall did not want to be on display for their mother.

Niall touches Ceil's hand, after rising to seat Elsa. "I am sorry mother." He releases her hand, sits again, and looks to Helena, holding her gaze with his eyes. "I did much thinking last night, after Helena and I ... talked. And I realized that she is right." His gaze falls from her, and now focuses on Elsa. Niall takes Elsa's hand. "I have not been a proper husband to you, Elsa.

And I apologize. I have no right striking you, or being mean to you."

Elsa smiles at Niall and nods, accepting his apology again. She is amused that he is apologizing before the family.

Niall let's go of Elsa's hand, and then focuses his eyes on his father. "I had to work out why it is that I am so mean to Elsa. And now, ... I understand that Elsa was never meant for me. I married her out of force and spite, because ..." Niall touches his chest, not caring about the shock that played over his wife's face, "I was hurt."

"Niall," Nicolaus calls to him with authority, not liking where this might be going. He wants his brother to stop his thoughts.

However, Niall continues, turning his whole attention to Deirdre. "It is not Elsa I want, it never was. It's you, Deirdre, ..."

"Niall ..." Helena interrupts him with sternness in her voice.

"Do you know what you are saying?" Ceil asks angrily.

Niall frowns, seemingly not to care that Nicolaus is present. For the moment, Nicolaus remains silent to see what else his brother is going to spew out of his messed up brain. He holds Deirdre's hand to assure her of her safety. "Of course I know what I am saying, Mother. I am saying that all along I have been in love with Deirdre."

"Niall, why are you doing this?" Elsa cries. "Why do you hate me? I've always only loved you, Niall." Tears well her eyes.

Deirdre cannot bring herself to look at Niall. She is not sure what to do, as he'd never been this bold in front of his parents. She remains silent, holding onto Nicolaus' hand. Elsa sits to Deirdre's right, and with her other hand, she touches Elsa to support her. Looking to Nicolaus, Deirdre knows her darling husband has a plan, as she could see in his face that the wheels of thought are turning.

"Deirdre, I declare this day that I love you with all my heart. If only I could know that you cared a little for me ...."

Nicolaus chuckles at the absurdity. "Well, that's all fine and good," he tells Niall, as he continues his meal. "You can love Deirdre as a sister, from afar. You don't put your hands on her, you don't look at her. If you behave, I might let you talk to her."

Deirdre takes her turn to chuckle. "You have such a beautiful and wonderful wife in Elsa, who is literally about to have your baby," her arm is outstretched to Elsa. Then her attention is on her love, "You should focus on that Niall, just as I focus on Nicolaus." Her eyes on her husband. Nicolaus kisses her hand.

"I don't care about that, Deirdre. I am mad for you."

"You're mad alright! That brain of yours has twisted thinking, again," Nicolaus comments. "You heard what I said, Niall."

Nigel sits back and laughs heartily. He has never seen Niall in such a state. Ceil stares at him to stop, as she does not think this to be funny. Nigel has another hardy chuckle, and finally stops. "All right now, Niall, that's enough. You are going too far. You may have been thinking, however, you are not properly considering everyone, or your given situation."

Helena agrees with Nigel and reiterates Deirdre's words, "Exactly! Elsa is about to have your baby. You've got to be joking about all this, right? I mean, you are not that much of an imbecile, ... or is my mind playing tricks on me?" Helena chastises Niall, frowning, internally feeling the sting of being a hypocrite, because she is in love with Nicolaus. Though she knows she'd never humiliate Deirdre such as this. And she wants Niall to do what is right by Elsa.

Nigel laughs heartily again. He is more amused than upset about his younger son. He is also very surprised at Nicolaus' cool attitude towards all this.

Niall answers Helena, bringing more embarrassment to Ceil, especially as he behaves this way before Nicolaus. "I just decided you were right, Helena. I was not being a man."

"This scene, Niall, makes you even less of a man than you were last night! I never told you to discard your wife. I told you to stop mistreating her!"

"I do not want Elsa. I want Deirdre."

"You cannot have Deirdre, Niall," Helena stands in frustration. "Obviously!"

Nicolaus stands with Helena and helps Deirdre up. "Don't bother yourself Helena, he knows better. This is just a childish ploy for attention. He's probably nervous about the baby." Nicolaus goes to Elsa and kisses her on the head, as she wipes the tears from her eyes. "Don't worry about it, Elsa," he pats her shoulders, "it will be okay." Nicolaus exits with Deirdre.

Elsa leaves the room and Helena walks out with her. Elsa cannot make her tears stop flowing. "I want to leave this place." Elsa grabs her suitcase out of the closet of her bedroom. "I don't want to stay here and be abused if he doesn't even want me."

"Oh Elsa. I'm so sorry," Helena tells her. Helena helps her pack some items.

Ceil continues to stare at Niall in despair, as she is beyond words at his behavior. She knew, and had previously told him, that his obsession with Deirdre would drive him to this.

Nigel feels he has to wrap up the situation. He clears his throat. "You know son, I do not give a damn what you have resolved, or what you declare," Nigel says harshly, "Deirdre is not for you to have. God help you if Nicolaus gets angry with you over this foolishness. Go away for a while if you must, Niall. I insist you stop this stupidity. You are doing great damage, and being very disrespectful to Elsa. It seems you have forgotten your place. You've been living long enough without purpose, and it's starting to get to you. You need to work on finding your purpose, which is more than about who you can have sex with." Frowning, "You have not been placed on earth to serve yourself!" he yells at Niall.

Feeling himself greatly annoyed, Nigel exits the room.

Niall meets the disapproving eyes of his mother, as they are the only two people remaining in the breakfast room. Her silent stare hurts him.

Chapter One Hundred Forty-Nine

The lives of Nicolaus and Deirdre are not the same since they returned to Austin from their honeymoon trip abroad. Even getting back to work meant something different than it did before their global endeavors against childhood homelessness. Both Nicolaus and Deirdre found themselves in international video meetings, and taking international calls from global leaders, global celebrities, and the wives of important people who wanted to help the cause to house homeless children.

Nicolaus and Deirdre began collaborative efforts in the countries they had not yet traveled to, such as Ghana, South Africa, Liberia, Brazil, Argentina, Guyana, Australia, and even New Zealand. Deirdre realized they'd be making future trips to some of these countries to assist with the children.

The couple is amazed at the global response to Nicolaus' challenge of the wealthy donating money. They received reports from all over the world of increased donations to local, national, and international charities, with a great thanks for their efforts.

Nicolaus and Deirdre are also both very thrilled and happy to help leaders who reached out to them from cities within the USA. Many of these leaders are from states VMC didn't have clinics, such as Mississippi, Louisiana, Arkansas, Oklahoma, California, Idaho, and Michigan. Nicolaus for sure thought this may bring future VMC efforts to these states.

Nicolaus is missing Alexander terribly, especially at every meeting he attended for which they usually attended together. Nicolaus is also doing additional work and taking on additional responsibilities. He realizes he might need to put someone in Alexander's position, though he isn't yet ready for this. He just cannot fathom anyone filling Alexander's shoes, though Daniel Araceli is certainly a shining star in their corporation. Nicolaus noticed Daniel seems to be going above and beyond to put the interests of the company first in his work.

Nicolaus finds that he is filled with boundless energy, sometimes working late into the evening. Deirdre naps on the couch in her office, waiting for her love to complete his day. Sometimes Nicolaus even brings work home, and works late into the night.

Without missing a beat, Nicolaus steps up his efforts at the children's home, regularly working with the older teens, helping them study for college entrance exams, certifications, high school graduation tests; anything they need. He also provides the funds to pay for anything required to get them to the next level. Each day he and Deirdre spend at the children's home, and each additional thing done for the children, feeds Helena's love for Nicolaus.

Additionally, Nicolaus and Deirdre continue their increased activities to support the church financially, and physically as well, assisting in a few of the social ministries; Nicolaus mentoring young men, and Deirdre assisting the single young women. Nicolaus also finally resumed his early morning runs with his comrades. And on top of all these activities, they still had to find time to attend social galas, community events and parades, celebrity parties, high society parties, and provide several press interviews, nationally and internationally, regarding their marriage and their work to end childhood homelessness.

Nicolaus and Deirdre are now the much sought after couple in the city, almost replacing Nigel and Ceil. Frequently, they invite Elsa and Niall to these events, to help elevate them in their networking circles, however, they routinely decline to participate.

Both Nicolaus and Deirdre keep a close eye on Elsa, as she is rounding into her eighth month of pregnancy. Ishani and Maggie are happy to throw a baby shower for Elsa, and they find party planning with Ceil both amusing and interesting. A good showing of ladies attend who are Elsa's friends, colleagues, women of the church, and some well-known elites from the city.

In the meantime, Deirdre insisted both Elsa and Helena be with she, Nicolaus and Constance, when they receive confirmation of her own pregnancy. She wants Elsa and Helena to be the godparents to their children.

Deirdre is overjoyed with the confirmation, Nicolaus pulling her into a kiss and hug. Immediately, his hand to her belly, "It's a boy!" he announces, to the laughter of the ladies, because of course, it is too early to know.

Staying in step with her husband, Deirdre begins her swimming and water pregnancy aerobic workouts in the Ravenell mansion pool, as Nicolaus is on his morning runs. Deirdre wants her body in tiptop shape for the birthing of Nicolaus' child. Each day, they arise together, after a time of being close to each other and daily prayers said, the only Ravenells up so early.

Chapter One Hundred Fifty

Excitement abounds in the family when Elsa is rushed to the hospital with labor pains. Helena, Nigel, and Niall are in the waiting room when Nicolaus and Deirdre arrive.

"Deirdre, Elsa says for you to go right in, she wants you to be with her," Helena tells her, glad for the opportunity of alone time with Nicolaus.

Deirdre looks surprised. "Oh, okay!" She stops and frowns, "Niall, why aren't you in with Elsa?"

Niall shakes his head, "I doubt she'd want me in there."

"Oh nonsense!" Deirdre beckons to him, "Let's go! You should be in there too. This is your baby!"

Reluctantly, Niall stands and goes back to the birthing room area with Deirdre. They are instructed to don on the head to toe clinical coverings, and to wash their hands and forearms to their elbows. They both follow the instructions in silence, then enter the birthing room.

Ceil is assisting Elsa, the best she knows how, in her cold way. Elsa is so happy to see Deirdre, who immediately hugs her, just as a labor pain hits, making her cry aloud. Niall stays by the door, waiting to see if he will be thrown out.

"Niall," Elsa reaches for him, a smile on her face. "I thought you might not show up." Quickly, Niall stands by Elsa's side, taking her hand.

"Okay, we've got nine centimeters of dilation!" the nurse practitioner tells them. "I'll page your doctor, Elsa, it's time for Elaine to be born."

"Elaine?" Deirdre asks with a smile.

Elsa nods, breathing through another painful contraction. "Elaine Marie."

Niall holds onto Elsa's hand. He holds her back, to support her. Ceil smiles at him, as if she approves of his actions. Elsa yells loudly as labor pain hits her, squeezing both Niall's and Deirdre's hands.

"Hold on, Elsa, the doctor is on the way. Keep breathing, you're doing great," the nurse tells her.

The obstetrician arrives, prepped, and ready to deliver Elaine into the world.

Elsa's labor is not difficult. Niall supports Elsa as she takes about forty minutes to push the baby out. Elaine is born with a strong baby cry, and excited fast movement of her baby body.

"My God!" Niall is in awe of the miracle of life that has just occurred before his eyes. He follows the baby to the staff who attend Elaine, as they clean her, take her vitals, and assess her. Niall wants to be the one to hand Elaine to Elsa. Smiling, the staff gently hand Niall his daughter after swaddling her in a warm blanket. "She's so little," he comments. He walks the baby to Elsa, who is exhausted, and hands her over.

"Oh, look at our little Elaine!" she tells Niall, as she cradles the baby in her arms, with a smile. Elsa didn't expect much from Niall, so she is surprised when he gently kisses her head.

"Yep," Deirdre giggles, "those generational Kiviste genes are strong all right. Elaine looks just like her daddy!" She giggles again.

"Mother Ceil," Elsa calls to her.

Ceil has a grateful look on her face, and gently takes her granddaughter. "Elaine Marie Ravenell. Very fitting." Elaine coos and yawns at her grandma, impressing Ceil. Ceil begins to gently rock Elaine from side to side. She looks up and sees Niall watching her. She smiles at him. "Now this little one, Niall, should definitely give you some purpose." Ceil hands the baby back to her son. The little newborn baby brought real hope to the people in that room.

Once the physicians complete the delivery process, Elsa is taken to recovery, and the family is invited in to see her. Nicolaus, Helena, Ishani and Maggie, who just arrived, follow Nigel.

Nigel kisses and hugs Elsa. "Oh my goodness!" he says of his first granddaughter. "She's beautiful!"

"Thank you, Pops. Elaine Marie meet your granddaddy."

Nigel chuckles. "Elaine Marie Ravenell. I like that!" He lovingly kisses Elsa again, knowing she probably wished her father were here.

"Elsa, she is beautiful," Helena tells her, looking upon the baby.

Ishani and Maggie are right upon Elsa. They both hug her together, and look upon the baby. "She looks like Niall," Ishani confirms again, "and she has your features too, Elsa, which makes her beautiful."

"Oh, thank you!"

Nicolaus hugs Deirdre to him, smiling on the baby, knowing in his heart soon they too would be having such a joyous occasion. He kisses Elsa. "How was your labor? Did my niece give you a hard time?"

Elsa giggles. "Not bad at all. About six pushes."

"Oh oh, you're a pro now!" Elsa laughs. "My niece is very pretty."

Elsa hands the baby to Niall again. He looks upon his daughter, realizing she is ... his daughter, his child, who will need protection from the world.

Nicolaus is abruptly by Niall's side, touching his shoulder, the brothers having a private moment. Nicolaus notices that Niall has a tear streaming from the side of his eye. "How does it feel to be a new dad? It's powerful, isn't it?"

Niall nods, "Yes." He continually looks upon his daughter.

"Elaine Marie Ravenell. A beautiful name for a beautiful baby girl. She actually looks like an Elaine."

"She does."

"You did good!" Nicolaus gently pats Niall on the back.

Niall briefly looks at Nicolaus for the comment, not sure if he'd ever heard such a thing from his brother. Then his attention returns to his baby daughter.

The hospital staff enter and subtly approach Niall. "Mr. Ravenell, we can provide the DNA test you requested now. We only need to swab your inside cheek, and that of the baby. It's painless."

Niall looks at Nicolaus, shaking his head. "I don't even need that anymore."

Nicolaus understands, he shrugs. "Well, they're here now. Maybe you should do it to remove any doubt you may have in the future. Give yourself peace of mind."

Niall nods, wiping the tear from his eye, while carefully holding his daughter. "Okay," he says to the staff. He and Nicolaus have their backs to the family. Niall actually hopes that Elsa does not see this action transpire.

Discreetly, the staff first take a sample of DNA from Elaine's inner cheek, and place the swab in a tube, attaching a label. Then they swab Niall's cheek, following the same procedure.

Elaine stretches herself again, feeling very comfortable in her father's arms.

Niall walks Elaine over to Elsa, and gently hands her to her mother. Nicolaus is in the background when Elsa calls to him. "Nicky, you want to hold her?" Elsa sees pain flash across Nicolaus' face as he hesitates. "It's okay, Nicky, you should hold her."

Nicolaus silently nods, and sighs, not having expected to hold his newborn niece. Gently, he takes her in his arms, reminding him of his own son. She is warm and cuddly. She stretches herself again, seeming to quite enjoy being passed around amongst family members. Though he'd held babies at Helena's children's home, holding Elaine is different. She is their bloodline. After briefly holding Elaine, Nicolaus hands her to Deirdre, who gently holds her, then returns her to her mother.

Nicolaus sighs again, then embraces Deirdre. "Elsa, Deirdre and I have been talking, and we were wondering if you might be interested in doing some grant writing work when you return to the office? That is, if you want to return. No pressure of course. We'd increase your salary, and you'd have your own space, or you could work from home if you want to stay with the baby. Even though I'm sure she'll have a nanny, a nurse, and ..."

"And a teacher. That's right! I've already got them on standby," Ceil announces.

Everyone laughs, amused. Niall is even a little shocked, thinking such treatment was only for Nicolaus.

"Wow, guys, that's so sweet and generous. I'm not sure what to say. I don't know anything about grant writing!"

"Oh, we'll develop you with first class training. There is a company that will provide one month of structured classroom training, and then a month of one to one training, and then they will be available for another year or two for support."

"My God, that sounds wonderful!"

Nicolaus nods at Niall, "Don't answer now," he tells Elsa. "You just had your little one. Think about it, talk it over with Niall, decide if you even want to keep working, then let us know."

"Oh, I do want to keep working, Nicky. And in the office."

Nicolaus nods.

"Sounds like a wonderful opportunity. Thank you for offering it to me."

Deirdre hugs Elsa to her. "Of course! You're the first person we thought of."

The family stayed with Elsa until visiting hours were over. Then Niall and Ceil remained with her. The private nurse arrived shortly after the family had left.

Chapter One Hundred Fifty-One

Nicolaus and Deirdre went to see about Rachel. "She didn't look right to me at our little party the other day, and I don't like that I haven't seen her around. That's just not like her," Nicolaus comments as he and Deirdre drive to Rachel's.

"Yeah, Francesca has been scarce too. She hasn't picked up my calls."

Nicolaus pulls close to Rachel's house. There are several vehicles there.

Deirdre frowns, "Hmm, Mom is here."

They enter the house, and Constance met them at the door. She hugs and kisses them.

"Mom, we came by to check on Auntie Rachel. Is she all right?"

"No." Constance touches Nicolaus on the chest and Deirdre on her shoulder. "She's ... dying, Nicky. She didn't want us to tell anybody."

He looks at her shocked to Deirdre's gasp. "Mom ... what do you mean?"

"She's in hospice care. She could go at any time."

Nicolaus looks down, then to Constance. "Can we see her?"

"Yes." Constance leads them to Rachel's elaborate bedroom, in her middle class home. The curtains are pulled back, and the sliding glass door is open to bring the cool Texas breeze into the room.

When Nicolaus enters, he could see that Rachel was made very comfortable by a nurse who is attending her. There are a few machines in the room, providing her medication. The priest from the church is also attending Rachel. He prays over her.

A crying Francesca flies into Nicolaus' arms, and she reaches for Deirdre, who rubs her back to comfort her. Nicolaus lovingly hugs his cousin.

"Mum is dying," Francesca whispers to him. "She has brain cancer," she tells them. Her tears flow. "She's been suffering, a lot."

"My God, Francesca."

"Sorry I didn't tell you. She didn't want anybody to know."

Nicolaus kisses Francesca's forehead. "How are you holding up?"

Francesca shakes her head, "It's been hard, Nicky. I'm glad you're here. She'd want to know you are here. She has trouble seeing now, but she'll recognize your voice."

The four of them move closer to Rachel. Despite their presence, the nurse continues to monitor and assess her. Nicolaus sits to the right of Rachel, and Francesca to the left. Deirdre stands next to Nicolaus, and Constance stands next to Francesca.

"Auntie Rachel," Nicolaus softly calls to her.

Rachel looks in the direction of Nicolaus' voice and weakly reaches her hand up. "Nicky, is that you?" She sounds very frail.

Nicolaus takes her hand. "Yes, Auntie Rachel, it's me, Nicolaus." He leans down and gently places a kiss on her face. Immediately he is struck with shock again. He can tell she is barely holding on. Of course, he'd seen this before in the military when one of his partnering team members was vitally struck down. He'd seen many men die in action, however, by the grace of God, Nicolaus had never lost a man on any team he led, in any locality.

Rachel puts her shaky hand up to Nicolaus' face. Nicolaus leans closer to her. "Nicky," she whispers his name. "Oh Nicky." She struggles to breathe. She struggles to speak. "I didn't get to ...."

Nicolaus takes her hand again. "It's okay, Auntie Rachel."

"Mum!" Francesca cries out, taking her other hand.

"I didn't get to tell you ...." She struggles. "Oh Nicky, Francesca, I didn't get to tell you ...." The strength and the light fades out of Rachel. Her arms go limp, as she breathes her last breath on earth.

Francesca shrieks, "Mum!" She can't believe it. She knew this moment was coming, yet it is still devastating.

"Auntie Rachel! Auntie Rachel."

"Mum! Oh Mum! Oh no, Mum!" Francesca cries, holding onto Rachel.

The priest intervenes and offers more prayers over Rachel. Then he puts holy oil on her forehead, preparing her for the end of life journey.

"I'm sorry, she is gone," the nurse informs them. Remaining professional and doing her hospice duty, she calls the time of death, closes Rachel's eyes, and folds her arms onto her chest. "The coroner will make everything official. She'll be here within the hour. You may take your time with Rachel," she informs them.

Deirdre clings to Nicolaus, and they both shed tears for Rachel. They hug onto Francesca, and with Constance, the four of them mourn Rachel.

Rachel's funeral is held at the end of the week, giving the overseas family time to arrive. Everyone is accommodated at the Ravenell mansion. The Bishop officiates the funeral services. The attendees are mostly family and her friends. Since an announcement went out and there was some news coverage of a Ravenell family member passing, some celebrity friends of Rachel also attended.

Ceil is shocked by Rachel's death, not having known she was sick. Janelle and Zoe flank Ceil during the church service, though she remains stone faced and unemotional. Everyone notices that Nigel seems to be immensely affected. He cries silent, non-stop tears, and is not his usual self. Francesca arranged the funeral just as she thought Rachel would like it. And she insisted that Rachel be buried with the rest of the Ravenells on the cemetery grounds of the mansion.

At the gravesite service, Nicolaus and Helena comfort Nigel. Nicolaus hugs his father several times, while Helena wipes Nigel's eyes. Nicolaus isn't sure why Ceil and Niall seem very distant. Janelle and Zoe hold onto Francesca who is broken up over losing Rachel. Elsa, Ishani, Maggie, and Deirdre also provide support to Francesca.

Later, at the repass, Nicolaus notices that Ceil is very quiet. She is just sitting as activity buzzes all around her. This is very unusual for Ceil Ravenell. Nicolaus approaches her, touching her shoulder, "Mother, are you okay?"

Ceil looks at him, "I told you I am not your mother," she coldly states. Not even this occasion diminishes her hateful attitude toward Nicolaus.

Nicolaus looks down, letting her behavior roll off him. He tries again, "Are you okay?" he asks gently with concern.

Ceil softens to him. She nods.

Nicolaus frowns, wanting to hug his mother. He doesn't dare take the action, although he can see Ceil needs a hug. Just then Janelle steps in. She touches Nicolaus' shoulder, and takes over, hugging Ceil to her. Nicolaus smiles at her, leaving the sisters to talk.

Chapter One Hundred Fifty-Two

It has been two months since Rachel's passing. Sometimes, time has a way of healing some pain of a person's passing, and sealing in the good memories we keep in our heart of the ones we love.

Niall and Elsa are getting along better, and Niall enjoys spending time with his little Elaine, Elsa having moved back into the mansion.

Deirdre and Constance kept their eye on Francesca. Janelle and Zoe were making plans for another visit at a more positive time. Nigel is glad about this, feeling Ceil has always needed the support of her sisters. He never liked that she had continually pushed them away, and had not let them have access to their sons.

Nicolaus finishes his session on career exploration with the teens at Helena's children's home. He believes the session went really well. As the staff attend the children, Helena pulls Nicolaus into her office. Immediately, she locks the office door, and closes the blinds to the little square window on that door. She then closes the blinds to her office window, as Nicolaus sits by her desk.

Nicolaus wonders why Helena is acting stealthily and strangely. "What's happening?"

"I just want to talk," Helena tells him. She places herself in a kneeling position, her arms on his knees, resting her chin atop her arms.

Helena isn't sure how to tell Nicolaus her true thoughts of him. She doesn't know how to express to him that she'd been dreaming of making love to him for over a year now, that she is strongly in love with him. And yet, he is right here before her. His delicate manly thing of pleasure she wants most from him, literally inches away from her. Her eyes affix to his crotch and her hands gently rub his muscular legs. She fantasized about watching his reaction as she made love to him.

Nicolaus stands, bringing her up with him. "What is it?" He is not completely oblivious to their attraction to each other, however, he had put that away, hoping she did as well.

Helena sighs, wanting to be assertive with him. "I ... I just want to ..." she rubs her hands over him, his chest, his shoulders, his torso. "I just want to give to you what I know Deirdre isn't capable of." Her hand skims his crotch, startling him.

Nicolaus takes her hands and kisses them, shocked at her boldness towards him.

Kissing her hands is an action which endears Nicolaus to her even more. She sighs.

He shakes his head, "I can't. It's taken too long for Deirdre and I to finally be together, and I don't want to do anything at all to mess that up. Anyway, I would never do anything to hurt Deirdre. And ... I'm not sure she'd want to share me." He looks into Helena's eyes, trying to be delicate with her, understanding she is being vulnerable with him. "I don't want to hurt you, Helena," he tells her softly, "I ... I can't. Deirdre means too much to me. I love her with all my heart, and have loved her for so many years. She's the only woman on earth for me, and we're finally together."

"I just want to be with you ... take care of you," she says softly, sitting on her desk.

Nicolaus can sense that Helena needs love. He feels a strong responsibility towards her, that same urge to look after her as he had when he first met her at her children's home. He hugs Helena to him, holding her tightly.

Helena is glad to be in his arms and her hands roam his muscular back, wanting more of him. His hug is warm and loving. Helena pulls him to her as close as she can get him. She can feel his crotch against her own, through their clothes. Her thighs encircling him, capturing him just below the hips.

Helena doesn't understand how he can be so calm and collected right now. Why is Nicolaus so different from other men? Normally, any other man would be working her clothes off, trying to get that very thing she is now offering Nicolaus, and yet, she feels no arousal about him. He is not breathing excitedly. He is not tugging at her body, or even at her clothes. She cannot understand his mind. Helena tries to stop thinking and she lays her head against his strength. She wants to enjoy the moment in his innocent hug, innocent on his part, not on hers.

Suddenly, her fantasy is interrupted by the smell of him. Helena wonders why Nicolaus smells of fresh baked sugar cookies. Nonchalantly, she sniffs near his arm pit and smells a hint of men's deodorant. She sniffs his neck to find a hint of men's after shave. Smoothly, she touches his hair, and the smell of her fingers are of coconut, very different from the smell of fresh baked sugar cookies.

Nicolaus hugs her tightly, wanting her to know she is loved by more people than the children she cares for. "I'm sure it's hard not having Joel."

Helena pulls back from him, frowning. "Joel? This isn't about Joel. I've already filed divorce papers on Joel. No, it's not about him. It's about you, Nicky!"

"Oh!" He is again surprised at her words. "What I mean is, it must be hard not having intimacy after so many years of marriage."

Helena raises her eyebrows, "I want to be intimate with you."

Helena grabs Nicolaus' clothes, and harshly pulls him in to kiss her. Nicolaus grabs her hands, this time resisting her, turning his head to avoid her passionate kiss.

Quickly and gently, Nicolaus kisses Helena's forehead, not wanting her to feel rejected or hurt. 'Oh Lord!' she thinks to herself. That little innocent kiss makes her body react with a passionate power towards him. Her temperature increases immensely.

This love torture is too much for Helena. She skedaddles over the desk, papers, books, and anything that lays there. The furniture is the safety zone between them. Helena wants to cry, she wants to scream, she wants to grab up Nicolaus and force herself on him.

Nicolaus is puzzled at her reaction. He knows he should extract himself before things go any farther. He notices how Helena is breathing heavily, as she looks upon him. He understands she wants more from him. "I better get going, my wife is waiting for me."

"Sure." Helena sounds defeated. She realizes he is running from her. She knows he should run from her, for Deirdre's sake, although she doesn't actually want him to run from her. Helena thinks herself a monster for wanting to be intimate with her best friend's man. She just can't help it anymore. She is in love, true love, with Nicolaus Ravenell.

Nicolaus observes her, "Helena, you okay?"

"I'm okay," she responds dryly.

"Helena."

"I have work to do," she tells him sharply, not looking at him. She holds on to her desk. She is so hot for him, she feels like she might not be able to control herself from jumping him. She sits down, pulls up her computer and begins to work.

Nicolaus doesn't feel right about leaving, now worried about Helena's state of mind. Before he gets to his car he phones Deirdre. "Babe, you okay?"

"Yes, all is fine. I'm here with your mom. How did your session with the kids go?"

"It went great. Hon, could you phone Helena? She seems a little down. I'm sure hearing from you will cheer her up."

"Oh, of course, sure. I'll call her right now."

"Thanks babe."

Chapter One Hundred Fifty-Three-TW

Deirdre's pregnancy is going along quite well. She does not have morning sickness, and she seems to regularly crave carrots and cookies. Nicolaus made sure the staff had plenty of whatever Deirdre wanted available to her at all times. For work hours, Nicolaus had the staff prepare them an insulated lunch tote containing carrots, and a variety of cookies. Deirdre giggles at his thoughtfulness, however, on many occasions when her cravings hit, she is appreciative.

Deirdre looks up from her work, as she'd just finished the contract document to be presented to the real estate agents for the future homes for children. Her idea is to create a partnership with one real estate company to assist them in finding the homes for the children, on the scale of Nicolaus' vision. Her attention is grabbed by Nicolaus, who is knocking on her office door. She sees great concern on his face.

"Deirdre, can you break from your work? We have an urgent call from Darfur."

"Seriously?" Deirdre saves her work on her computer, and bounces out of her office chair to join Nicolaus. He has their assistant put the video call through to the conference room, so they can both be seen by the caller on camera, and they can see the caller on the large video monitor on the wall in the conference room. Nicolaus asked Daniel to join them as well.

"Nicolaus and Deirdre, thank you so much for taking my call. It is very well to see you both. My name is Ibrahim Ahmed, and I am with Over the World, the nonprofit children's agency. Our agency works to save children out of conflict zones across the world. I am stationed here in Sudan, Africa, in the Darfur region."

"Ibrahim, it is very nice to meet you. This is my Chief lawyer, Daniel Araceli, as well. Tell us, how can we help you today?"

"Thank you, Nicolaus. We have seen the reports of how you are helping children all over the world. This is very impressive. And I'm sure you know about the conflict here in Darfur, and I am reaching out to you ... no, I am begging you ... to help us." Ibrahim's emotions quickly surfaced. "The children are suffering greatly here. The families that could get away from the murdering militias have fled as far as they could. If you can imagine, fleeing across the desert with nothing, no water, no food for your children, having to trek fifty to a hundred miles or more on your bare feet, to get to an open makeshift camp. A camp that has no shelter from the blistering sun, no water, no food. Your children are hungry, and thirsty, and they begin to die. And they are still not safe. The murdering militia could arrive at any time. We have lost so many people, Nicolaus."

Ibrahim pauses at the thought of the loss of the women, children, and elders to the vicious hands of militia men. "It is unspeakable ... what they have done."

Deirdre sheds tears at the thought of the suffering of the families and children. Nicolaus also becomes emotional at the description of desperation of the families and the suffering of the children.

"The children," Ibrahim continues, "all they can do is cry. Basically, they cry until they are so weak, they no longer can, and then death takes them. Or their mother's die of starvation. So these people ... they either die at the hands of vicious killers, or they starve to death in the desert ... a desert that is not meant for making a home to live."

Deirdre, Nicolaus, and even Daniel, use tissues to wipe their eyes. Nicolaus takes a breath, nodding to Ibrahim in understanding of the predicament. "What can we do to help? Is our government already involved?"

"No. No one is helping us. We seem to be all alone in this plight, just waiting to die one way or the other. It seems that the world has closed its eyes to what is happening, acting as if these people don't exist, as if these suffering children don't exist. Nicolaus, I am begging for your help. I'm literally begging you."

Nicolaus clears his throat. "My new friend, you don't have to beg us." Nicolaus looks to Deirdre and Jonathan who are both nodding in agreement with him. Deirdre can immediately see the look on Nicolaus' face change. She knows plans are forming in his brain. Nicolaus crosses his arms and puts a tapping thumb to his upper lip in thought. "Why don't we try to get some of those families out of there?" Nicolaus got about strategically thinking this through.

"Ibrahim, is it possible to move the families with children from where they are to another place. So currently, in that camp, they are still at risk. Can they be moved to the north or the east of where they are?"

Ibrahim thinks about this for a moment. He frowns and nods. "Yes, perhaps we can move them. But how? Our agency has no access to such vehicles or planes?"

Nicolaus quickly pulls up a map of the region. "Where exactly are the children? Where is the camp?"

"We are outside of Khartoum, to the north."

Nicolaus breathed out, thinking. "Okay. For obvious reasons we cannot go in there. I'm thinking we can help to get one hundred families out. You'll have to bring them to us, though, Ibrahim. Somewhere further beyond the conflict zone of where you are. I cannot send helpers into danger. However, we do have contacts that can help to meet those families at a point beyond the fighting, and then get them out of the country."

"Nicolaus, you can do that?"

"What do you think, Deirdre? Daniel?"

"Yes, we should be able to do that," Deirdre confirms.

"We have partners in Egypt, though I'm not sure they are willing to go into Darfur," Daniel notes.

"What about Eritrea? We have partners in Eritrea, helping us reach out to Ethiopian children," Nicolaus voices.

Daniel nods. "That could work."

"Ibrahim, what do you think? Can you get families to Eritrea?"

Ibrahim gets choked with emotion again. He shakes his head. "Eritrea is too far from where we are. Those families would die from the walk there. It is just too far."

"Nicky, what about Atbara? Can we get our partners from Eritrea to get to Atbara to pick up the families or to set up a camp? Isn't that an open border?"

Nicolaus and Daniel think about the suggestion, and they both nod. "Yeah, I think that could work. What about Atbara, Ibrahim? That is closer. If you can get the families there, we can have our partners either set up camp or try to bring those families by bus to the camps in Ethiopia. We have food, water, shelters, and physicians at this camp."

Deirdre touches her love on the shoulder. "Nicky, those families and children will be too weak to make a journey all the way to Ethiopia. We need to get them out of that conflict zone, set up camp in Eritrea with food, water, shelter, and medical care, first. Then we can offer the trip to Ethiopia once they are stronger."

Nicolaus smiles at Deirdre. "My wise wife has spoken."

"Nicolaus, Deirdre is right. Once they get stronger, perhaps we can offer more options of bringing some here to the U.S.," Daniel offers. "Well, not here, Texas appears too cruel and adverse to immigrants of color, however, we can set up other places for them, maybe in New Mexico, Colorado, or California. Getting them to Eritrea provides us some time to get things ready."

Nicolaus nods with a smile and jousts his arms out to Deirdre and Daniel. "Ibrahim, now you see why I have these two brilliant people on my team. Okay, so how does that sound? You think you can get one hundred families to Atbara? I wish we could help everyone all at once ... it's just not possible. I know there are thousands in that camp there."

"Nicolaus, Deirdre, and Daniel, we are so grateful for any help you can provide. Yes, we can get families to Atbara. We will have to walk, but I believe we can get there. How do I pick the families though?"

"That will be the hard part," Deirdre chimes in. "I suggest, start with the families who have been there the longest. That only seems right. And if there are more than one hundred families, your agency will need to find a way to have a fair lottery within your culture there."

"Yes, Deirdre, that is wonderful," Nicolaus tells her. "And let them know that once we rotate those hundred families out, we'll take another hundred families. We'll do this as long as we can. We don't have unlimited resources, though, we will help through our partners where we can. I think a good goal for us is to try to save at least five hundred families. I think though, Ibrahim, if your agency can get most of those families out of the conflict region, and get them to Eritrea, they will have a better chance of surviving. Hopefully those militias will not cross the border. Already, we understand this is going to be a long term project of saving families. We will also try to bring others into the cause, and perhaps this will increase the numbers of families that can be saved, and could speed up getting them out of the conflict zone."

While Nicolaus is speaking, tears flow from Ibrahim's eyes at the level of help for the desperate and dying population. "I cannot thank the three of you enough." He wipes his eyes. "My young staff told me to call you. And I told them they were crazy ... that you are celebrities, and that you would not help. First I couldn't believe I got through to you, just by dialing your number. And now this ...."

Tears flow from him again. "On behalf of my agency, and all the children of Darfur, I thank you for being open to helping us. For being willing to try to save some of these children."

Deirdre also had tears flowing again. "Ibrahim, we hope this is only the beginning of what we can do. We will continue to make plans and work to get families out of there. We promise. Please write our numbers down, and call us any time. These are our private cell numbers, and you can pass them to your staff as well." Deirdre proceeds to provide Ibrahim her and Nicolaus' private cell numbers, and they took down Ibrahim's numbers as well.

"Ibrahim, do you think you can get the families to Atbara in five days' time?"

"Yes! Yes, Nicolaus, I believe we can be there in five days. I will call you if anything changes."

"Okay. And as my wife has stated, you and your staff can call us anytime."

"Nicolaus, Deirdre and Daniel, thank you ... thank you ... thank you," Ibrahim tells them with prayerful hands.

As the call ends, Deirdre jump hugs her husband, not caring that she is at work. She appreciates Nicolaus' loving heart. Daniel gives them a high five, and they get to work on these important plans to save the families of the Darfur region.

Chapter One Hundred Fifty-Four

Just before dinner, Elsa gave the news of her second pregnancy to the family. Everyone seems excited, including Niall this time. Deirdre is glad to see that Niall appears to have a change about him, and has settled down. She believes the birth of a daughter did this for him, though she didn't tempt him in any way with hugging or touching.

Niall no longer has access to Deirdre because she is with Nicolaus all day, every day. He only sees Deirdre during mealtime with all the family present. Both Deirdre and Nicolaus agree that his limited access to her, and the birth of Elaine may have squelched his obsession of her.

Deirdre hugs Elsa. "I'm so happy for you!"

"This time we truly will be pregnant together!" She holds Deirdre's hands. "I cannot thank you enough for helping me with my dreams of having a family with Niall, and for my promotion at work."

Ceil touches Elsa's shoulders, wine glass in hand. Ceil knows that Elsa has proven herself good for Niall and another child is one up on Nicolaus. "Let's have a toast. Everyone get a drink." Everyone quickly receives a drink from the staff, Deirdre and Elsa are given apple juice. Ceil smiles and holds her glass in the air to toast the happy couple. "To my Niall and Elsa! Our most productive Ravenells!"

Everyone immediately understands the insult Ceil is leveling against Nicolaus and Deirdre. No one is sure if they should drink. As Ceil put her glass to her lips, Nigel pulls her arm down, stopping her from drinking, clearing his throat. "To Niall and Elsa! Congratulations! And may this baby be as happy and as healthy as Elaine!" Glasses clang, and everyone drinks to Nigel's toast.

Nicolaus wonders why Ceil is jabbing at him again. Her attitude changed towards him since Rachel's funeral. He tried not to let it bother him, however, he did not like that she insulted Deirdre as well. The family sits down to dinner, and the atmosphere is more quiet than usual.

The following week, Nicolaus encircles his arms around Deirdre as she lay on the exam table to get her first ultrasound of their baby. The advanced 4D imaging shows the baby very clearly. Helena and Constance are present. Constance holds onto Deirdre's hand with great joy. The technician confirms that the baby is indeed a boy.

Nicolaus chuckles, hand in the air, "I told you!" Everyone laughs. He kisses Deirdre's head and looks at the monitor again. "That's my son, right there!"

Nicolaus and Deirdre continue their work. Deirdre has much of the planning for the children's homes complete. She met with real estate agents from different companies to decide who she wanted to bring aboard for partnering and assisting them.

The Darfur rescue is also moving along well, so far no issues. With the help of partners in the surrounding regions, they have assisted two hundred families out of the conflict zone, thus far, with more to follow. Nicolaus was even able to get their partners in Egypt to help at the Eritrea camp.

At the VMC office, they promoted a lower-level staff for their administrative assistant, since Elsa moved into her new role, and she is completely loving it. Deirdre is ecstatic, knowing that she was right about Elsa's ability for the role of their grant writer.

Nicolaus is analyzing investor prospects, when he receives a call from Francesca. She sounds very upset. "Francesca, calm down." She's speaking so fast he doesn't catch what she is saying.

"Nicky, do you have your birth certificate? Your birth certificate," she says impatiently.

Nicolaus sighs, "My birth certificate?"

"Nicky, do you have it or not?" she frantically, half yells at her military hero cousin, in her British accent.

Nicolaus thinks for a moment, frowning, wondering why she is asking this of him. "Sure. At the house."

"Have you ever read it, Nicky?"

"Francesca ..."

"Nicky, answer the question," she half yells at him, sounding panicked.

Nicolaus frowns. "Well ... yeah, ... sure. Francesca what's going on?"

"Nicky, I think I have it here. I'm going through Mum's papers, and ... and ... you better get over here. Now, Nicky, now!" She sounds frantic again.

Nicolaus looks at his desk calendar, then checks his computer calendar. The rest of his day is clear, and it is noon time. He looks at the stack of work on his desk. Not only does he need to vet the investor prospects, he also has financial reports, the end of year report, and ...."

"Nicky!" she yells into the phone at his silence, knowing he is thinking about work.

"Francesca, calm down!"

"Cancel whatever you're looking at, Nicky. Get over here now!" she yells at him.

He sighs, "Okay, okay. Where are you, at Aunt Rachel's?"

"Yes. Get over here now, Nicky!"

"All right, I'm on my way. Just stay calm."

Nicolaus leaves his papers on his desk, and locks his door. Deirdre and Daniel both have keys to his office for emergency purposes. He goes into Deirdre's office. They were to lunch together. She too is pouring over financial documents. He sits in the chair before her desk.

Deirdre looks up and sees the expression on his face. She frowns, "Everything okay?"

"No, Francesca just called, and she sounds very upset, something about my birth certificate. She needs me to go see her right away."

"Nicky, that sounds really important. You need me to cover any meetings for you?"

Nicolaus' frown turned into a smile at her question to him, his heart warmed. "No, I'm all caught up, thank you, hon. What about lunch? You must eat."

Deirdre touches her pregnant belly. "Nicolai and I will be heading to the café in a few minutes."

"Nicolai?" Nicolaus asks, amused.

Deirdre nods. "Yep. I want him named after you, his wonderful father, and to also have his own identity."

Nicolaus chuckles, "When did you decide this?"

Deirdre smiles. "This morning on our drive in, while I was admiring you."

He stands and walks to his wife, placing a gentle kiss on her lips. "Nicolai Ravenell." He nods in approval. "I like it. And I surely appreciate your sentiment, babe. Thank you." He kisses her again, touching her belly. "You working until five today?"

"Until five thirty. Don't worry, babe, I'll wait right here until you get back."

"Okay. Hopefully this won't take too long."

Nicolaus enters Rachel's house, and finds Francesca sitting on the floor, with boxes of documents and papers sprawled out everywhere. He sees that she is crying, and immediately, he is on the floor with her, hugging her. "Francesca."

"Nicky, I don't understand what she was doing. I don't get what she was thinking. Mum was holding too much."

Nicolaus frowns at her, "What do you mean? What have you found?" Francesca hands him a folder. Slowly, he opens it. There are two birth certificates inside. One is for him, and one is for Francesca. He frowns again, shaking his head, "Auntie Rachel had my birth certificate? I don't understand. I have my birth certificate. There are two documents?"

"Nicky, read it! Read it!"

Nicolaus stands, and slowly reads the birth certificate. He reads it again. He looks at Francesca. "Auntie Rachel was my mother?" he asks in disbelief.

"Now read mine."

Nicolaus pulls Francesca's birth certificate to the top, and slowly he reads. "What?" With astonishment he reads it again. "My father is ... your father." Nicolaus looks at Francesca. "Oh my God, this is what she was trying to tell us before she died."

Francesca wipes her face, trying to calm down. Hearing someone else say it helps her be able to somewhat accept it. "So that makes you my ..."

"Brother."

"Why would Mum lie to me like that? For all these years? My whole life!"

Nicolaus sits himself on the floor again, next to Francesca. He hugs her. "I don't know, maybe she had a good reason."

"A good reason? To lie to me? Me, Nicky, me!"

"Okay, okay. I hear you."

"Uncle Nigel ... I mean dad .. ugh, whatever, ... is going to answer to me for this."

"Francesca, look we both need answers, we don't know the whole story. We have to approach this strategically. We don't want to shut my father down and he not tell us anything. Believe me, he hasn't been straight with me on many things either. If you push too hard, he'll just shut down and won't tell you anything."

She leans against her strong, strapping brother. "There's more. I found medical records. She had some mental issues she never told me about. For a while, she was taking medication. Just like the cancer. She'd been sick for a while. I only found out when I found her on the floor with a pain attack."

Nicolaus hugs Francesca to support her emotional upheaval. He sighs, "There seems to be many family secrets."

Chapter One Hundred Fifty-Five

Nigel receives a surprise as he arrives home early from golfing with Dwight. He opens the door to his bedroom to change clothes and to invite Ceil out for lunch. When he enters, he finds Helena in the bed with Ceil. Both ladies are disrobed and frozen at his appearance. Nigel laughs to himself, notices how beautiful Helena is, and backs out of the room.

Nigel knew Ceil was taken with Helena, however, he did not think she would go this far. This situation doesn't bother him, it more fascinates him, and he wonders how this would play out. Will Ceil treat Helena properly to keep her around, or would she turn mean and run her off? More importantly, Ceil can no longer badger him about his infidelity with Rachel.

Nigel walks to the drawing room and pours a drink. He sits down to relax when Francesca and Nicolaus enter together. He sees that Nicolaus is attempting to hold Francesca back, and she isn't having it.

"There you are Nigel, ... Pops, ... Dad, ... I don't even know what to call you these days," Francesca scolds him.

Nigel eyes Francesca, swallows his perfectly tasteful drink, and sighs. He pats the couch for Francesca to sit next to him. She does so. Nigel side hugs Francesca to him, and she bursts out crying, bringing up his own emotion. Nicolaus frowns, thinking Francesca is completely ignoring what he told her to do. He closes the door to the drawing room, and hands Francesca some tissues before sitting.

"Sounds like you may have found some documents in your mother's things," Nigel gently says, hugging her more, controlling himself. He knows if he begins to shed tears over Rachel, he may not stop.

Nicolaus hands Nigel the folder with the birth certificates. "Are these correct, father? One of these is different than what I have."

Slowly, Nigel opens the folder, revealing the documents. He looks over both birth certificates. Reluctantly, he nods. "Yes."

Nicolaus frowns, another shock. "How's that? Then ... the one I have is not real?"

"Well, ... not exactly," Nigel elusively answers his son.

"So, you both been lying to us! All these years!" Francesca bursts out crying again.

Nigel hugs Francesca again. This is painful for all of them. "You both have to understand that we made the best choices to protect you. Ceil is very difficult at times, so we had to keep this a secret. And Francesca, she still mustn't know about you. You already understand how vindictive Ceil can be. What you have found changes nothing. I'm still your uncle. Nicolaus, you will still refer to Ceil as your mother. Rachel and I have always loved both of you."

"And you were in love with Rachel?" Nicolaus poses the half question, half statement to his father. He suddenly understands his father's unusually distraught behavior at Rachel's funeral. "Same situation as Deirdre and I, what you told me about previously, without naming names? Auntie Rachel is the woman you were to marry?"

Nigel nods one time. "Yes. I was to marry Rachel, and then betrothed to Ceil."

"So ... why didn't I live with her? She gave me up?"

"She couldn't take care of you, son, she was ill. In actuality, I insisted she give you to me, for Ceil and I to raise you."

"Mental issues?" Francesca asks, more calm.

"Yes." Nigel doesn't elaborate.

"So ... this is the thing you did that has mother ... Ceil ... coming after me? This is why she hates me? It's not that I did anything, it's just that I was born?" Nicolaus reasons, starting to feel very upset.

"It's why she treats you so poorly, Nicky," Francesca states.

Nigel nods, agreeing with what is being said. "Yes, I'm very sorry for that, Nicolaus. If I could fix it I would. I have tried to fix it, and thought it was patched up, and yet Ceil continues to go back to it. She won't let it go. She won't ..." he stops talking, realizing his explanation isn't helping the situation when he sees the look about Nicolaus.

Nicolaus stands in his upset. "I lost a lot of time with Deirdre because of all this," he sounds perturbed. He sighs, "I was forced to marry Marguerite ..."

"Not to mention Auntie Ceil tried to get Gwen to kill Nicky with drugs!"

"Oh yeah, and that too!" Nicolaus agrees with Francesca.

"Well, that is exaggerating." Nigel tries to downplay what they are discovering.

"I lost a child ... I lost time that I can never get back!"

"Son, don't. I'm sorry. We can't change any of that."

"None of it should have ever happened in the first place!"

Nicolaus goes to the sidebar and pours himself a drink. Quickly, he swallows it down, hoping to calm himself. He rubs his forehead, feeling very stressed. "I should have known that Rachel was my mother." He turns to face Nigel again. "I should have known, father." Nicolaus gasps in sudden realization. "Oh ... my ... God! All these years. That's been why Niall ...." Nicolaus sits down, taking another shock.

"Auntie Ceil has always preferred Niall over you, no matter what you do, Nicky. She doesn't accept you. And she's never respected you ... and now we know why." Francesca confirms Nicolaus' thoughts.

"Now Nicolaus ..."

"No more lies father," Nicolaus says evenly, "please, no more lies."

Francesca sits next to Nicolaus, seeing he needs support. He frowns deeply, a tear falling from his eye. "You know, I can't change any of this. I can't change what my mother ... Ceil ..., thinks of me, or why she hates me." He sits back in thought. "When I had people under my command, the one thing I learned is that you cannot change people. You may be able to get them to follow rules, or policies, or guidelines, but you cannot change them. The only ones who can make a change is they themselves."

Nicolaus wipes the tear from his face, sitting forward, resting his elbows on his knees. He breathed out some stress. "At least now I know I didn't do anything to Ceil to make her hate me. I was just born. None of us can control that! Makes me think of my son, Thaddeus. He didn't ask to be born. His mother never loved him. She decided she didn't want him again, and could have handed him to those who were willing to help her, instead she decided to kill him." His tears are back. He wipes them. "The person themself has to be willing to change." More tears appear. "I do wish I had known that Rachel was my mother, while she was here with us. I'm very sure it would have made a difference in my life."

"Nicky, don't do that. She saw you. She loved you, just like she loved me. I could see her love for you." Francesca hugs her newly found brother. "I understand now that she watched you grow up. She was always very proud of you. She wanted to see you run the company, and she got to see it. She wanted to see you married to Deirdre and happy, and she got to see that too, and help to arrange the marriage ceremony. That really made her happy. She knew you were all right, Nicky. That's all that really matters, Love. Right?"

Nicolaus nods, and they hug each other tightly. Tears flowing from both of them.

Nicolaus is calm by the time he picks up Deirdre from the office. However, he does not want to discuss any of what he'd learned with her. He knows this new information will upset her, and he doesn't want to stress Deirdre. Additionally, now he is worried that Ceil might do something to harm Deirdre, just to spite him.

However, Deirdre is aware that something significant happened for Nicolaus today when she hears him vomiting in his office bathroom. He had only told her that Francesca was upset over some documents she found, and would say nothing more about the matter. She heard him cleaning up and brushing his teeth before exiting.

"Nicky," she touches his chest, "you okay, honey?"

He smiles at her, nodding, "Of course. You ready for dinner?" He asks as if nothing were wrong, not realizing she heard him vomiting. Everything he knew about his life has been changed from looking at one document and getting some truth from Nigel. Somehow, he must get through dinner without getting upset. This will be something he'd have to manage from this day forward. He must protect Deirdre as well as Francesca.

Chapter One Hundred Fifty-Six

D uring the week of the September Labor Day Holiday in the U.S., Nicolaus and Deirdre are spending this holiday time away from their families. Nicolaus needs a break from everyone, and decided he and Deirdre will take a little vacation, though he did try to talk Constance into joining them.

It just so happens that Nicolaus and Deirdre want to scout out properties for housing the Darfurian refugee families. He surprised her with airline tickets to Denver, Colorado. Not only can they conduct business, they can also enjoy celebrations within a different culture, and see some beautiful wilderness of the western region of the United States.

They really like the city, which is completely different than Austin, and they are inspired by the huge Rocky Mountains which are a backdrop to the city. They notice that everything seems different, the environment, the people, the region.

This is the third apartment building property they have looked at. Nicolaus is not satisfied. Deirdre touches his chest. "What is it babe, what's the matter?"

They are standing outside the three story apartment building. "I just don't think this is big enough for what we need. It just doesn't fit." Nicolaus helps Deirdre into the rented top of the line vehicle. He gets into the driver's seat, looks at the building again, then looks at his wife, with a twisted mouth, and squinted eyes.

Deirdre giggles, knowing for sure her husband is thinking about something big. "Nicky!"

Nicolaus takes her hand in silence, then he kisses her hand, and then her cheek. "You know what? I want to give you everything you want, and take you to extravagant places, and ..."

Deirdre touches his face, and his lips to hush his words. She shakes her head. "Nicky, I don't care about any of that. I only care about being with you. All that money we can use to help these families. Anyway, I'd be really unhappy if we spent thousands on a trip when we could have spent those same thousands to help save children, for what has been placed in our care, by divine intervention. Right now, those families are our duty."

Nicolaus kisses her hand again. "I can't believe how much we think alike. We're on the same page, honey. I was going to say that I want to do all those things for you, and yet my heart tells me I've got to use that money differently. We are so blessed for all we have. I am blessed, even though I know my family is ... difficult, for the most part. And I've got you, and you're my wife now, and we have little Nicolai on the way. I think about the suffering families ..."

"Me too, Nicky. So, what are you thinking?" She knows his thoughts are leading to his plan.

"Well, I think we should buy a hotel."

"A hotel?"

"Not a rickety run down place, a nice, midpoint hotel. We buy a hotel that can house at least one hundred families. Just think, they'd each have privacy of the hotel room and with a bathroom."

"A little kitchenette?"

Nicolaus nods with a smile, as he knows Deirdre can already see his vision. "Yes, a kitchenette. And I'm thinking the children begin with private schooling, right in the hotel. We can turn the conference rooms into classrooms. They'll have a big kitchen for meals along with the communal eating area, and the lobby for the gathering place. We can put in a playground for the children."

Deirdre squeezes his hand, "Oh my gosh, yes! And an internal no cost store so they can get whatever hygiene supplies they may need for men and women, or food and snacks that they want."

"Well, and we'll need helpers, cleaning staff, cooking staff, social workers, an Imam, teachers ...local resources to help them integrate into society ..."

"We can make it like a village for them, but not closed off. And of course they can go out, and like you say, we'll have agencies and others present to help them. We can connect them with a mosque or a church, whatever they want." Deirdre adds.

"Yes, we can have a van and driver to take them where they need to go."

"They can be comfortable and safe while we work with immigration."

"Yes, they will have to have immigration hearings, and we will sponsor all the families this way Deirdre, you and me. We'll be their sponsor. And if they are approved by immigration, we'll need to work on getting employment for at least the men."

"Wow, Nicky! You've been thinking about this for a while. Haven't you, babe?"

Nicolaus smiles, "Well ... yeah, you could say that. I think it hasn't really all been pieced together in my mind until now, though. Talking it over with you helps me think things through." He sighs, "Deirdre, we'll have to take a hit to our budget. I mean, it's going to take a lot of money."

"Babe, it's okay. It's worth it. Though ... I think you should see if the foundation will provide the down payment for the hotel."

"The foundation? It's not their mission. I don't think ..."

"Nicky, ask! The board might approve it as a special project to help desperate children. We should ask for the down payment, and then you and I will make the payments."

"Hmm!" Nicolaus sat back into the car seat, putting his head on the headrest. Deirdre could see him formulating something in his mind, she could see he is thinking the next move. "Hmm!" he says again. "What if ... hmm!"

"Say it, babe."

"I'm just thinking, what if we do as you say. We ask them to help, not only a down payment, we ask them to pay half, and you and I pay the other half. This way we'll outright own the property and that will give us cash flow for the support services we are talking about. Then we give the board a return on the investment by putting the property into a trust back to the foundation. In other words ..."

"Of course, since it would be a charitable donation with no money revenue, the building itself would now be their investment. Darling, I think this would be a good push to get them to do it! Property for future sale, or whatever. That property, a nice hotel, turns into an asset for the foundation, and looks really good on the balance sheets."

"Exactly! Oh my dear Lord! Deirdre, my love, you are a genius."

"Babe, we came up with this together."

Their hearts rejoice, as they seal their plan with a passionate kiss.

Chapter One Hundred Fifty-Seven

Nicolaus and Deirdre work feverishly to get things ready for the Darfurian refugee families. They work their VMC jobs during the week, maintaining what needed to be done, and preparing the children's homes to release children out of foster care, and then on the weekends, they work in Denver to get the hotel ready. Nicolaus takes care of the administration issues such as interviewing and hiring staff, while Deirdre takes care of accentuated details such as towels, bedcoverings, supplies, and furniture. They both work on setting up the school for the children. Then on Sunday nights, they'd take the latest flight back to Austin, and get ready for the work week at VMC. Everything they did, they did together, as a labor of love for all involved and for the greater community overall.

"Ibrahim, it is so good to see you. You look well my friend," Nicolaus tells him.

"Yes, yes, we are doing pretty well."

"Yaaaaay!!" Darfurian women with young girls jump into the view of the camera phone to greet Nicolaus and Deirdre with great excitement. "Hello!! Hello with love! And blessings! Thank you, thank you!"

Deirdre and Nicolaus chuckle and waive to the extra guests on the phone call. They love seeing the smiling faces of women and children they have helped.

Ibrahim returns onto the call. "They have been waiting to see you, and to thank you. The children are doing so much better at this camp here in Eritrea. We cannot thank you enough."

"It fills our hearts with joy to hear this, Ibrahim." Nicolaus takes Deirdre's hand. "It's all blessings from God and help from our partners on the ground out there. We cannot take any credit for any of that. We thank God, truly, that the families are doing better."

"Yes, we thank God as well. For putting you in our path, Nicolaus and Deirdre."

Deirdre smiles, "Ibrahim, we are calling with good news, great news today. We have receive permission from our government for our plans to bring families here to the U.S. We are so very thrilled about this."

Ibrahim beams with joy and tears, so very happy to hear this news. He is amazed at the length this couple has gone through to save these families.

"Ibrahim, we have a place, a nice place, support people, a school for the children, just really everything we could think of that they might need."

"Oh they will not believe it when I tell them this!" He laughs at the thought of how the mothers who have suffered so much may react to him telling them this good news.

"With your help in coordination, we can begin receiving the first hundred families next week."

"Nicolaus, did you say next week?"

"Yes. And then you can rotate the next families to the Eritrea camp." Deirdre interrupts Nicolaus to show him her phone. They received a resounding yes on help from a group of celebrities, led by their favorite shareholder, Ms. Winfree, to get more families out of Darfur. The celebrities decided to combine their money to buy three large hotels to assist. Deirdre begins to cry. She couldn't believe it.

"Ibrahim, hold on there." Nicolaus hugs Deirdre to him, and he looks at what the phone says again. "Oh my God!" He too is in awe. "Ah ... Ibrahim ... we just received word that many celebrities will be helping us bring families out. Oh my God! Ah .. we need to verify all this before we tell you more, looks like ... my friend ... it's happening. We're getting movement from others to help. I promise I'll tell you what we can do."

"Nicolaus ... I'm speechless! My God! My good God!" Ibrahim dances around filled with joy for the children. His dancing brings attention to the mothers who soon join him.

"I promise, I'll call you back with all the details."

Chapter One Hundred Fifty-Eight

Within several weeks, Nicolaus and Deirdre had reached and surpassed their goal of helping Darfurian families survive the vicious conflict, bringing them to safety, giving the children an actual future. With celebrity help, and government assistance, they settled seven hundred families into the U.S., in Colorado, New Mexico, and California. The governors of each state are more than welcoming to the Darfurian families. With love and understanding, the people and many children of several cities pitch in and helped as well, having heeded the encouragement from the mayors and several city leaders. The families have full support in each state, and the Darfurian children are already receiving schooling.

Nigel is extremely impressed by what his son and daughter-in-law have done for others, especially the African families. They are so humble about their actions. Nigel only found out when Nicolaus asked for bedding, linen, and kitchen ware items from the church congregation. Then he saw the extent of their project in a news report about their efforts. They had not mentioned their work to the family, nor talked about it at VMC. Nigel knew they were traveling back and forth to Denver, however, he had not understood the depth of their weekend work. "I'm so proud of both of you!" he tells them at dinner, with Ceil and Helena present. He is so surprised when again their response is very humble.

Nicolaus smiles, "It's not us. God brought people together to help those families." His smile fades. "So many more need saving." Deirdre touches his hand and nods in agreement. Nicolaus has made many trips to the church to offer prayers about the whole situation. He also prayed for sustained strength for he and Deirdre during this very busy season for them.

The following week, Deirdre has an appointment at the clinic for the second ultrasound, now that she is six months pregnant. Nicolaus helps Deirdre to the vehicle, and she is pleasantly surprised to see that Nicolaus has traded in his sports car for a Sports Utility Vehicle.

"We've got to get ready for Nicolai's arrival!" he excitedly tells her. "And our other children!" Instantly, Nicolaus feels the reward of trading in his sports car for this high end, luxury vehicle, as right away he can see that his wife is more comfortable.

Constance met them at the clinic, and they are really able to see the baby's development and features in the 4D imaging. Their son looks exactly like Nicolaus. All three of them are very excited.

When Nicolaus and Deirdre arrive back at the mansion, they are happy to see Francesca, as she intended to join the family for dinner today. She'd been away for a while, going through Rachel's things, and tying up loose ends. They both hug her.

"Wow, look at you!" Francesca observes Deirdre. "This baby is really happening!"

"Nicolaus," Elsa begins halfway through the meal, her three month baby bump just showing. "I haven't heard from my father for quite some time. I am very worried."

Nicolaus nods, "It has been a while. Do you know where he is?"

"No. He never tells me where he's going. Usually, he returns my calls when I leave him a message."

"Hmm. Who does he work for?"

Elsa chuckles, "I don't know. I've never known. He's never discussed it."

"Gosh, he could literally be anywhere in the world."

"Niall and I went to the house, and no one is there."

Nicolaus nods, "So he's probably on assignment ... or whatever he does."

"Or maybe he's on vacation and doesn't want to be bothered," Ceil states the polar opposite of Nicolaus' thoughts.

Nicolaus nods to acknowledge Ceil. He chuckles, "It's true, he could be anywhere."

"What if something bad has happened to him? I mean it's been months since I've heard from him."

"Well, I can make some calls to the state department to see if anyone knows anything."

"Would you, Nicky?"

Nicolaus nods. "If your father happens to work for the government, they may know where he is."

"Oh Nicky, we'd be so grateful," Elsa said of herself and her husband. Niall nods without words.

"There's that James Bond characteristic again," Francesca notes, getting laughs. "Deirdre, didn't you have a birthday, Love? I've been waiting to see a party invitation."

"Oh, I didn't want a fuss. Nicky and I have been busy. And I'm just happy and focused on Nicolai." Deirdre touches her baby belly.

"Nicolai? That's cute! Well, and then Nicky did something for you?"

"Of course!" Deirdre touches the beautiful diamond necklace around her neck, the stone is cut into the shape of a heart. Then she displays her arm with a matching diamond bracelet. "And Elsa, Ishani, and Maggie are sweet, they took me to lunch. Francesca, you and I can go to lunch if you'd like."

"Oh sure, always. We'll just have to go before my trip. I've decided I need a break, so I'm going to the Cayman Islands for a couple weeks, maybe a month. Or two."

"Francesca, you're going by yourself?" Nicolaus is immediately alarmed.

"Ah Nicky, I'll be fine. Anyways I'm leaving in two weeks."

"Hmm, that actually sounds very nice, Francesca," Nigel comments.

"Well, you're going to check in with me regularly, so we know you are all right."

Deirdre touches Nicolaus' hand. "Nicky," she whispers disapprovingly to him.

"I'm serious! I want two calls a day, one in the afternoon, and one before you go to sleep. Every day while you're away. And you let me know when you decide to return."

Francesca laughs at Nicolaus' demand, and bossy disposition.

"I'm serious, Francesca! If I don't hear from you, I'll be down there looking for you."

"I know you're serious! That's why it's funny, Love."

Chapter One Hundred Fifty-Nine

"DeeDee, what are you doing?" Cecil asks Abigail as he watches her packing her clothes into two suitcases. He called her by her endearing nickname, hoping to make her stop.

"What does it look like father? I'm packing! I'm going to Austin to meet Nicolaus and Deirdre. They both run a company called VMC. I have the address. I'm going."

"Abigail, you cannot go there." He sounds panicked.

"Well ... whose going to stop me? You? You cannot stop me, father. Anyway, perhaps I can get some answers from them, since I'm getting none from you."

Cecil grabs onto his daughter's arms to stop her from packing. "Okay, okay. I'll tell you. To keep you safe, I'll tell you."

Abigail looks at her father with searching eyes. She'd never seen him like this before. "I want the whole truth, father. A journalist's truth."

"Yes," Cecil nods, understanding the time is now to tell all to his daughter.

Chapter One Hundred Sixty-TW

T he very first chance he got, Niall seized on the opportunity to capture Deirdre. No one else is around as he forces her in the library, locking them inside.

"Niall, what are you doing? Stop this! Let me out!"

Deirdre screams as Niall shoves her against the corner wall, trapping her, where he previously had her cornered many months ago. She can't believe that she has to endure this again. After all she and Nicolaus have accomplished, she just cannot understand why Niall has not progressed himself beyond this. He has a daughter now.

The exquisite smell of Deirdre, which he'd missed, and her pregnancy which enhances her beautiful features, increases Niall's arousal and illogical reaction to her. He feels incapable of keeping himself from Deirdre any longer. Ignoring her pleas, he intends to take liberties with her.

Niall is oblivious to everything else going on, having found Deirdre alone. His mind is only on taking Deirdre. He'd grasped the realization that he'd have to take her by force, and he seems to have made up his mind to do so, as he places a tight grip around her delicate neck.

Niall is unaware of Nicolaus' presence in the mansion. He didn't think of Elsa; he didn't think of little Elaine; he didn't think of his mother; and he clearly doesn't care about his brother. All he can think about is copulating with Deirdre. He knows he only has limited time to move through his plan. With obvious intent, Niall attempts to rip Deirdre's clothes, wanting to expose her body.

Deirdre screams again, "Stop! Let me go!" She continues fighting Niall and resisting his force, feeling as though Niall has gone mad.

The push of Deirdre's dainty arms against him could not keep his determined force from her. Harshly, Niall slaps Deirdre's delicate face, making her cry out. He is intent on violently taking her, as he roughly shakes her to make her quiet down, not caring about her pregnancy.

Suddenly, Deirdre sees Nicolaus pull Niall away, with his arm wrapped around his brother's shoulders. Like a giant knight in shining armor, Nicolaus easily snatches Niall off Deirdre and throws him across the room to the floor.

Enraged, Niall jumps to his feet and charges his brother. Nicolaus shows no mercy as he calmly gives Niall one quick punch to the meaty part of his throat, a special military technique exclusively taught to specific military members, normally reserved to incapacitate enemy combatants. Immediately, Niall falls backwards to the floor, grasping at his throat for air, his breath painfully knocked out of him.

Nigel enters to see what is going on as he'd heard screaming. When he steps through the door, the scene is self-explanatory as Deirdre looks terrified, and Niall is being disciplined. Nigel stands and watches without uttering a word. He leans against the doorframe and folds his arms, knowing he'd do the same, justifying Nicolaus' actions.

Nicolaus attempts to approach Niall again, however, Deirdre grabs Nicolaus' muscular arm, feeling his enormous strength, as she could see the wrath within her husband. "Nicky, enough! You will kill him! You have to stop," she pleads for Niall who is having serious trouble trying to inhale, never having received such a painful punch to his throat.

Nicolaus is in control and has no intention of killing Niall, however, he considers his wife's words. Nicolaus grabs up Niall, "I warned you!" Through gritted teeth, "I will hurt you if you *ever* touch Deirdre again." He shakes Niall by the collar. "Brother or not. Make no mistake, Niall, I will not tolerate this behavior from you." Nicolaus replaces Niall back to the floor with a shove.

Grim faced, Nicolaus meets the eyes of his father, who neither approves nor disapproves, and says absolutely nothing. Shocked devastation overcomes Deirdre, and she cries as Nicolaus takes her into his protective arms. In silence, they leave the room.

Niall sits on the floor, still holding his throat, taking short breaths to get air, it slowly occurring for him. He feels stupid. His dream of taking Deirdre did not go exactly as planned.

He looks to Nigel for sympathy, and receives none. Remaining silent, Nigel turns his back and leaves the library.

Chapter One Hundred Sixty-One

Deirdre knows Nicolaus is very bothered by what happened with Niall. How could he not be? He comforted her to calm again, and she feels safe with him by her side. She watches Nicolaus as they lay in bed, she with ice on her face, and he staring at the ceiling.

Deirdre lays herself on his chest, hugging his torso. His arms immediately encircle her. "Nicky, you have to let this go." She is very worried about his psyche.

He scoffs, "Let it go?"

"I don't want to see you like this."

"I'm livid!"

"I know babe, but it's over now. You took care of it. He won't ..."

"What was he planning to do? Rape you?" Nicolaus interrupts her, frowning, asking with unbelievability in his voice and manner, his hand in the air, as if such a thing is improbable.

"Nicky, you took care of it. He won't bother me anymore."

Nicolaus sighs. "I can't understand why Niall has no boundaries. He must have damn well known I would go after him. I don't understand his twisted thinking."

"Honey, maybe it's not for us to understand. Maybe we just have to keep praying for him. I've been praying for him and Elsa."

Nicolaus sighs again. "I think you should go to the hospital to make sure you don't have a fracture. Let them x-ray your cheek bone."

Deirdre shakes her head. "No, I think I'm okay. It's sore, but I think I'm okay. Let's see how it is in the morning. However, babe, did you hear what I said about praying?"

"Yes, I heard you." He pulls Deirdre closer to him.

"Promise me, you'll let this go. I don't want to see you upset like this."

Nicolaus sighs. "I'll work on it."

Nicolaus holds Deirdre tightly, as close as he can, valuing her virtuousness. At this very difficult moment, he realizes again how much Deirdre's character compliments him, as she can see and understand situations he cannot.

Chapter One Hundred Sixty-Two

The following morning, there was to be no peace for the Ravenell family. Elsa looks sad, as she sits next to Niall, who has a large, swollen, red bruise on his throat. Nevertheless, he is breathing normally and otherwise seems fine. Nicolaus knew where he placed the punch would superficially hurt Niall, and give him time to calm down to get ahold of himself. Elsa is sorry that she is not enough for Niall, whom she loves very much, despite his abuse of her. She moved back in to live with him and make a family, however, she realizes that it just does not seem to matter to him.

Nicolaus assists Deirdre to sit down. The bruise on her face shows darker, and is still swollen.

As soon as Deirdre is seated, Ceil runs upon Nicolaus. She aims to strike his face. "You brute!" she yells her favorite insult at Nicolaus, completely ignoring what Niall has done, demonstrating her extreme devotion for her younger son. Ceil didn't seem to care that Niall struck Deirdre and tried to tear her clothes from her. She is only angry that Nicolaus' response to the aggression hurt her Niall. She swings her arm for a hard hit.

With ease, Nicolaus catches her arm, holding onto it. He moves back from Ceil, as she wildly struggles against him, swinging her other arm and trying for a kick to his forever injured knee. The knee that she permanently damaged when he was just a small child.

None of her tactics are working. She cannot reach him. "Let go! Don't you touch me!" Ceil yells at him, all eyes on them.

Nicolaus releases his hold on Ceil, and she moves away from him, understanding he is not going to let her strike his face, or strike him anywhere else.

Nigel remains silent and offers no help. Elsa and Niall quietly watch the dramatic exchanges.

"You disgust me!" Ceil yells at Nicolaus. "I hope you get beaten within one inch of your life!" She points at Deirdre, "And she does not belong here."

Deirdre touches Nicolaus, seeing the hurt on his face at Ceil's words. "Nicky, she doesn't mean any of that!" She tries to soften the blow of the harsh words.

Nicolaus nods, not taking his eyes from Ceil, as she sits in her chair on the other side of the breakfast table. Nicolaus sits beside his wife, his eyes still on Ceil, "She does mean it. She always means everything she says. Isn't that right, mother?"

Ceil looks at him with her usual cold stare, "I told you, I'm not your mother," she clearly announces to everyone present. "Stop calling me that!" she severely demands of him.

"What?" Elsa says shocked. She looks to Niall, who shrugs, not understanding.

Nicolaus and Ceil lock eyes at this time. The punitive treatment badly stinging him. Ceil is undoubtedly demonstrating that no matter what he did, her dark feelings for him would never change. "Okay then. What would you have me call you? After all these years, what is it that you want me to call you?"

Ceil stands. "Nothing! How about not calling me at all. Ever!" She turns her back to him, and walks out the room. Everyone remains silent.

This is too much for Nicolaus. Her words have the intended effect. Nicolaus put his fingers to his eyes to try to stop the tears. "Excuse me," he says getting up from the table and leaving the room, the opposite direction of Ceil.

Deirdre follows him out. He'd gone into the drawing room. "Nicky."

He put his hand up to her, "I just need a minute." He stands by the fireplace, his arm stretched forward to steady his weight with his hand on the wall. Nicolaus knows that whatever goodwill he'd made with Ceil for the last year is now broken, and that she is probably going to be worse than ever in her behavior towards him. He dreads it.

Deirdre grabs on to her love's arm. "Okay, I'll stay right here with you." She can see tears falling from Nicolaus' eyes. She hates it when Ceil is so mean to him. This is the kind of thing, such harsh emotional abuse, she is worried about happening to her own children. Deirdre decides she would talk to her mother and find a way around Ceil to soften her up for Nicolaus.

Chapter One Hundred Sixty-Three

L ater at the office, Deirdre notices that Nicolaus seems somber as he prepares for his board meeting. Today he is to present figures, and she knows he'd been working on the report for a few weeks. She knocks and enters his office. As usual, Nicolaus is smartly dressed in his expensive French suit, looking fine, sitting behind his desk, serious and studious over reports and figures. "Honey, are you okay?" she half whispers to him.

Nicolaus looks up at Deirdre. Her appearance is the thing he needed. Her pregnancy beauty is all about her. He smiles at his wife, happy that she cares about him as such, though she's always cared about him this way. He nods, "Yes. Thank you." He stands and goes to her. They hug each other as if it is just the very natural thing to do. "You are so beautiful," he tells her, as he often does.

Deirdre smiles up at him, wishing she could take away his emotional pain, and hopes she is helping him feel better in some small way. She knows his biggest hurdle in that meeting today is going to be the presence of Ceil.

The meeting got underway at half past ten in the morning. All twenty-five board members are present, including Ceil. Nicolaus has their new administrative assistant, Vinatalie Yeung, pass out the reports and exhibits to each board member. There is much chattering until Nigel calls the meeting to order. After stating there is no new announcements, Nigel gives Nicolaus the floor.

"Good morning! First, I'd like to acknowledge the passing of our dear Vice President, Alexander Collins, as all of you know. Dwight, the company and the board appreciate all the effort, time, and brain work Alexander gave to us. I miss him greatly, every day. He was my lifetime friend, more so, ... he was like a brother to me." Nicolaus frowns, feeling emotional again. He swallows the emotions down, sensing Ceil's eyes on him.

Dwight nods, with a painful smile, "Thank you for that, Nicolaus."

"We'd like to present you with this plaque." Nicolaus motions for Vinatalie to give the sealed wrapped box to Dwight. Dwight thanks her. He opens the nice packaging to find a beautiful wooden plaque with a blackfacing. The trade symbol of lawyers is engraved in deep gold over Alexander's name, title, and dates of life, which are also in gold.

Nicolaus continues, "To honor Alexander, we'd like to place the plaque on the wall, here in the conference room, next to a large photo of him. We'd like to honor Alexander, and ensure future generations of staff and lawyers have knowledge of him."

The board members clap and nod in support of this previously unknown and touching action to honor Alexander. Ceil remains silent, unmoving, and observant.

Dwight smiles and wants to cry. "Very sweet. Thank you all."

Some of the board members arise and go to Dwight to provide support, as Dwight is now full on crying. He receives hugs, handshakes, and shoulder squeezes. Nicolaus pauses the meeting to let this play out. He and Nigel go to Dwight, and hug him as well.

The meeting then resumes. "Second, I'd like to thank each of you for your votes in the last meeting to approve the directorship position for the foundation. I did see that additional funds were included for an administrative assistant for the department. Thank you. We currently are recruiting for this position.

Now, we can review the third quarter financial reports, which you have before you. You will see that we did very well in the third quarter, outperforming our second quarter, and we shot past our projected growth."

"Hold on here, Nicolaus, are these figures correct?" Nigel asks, sounding astonished.

Nicolaus nods, fully prepared for the questions he knew he'd be receiving. "Yes. I had accounting go over the figures three times, and then two additional times with me."

All the board members are looking at the figures. Some members make noises of shock, others smile, and some chat with their colleague.

"This says our profits are a billion, with a 'b'," one of the board members points out.

Nicolaus nods. "Yes! One point three billion. It's exciting!"

"For the third quarter, only?" Nigel questions him again.

"Yes. Now some of this profit is from the new clinics. Some of it is also from investors. And another portion is from our own investments. If you turn to page three of the report, there is a bar graph and a pie chart which breaks that down for you."

Nicolaus gives them some time to look over the data and digest the information before moving to the next item. Nicolaus expected flak from Ceil. Her silence makes him nervous.

"This is fantastic! We have never been able to reach figures like this for one quarter." Nigel is astounded.

"Well, we do have additional clinics, and new investments since you ran things. We have promoted Elsa Ravenell as a grant writer, and she will be seeking out grants for the foundation. As that grant money flows in, I'd like us to put less profits into the foundation, and re-invest those same profits back into the company. We'll have to do some analysis, and I don't want to overstate any figures, ... I think we should probably invest about twenty-five percent of our profits into growth guarantee and sustainable stocks such as gold, oil, and electricity."

The board members make affirming sounds.

"What type of return are we looking at if we do this Mr. Nicolaus?"

"Hmm, well, again, I don't want to make any overstatements. We'd have to do some research and studies to give you approximate projected numbers, ... we could probably expect a return of five to ten percent or more. I can get a workup for us."

"I don't know about electricity investing. Our has so much trouble with this."

"Yes, it's true. We would be looking at other states that are connected to the national grid, such as Colorado, New Mexico, and Nevada."

Dwight nods with approval. "Again, it's amazing how you are leading this company into the future, Nicolaus."

"Thank you, Dwight." Nicolaus smiles, "I'm trying."

Nigel is stuck on the third quarter profits. "This third quarter profit margin is ten times the amount we use to pull in. This is amazing, Nicolaus! Very well done, son, very well done!"

Humbly, "Thank you, father. Of course I cannot take full credit. We have a staff of wonderful, hardworking people, who are very professional, and they know their fields well. They certainly deserve most of the credit."

"Yes. Agreed!"

"What about the Drone Pharma merger? How is that doing?" a board member inquires.

Nicolaus sighs, "Well, we were supposed to have shipments of our requested list of seventy-five drugs for disbursement through prescriptions for the local partner pharmacies. We have a stall on this ..."

"Because of all the family drama?" interrupts a board member, trying to be funny.

"No, because of red tape, actually. We have a regulatory issue with the shipment. I have been in contact with government leaders, and as soon as I have an update, I'll send out an email to everyone.

It may need to be a little cryptic. I'll make sure you can understand it."

"Thank you, Mr. Nicolaus."

"Sure. And I'll get a workup of the investment figures. I'd like for us to have a vote on the investment plan, as I would like to see a group effort for decision making on this. I don't want it to be all me. And also, if you have investment ideas, please present them in our next meeting so we can discuss it. And I am open to helping with any research you may need. We don't have to rush into any of this. If we need a few meetings to arrive at a consensus, that is fine. We do have time."

"Nicolaus, this is great! I think we're impressed! Again!" A board member tells him.

Nicolaus chuckles, "Thank you." He sighs. "Well, that's all I have. I'll turn the meeting back over to my father. Father."

Nigel is still focused on the figures in the report. "Hmm? Oh! Thank you, Nicolaus. Anyone else have any business they'd like to discuss?" No one has anything. "Ceil?" Ceil shakes her head negatively. She is unusually quiet this whole meeting. "Okay, folks, meeting is adjourned."

Nicolaus stands and accepts compliments, and speaks with the board members as they shuffle out the boardroom. They are impressed with him. Some even acknowledge the good work he and Deirdre are doing abroad, separate of VMC. Nicolaus conversates with the board members for about a half hour more. Once they are all gone, Dwight, Ceil, and Nigel remain in the conference room.

Dwight brings Nicolaus into another hug. "Thank you so much for thinking of my Alexander. This is a wonderful gesture."

Nicolaus nods. "He's my Alexander too. I'm going to have a really hard time filling his shoes. I can't even think about that now."

"No, and it's okay. It takes time to get over tragedy. Neither of us is ready." Dwight hugs Nicolaus to him again. "Well, I'm going to show this to the wife, and I'll bring it back for mounting. Again, thank you, Nicolaus. This is very thoughtful."

Ceil continues to silently observe Nicolaus, even after Dwight leaves.

Nicolaus busies himself with straightening to quell some of the anxiety Ceil is causing inside of him. When he runs out of things to straighten, he faces up to Ceil, who is still sitting and watching him. He is glad his father is present in the room.

"Well, is there anything else either of you need?"

"Son," Nigel finally drops the report onto the conference table, "I'm very proud of you. My goodness, proud is an understatement! This is ... this is ... I can't even believe it. I don't have words. It's ... amazing!"

"Thank you, father. Hopefully, this trend will continue."

Nigel stands and hugs Nicolaus, really holding on to him, trying to make up for Ceil's nastiness and bullying behavior. "I'm very proud of you, son," he tells him again, breaking the hug, and giving Nicolaus a man pat to his back. Nigel turns to Ceil, "Let's go, Ceil. I'll buy you lunch downstairs."

Remaining silent and statuesque, Ceil finally stands and leaves the conference room with her husband. She finally sees Nicolaus as Nigel had seen him two years ago. She is also very much in awe of the success he's created within the company in such a short amount of time since he's taken over. However, there is no way she is going to let him know her thoughts. Continuing her disdain for him, she knew if she silently stared at him, it would make him uncomfortable and nervous. She wants to dismantle his confidence. The confidence and the success she knows Niall would never be able to obtain. Most certainly, Niall could not even closely acquire such confidence without her help.

As his parents leave the conference room, Nicolaus stares out the window upon the city below with arms crossed. He wants to take Deirdre and Constance and leave everything behind: his emotional pain, his family, his prominence, and the company. He wants to run from the massive responsibilities he carries, and just focus on Deirdre and the baby. He knows he can't leave the prestige garnered by his family and his ancestors; he cannot dismiss the power of his military experience and current position in life, nor can he walk away from the money that he has been blessed with in order to help others. He knows he must remain and carry on what he believes is God's will for him. His stress emerges again, and this time, instead of vomit through his guts, it is uncontrolled tears that spill from his eyes.

Chapter One Hundred Sixty-Four

Nicolaus insisted on taking Deirdre out to dinner to a fancy restaurant in downtown Austin. They want to take time to be away from everyone and spend time together, and also want to celebrate their many recent successes.

Nicolaus is always amazed when he and Deirdre are recognized, and even though they try to be discreet like regular people, at times like this, they are treated special. They are offered one of the best tables, and assigned the best server.

After about an hour, Nicolaus receives a text from Braylin of the state department, for a phone call at the next hour regarding Jonathan. Deirdre sends a text to Elsa and Nigel to alert them of the expected call.

Everyone is gathered in the sitting room when the call is received. State Department staff verify Nicolaus' identity, then pass the phone to Braylin.

"Hey Braylin, thanks so much for following up on this with us." Nicolaus loosens his tie and removes his suit jacket. "I've got all parties here, my father, Nigel Ravenell and his wife Ceil, my wife, Deirdre, Jonathan's daughter Elsa and her husband, also my brother, Niall."

"Great! Glad everybody is there. Makes it easier."

"Yes. So ... what were you able to find out?"

"Well, even though Mr. Baird does not work for any governmental agencies, we did find him, miraculously. And the good thing is, at the time of reach, he is alive."

Nicolaus nods. "Where is he?"

"He's in Glavischtein."

"Glavischtein? Where is that?" Nicolaus couldn't place the location.

"It's outside of Spain. A scarcely heard of, independent country."

Nicolaus frowns, "What's he doing there?"

"Well, we don't exactly know what business he has there. Apparently, ... and this is the bad news, he is being held by a drug cartel who hides in the mountains. He's being held in the mountain closest to Benlloch village. He's been there for some time, our source tells me. The militia he usually carries with him is not seen. So we don't know if he was there on business, if he was making a drug deal, or if he stumbled upon them. And we do not know about his men, if they are imprisoned as well, or if a worse fate has occurred."

"Jesus! Will you be sending a team to get him out of there?"

"Mmm, not exactly. There is more bad news. We can't, Nicolaus. If I send a team, the president has to sign off on it. And we have a delegate treaty with both Spain and Glavischtein, which actually prohibits such actions. So guess what, the president will never sign off on it."

"Wait a minute. He's an American citizen. You can't send active duty to rescue him? What about retired ops?"

"Nicolaus, we can't send anybody. Sending equals a mission, and a mission has to be signed off by the president."

Nicolaus sits back on the couch. He sighs, putting his hands behind his head.

"Is my father all right?" Elsa asks.

Braylin hesitates. "Ah, ma'am, ... we cannot say for sure. We do know he is being tortured. This has been confirmed."

"Oh my God, why would they torture my father?"

Nicolaus sits up. "It's standard procedure for a cartel, Elsa. Sorry about that."

Elsa frowns, and feels very bad for her father. She wants to cry, thinking of his suffering, even though she knew he had caused others to suffer in his lifetime, as well.

"And sorry, but there is more bad news. My source tells me they will be moving him in seven, now six days. We know where he is today, however, once they move him ... we won't know where he'll be. We'll most likely lose contact."

"So then, Braylin, this is Nigel, what can be done?"

"Well, Sir, this is the very difficult part to hear. We, the state department, cannot do anything. I noted our restrictions. However, you can either try to go get him yourself, or hire someone to try to extract him. We cannot stop you from doing this. You can try to negotiate his freedom, however, we will not be involved in any way, and will not help with any communications. And please understand, dealing with a cartel is very dangerous and deadly business."

"Oh my God! Those are our only options?" Nicolaus asks.

"Yes. And unfortunately, it will be very difficult and costly to hire a team to go where most people have never heard of, to deal with a drug cartel. And you only have a small window. I doubt you'd get anyone, and honestly, not before four weeks."

"Well, that is not going to work," Nigel comments.

"Luckily, for your family, you have an expert on hand in Nicolaus, who has faced these types of situations before."

"Me?" This discussion took an unexpected turn. Nicolaus shakes his head. "I can't go, my wife is about to have our baby. And I have a business to run, and projects to oversee."

"Oh Nicky! Please!" Elsa pleads with him. "They're torturing my father. They will probably kill him."

"I've never even heard of Glavischtein. I know nothing about that place."

"Well, of course we'd give you access to all resources. We can even supply you with up to four assets."

"Wait a minute, you can do all that, including give me guys, but you can't send them over to extract him?"

"Remember, we cannot send anyone. However, we can assist you, Nicolaus. Or whomever you get to extract him."

Nicolaus sits back onto the couch again. His stress level just went through the roof.

"Oh my God! Anything else for us, Braylin?" Quickly he sits up with another thought. "What about the local law enforcement in Glavischtein? Can't you partner with them for an extraction? That seems more ... efficient."

"The complication here is that the cartel provide for the locals, which is not uncommon for cartels to do, to keep the people loyal in the city where they operate. We have tried and we did not get movement on this from the local law enforcement. And, they are in a village, so any law officers would be small in number, the cartel members would heavily outnumber their force. Most likely why the cartel picked this place for operations to begin with."

"Nicky, you have to help my father. Please!" Elsa pleads again.

"Braylin, can we call you back? We need to discuss this."

"Of course! You have my number there on your phone. I'll be on standby."

"Thank you."

Nicolaus ends the call. "Elsa, I appreciate your belief in my abilities, but ... I couldn't even begin to think about how to do this." He pulls Deirdre to him. "And Deirdre is too close to delivery. Four weeks away. I can't leave her." He frowns.

"Nicky, I know my father is not the best person. And that you've had your differences with him, ..."

"Differences? Your father doesn't even like me! He forced me away from Deirdre," he reminds everyone. "I'm not really sure I'd be willing to risk my life to extract him. Look, this would be really dangerous. And in a mountain? God knows what that means. Are they at the top? In a mountain side? On a steep slope? Off a cliff? Too many variables."

"So, we're willing to just ... let my father die over there?" Elsa poses the question to the family with anguish. She does not want such a fate befalling her father.

Nicolaus shrugs, "It's a calculated risk that he chose to take, Elsa. He's not a child."

"Nicky, I once heard you say, that if one of us was captured, you'd want someone to rescue us. Doesn't my father deserve the same? He is one of us. He's family. Mine and yours. And now we know he's being tortured." Elsa eloquently argues for her father.

"Well, maybe we can find somebody to hire to go over there," Nigel offers.

"Oh Pops, thank you. Anything!" Elsa pleads again.

Nicolaus sighs. "That's really a non-starter, father."

"Well, what else can we do? We really don't have a choice. How do we even go about finding someone for something like this?"

"You have to put feelers out to retired ops, and see if anyone responds."

"What's that again?" Nigel frowns, not exactly understanding what Nicolaus is saying. "Retired vets, who were in operations or special forces, like I was."

"Oh! How do we do this?"

Nicolaus and Nigel rise to get moving on a process. Nigel stops Nicolaus by the shoulder, and looks back. "Ah, Niall ... you joining us?"

Niall and Ceil had not said one word. Niall feels out of the loop, because he knows nothing about any of this. He stands, and joins his father and brother, as they go into the library. Immediately, Niall's mind wonders onto Deirdre. Being in this room reminds him of ... not the discipline he received from his brother for putting his hands on Deirdre, it reminds him of what his twisted plans are for Deirdre.

In the other room, Deirdre comforts Elsa. She texts her mother to let her know what is happening.

Chapter One Hundred Sixty-Five

A nother day passes, which is closer to the window of rescue opportunity closing in on Jonathan. Nigel receives several responses to his request for help from retired ops members, however, they each declined, and several noted there is not enough time to prepare for such a rescue. Not enough time to pull a team together.

Deirdre notices that after work, Nicolaus has taken to his office space within their massively large bedroom. She stands behind him, encircling her arms around his shoulders. Suddenly she sees that he has several maps of the area where Jonathan is being held on his computer screen, also, she see several tabs open to webpages, and books strewn across the desk. She can see that he is studying one of the maps.

"Nicolaus, what's happening? Are you going?"

Nicolaus sighs, and pulls his wife onto his lap. "I don't want to leave you," is the first thing he makes clear. "None of this feels right." He looks down in thought, then back to his wife. "We aren't having any luck with the responses from retired special ops individuals." He sighs again with a frown. "I don't know what to do. I should at least be prepared."

Deirdre gently takes his face in her hands. "Nicky, I don't want you to go either. No more missions, remember?" She put her forehead to his. "I ... I don't want you not to go because of me. You have to do what you think is right, what you think God wants you to do. We have to make a decision that we can live with if something worse were to happen to Elsa's father."

"None of this feels right," he complains again, frowning.

"Do you think you can get to him, and get out of there quickly, without getting hurt?"

Nicolaus shakes his head, moving his wife off his lap. He stands, sighing again, feeling very stressed. "That's never a given. In all rescues there is a risk of getting hurt, or even killed. And having to deal with mountains is very tricky, and who knows how long that could take. And if Elsa's father is hurt, carrying him out would take even longer. I think all this feels blind, like pieces are missing. I'm not sure the state department is being completely straight about this situation. Or maybe they just don't have enough information to pass along."

He and Deirdre embrace, and then he gets back to studying the materials.

When Nicolaus finally joins Deirdre in bed, he holds her tight and very close to him. Deirdre finds herself already very worried. She holds onto Nicolaus. She does not want him to go to Glavischtein, or Spain, or anywhere else. She does not want him to have to risk his life.

She prays that another path forward would reveal itself to them in the morning.

Chapter One Hundred Sixty-Six

When morning arrives, Deirdre knew when Nicolaus cancelled his early morning run, and instead is on the phone with Braylin, that he'd decided he had to be the one to go get Elsa's father. He made calls to leaders at VMC to inform them of the emergency situation, and he provided them instructions. He made a call to the Bishop to ask for prayers, which they both receive over the phone. Deirdre does not argue or plead with Nicolaus not to go, though she really wants to. She can see that he is already in his special forces frame of mind, which meant for him, there is no turning back, no changing his decision.

Deirdre watches Nicolaus dress himself in his unofficial camouflage military fatigues, including the bulletproof vest he wore underneath, which she knew meant he intended to be very quick about the rescue. She also knew the military fatigues with the American flag patch on the arm is also a scare tactic to enemies.

Nicolaus gave her directives with an authoritative tone of his voice, knowing she'd understand this meant she needs to follow his instructions to the letter. "Roddy is on vacation in France, and Manfred is unavailable. So, until father hires security for you, I don't want you by yourself. You must have Mom, Ishani, or Maggie with you at all times until I'm back. You should get Ishani and Maggie to move in so they will already be here to help you. If the security arrangement falls through, just go to your house, with Mom present. I don't want you to be alone, Deirdre."

"Yes, darling."

"And no driving to work. Have the driver take you and bring you home."

"Yes, darling."

He takes Deirdre in his arms, and looks at her seriously, "And no working overtime." He touches her belly which encased Nicolai, his soon to be born son. "Try not to stress too much. And make sure you eat normally. I want my son born perfectly healthy."

Deirdre lays her head on his strong shoulder. "Yes, darling." She wills herself not to cry. She wants to be strong.

Nicolaus moves her to face him again. "And of course, I know you'll handle any matters for the Darfurian families. I don't want you traveling, whatsoever, Deirdre. You delegate."

"Yes, darling." Deirdre replaces her head on his strong shoulder. She knows he is trying to think of everything.

Nicolaus pulls Deirdre to sit on the nearby chair. "Now Deirdre, I have to go completely dark for this rescue. That means I can't have any electronics on me. I'm not even taking my phone. I'll send you communication once I am in Spain, close to Glavischtein, but then I can't contact you again until we are completely out of danger."

Deirdre touches his face. "I understand."

"I'm sorry I have to miss the baby shower on Saturday. I want you to have fun. Have them take lots of photos for me."

"Of course, darling."

Nicolaus pulls Deirdre into a full embrace hug. They kiss passionately.

Nicolaus grabs his duffle bag which has all his essentials, and he effortlessly swoops Deirdre into his muscular arms, as he loves to do. They kiss passionately again before he carries her and Nicolai down the stairs, not taking his eyes from her.

Constance made it to the mansion in the early morning hours, worried about what may be taking place. Nigel filled her in. She enters the kitchen to help with breakfast. When Nicolaus arrives at the breakfast room, he is surprised to see all the family and Helena gathered, even though it is early. He figures his father had alerted them.

Nicolaus carefully places Deirdre on her feet, and sits her in her usual place next to him. He is greeted by a kiss from Constance and a plate of her special pancakes.

"You did this for me, Mom?" He returns the kiss. "These are my favorite." With a smile, Constance sets a plate for him and Deirdre. The staff bring in more plates of pancakes for the rest of the family, along with add-ins of meats, fruits, and potatoes.

"Oh, I remember these!" Nigel comments with delight as he tastes the pancakes.

Deirdre watches Nicolaus, as if this may be the last time she sees him. She observes his beautifully handsome face, his thick soft wavy hair which is cropped on the top with a semi-short fade, his light brown eyes, his strong jaw line which holds straight, white teeth, his smooth light caramel skin coloring, his muscular shoulders, his sturdy back, his capable arms, his soft hands, his powerful torso, his solid legs, his large masculine feet. She thought about the things she couldn't see which is within Nicolaus; his pious spirit, his strong work ethic, his good heart, his love for people, his integrity, his intelligence, his generosity, his love for her. She wants to sob her heart out all over the place. She controls her emotions, as she does not want to make Nicolaus feel bad about leaving. In the end, he is doing the right thing. He always chooses to do the right thing.

Helena is sitting to the right of Deirdre, she touches her hand, wanting to cry herself. She could feel Deirdre's desperation, and sees that she is keeping it in check, trying to be strong for Nicolaus.

"Nicky, you know it's not your responsibility to go do this," Helena notes aloud, hoping to change his thinking, not wanting him to go on such a dangerous rescue. Nigel and Ceil had filled her in on what is happening.

"Helena, please, don't. We've already been through this, as a family," Elsa chastises her, not wanting her to try to change Nicolaus' mind, or put a bad jive on things.

After a few bites, Nicolaus notices Deirdre isn't eating. He picks up her fork and puts some food on it, placing it to her delicate mouth to feed her. "Okay babe, you've got to nourish my son. He wants some of these delicious pancakes too!"

Deirdre giggles to keep from crying. She eats the food on the fork before her, bringing a smile to him. They peck kiss.

Nicolaus takes more bites of food, then addresses Helena. "Well ... Helena, I thank you for your words." He nods. "I have taken on the responsibility. We were not able to hire anyone, we tried." Nicolaus eyes momentarily land on Niall, who has remained completely silent on the issue of rescuing his father-in-law, "and someone has to try to retrieve him. I think it will be okay. Don't worry." Nicolaus continues eating.

Deirdre has her father's necklace in her hand. Without words, she puts it on Nicolaus.

He touches it, smiling at her, remembering the intention. He remembers this is the lucky necklace that always brought her father home, the one he was not wearing when he left so many years ago. Nicolaus knows Deirdre expects him to bring it back, to return with the necklace.

Not wasting a moment of time, as Nicolaus finished his plate of food, he phones Francesca. "Francesca, thanks for checking in with me while you've been gone. How is everything over there?"

She balks and chuckles. "As if I had a choice about checking in! Why are you ringing so early? I'm chilling with a special someone. And he's gorgeous too."

"What? 'She's met someone'", he whispers to the family, his hand momentarily over the receiver. "Don't go rushing into anything, Francesca."

She chuckles again. "Does Deirdre know you're this bossy? Good Lord, man!"

"Hey, I have to leave for a while, and I'll be off the radar, so you check in with father or Niall. Okay?"

"Off the radar?" She sits up, recognizing that military term. "Nicky, where are you going? What's happening?" She asks frowning, suddenly feeling worried.

He sighs. "Look, I can't really talk now," he looks at his watch, "I've got to go. Deirdre and Elsa will fill you in. Just know that I love you, and I'll see you soon. And be sure to check in every day, Francesca."

"Okay, wait, ah ... well ... I love you too, Nicky." She skips her thoughts to the most important part of the call. She hated being rushed, as she needs to discuss what she'd found in the family history. She wanted to talk to Nicolaus about it later today. She'd found the word 'needus' (curse) in the writing. She is not sure of the rest of the translation, though somehow, this issue seems to veil the day. And now, this call. "Nicky, whatever you're doing, please ... be careful."

"Always."

Nicolaus ends the call and hands his phone to Deirdre. "Well, it's time to go." He pulls the duffle bag on his shoulder.

Elsa takes his hands. "Nicky, thank you. I know this isn't easy. I thank you."

Nicolaus nods. "Sure." He gives Elsa a quick peck to her face cheek and a hug.

Nicolaus receives a shoulder squeeze from Nigel.

Helena hugs him, feeling his muscular body upon her. She kisses his face, then smacks his lips, and hugs him again.

Constance touches Nicolaus on the face and smiles up at him. They hug and he gives her a forehead kiss.

Niall and Ceil mill around somewhere in the background of things.

It is Deirdre who lands in his arms for the last goodbye. They go outside on the breezeway to the front of the mansion for privacy. Nicolaus hugs Deirdre tightly, and grasps her lips, touching her belly. "I love you so much!" he tells her.

"And I love you, my darling. Be careful, my love. Return to us."

They kiss passionately one last time before parting, Nicolaus having to tear himself away from her, as usual.

Nicolaus gets into the limousine and the driver steers the vehicle down the cobblestone path out the gates, and towards the airport. Nicolaus expects to return with Jonathan in about a weeks' time. More than enough time to see his son born into the world.

Deirdre re-enters the mansion with a mass of tears streaming down her face. She hugs Elsa, who looks worried and sad. "It's going to be okay, Elsa," Deirdre comforts her, barely holding herself together. "Nicky will bring your father home."

Chapter One Hundred Sixty-Seven

W hen Nicolaus arrives in Glavischtein, he meets up with his team, who will be helping him rescue Jonathan. They meet in the hotel lobby. Four young men, two dressed casually, the others, the youngest and the oldest, dressed in military fatigues. For a nominal fee, Nicolaus secures a small meeting room so they can talk. He closes the door.

"Nicolaus Ravenell!" the youngest man sounds like he is star struck. His eyes are wide, and his hand is out toward Nicolaus, waiting for a handshake. "I can't believe I get to serve with you, Sir!" He says loudly, chest out and standing tall. He has the utmost respect for Nicolaus Ravenell, the military hero, who is decorated four times for valor. "It's the honor of a lifetime, Sir!"

Nicolaus takes his hand to shake it. "Son, how old are you?"

"Nineteen, Sir! Just turned."

"Okay, this will not be that formal. Serious yes, formal no. You can call me Nicolaus."

The young man relaxed. "Wow! Yes Sir! I mean ... Nicolaus."

"What's your name, son?"

"James."

"James, you're very young," Nicolaus frowns.

The other young men step up to meet Nicolaus, with hands out to greet him. Each introduce themselves, and state their age, seeing that is of interest to Nicolaus.

"I'm Sergey, nineteen."

"Joshua, twenty-five."

"Manny, Sir, nineteen."

"Wow. Any of you seen combat?"

Joshua is the only among them to raise his hand.

"Mission work?"

Again, Joshua is the only one to raise his hand.

"Field training?" Nicolaus is hoping they at least had that. All their hands go up, however, Nicolaus is not relieved. He sighs, realizing the state department sent him newbies. This would be a first mission for James, Manny and Sergey. This is no time for training fresh, snot-nosed recruits, as the military training camp leaders would call them. There is not time for anything, except to get going.

Nicolaus sighs, his stress level going up again. He puts his hands to his hips as he looks over the assets, and wonders if he should take them at all. Perhaps only Joshua, and send the rest back home.

"Nicolaus, I know what you're thinking, Sir," James starts at him. "You think we cannot get this job done. Sir, we are trained. We know the mission. We are willing to go. We are willing to risk our lives to serve our country and to rescue your father-in-law, Sir."

Nicolaus smiles, and puts his hand on James' shoulder. "You can knock it off with the sir stuff. So you feel like you can do this?"

"Yes." James answers, standing tall, with great confidence. "I've been hunting and fishing since I was young. I'm first in my training class, first in my cadet class, first in my academic class."

"Oh, so you could be somewhat helpful," Nicolaus half jokes with him. He sighs. "What about the rest of you? Sergey and Manny?"

"Oh, I'm willing to go sir, ... I mean Nicolaus. I'm ready. I'm not afraid," Manny makes clear.

"I'm ready!" Sergey agrees.

Nicolaus looks to Joshua. "What do you think, Joshua? If I put you second in command, you think you can handle these guys?"

"Oh yes Sir. I've managed and led squadrons of ten to twelve before."

Nicolaus nods, deciding to put his trust in the young men. They seem to be willing to give their lives for the job, which is what is asked of each and every military person, no matter their age, rank or military branch.

Nicolaus remembers when he'd joined up when he was eighteen, fresh out of high school. He was also willing to put himself out on dangerous missions, which is partly why he was promoted through the ranks so quickly.

"Okay, so unfortunately, I don't have the full picture of what we will be stepping into. We must be quiet and discreet this whole mission, even in this hotel. Do not draw any attention to yourselves. We will start early in the morning, at five a.m. We will hike five miles up the north side of the mountain. We'll see a compound with a red house. The red house is where Jonathan is being held. I don't know what shape he'll be in. He's being tortured, so we'll need to prepare to carry him down. I don't know how many guards they will have. For sure they will have firepower. I always prefer not using our weapons, however in this case, we take out whomever we need to, there will be no love lost. This is a cartel, and for sure they will use their weapons against us first and foremost. We'll take them all out if we have to. Any questions?"

No one has questions. "I'm putting Joshua as second in command, so you will address him with any problems. There will be absolutely no alcoholic drinking. For this evening, we will eat our meal together, then retire to our rooms and get rested. Tomorrow is going to be tough. In the morning you pack fruit, protein bars, and lots of water. Make sure we have the soft stretcher, and we should each have first aid kits." They all nod in agreement.

Nicolaus touches each of their shoulders, then they stand in a circle and pile their hands in solidarity and teamwork.

Chapter One Hundred Sixty-Eight

I shani and Maggie did a wonderful job on the baby shower for Deirdre, and it is hugely successful. Over one hundred guests attend, not only colleagues and friends, also celebrities. Deirdre has her curly, thick dark hair done up, and she is dressed fashionably in a light blue, leg slit maternity gown, looking stunning, yet elegant. The dress has long, chiffon tailored sleeves. The bodice accentuates her bosom and wraps around the baby. Long material streams from the bodice to the floor, with perfectly creased vertical folds, flowing as she walks. She appears as a princess.

Niall lurks in the background and watches everything. He cannot take his eyes from Deirdre. Observing her emphasized beauty increases his want for her one hundred fold. He is having trouble keeping control of himself, despite the presence of all the guests and his wife. Even though Deirdre's standing in the elite community is higher than ever before, Niall cannot think of her beyond a sexual conquest.

Jeune Tran, who recorded Deirdre's first interview, when she was first preparing to marry Nicolaus a few years back, before they were forced apart, attended as a friend and not as a reporter. Jeune is truly happy for Deirdre. Ms. Winfree is in charge of the baby games, and she brought the biggest gift. Down to the last gift item, Ms. Winfree gestures for the staff to roll out the top of the line baby food maker. Deirdre gets up from her chair of honor and hugs Ms. Winfree.

Deirdre had assigned one of the staff to take the pictures of each item and with the person who gifted it. As Deirdre hugs Ms. Winfree, she calls her mom and Ceil over to get into the picture. Mostly, Deirdre had the two mothers join in all the pictures.

The love for Nicolai is very strong in the room, as he is one of the most anticipated babies in Texas, and in the nation. Deirdre and Nicolaus would not have to buy him anything. They received bottle warmers, diaper wipe warmers, strollers, a baby gym, a top of the line baby swing, lots of cute clothes, and many, many more gifts. She even received handmade cards and pictures from the young Darfurian girls they helped to rescue. Deirdre could not have imagined all this. She knows God is blessing Nicolai, who she and Nicolaus believes is a gift to the world.

During the baby shower, just before the cake cutting, three dozen beautiful large Darcy roses are delivered to Deirdre from Nicolaus. The roses are overwhelmingly beautiful. In addition, Nicolaus sent a special delivery letter to coincide with the arrival of the roses.

"We also have a letter from Nicolaus! It's from Spain! He sent it through an international courier service," Nigel loudly announces to the crowd of ladies, while holding the letter in the air so they could all see it. Happy hoots and hollers and joyful noises are heard throughout the large crowd of women. Nigel hands the unopened letter to Deirdre.

Deirdre holds the letter to her chest. She seems to be frozen in time. Constance sees that Deirdre is now trembling. To take the attention off her daughter, Constance begins the cake cutting.

The rest of the party is a blur for Deirdre. All she can think about is the letter she holds in her hand, and to her chest, from her love, her Nicolaus. The baby shower came to an end. Deirdre remained sitting in the honor chair, as the guests kiss her face and bid her goodbye with well wishes for the baby. Deirdre accepts their hugs and kisses, even though her mind is solely on Nicolaus.

Once all the guests are gone, Deirdre remains sitting, staring at the beautiful flowers, holding the letter to her chest, over her heart. She had been doing so well to hold herself together, though now she is about to fall apart. The silent tears stream, as she seems to be shaken.

First Constance and Helena are next to her, supporting her, then Ishani and Maggie. Elsa, and even Ceil rush to Deirdre as her crying blurts out in hyperventilation. Nicolaus' love for her literally takes her breath away. The separation is too much, and she is unable to breathe, unable to get air.

"Okay, Deirdre. Calm down, now, honey. Take deep breaths," Constance instructs her.

After a few minutes, Deirdre is breathing normally again. She points to the roses. "It's the trinity," she tells them. "Three dozen roses. The trinity of protection, the Father, the Son, and the Holy Spirit."

"Isn't ... that clever of Nicky." Helena comments, staring at the beautiful flowers, suddenly seeing them differently. She is always amazed at this couple and their wonderfulness. She realized she'd never received any such thing from Joel. Once he gave her roses, ... only once, in their twenty year marriage. Her heart pines for Nicolaus.

Deirdre stands to go to her room. She wants to be close to Nicolaus. She has spent much time there, since he's been gone. All the ladies walk along with her, including Ceil. Deirdre sits on the romantically draped bed, and several of the ladies follow her lead.

Elsa lays back, her arms over her head. She imagines the romantic magic that happens in this room. She laid on the bed where she knows Nicolaus makes sweet, gentle love to Deirdre. She could only wish this for herself.

Helena had not been in their bedroom, as no one had, until recently. Nicolaus and Deirdre kept this room private for themselves. Helena's mind goes wild with desirous thoughts of Nicolaus. Tenderly, she sits on the bed, imagining him there.

Deirdre doesn't notice any of the fantasizing about her husband going on around her. She is still trembling, the letter clenched to her chest. Constance sits next to her, with Ishani and Maggie close by.

Ceil stands on the other side of the room, near the dresser. "Well, aren't you even going to read the letter?" She asks Deirdre, in a somewhat cold tone. "You'll probably feel better if you read it."

Deirdre shakes her head, "I can't!" she cries out, her trembling more visible.

"Oh, now." Constance puts an arm around her daughter.

Suddenly, Deirdre sees an opening to Ceil for Nicolaus. Trembling hands hold out the letter to Ceil. "I can't. You read it."

Ceil is taken aback. "Me?"

Deirdre nods. "Please. You read it. I can't."

Silence falls over the room. Constance nods to Ceil. Gently, Ceil takes the letter, treating it carefully, as Deirdre would. Cautiously, she removes the letter from the hotel stationery envelope. She sees the handwriting of Nicolaus. The letter is several pages, tri-folded, and sealed with a red heart sticker. Ceil breaks the seal and opens the letter.

Deirdre lays her head on Constance's shoulder, in preparation to listen to the words of her loving and kind husband, her Nicolaus, who she greatly misses, and has extreme worry for his safety. The ladies intensely listen as Ceil begins to read the flowing words of love Nicolaus has written, the love weaved words of a devoted husband who immensely loves and cherishes his wife, words which were only meant for Deirdre's eyes:

To my most precious, heaven created, truly one and only wife, Deirdre,

> *I hope this letter has found you on the day our community has come together to shower their love on the human result of our love union, Little Nicolai. Inside, I am exploding with anticipation of his arrival. I cannot wait to greet my*

son with a loving kiss to his head, which will be holding the brain of a genius and one who will love humanity. Of this I am certain.

Every day, I am so very grateful that you are in my life and have been in my life for years. I am also very grateful that you agreed to be my wife, and I look forward to the many years that we will be spending together, God willing. I'd be nothing without you, Deirdre, my sweet, sweet love.

I may not be near you at present, however, I do see you as if you were standing right here beside me in Spain. I see your beautiful heart-shaped face, your perfectly shaped eyebrows, your half inch long eye lashes that flutter when I kiss you on the neck or when I touch your womanly sweetness. I see your beautiful light green eyes, the eyes that melt my heart whenever you look at me. I see that beautiful nose that is inherited from your Greek ancestors. I see your little ears that hover over one of my favorite parts of your body, your long soft neck. I love to kiss your neck because I know what kissing you there does to you. I see that beautiful tanned colored skin that covers the beautiful heart in your chest. The beautiful heart that belongs to the lost children of the world, and has a little room left for me and our own children to be. Then the next of my favorites I see, your soft, beautiful bosom. The only bosom in the world that I love to touch and kiss, that were created just for me. I also remember what touching you there does.

The ladies couldn't help making positive noises and fan themselves at the words of hot passion and love sent through that letter. Deirdre is all smiles with tears, her heart beating very fast for Nicolaus.

And then your womb, which holds the embodiment of my love for you, our son.

I prayerfully think of you every minute of every day since I have been away. I'm hurt to my heart to be away from you. Every day I am separated from you tears at my soul. I miss being near you as we breathe the same breath. I miss hearing the rhythm of your heart, making mine beat with joy. Your very presence advances me through each day. For now, being away from you, I hold on, waiting to take you in my arms, waiting to kiss your God created sweet lips, and waiting to remind you how much I love you.

I know you are praying for me because I can feel your prayers. I am certain you received my message of the trinity through the flowers. You have always been and always will be the love of my life. Though I understand that my life is small compared to others, and some may not think much of me, it is all I have and what I pledge to you, my life, my love, my being, to love you always.

Tears flow from more ladies than Deirdre in that room. Even Ceil is touched by the words.

Please remember my instructions to you, keep yourself safe. I plan to return before the birth of Nicolai. I want to hold you, and help you through the birth of our first son. I can only imagine his siblings being born soon behind him.

With love from all of my heart, which beats only to love you and to serve God,

Your most devoted husband, Nicolaus.

Ceil sighs. She'd never read any such words of love addressed to herself from her own husband. She'd never read such words of love at all. The room is very quiet, the ladies wiping their tears, as Ceil gently refolds the letter and places it in its envelope. In silence, and with a smile, Ceil hands the letter to Deirdre. She feels regretful for having tried to break them apart, now seeing how strong their love is for each other.

"Thank you, Mother Ceil." Deirdre tells Ceil, with a smile, knowing the gesture touched her as did Nicolaus' words. Looking at the letter with Nicolaus' handwriting, Deirdre places it over her heart again.

Chapter One Hundred Sixty-Nine-TW

L ater that night, Deirdre has the staff draw her a lukewarm
bath. She places several of the rose petals of the flowers from
Spain, into the water. Her mind is filled with thoughts of Nicolaus.
Worry is at the surface of her thoughts as she lays back into the
bathwater and tries to relax. Exhausted from the wonderful day of
love and caring from so many friends and family, Deirdre sits back,
closes her eyes, and meditates on thoughts of her love for Nicolaus.

A smile beams across Deirdre's face when she remembers them
being together. She thinks about the first time he proposed
marriage to her when she was only fifteen years old. Deirdre
remembers that she'd always known that she would marry
Nicolaus, she'd always felt that they'd be together. She visualizes
their wedding day in Estonia, and chuckles about how surprised
Nicolaus was on that beautiful day. Deirdre thinks about when
they were in Denver, thinking about how to help the families of
Darfur, and how they made plans together for their biggest project
yet. She smiles when remembering the looks on the faces of the
families from Darfur when they greeted them into their hotel
shelter. Deirdre's mind goes into prayers for Nicolaus. She prays for
his protection and for success at retrieving Elsa's father.

Meanwhile, across the ocean, Nicolaus and his team begin the
five mile hike up the north side of the mountain. They should
have a good head start under the cover of darkness so that the
villagers do not notice them. By the time the sun is fully up, they
will be more than a mile up the mountainside. In the darkness, they
must be careful and watch their steps, and be mindful of snakes,
scorpions, and wild animals that may be lurking.

At this same time back in Austin, Deirdre opens her eyes and
finds Niall standing over her. She's shocked that he would enter
her private space. She gasps of fear, however, before she can get any

593

words out, his hand is tightly around her neck, and he shoves her under the water. Deirdre fights against him, and he lifts her up for a second or two to let her get air, then pushes her completely under the water, his grip tight around her neck, in full control of her.

Smiling at the power he has over her, Niall easily takes the action to assault Deirdre with his other hand, not caring what special day it is for her, or that Nicolaus is in harm's way to rescue his father-in-law.

Niall pulls Deirdre up by the throat for a second, for which she tries to breathe with great difficulty, then he plunges her under the water again, while fully assaulting her. Without mercy, Niall repeats this action several times.

Deirdre believes he intends to drown her.

In bed, a world away, in Johannesburg, Abigail is suddenly awakened from her sleep. She has trouble breathing, as her twin reflex kicks in, however she does not know the reflex is what is happening to her. Abigail grabs her throat and gasps for air.

Dominique is in the bed across the large room they sometimes share in sisterhood. She sits up with her fashionable, furry sleep mask on, just now remembering to pull it up. Her golden silk pajamas glow in the dark room, lit by the moon that shines through the oval glass ceiling windows. Dominique sees that Abigail is having trouble, and she goes to her.

On the other side of the Ravenell mansion, Ceil wonders why Niall went to Nicolaus' wing of the mansion at such a late hour. When he hadn't returned, she went to investigate. She grabs Constance, and they go into the bathroom to check on Deirdre, only to find the horrid scene.

Constance rushes over. "Deirdre!" she screams in fright.

"Get your hands off her," Ceil yells at Niall. "Release her! Now!"

Embarrassed, being caught in the act of assaulting Deirdre, Niall immediately releases Deirdre, with a finger lick of defiance toward Ceil.

Deirdre chokes on water, as air enters her lungs, causing her to harshly cough.

Constance covers Deirdre and helps her out of the bathtub. She looks at Niall with harsh disdain, but says nothing.

Ceil shakes her head, feeling grave disappointment, standing a distance from her younger son. "I told you!" she shouts at him. "I told you, that girl will drive you to madness. And here we are ... you acting like a buffoon!" she shouts at him. "You cannot possibly think your actions are okay."

Niall does not know what to say. He looks in the direction of Deirdre's whimpering.

"You get out of this house," Ceil tells him sternly. "You get out!" She shouts at him. "And I don't want you back here until Nicolaus has returned. Do you hear me?"

Niall looks at his mother in shock. He frowns, having a sudden understanding that she is throwing him out of the house. For the first time ever, his mother is throwing him out.

"You have caused harm. You will get out!" Ceil furiously shouts at him.

Niall nods in silence. He leaves.

Chapter One Hundred Seventy

"Well, did you swallow some gum or a mint or something?" Dominique questions Abigail. All of a sudden she seems fine.

"No, I didn't have anything."

"Maybe you're having an allergic reaction to something."

Abigail looks at her best friend with a side-eyed frown. Abigail grabs up her phone and begins to search the internet for happenings with Deirdre and Nicolaus.

"Oh my God, Abbey, what are you doing?"

"Maybe something happened today."

Dominique grabs the phone out of Abigail's hands, and slaps it on her nightstand. She takes Abigail by the shoulders. "Okay, you are going to stop this! I have known you all my life, and you have never had weird symptoms like this before."

"I think something may be wrong with Deirdre."

"And what ... you can feel it?" Dominique looks at her with doubt.

"Yes ... I think so," Abigail frowns, knowing she sounds crazy.

"How so, Abbey? You didn't feel anything before. This doesn't make sense."

"Dominique, maybe I did and just didn't know it. Or maybe nothing happened to her before," she reasoned.

Dominique sighs, and hands Abigail her water that is on her nightstand. "Hon, it's late. If you are okay now, let's try to figure this out in the morning. Okay? This diva needs her beauty rest," she says referring to herself.

Abigail nods. She sips the water, her throat feeling better. She is certain she is not going to be sleeping for the rest of the night. Her investigative mind is now filled with worry.

. . . .

Chapter One Hundred Seventy-One

Ceil actually apologizes to Deirdre for Niall's appalling behavior. She let the ladies know that she had made him leave the house, and that he would not be bothering them again. This certainly put them all at ease, as Ishani and Maggie remained with them overnight.

Unfortunately, as Nicolaus and his team trekked five miles up the side of a mountain to get his father-in-law, Niall returns to the house in the early morning hours, as Ceil had not taken his keys, nor alerted security, nor the staff. She expected Niall to do what she told him; however, she is mistaken. The reality is, he's never done what she's told him to do.

Niall's lust for Deirdre is excessively strong, as he'd forgotten all about making a change in his life, his obsession for her completely taking over him. He'd grown angry about the baby, and about the way Deirdre ignores him at every turn. He is determined to have Deirdre while Nicolaus is away.

Everyone is fast asleep in their respective bedrooms when Niall enters the mansion, shewing the staff away, after they let him in. Quietly, he makes his way to where he knows he should not be. Niall quashes the consciousness of his mind that tells him to turn back, or to at least go to his own wife. His feet, and maybe a streak of twisted darkness, leads him into transgression.

Deirdre stirs from unease and uncomfortableness. She is dressed in the special nightgown her mother bought her for her pregnancy. Constance sweetly bought Deirdre designer gowns for each night of her last month of pregnancy to accentuate the specialness of finally being married to Nicolaus, and them finally beginning their family.

Stirring, Deirdre sits right up into the arms of Niall. Immediately, his hand goes around her throat again, in a tightened grip to keep her from screaming for help.

On the other side of the world, Nicolaus decides to rest the team, as the hike is moderately difficult, and the strong sun is beaming on them, heating them up. They can see the compound from where they are. They quietly rest and refresh with water. Soon they will be entering the cartel's compound in attempts to rescue Jonathan.

Back in Austin, Deirdre became very frightened of what Niall might do. She is so shocked at his behavior towards her. She cannot believe he had entered her bedroom, the sacred space she shares with Nicolaus, only to attack her.

Niall violently shakes Deirdre. "You think you're better than me?" Niall harshly whispers to her. "Women all over the city worship me, and want my autograph, and they want to be with me. At every race show I go, all kinds of people want pictures with me. They want to touch me and stand next to me. But you ... you don't even look at me anymore, Deirdre. You reject the love I have for you. You completely ignore me, Deirdre." He shakes her. "No longer will I allow you to ignore me! You're going to see me today!"

In a fright, Abigail sits up in bed. She holds her throat feeling something is very wrong, as she has trouble breathing again. "Dominique, wake up! Dominique!"

Startled, Dominique sits up, and removes her fuzzy eye mask. "Abbey?"

"We've got to go to Austin. Right now!"

• • • •

END OF BOOK TWO

Other works by this Author:

Enduring Love
Book one of The Ravenell Dynasty Trilogy

• • • •

SIGN UP FOR ALERTS: https://www.ravenelldynasty.net

Don't miss out!

Visit the website below and you can sign up to receive emails whenever Kamrynn Bellary publishes a new book. There's no charge and no obligation.

https://books2read.com/r/B-A-FNSCB-OFRTC

BOOKS 2 READ

Connecting independent readers to independent writers.

About the Author

Kamrynn Bellary lived much of her life in Texas, and now happily lives in Colorado, in the USA, where she contributes to the field of healthcare. Kamrynn accomplished a Master's degree in Public Affairs, and a Bachelor of Science degree in Social Psychology. Kamrynn has one daughter, who has made wonderfully positive impacts upon society. In her spare time, Kamrynn likes to take in the beautiful scenery of Colorado, travel, learn about history, and assist in charitable causes for children.

Read more at https://www.ravenelldynasty.net/.

www.ingramcontent.com/pod-product-compliance
Lightning Source LLC
Chambersburg PA
CBHW030740030726
47497CB00001B/67